South San Francisco Public Library

S.S.F. Public Library
Grand Ave.
306 Walnut Ave.
South San Francisco, CA 94080

D0373749

# MAGGIE WELLS

sourcebooks
casablanca

Copyright © 2018 by Maggie Wells
Cover and internal design © 2018 by Sourcebooks, Inc.
Cover design by Damonza
Cover image © Kontrec/Getty Images

Sourcebooks and the colophon are registered trademarks of Sourcebooks, Inc.

All rights reserved. No part of this book may be reproduced in any form
or by any electronic or mechanical means including information storage
and retrieval systems—except in the case of brief quotations embodied
in critical articles or reviews—without permission in writing from its
publisher, Sourcebooks, Inc.

The characters and events portrayed in this book are fictitious or are
used fictitiously. Any similarity to real persons, living or dead, is
purely coincidental and not intended by the author.

All brand names and product names used in this book are trademarks,
registered trademarks, or trade names of their respective holders.
Sourcebooks, Inc., is not associated with any product or vendor in this
book.

Published by Sourcebooks Casablanca, an imprint of Sourcebooks, Inc.
P.O. Box 4410, Naperville, Illinois 60567-4410
(630) 961-3900
Fax: (630) 961-2168
sourcebooks.com

Printed and bound in Canada.
MBP 10 9 8 7 6 5 4 3 2 1

# Chapter 1

With her feet spread wide and her lucky clipboard clutched tight to her chest, Coach Kate Snyder tipped her head back and gazed at the scoreboard suspended over center court. She didn't need to check the display to know they were up a mere three points in these final seconds, but superstition kept her chin up and her eyes locked on the garish display.

She never watched the last play of the game.

The LED display exhorted the crowd to "MAKE SOME NOISE." The timer switched over from minutes and seconds to seconds split down to hundredths. Her heart beat as hard as the sneakers pounding hardwood.

Without looking, she knew the opposing team's point guard was driving the ball down court with little impediment. Kate's players wouldn't risk a foul at this point. The Wolcott University Women Warriors played smart. They weren't about to give up any free shots. She'd made it clear she'd prefer to play it out in overtime rather than witness her Warriors exhibiting any self-defeating behavior.

*Guard the perimeter. Make them shoot for the tie. Keep it out of the hot hands of the other team's lethal power forward.* These were the key points she'd driven home in their final time-out. Now, she had to trust her team to execute. The increase in noise level told her their defensive strategy was working.

A collective gasp signaled the Huskies had finally succeeded in getting the ball to their shooter. The roar of blood in her ears muffled the mixture of cheers and groans. Two and three-tenths seconds left on the clock.

Then, a sharp slap shattered the preternatural calm. Cheers erupted into unchecked screams. Kate heard the lazy *thump-thump-thump* of a loose ball and tuned in just in time to see the basketball bounce to a roll, heading for the other end of the court.

The buzzer sounded and the bench emptied.

Staring up at the screen, hoping for a replay, Kate allowed herself to be carried along on a swell of people. Assistants and trainers pummeled her shoulders and back. Three of her senior starters enveloped her in sweaty, tearful hugs. Reporters tried to muscle their way into the throng, but her Warrior Women formed a wall around her.

A stepladder was set up under the home team's basket. They moved toward it in a clump of jubilation. Someone plunked a hat atop her head. One persistent reporter snaked a microphone through the mass of bodies, but the question was lost in the shuffle. Kate kicked her pumps off at the foot of the ladder and started to climb. One step, two. She'd been able to touch the cool, smooth iron of an orange-painted rim since she was fifteen, but the sensation never grew old. Perching a hip on the highest step, she reached for the gleaming gold-plated scissors her boss, Wolcott University Athletic Director Mike Samlin, passed up to her.

Security tried in vain to herd the players toward center court, but it was no use. They weren't moving until the net came down. Reporters continued to thrust their microphones in her direction, though how they'd isolate her answers in the cacophony of celebration, she'd never know. Still, she answered one inane question for each loop of nylon she cut through.

*Snip.* How big a role did strategy play in their victory?

She bit back the first sarcastic answer that sprang to mind. Her friend and university public relations guru, Millie Jensen, would be so proud. "Like flattery, strategy will get you everywhere," she called down to the milling crowd. "You can't win if you don't know how you're going to play."

*Snip.* "Yes, I am incredibly proud of these young women."

*Snip, snip.* "God yes, I'll miss those seniors. We've been through a lot of battles together."

Already impatient to move on to the trophy ceremony, she started hacking at the loops on the far side of the hoop. *Snip, snip, snip.*

"Of course we expected a fight out of the Huskies," she answered, trying to hide her irritation with a wide smile. "This is the championship game. We wanted a fight."

She pretended not to hear the garbled questions coming at her as she worked her way around the rim. There'd be a press conference immediately following the presentation of the trophy. They could wait until then to pepper her.

Mike Samlin beamed at her from his spot at the foot of the ladder. As he should. They'd done it. The Wolcott Warriors were the NCAA Women's Basketball champions again. Their boosters would be ecstatic. Alumni donations would roll in fast and furious. At least, for a little while. They'd gain a smidge more respect in the conference and leverage within the NCAA as a whole.

Millie gave her a squinty-eyed glare, but Kate knew her old friend well enough to be certain she was doing mental backflips behind that mask of imperturbability. The other member of their unholy triumvirate, Professor Avery Preston, was most likely scamming leftover nachos from one of the snack bars. Athletics weren't her thing, but Avery was a good friend. She accepted her ticket to the game with only a few grumbling words about the possibility of bleacher butt.

Kate skimmed over the crowd of reporters, looking for one familiar face, but came up empty. Tamping down a sharp pang of disappointment, she sliced through the final strands, then waved the net high over her head.

Mike took the severed net from her as he handed her down from the ladder. Kate wriggled her feet into her pumps, then started toward the hastily stretched-out red carpet at the center of the arena to accept her prize.

There'd be no denying her legacy now. Kate Snyder was the winningest coach in the history of Wolcott athletics. Period. No need to add any pesky sport or gender qualification to the accolade.

Anxious to score good positions, the reporters scurried off to the press room while the NCAA commissioner took his spot next to the table holding the trophy. Her players slipped championship T-shirts over their heads and snapped selfies. Unlike the endless hoopla surrounding the men's tournament, this celebration was already winding down. Only a few die-hard fans would stick around for the presentation.

"You ready, Coach?" Director Samlin asked, taking his place beside her.

Kate smiled, then plucked her net from his hand. She liked Mike, but winning this tournament meant she had the balance of power firmly in her grasp. This particular battle was over, but the war wasn't won. Yet.

"I'm more than ready, Mike," she said as she draped the net over the corner of the trophy. "More than ready."

———

"I can't tell you how proud the entire Wolcott Warrior nation is at this moment…"

The athletic director's words faded to background noise as Kate surveyed the crowd crammed into the too-tiny conference room. Never in all her days as a player or a coach had she seen so many media outlets assembled in one spot. Well, maybe when she played in the Olympics, but certainly not here in America.

She didn't see Musburger or Costas in the crowd, but National Sports Network had sent their golden boy, Greg Chambers. She hadn't seen him live and in person in years. Something was up. Something juicer than an NCAA Women's title.

A lump of apprehension formed in her stomach. Cameras whirred and flashes blinked like strobes. She shifted on the utilitarian metal folding chair and squinted into the glare of the portable lights set up on either side of the stage. Needing something to ground her, she reached out to touch the severed net dangling off the edge of the trophy. Ironic that something that usually hung nine feet off the floor should make her feel more secure.

"…Coach Snyder's unwavering dedication to the Warrior athletic program is an inspiration to me and everyone who has known her as a player, leader, mentor, and role model."

Kate plastered a gracious smile back on her face and promptly zoned out as Mike launched into the usual spiel. She didn't need to be reminded of her accomplishments. The proof of her hard work and determination sat front and center on the table.

The Wolcott University Warrior Women were the national champions, and she, Kate Snyder—Wolcott alumna, WNBA all-star, and Olympic gold medalist—was the one who'd led them there. Again.

This was her moment. The net-draped trophy was her third Division I championship as a women's basketball head coach. A stat that placed her a half dozen wins behind the current king—Geno Auriemma, from the University of Connecticut—but next in line after her idol, the late, great Pat Summitt, in the record books.

A banner achievement. One more personal milestone. She just never imagined it would garner this much press attention. Kate drew a deep breath, trying to calm the nerves making her heart stutter-step, and tuned back into what the AD was saying.

"Kate Snyder is the personification of the title 'Coach.' Grace under pressure and the instincts of a born champion…"

His voice held a slightly too-enthusiastic edge. Kate shot him a curious glance. Mike was a former NFL player turned collegiate program builder. Women's basketball probably wouldn't have even registered on his radar if his first gig as athletic director had landed him anywhere but Wolcott. But the Warrior Women held the only bragging rights the university had reaped in decades. That meant it was time for Mr. Former Football Star to suck it up and sing the praises of women's hoops.

"We are honored that Coach Snyder continues to call Wolcott University home…"

Ah, a shot across the bow. Her contract was up this year. He knew it, she knew it, and the handful of people in this room who actually cared about women's basketball did too. Kate Snyder was no longer willing to be treated like the protégé she'd once been.

No more jokes about the salary differential between her and her male counterparts being her contribution to the alumni fund. If Mike thought he could bamboozle her with a charming smile and a hefty dose of sentiment, he had another think coming. She was done shooting from the outside. He'd better be prepared to pay her what she was worth or be ready to take a charge, because she was coming at him straight down the middle.

"Kate Snyder is the epitome of a warrior, and I, for one, am damn glad to have her on my team." He turned his smooth-operator smile on her. "Coach, on behalf of the Warrior nation, I congratulate you on another fantastic season and thank you for doing us proud."

The two of them exchanged smiles and nods. She reached out to touch the net again, and a barrage of flashes nearly blinded her. Kate hoped the cameras captured every morsel of Mike's sincerity. Her agent was most likely recording the press conference, but Kate wanted to be sure they had a good record of the depth of his gratitude. Those things were easy to forget once contract negotiations began.

"Thank you, Director Samlin."

Squashing the rising tide of nervousness building inside her, she scanned the crowd, looking for a friendly face to focus on while she gave her statement. She didn't need to look any farther than the front row.

Jim Davenport from the *Sentinel* held his micro recorder pointed directly at her. She stifled a smirk when she noted the grim expression on his face. It seemed out of place. Jim was Wolcott's hometown sports reporter and a die-hard basketball junkie. You'd think that would make him the friendliest face of all, but no. He frowned every bit as fiercely as he glared at the other reporters, clearly peeved by the additional media coverage. Why hadn't he been out on the court?

A hot flash of annoyance fired in her gut. Jim ought to be happy. He was the guy with the inside track after all. He should have been the first clamoring for a quote. Pushing through her irritation, she ignored Jim's snit and scanned the room until she landed on the familiar face of Steve Bishop from one of the Nashville news affiliates. When their gazes locked, she turned on her brightest smile and dredged up a little of the drawl she'd never quite shed.

"And thanks, y'all. My, I never imagined a turnout like this. I thought I'd just let y'all catch a couple of pictures of the new hardware and then hop on the bus."

Her comment was met with a low rumble of chuckles. Though she'd been dealing with the press for years, it still took her some time to get her feet under her at media events. She zoomed in on Jim for a moment, allowing herself to dally in her comfort zone before making eye contact with the bigger sharks in the tank.

"I appreciate Director Samlin's praise, and trust me, I'll be playing that sound bite over and over on my DVR," she added, flashing her boss a cheeky grin. "But I'm not the one who won the game, am I?"

Lifting a challenging eyebrow, she turned her attention to Greg Chambers. She hadn't had the pleasure of seeing the National Sports Network's lead basketball commentator since she'd been in the WNBA and he'd been hanging around the sidelines hoping for a quote. Well, she had one for him now.

"Most of y'all didn't expect much out of us this year, and I want to thank you personally for giving these twelve phenomenal young women the kick in the long baggies they needed to get the job done. Just imagine: if we'd believed our own press, we could have been watchin' the game from home."

The press corps gave another appreciative chuckle, and she plowed ahead, confidence growing. "Then again, if we were watching from home, we would have had snacks." She pressed a hand to her stomach and grinned at the assemblage. "I don't suppose anyone thought to bring us any Ro-Tel dip? Maybe one of those six-foot sub sandwiches?"

That earned her a heartier round of laughter, but it was laced with discomfort she couldn't quite identify.

"Of course, it's also nice to be able to wrap this one up so close to home. The Music City has been awful good to us, but I hope that the good people of Nashville won't be offended when I say I think we all look forward to sleeping in our own beds tonight."

She went on to praise a few individual players for outstanding performances and heaped the usual load of

"I couldn't do it without you" on her assistant coach, but still an undercurrent of impatience hummed through the room. Reporters tapped pens and repositioned equipment. Onlookers gathered along the walls shifted their weight from foot to foot. Her words came slower, but her mind raced.

Was she missing something? Forgetting to thank someone critical to the process? Was her blouse buttoned correctly? Or maybe she was committing the kind of unwitting gaffe that would turn her into an internet GIF before the evening was out?

Watching the crowd warily, she wound down with a self-deprecating chuckle. "I guess that's all I have to say."

She glanced at Mike and found the athletic director sitting rigid in his seat, his eyes fixed on someone at the very back of the room. She squinted, but like ninety percent of the guys in the room, the object of Mike's attention was dressed in the off-duty jock uniform of khakis and a knit polo shirt. He wore a ball cap pulled low over his eyes, but it didn't bear the Wolcott Warrior logo or the logo of any media outlet. No, his hat had what looked like a coiled snake appliquéd just above the bill.

A jolt of unease fired through her belly as every reporter's hand shot up, but she kept her smile firmly in place. Director Samlin gave his head the tiniest shake, but she wasn't about to be waved off. They'd won. This was her night, and damn it, she could alley-oop any question the jackals threw at her. Her team had played strong and clean. She had nothing to hide.

So she went straight to the biggest jackal of them all. "Yes, Greg?" she said, giving NSN their due by nodding to Chambers first.

To her surprise, he didn't direct his question to her but spoke to the man sitting next to her.

"Director Samlin, at five forty-three this evening, a private plane owned by Richard Donner, one of Wolcott University's biggest boosters, touched down at Nashville International. Witnesses at the airport confirmed that the plane was carrying former Northern University football coach Danny McMillan."

Kate's gaze immediately flew to the mystery man at the back of the crowd, but the snake charmer was gone. Everyone in the room seemed to be waiting for Mike's reply. Turning to look at the AD, she found Mike wearing a mildly curious expression. But the man's eyes were sharp.

He offered an apologetic but confused smile. "I'm sorry, was there a question I missed?"

"What is he doing here?" Chambers asked. "Are you thinking of hiring him to replace Coach Morton when he retires?"

"Coach Morton has not informed me of any retirement plans, so I think it would be a bit presumptuous to start looking for candidates to fill his job," Mike answered smoothly.

"Then what is Coach McMillan doing here?"

The smile Mike turned on the reporter probably got him laid back in his playing days based on wattage alone. "Perhaps he wanted to come watch the game."

"But you and Coach McMillan played together—"

Mike held up a hand to stop the reporter. "People, I can honestly tell you that no one employed by the Wolcott athletic department is thinking about anything but basketball tonight. This is Coach Snyder's and her team's night, and if you don't have any further questions pertaining to tonight's stellar championship victory, I'm going to thank Coach for doing us all proud once again and let her get back to the celebration she so richly deserves."

The room exploded with shouts and calls, but Mike ignored them all as he pushed his chair back and rose. She stood too, and the moment their eyes met, she knew every word he'd just said was complete bullshit.

---

A week later, Kate stood inside the Warrior Center, her back to a spanking-new trophy positioned under a glowing spotlight. The damn thing had just been placed on its pedestal two days ago. There hadn't even been time for a layer of dust to settle on it. She should have been on top of the world. Yet here she was, watching a train wreck unfold right in front of her.

She assumed her sideline stance—arms crossed over her chest, chin up, eyes wary and watchful. Her shoulders ached from the exertion of keeping her spine straight, and her fingernails bit into the thin knit of her sweater. But all the while, she was plotting. Planning. Sketching out plays in her head and wiping them away in the blink of an eye.

She was a fast-break girl. A woman unafraid to attack the goal. And somehow, this game was moving slowly and disconcertingly fast at the same time.

"A rolling stone and all that crap."

Kate jumped and turned, grimacing as she rubbed at the knot of tension below her ear. The Wolcott men's basketball coach, Tyrell Ransom, lounged against the corner of the massive display case. His posture was as casual as Kate's was taut, but his dark eyes were focused on the small cluster of people gathering on the steps just beyond the athletic center's glass doors, like hers had been moments ago.

"Rolling stone?" she asked, quirking an eyebrow.

"Gathers no moss, right?" Ty kept his eyes locked on the commotion on the front steps as he straightened. The man was long and lithe, nearly six foot eight and as graceful as a panther. Sleekly handsome to boot.

Aside from his looks and grace, Ty was talented. Not just on the court, but on the sideline as well. It might take some time, but he'd get the men's program up to snuff. There were few men who'd made the transition from the NBA to coaching look as seamless as Ty did. Just as there were few people in the world who might recognize the restless gleam in the man's eyes. But Kate did. The man practically shimmered with the impatience of a person who was used to winning and hadn't been lately.

"Mike already had an ace in the hole when he took the job as AD." He smiled as he turned to look at her, but it didn't reach his eyes. Shifting his attention back to the scene beyond the doors, the smile faded. "Within just a few years, he's managed to bring me in, and now this guy."

His brow puckered. "You're a no-brainer, of course. Alumna, all-star, winner of all things great and good. But me and this guy?" He wagged his head in bewilderment. "I'm thinking Mike must have had a thing for nursing broken birds when he was a kid."

"You're hardly a broken bird," she retorted.

"I could have scored major endorsement deals for splints, and we all know it," he shot back. "Funny how after that meeting with Donner, all Stan could talk about was retiring." His eyes narrowed as if searching his memory for any clues the old football coach might have dropped. "I don't remember him mentioning any desire to buy an RV and explore the campgrounds of the world."

Kate's snort faded into a chuckle as she pictured Stan Morton, Wolcott's pudgy, pugnacious football coach, wedged behind the wheel of a luxury motor home. "No. Last I heard, he was having a hissy fit over the fact that his daughter was trying to set a wedding date for a Saturday in late September."

Ty laughed. "That had to be intentional."

"Of course it was." For the first time since she'd walked out of that jam-packed conference room, Kate smiled and actually meant it. "The man named his only daughter Lombardi, for cripes' sake. He had to know retaliation would come at some point."

Kate stifled a sigh when Ty moved to stand beside her. At six two in her stocking feet, there weren't many men in the world who made Kate feel small, but this one did. Ty was living proof all the good ones were taken. Most of them by women more than ten years younger and about fifty shades blonder, like Ty's wife, Mari.

His chuckle went a long way toward dispelling some of her tension. They'd become friends since he'd come to Wolcott, but that didn't mean the sight of his thick gold wedding band didn't ding her battered heart. To this day, Ty had no idea that his hiring had thrown a wrench in her ex-husband's ambitions and pounded the final nail in the coffin of Kate's marriage.

"Not much of a turnout for a press conference," he commented, nodding to the small knot of reporters gathered at the base of the steps. "You'd think there'd be more, what with all the scandal he stirred up a few years ago."

About halfway down the stairs, Millie Jenkins, Wolcott University's public relations guru and one of Kate's closest friends, flitted around the two men positioned at dead center. The woman was in her element. Millie was born to direct, position, and basically boss people around. She was a master of spin, and this little one-act play was her brainchild.

"It's not a press conference," Kate murmured, not taking her eyes off the two men at the eye of the storm. Mimicking the self-proclaimed PR goddess, Kate gave a fluttery wave as if wielding a magic wand. "It's an impromptu gathering of select members of the press."

Ty barked a laugh. "Right. Of course it is." He pursed his lips as he watched the small throng of reporters shift impatiently. "Frankly, I always thought the guy was kind of a scapegoat."

Kate raised her eyebrows. Was Ty actually going to stick up for a man who'd been ridden out of Division I coaching on the proverbial rail? "He admitted to having an affair with a grad student."

Ty waved the point off. "Not that. The recruiting violations, sanctions, and that stuff. He wasn't doing anything everyone else wasn't doing. He just got caught, and they needed to make an example of someone."

Kate snorted. "I can't believe you're defending him."

He raised both hands. "Not defending him, just saying I'm not sure I believe everything I hear about the guy, that's all."

"Where there's smoke—" she began.

"There's usually someone like Millie fanning a match," he concluded.

Kate laughed. How could she not? He was right. So much of their world was little more than smoke and mirrors. "Point scored."

Grinning, he pushed off his pivot foot and nodded to the shiny new trophy. "Beautiful prize there, Coach." He turned in the direction of his office and called over his shoulder, "Enjoy the circus. And be careful. Don't let the clowns in tiny cars run over your feet."

Kate pursed her lips as she watched Ty walk away, his gait thrown off by a slight limp that favored his right leg.

The minute he rounded the corner, she returned her attention to the scene unfolding beyond the tinted glass doors. Circus was right. Millie was damn good at her job, but soon it would be three rings around here—with one guy at the center of it all.

Her eyes narrowed as she homed in on the man of the hour. Danny McMillan was a fine-looking fella in his own right. Dark-haired, tall, and solid. Not beefy, like so many former football players. Of course, he'd been a quarterback in his playing days. Those guys were expected to be trimmer, more agile than the guys paid to put up a protective barrier around them. Still, he looked like a man who could take a hit and keep his feet under him.

And he had taken more than his share. She had to admire his stamina. If only grudgingly. This guy had the balls to step foot into her press room, walk onto her campus, and stand on the mica-studded steps of the athletic center her program had built as if he owned them.

He was the savior they'd all been waiting for—the

man who could make Wolcott football something more than a sports radio joke.

She moved to the doors for a better look, gratified to note that the assembled members of the media looked unimpressed. Jim Davenport was there, of course, but she didn't recognize the painfully young blond wearing NSN credentials on a lanyard around her neck.

Did Mike Samlin truly think he could hire the bad boy of collegiate athletics, at a purportedly astronomical salary, and not have that come back to haunt him at contract time?

Oh, hell no.

She was a Wolcott Warrior and a champion. These men thought they could waltz into her world and take what they wanted? Not likely.

The heels of her palms came to rest on the door's crash bar. She watched as McMillan spoke, trying not to notice the way his eyes crinkled when he squinted against the sun or the open hopefulness in his smile. Attractive he might be, but this man was a rule breaker and a cheat. He didn't deserve to stand on the steps of the house she built.

This was her time. Her turf. The center ring belonged to her.

And she'd be damned if she let some clown run over her to get to it.

# Chapter 2

FEELING A BIT LIKE A SIDESHOW FREAK, DANNY MCMILLAN ignored the small group of people staring at him and took a second to drink in the scenery. The sky was blue, the spring sunshine bright, and the Wolcott campus looked like something Hollywood had nailed together on a back lot. The crowd gathered at the base of the steps appeared to be marginally friendlier than the lynch mob that had converged on Coach Snyder's conference at the Bridgestone Center in Nashville. That was as optimistic as he could get about this little dog and pony show.

The last time he'd held a press conference, camera shutters clicked like machine gun fire and flashbulbs flared. This time, the assemblage came equipped with exactly one shoulder cam and a smattering of cellular devices. Hell, the smirky, white-blond cheerleader with the National Sports Network credentials dangling from her lanyard didn't even bother pointing her phone in his direction. She was too busy thumb-typing. He stared at the razor-thin part on the top of the young reporter's head and rattled off the usual string of gibberish.

"I can't tell you how excited I am to be a Wolcott Warrior."

No lie. The last four years were a testament to his mental strength and endurance. It was a good thing he had age on his side. He'd once been one of the youngest coaches to ever lead a major program. Maybe they'd forgive him for being nearly junior-high-girl giddy at the prospect of being restored to Division I collegiate athletics—even if it meant coaching a team that hadn't won a single game in four seasons. Not even against the Division II teams the school paid to play in their preconference games.

Though they were a member of the revered and feared Mid Continental Conference, the Wolcott Warriors were perennial cellar dwellers. But it didn't matter. Division I was Division I. He was back, damn it.

Pale spring sunlight glinted off the camera lens. There wasn't a cloud in the sky. Once again, his future was bright.

"Athletic Director Samlin and I met with the team this morning, and I can say these young men have made quite an impression on me."

Again, the truth. The world at large didn't need to know that the program would have more success if they channeled their playoff ambitions into the action offered by a couple of well-oiled foosball tables.

"Smart players playing smart, fundamentally strong football. It's hard to beat a team that plays with their heads and their hearts."

More home truths. The team had an admirably high grade point average as a whole. Surely a group of young men who excelled in Wolcott's high-flying academic environment could be taught how to convert four downs into six points. As for the kicking game, one of these boy geniuses must have played a little soccer at some point.

"Trust me, I have every confidence the Wolcott Warriors will make their mark on collegiate athletics."

The tiny cluster of reporters snapped to attention, and

he clamped his mouth shut, wishing the words back. He hated himself for asking for their trust. Only used car salesmen asked people to trust them. Well, car salesmen and men who'd publicly fallen from grace. And only a fool thought that football meant squat around these parts. He was still scrambling for a way to rephrase when the question zinged him right between the eyes.

"*Make their mark?* Coach Snyder has won four national championships in the past decade. Wouldn't you say that made a mark?"

Danny hid his cringe as he scanned the sad group of reporters. The question came from a tall, nerdy-looking guy standing at the back of the pack. At first glance, Danny had pegged him as an easy target. He looked like a former athlete. The type who didn't quite have the talent to play beyond college. The glory-days guys used to be his specialty, but it didn't look like this one could be wooed with a sideline pass and a date to speak to the Rotary Club.

Shit. How could he have slipped up like that? This was a basketball school. Women's basketball, of all things. Wolcott University was home to Kate Snyder — basketball star, coaching legend, and media darling. "No. Right. Of course." He stumbled over the acknowledgment. "I meant in football."

Thankfully, Mike decided to put him out of his misery. His old friend, former teammate, and new boss stepped forward and held up a hand. "Coach McMillan will take just a few more questions. He's got a hot date with some game film lined up for this afternoon."

If he didn't have to be the guy to answer the damn things, Danny would have found the predictability of the questions laughable. But he did have to answer them. Every single time he took a new coaching job. Danny clenched his abs and stood straighter in a Pavlovian response. And here it came…

"Coach, do you truly think you can build a winning program at a school like Wolcott without resorting to the kinds of…questionable tactics you used at Northern?"

He didn't blink. No point in denying the recruiting violations he'd already owned. Even though his staff had only done what everyone else was doing. Because he was their leader and ultimately responsible for the entire program, he'd fallen on his sword when they got caught. At any other time, in any other place, he would have gotten a few wins vacated from his record and a slap on the wrist. His people just happened to step in it at the wrong time.

He didn't dare give anything but the faintly puzzled smile he'd perfected in front of the mirror. "Yes. Yes, I do."

Damn straight he could and would. He'd been the NCAA's whipping boy for too long. He had something to prove, and what better way to stick it to them all than to turn one of the worst programs in the division into one of the best?

Danny waited, but the follow-up question never materialized. For one blissful moment, he thought maybe they'd forgotten about the girl. But reporters were like elephants. They never forgot. They'd remember the rest of the scandal that had gotten him fired and essentially blackballed. It was just a matter of time. Instead, this hard-hitting journalist decided to make a name for himself by being completely ineffectual and innocuous. God bless him.

The beanpole reporter waved away the ethics questions in his rush to state the obvious. "Unlike the other Division I schools you've coached for, Wolcott athletics have historically focused on the basketball programs."

Once again, no actual question followed. Rather than wait for the attack, Danny decided to grab the bull by the horns and wrestle his way out of this meet and greet as best he could.

"That's true. This is one of the reasons I'm so excited to be here. History is the past. I think what Director Samlin is trying to do is look to the future. My goal is to generate the same kind of support for the football program that Coach Snyder and Coach Ransom have for basketball. We're playing in the big-boy conference. I want to see Wolcott claim its rightful spot."

The metallic clunk of a crash bar filled the silence as the reporters dutifully noted his ass-kissing. He heard one of the heavy glass doors behind him hiss a hydraulic sigh, but he paid the commotion no mind. He had only a few land mines to navigate between him and the safety of seventy hours of film analysis.

A few reporters straightened when they spotted whoever came through the door, but he didn't dare turn his back on the wolves gathered on the steps. Good thing he didn't, because the NSN reporter chose that moment to spring into action. She waved her arm to get his attention. "Coach! Coach!"

"Yes"—he scanned the name on the badge dangling just above her navel—"Brittany?"

The woman shot him a dismissive glare and gestured to the steps behind him. "No, I have a question for Coach Snyder."

Danny turned to find Kate Snyder standing at the top of the steps. He'd seen enough of the basketball legend on television to know she was attractive. He'd prepared for that. But he hadn't expected beautiful.

She wore snug pants that clung to her mile-long legs and a sweater so loose and delicate it looked like it would unravel with one tug. The spring breeze caught strands of her dark hair and tossed them like streamers. Her wide mouth stretched into a saccharine-laced smile. The sharp glint in her eyes should have put him off, but it didn't. If anything, it made his pulse jump like a twitchy offensive lineman.

She was feminine but formidable. Bathed in sunlight and framed by the silvered glass doors, she packed the wallop of a knee to the nuts. Tall and slender, she had the kind of regal bearing and willowy grace that made a man think she might have been a fashion model rather than an athletic prodigy. But the set of her jaw and the steely determination in her eyes warned him not to buy into the lithesome ease. He recognized the trap.

Kate Snyder was a damn warrior.

The welcoming smile and silky sweater were calculated to make people underestimate her. The way she tucked a wayward lock of hair behind her ear was nothing but a pick set to trip him up. This woman was a competitor. A champion. A friggin' hall of famer, and she wasn't even in her prime yet. She played to win—at all costs.

Mike had warned him about her. Kate Snyder was one of the university's greatest assets and most powerful people. He claimed she had the board of regents and the entire student body eating out of the palm of her hand.

The media stumbled all over themselves to get a sound
bite from her. Rumor had it she managed to snare a solid
twenty percent of the vote for homecoming queen each
year since she'd returned to her alma mater to coach.
Now he could see why. The woman was as hot as Hades.

The wary expression creasing Mike's brow told
Danny that Kate was also a woman who wasn't the least
bit afraid to wield that power. Unfortunately, dire warnings weren't enough to quell the spike of lust that embed-
ded itself in Danny's gut the second his eyes met hers.

He had to look away. The pack of jackals was safer
than this woman. At last, his instinct for self-preservation
kicked in, and he turned back to the reporters, a smile
stretched taut across his face.

The perky blond preened just a little, happy to be in
the spotlight no matter how small it might be. "Coach
Snyder, you've been instrumental in building the university's athletic and booster programs. How do you feel
about the exorbitant salary Mr. Samlin attached to the
contract Mr. McMillan signed?"

Danny bit his tongue to keep from scoffing at her use
of the word *exorbitant* in reference to the comparatively
moderate contract he'd signed and to stop himself from
demanding the reporter address him as Coach. Her wide
china-doll eyes narrowed speculatively as she glanced
from Danny to the AD and up to Coach Snyder once
more. A sly smile curved the junior journalist's mouth.

Kate's lack of reaction told him she'd expected the
question. She matched the reporter's smile and then
upped the ante, adding enough warmth to ensure the
small assemblage of press focused solely on her. "Why,
Brittany, I hadn't even thought."

She drawled the words with Southern-bred deliber-
ateness, making it clear she was *all about* renegotiating
her salary.

"I just wanted to take a moment to welcome Coach
McMillan to Wolcott and wish him the best of luck with
his program." She shifted her focus to him, and everything
locked up. Heart, lungs...everything frozen by a pair of
amber eyes set to stun. Cat's eyes. This woman was preda-
tory, not prey. "We hope to see great things from you."

The skeptical lift of one perfectly arched eyebrow
conveyed the message loud and clear: they hoped but
did not expect.

Danny's fingers curled into loose fists as she flashed a
challenging smile. Air exploded from his lungs. The classic profile and long, lean body were tempting enough,
but the air of confidence that radiated from her was such
a turn-on, he had to resist the urge to adjust himself.

"I have great plans," he replied.

Danny clamped his mouth shut and cleared his throat,
shocked by the low, gruff rasp of his voice as much as
the promise. He wanted to kiss the smugness out of her,
press her up against the smoked glass doors and take her
hard and fast. Show her straight off the bat the kinds of
"great things" he had in store for her.

Mike was right to be worried. One look from Kate
and Danny's tongue jumped offside before his brain had
even called the play. But there would be no dropping
back into the pocket now that the rush was on. Instead,
he stepped up to the line she'd drawn between them.

Her smile widened, crinkling her eyes and triggering
the most attractive set of brackets around her mouth. "I
can't wait to hear all about them."

His thoughts went to a fantastically filthy place. This
time, he didn't bother trying to clear the huskiness in his
voice. If she wanted to play, he'd play. "I'd love to tell
you all about them…Coach."

Her eyes flared with amusement, and she touched the
tip of her tongue to the center of her upper lip. With a
nod heavy with mocking solemnity, she stepped down
to offer him her hand. He was vaguely aware of the whir
and snick of photos captured but intensely tuned in to the
feel of her slender fingers wrapped around his hand. Her
palm was soft. The spring breeze caught the fresh floral
scent of her perfume, and silky strands of hair clung to
the pale lipstick she wore. Everything about her was
simple, elegant, and as blatantly arousing as a lap dance.

"I'd be happy to offer any advice you might need."
She pitched her voice loud enough for their audience to
hear. "You know where to find my office, right? Straight
down the hall past the four NCAA championship trophies and turn right at the Naismith awards."

Turning her brilliant smile on the rapt reporters, she
gave a jaunty wave and bounded up the steps, her long
legs eating up concrete with the same gusto she'd exerted
in smashing his ego. The sunlight cast a halo around her
head as she paused on the top step once more.

"Oh, and if you reach the case with my old jerseys
and the Olympic team photo, you've gone too far. But
don't worry. You'll find your way eventually." She
winked at the reporters, nodded to the athletic director,
then gave Danny McMillan a patently insincere grin.
"Welcome to Wolcott, Coach."

Kate dropped the pen she'd been clicking manically and glanced toward the window. Intruding on Coach Hotshot's press conference wasn't the most mature way to introduce herself, but damn it, this was her turf. She'd spent her entire adult life representing Wolcott University athletics, and she wasn't about to be brushed aside for some smarmy has-been with a shoulder-pad fetish.

Her phone rang, and she reached for it without looking. "Kate Snyder."

"That was gold, Katie! Gold! Check the website."

Twisting in her seat, Kate smirked as the Wolcott Athletics home page loaded on her computer screen. It hadn't taken Millie long to get a snapshot of Kate nose-to-nose with Danny McMillan posted and released to the press. The university's media maven was as industrious as she was insidious. Once Millie wrapped her arms around an idea, it was almost impossible to pry it from her grasp.

Kate fell back in her chair. "Does Jerry Seinfeld know you're stealing his lines?"

"It's Kenny Bania's line." The older woman's raspy voice might have indicated a three-pack-a-day habit, but Kate knew for a fact Millie had never taken a puff. The woman ran marathons as often as others ran errands.

Heaving a sigh, Kate tucked the receiver under her chin. "I'm glad you enjoyed it."

"Enjoyed it? NSN called. They're sending the crew in to talk to you this week. Not Brittany, the documentary crew." Kate's eyebrows shot up. "They want to shine their Sports Spotlight on you ASAP, Coach."

Kate rolled her eyes. "I bet they do." It was hard to keep the edge of bitterness out of her voice. The network had already pitched the documentary idea, and she had signed the papers nearly two years earlier. Somehow, there was always a bigger story to be told. A man-sized story. She tapped her mouse to minimize the screen. "Tell them to bring it on."

"Done." She heard the click of Millie's pen. "And, Kate?"

"Yeah?"

"Avery said to remind you that you built this athletic program. Don't let them marginalize you. Keep giving him hell."

Kate smiled, seeing straight through the moment of sisterly solidarity to the media circus that was sure to blossom at the center of this hiring fiasco. "Will do."

"Good girl. You can't buy this kind of publicity."

Millie's rasping cackle blared from the receiver as Katie hung up, but the second she pulled her hand back, the phone rang again.

Heaving a sigh, she answered with a simple, "Snyder."

"Coach Snyder, it's Davenport with the *Sentinel*."

The tersely professional greeting both amused and annoyed her. "Davenport from the *Sentinel*" had kissed her good night at her front door a few nights ago. Choosing to let the flash of irritation go, she rocked back in her chair and tucked the phone between her ear and shoulder.

"Yes, Mr. Davenport, what can I do for you?" she asked, a smile adding some lilt to her voice.

The head of the sports department for both the local newspaper and television station, Jim Davenport also happened to be number one on her roster of potential lovers. Not that the bench was deep at the moment. When one lived and worked in a college town, men of appropriate age and unencumbered marital status weren't exactly thick on the ground.

Jim was handsome, if a bit pedantic. She figured sooner or later, he might grow into the suave newspaperman persona he swiped from Cary Grant in *His Girl Friday*. He just needed to cultivate a bit of charm. They'd flirted with becoming something more than friends for years, but the timing was never quite right. First, she was married. Then, by the time she was divorced, Jim was involved with someone else. In the months since his messy breakup, they'd established a semiregular routine of drinks or dinner, but things were slow to develop from there.

The stagnation left her feeling both frustrated and oddly relieved. She liked Jim, and if things didn't work out between them…well, alienating her closest ally in the press wouldn't be a prudent move. Not that she worried he'd abandon the team. The guy was a basketball fan through and through. He'd continue to be a fan as long as she continued to win.

"Listen, I need you to get me an interview with McMillan."

Her head jerked back. She gave the receiver an incredulous glare. "Excuse me?"

"I need a one-on-one with him," he persisted.

Agitated, she turned back to her desk and jiggled her mouse to wake her computer. The website's banner screamed "Danny McMillan to Lead New Warrior Uprising." A hot flush of annoyance prickled its way up her neck. "And you got confused and dialed my extension instead of the press office?"

"Millie just laughed and hung up when I called. If

Mike Samlin thinks he can tuck Danny Boy away until the season starts in the fall, he's mistaken. That last-minute press conference was bullshit."

Last-minute or not, Jim had come running when the athletic director called. Touching her toe to the floor, Kate pivoted just enough to shift her focus to the dark hunter-green jersey framed and mounted on her wall. If she counted back to the day she signed her letter of intent, she'd spent almost a quarter of her life as a Wolcott Warrior. She could lay claim to one championship and a handful of prestigious awards as a player, as well as three titles and even more accolades as a coach. And now, this man wanted her to play social secretary for a man whose salary made hers look like tip money.

"I'm sorry your inability to seduce a woman with a rerun addiction is impeding your ability to find an angle on the biggest story in the history of Wolcott athletics," she drawled, each word dripping sarcasm as thick as Spanish moss. "But I'm afraid I won't be able to help. The folks from NSN will be here soon to start filming me for the *Warrior Woman* documentary they're so hot to do—"

"I didn't say he was the biggest story—"

She had to give him credit. Jimbo recognized a blunder when he made one. Too bad he was better at giving offense than launching it. There was no way she would let him off the hook without making him squirm first. "Why don't you give Cheryl Miller a call and see if she can use her pull to set up a playdate with Reggie for you?"

Without giving Jim a chance to sputter, she took a cue from the university's media officer and hung up on him. Whirling away from the computer, she propped her feet on the windowsill and narrowed her eyes against the vivid green of the spring leaves as she sank into a sulk. The quad was crawling with students happy to bask in the sunshine, but all she could do was wish away the months until the season started in November.

At least the multiyear, multimillion-dollar man got to hold spring scrimmages with his team. All she had left on her agenda were her usual appearances at commencement ceremonies, basketball camps, and a month or so on the lecture circuit. The sad fact was, a couple weeks of delivering motivational speeches to middle managers earned her more than a championship season.

Eyes fixed on an old team photo, she counted to fifty in her head as she drew air in through her mouth and expelled it from her nose. Her one-time coach Buzzy Bryant had taught her that trick. In the years since, she'd discovered it worked just as well when one wasn't standing at the free-throw line. She closed her eyes, absorbing the stab of pain that always accompanied thoughts of her late mentor.

But she'd done Old Buzzy proud. He'd visited her the day the surgeons informed her there'd be no repairing her knee and coaxed her into coming home to Wolcott. In a little over a decade, she'd experienced unprecedented success. Only a handful of coaches could claim a better win-loss record. She was nationally recognized for her excellence as a player and a coach, a living legend, a champion who didn't allow such pesky details as limited resources or the gender bias inherent in collegiate athletics to hold her back.

And she wouldn't let it now.

She scowled at the play of sunlight on newly unfurled

leaves. It was the quintessential early April day, and all
that spring green and golden sunshine depressed the hell
out of her. She and all the other nonbaseball fanatics
called the time between postseason tournaments and the
first tip-off in the fall the *dead zone*. For people like
her, the kind who lived for basketball, there was no such
thing as the off-season, no matter what the schedules
said. Life without basketball wasn't any kind of life. The
truth was, she barely felt alive outside of the season.

Until Danny McMillan's hand closed around hers.

Something had happened when he'd touched her.
Something she didn't want to examine too closely.
She dropped her feet to the floor and crossed her legs,
squirming in her seat until she sat up straight and tall.
She might have assigned the tingling in her nether region
to the molded seat cushion on her ergonomically correct
desk chair, but she wasn't a woman who lied to herself.
At least, not often. Visions of black hair and icy-blue
eyes danced in her head.

She briefly entertained thoughts of running home
to her handheld showerhead but opted to squeeze her
thighs together instead. She peeked at the picture of her
facing down Danny McMillan again. It was as irresist-
ibly painful as touching a bruise. She could still feel the
sizzle, but she ignored it as she stared hard at his face.
The cocky smile cut unspeakably attractive grooves into
his skin, and bright-blue eyes glowed with intensity.
She knew that gleam. Had felt the warmth of the same
burning ambition. The man was a believer. A zealot. A
champion in the making.

The hot bloom of lust in her belly hardened into a
lump and dropped to the pit of her stomach. He was also

a ruthless competitor with nothing to lose and every-thing to gain. She'd be damned if she'd let him crawl over her to get to the top. The administration might think he was worth a bunch of zeroes, but as far as she was concerned, the guy *was* a zero. And she would prove it.

# Chapter 3

"I'M TELLING YOU, THE PRESS IS EATING IT UP," MILLIE crowed.

"Eating what up?" Kate asked. She tossed the clipboard she'd been grasping like a lifeline onto her desk and planted her hands on her hips. "There's nothing to eat. You'd get more rummaging through my kitchen cabinets, Millie."

Her friend grinned and tossed her artfully streaked hair as she looked up. "Isn't it great? All I have to do is release a picture of you somewhere in the general vicinity of Delectable Danny, and they gobble it up."

The woman clapped her bejeweled hands with glee, as if the shit-eating grin wasn't hint enough that Millie was pleased with her machinations. Zebra-striped readers perched on the tip of her nose. She wore a pair of purple skinny-legged pants and a matching flirty top that should have looked ridiculous on a woman over forty, but as always, she ended up looking chic and stylish.

Kate was fairly certain she'd look like a freezer pop in that particular outfit. "You think he's delectable?"

"Everyone thinks he's delectable." Millie's smile didn't fade one watt as she turned her attention back to the tablet in her lap. "I'm thinking I'll leak this one next."

Kate's jaw dropped as the contents of the photograph filling the screen registered. That was her black racer-back tank top, her butt encased in a pair of electric-blue

Lycra shorts. She could barely acknowledge the haphaz-
ard ponytail and damp strands of hair plastered to her
cheek and neck.

The muscles in her arms and back bunched, and a
weight bar rested on her shoulders. Other than the
outdated workout wear and the tragic hair, she had
to admit she looked damn good. And so did Coach
Danny McMillan. She squinted at the picture, trying to
remember if she'd seen him in the weight room that day.
Wondering how she could have missed him. The man
was all tanned muscle and sweat-dampened dark hair.
And he appeared to be staring right at her, a sneer twisting his handsome features.

"What the hell?" She caught the mischievous gleam
in Millie's eyes. "When did… How…"

"One of the students posted it to his PicturSpam this
morning." Millie rose gracefully from the guest chair,
every hair in place, every fingernail perfectly polished.
As it should be. Women like Millie didn't sweat—they
glistened. And men certainly didn't scowl when they
looked at her.

Kate squashed the stab of envy by dropping into her
own chair with a huff. "You are not going to post that."

Millie cocked her head, smiling wistfully as she
tapped the tablet's screen. "God, I love these kids. They
can snap a picture faster than I can blink, and I've got
dry eye syndrome."

"You can't…" Kate sputtered. "You wouldn't!"

"Oh, yes, I could." Millie's smile simmered to a
smirk as she switched off the screen. "But you're right.
I wouldn't. Why would I want to release a picture with
you looking like that?"

"Hey!"

Millie brushed off her indignation. "Whose side do you think I'm on anyway?"

"It's not a matter of sides," Kate protested.

"Bullshit." The smile was gone, chased off by the hard-bitten sentiment. Millie's lips tightened into a thin scarlet line. "It's always a matter of sides."

"Millicent is right."

Both women looked up. Avery Preston—Wolcott's first and only women's studies and feminist literature professor and the third member of their unholy alliance—stood in the doorway. With her flowing skirt and flyaway hair, Avery reminded Kate of the holy-roller mother in the film version of Stephen King's *Carrie*.

Millie blinked as if their friend's appearance was painful to behold. The two women rarely agreed on anything beyond their mutual affection for adult beverages and the undiluted sexiness of Alan Rickman's voice. "I am?"

"Life is all about choices. Knowing which side to choose is a valuable skill," Avery asserted. "We're on yours."

"I always back the winner," Millie said with a decisive nod.

Kate barked a laugh and wagged her head at the pair of them. "I don't see the big deal. I've hardly exchanged more than twenty words with the man."

"Yeah, well, I wish you would," Millie said as she tucked her ever-present tablet under her arm. "Wolcott is a guppy in a pool full of sharks. The school needs all the free press we can get, and if Coach Stud Muffin is what it takes to get it, then I'll do what I have to do to keep him in the news."

"That's our Millie," Avery said with an amused laugh. "Do we need to buy you a big pimp feather for your hat?"

Turning on her stiletto heel, Millie exaggerated the sway of her hips as she strolled to the door. "I bet I could rock that feather. Are we meeting at Calhoun's?"

Avery nodded. "I'll be there. Shaping young minds gives a woman a terrible thirst."

Millie gave Avery a slow once-over, then gave her a syrupy sweet smile. "I wish they could figure out exactly what causes a woman to choose such a terrible skirt."

"Ladies," Kate warned. "No bickering until we have fuel to throw on the fire."

"Oh, I have fuel." Millie held the darkened screen up in silent reminder.

Kate sat up straighter. "You promise you won't release that picture?"

Millie glanced at Avery, then turned back, her eyes alight with challenge. "Get me something better, and I won't have to."

"Blackmail."

"Incentive."

"Extortion," Kate shot back.

"On that note," Avery interjected, "see you two love-birds at happy hour."

The moment their fashion-flouting friend was out of earshot, Millie refocused on Kate. "Buy yourself some new workout clothes, Kathryn. You look like a refugee from the nineties."

Falling back into a sulk, Kate crossed her arms over her chest and slumped in her seat. "I *am* a refugee from the nineties."

Millie shook her head in disgust. "Looks like it's time we had another shopping excursion. I can't have you delivering commencement addresses in your shorts and sneakers."

"But I rock the shorts and sneakers look."

Millie's expression softened, but she glanced warily at the wall rack that held Kate's extensive collection of athletic shoes. "You do, but…no."

"Lunch too?" Kate would submit to thumbscrews rather than say it aloud, but she loved shopping with Millie. The woman was flashy and irreverent and Kate's personal heroine. Kate never failed to return from one of their expeditions feeling a little brighter.

Millie inclined her head, her ever-perfect pageboy curling over one cheek. "We will need food."

"And wine?"

"I *have* been trying to consume more fruit." Millie bit the inside of her cheek. "Think we can get Avery Steinem to join us?"

Kate snorted. "Not likely."

Tapping the pointy tip of one glossy fingernail against the dark screen, Millie sent her a stern but sympathetic look. "I promise I'll never leak a picture of you without lip gloss, but remember, I have to feed the beast."

"Duly noted."

"And I *am* on your side, doll."

"I appreciate that."

Millie raised her fist, then waggled her fingers in a girly wave. "Solidarity, sister!"

Kate chuckled as she jiggled her mouse to wake the computer. A document with the usual rhetoric half filled the screen, but even the daunting task of writing yet another speech failed to dampen her spirits. An afternoon of basking in Millie's brashness was exactly what she needed to shake the fog that had enveloped her for the last few days.

Two weeks had passed since Danny McMillan's hiring was announced, and the whole campus was abuzz. All questions of ethics and integrity were swept aside. Danny was the anointed one. The man destined to bring their never-a-contender football team to glory. Kate snorted and shook her head as she placed her fingers on the keys. Coach McMillan was going to need more than Millie's manic publicity grabs to meet that goal. He needed a freakin' miracle.

―――――

Wolcott University's football facilities left something to be desired. Truthfully, they left a lot to be desired. Like a practice field that wasn't actually a field.

Mike shifted his weight from one foot to the other but kept his gaze locked on the action on the field. "Not exactly what you're used to, I know—"

Once upon a time, Danny's scrimmages had taken place in a two-story, indoor practice arena carpeted with the latest and greatest in synthetic turf and boasting a weight room that spanned the length of the field. Today, he stood in a field of mushy weeds watching a ragtag bunch of walk-on wannabes play hot potato with a football. And it still wasn't the worst he'd seen in the last few years.

"Yeah. That sandy hardpack the boys at Rio River Junior College played on was sure nice," Danny murmured, his eyes trailing after a running back who wasn't completely without promise. "Go Rattlers."

"Danny—"

"Stop fretting. You sound like my mother."

"How is your mom?"

Danny had to smile at Mike's eagerness to change the subject. "Relieved." Wolcott might have been a step up from his last couple of jobs, but his had been an extremely long fall from grace. "And still too much woman for you."

Mike sighed. "Probably always will be."

But as much as Danny liked to brag about her, his public humiliation had taken a toll on his indomitable mother.

"And Tommy?"

*Take care of Tommy. Protect Tommy.*

*With my life, Ma.*

At the mere mention of his little brother, the ache in Danny's jaw came back with a vengeance. He hadn't been the only McMillan to lose his job that day. "Doing fine," he replied tightly.

And it was the truth. After the shitstorm finally died down, Danny had made a few calls. His baby brother had come out a damn sight better than he had, career-wise. Hell, Tommy was a hot commodity these days. One of the best specialty coaches in the business. Ironic, considering his little brother was the one who screwed everything up in the first place. But Danny spent a lot of time and energy trying not to think about all the ways Tommy had fucked him over.

"Your office okay?"

His office was little more than a shoebox filled with shipping cartons, but he couldn't care less. "It's fine."

"I think you have some potential in the backfield."

Danny winced. The needy edge in his friend's

voice both annoyed and shamed him. The fact that Mike had taken a risk in hiring him wasn't lost on either of them. "Possibly."

"You can do what you want with most of the staff, but I'll ask you to keep Mack Nord if you can find a spot for him. The guy is one of Wolcott's longest-tenured employees and kind of an institution."

"Seem to have a lot of those around here."

"Tradition is important at Wolcott. It's a pretty, uh, conservative community overall, and you know people will be watching…"

Mike trailed off, and the awkwardness grew thick between them.

Danny fixed him with a level look. "Watching what?"

"Everything."

The word fell to the spongy ground with a thud. Shoving his hands deeper in his pockets, Danny zeroed in on a cornerback who seemed to have no clue how to defend the post. But instead of mentally tracing the route, his thoughts churned through the clues Mike trailed through their conversations.

They were as simple to decode as a Cracker Jack mystery. The kinds of shenanigans that got him sent to Division II purgatory would get him exiled for good next time. This was his second chance at the big time. There wouldn't be a third.

As if he would risk this opportunity. Not only had he gotten older while he was wasting the best years of his career at the JuCo level, but he had also managed to grow wiser. A part of him wished he'd thrown his staff under the bus, but that wasn't how things were done. The head coach was responsible for everything that went on under him. He wasn't the first coach to own up to a laundry list of NCAA recruiting violations. Hell, most of the big guys had. Taken in context, his indiscretion was small potatoes.

But then the shit hit the fan in college athletics, and suddenly, zero tolerance was the rule of the day. No one wanted perspective; they wanted blood. The NCAA had been poised to make an example of someone, anyone. He was just the first to own up to committing some sins after college football was rocked by a series of scandals so salacious no breach of ethics could or would be forgiven. Particularly not when it was discovered that the coach in question was also involved in a relationship with a gorgeous red-headed grad student.

He turned to face his new boss. "Mike, I'm really glad to be here." The simple statement seemed to put the AD at ease, but even thinking back to those jumbled, frantic days still twisted Danny's gut into knots. "I think I'll get a dog."

The lack of segue didn't seem to faze Mike in the least. "As long as it's not one of those little yappy ones."

Danny crossed his arms over his chest as he watched a wobbly spiral arc through the air. "You think I look like the type to carry a dog around in a purse?"

"I'm just saying." Mike shrugged. "A Lab or a shepherd maybe."

A lazy wide receiver loped down field, still chasing the ball as it bounced end over end toward the far sideline. "I'm cutting that kid," Danny said without a glance in Mike's direction.

"Your roster isn't deep."

The statement was a reminder, not a warning, and

Danny knew it. "I'd take an enthusiastic water boy over a slug like that."

"You're the coach." For the first time since Danny had stepped foot on campus, his friend broke out a genuine smile. "So, Millie wants you to—"

He didn't bother to hide his wince. The conversation he'd had with the head of the PR department had been oddly confrontational, though he couldn't for the life of him figure out what he'd done to offend the woman. "Yeah, I talked to her, I don't see how—"

He was cut off by a shout of, "Hey, Coach!"

His head popped up automatically. He scanned the overgrown field looking for who'd called him, but every player was facing the road, not him. He shot Mike a puzzled glance, then searched the field again. "The hell?"

Shielding his eyes from the slanting afternoon sun, he caught sight of a slender, shapely silhouette set off against the fender of a classic Mustang convertible. Recognition kicked in, and a burst of warmth pulsed through his veins.

Two weeks had passed since he'd started picking apart the film on his half-assed football team. He'd tried to erase the image of Kate Snyder sauntering down those steps, her hand extended and her sharp jaw set. The sight of her lifting weights encased in nothing more than a yard or so of skintight spandex fired his imagination to the point that he'd skipped his workout three days in a row, something he hadn't done since…ever.

He'd been avoiding her. Fat lot of good that did. Even from this distance, he could tell he'd failed at banking the inferno her cool handshake sparked in him. Dangerous. The woman was dangerous. He needed to remember that. Career suicide on legs.

His pulse rate kicked up when she pushed away from the car and started toward the field. Danny rolled his shoulders back and widened his stance. Fit as he was, he clenched his abs just a little bit as he watched those long legs eat up the ground. In a gesture he was coming to realize was habit, she tucked her shiny, brown hair behind her ear, then shooed the slackers away.

"Back to work, or I'll have all y'all running laps," she called to his players.

Beside him, Mike stiffened and shot him a sidelong look, but Danny wasn't about to take the bait. He wasn't an impressionable young player or the hot-headed prima donna he'd once been. He wasn't about to let a woman trip him up. Never again.

"Afternoon, Coach Snyder," he called as she approached. "What brings you here?"

"I was just driving by on my way home, and I saw you boys out here."

She made one of those flirty, fluttery gestures meant to deflect and distract. It wasn't until Danny caught himself staring at those graceful fingers that he realized how powerful a weapon it truly was. Giving himself an internal shake, he forced himself to step forward rather than retreat. This was his turf, damn it. Literally. He wasn't about to challenge her on the basketball court. She needed to stay the hell away from his practice field.

What little action he had happening on the field ground to a halt. Only old Mack Nord had the ability to keep his head in the game when Kate Snyder happened past, and he'd returned to the drill he was running with a friendly wave. The other two guys Danny had inherited as assistant coaches weren't so cool. Neither were the players who were pulling cell phones out of he didn't want to know where and snapping photos as if her appearance marked the start of coffee-break time.

He nodded to the milling players and raised his voice. "As you can see, we have our work cut out for us. Don't we, fellas?"

The phones disappeared, and his team snapped back into action. After all, they had an audience to impress now. Danny focused his attention on the woman in front of him. That was both a blessing and a curse. Her eyes were big and thickly lashed, a medium brown that might have looked muddy if not for liberal flecks of gold. The healthy glow of her skin was the kind no cosmetic could mimic. Her lips were bare and pink and fucking perfect. He forced himself to look away as he grappled to gain the upper hand.

"Nice of you to stop by." He managed a smile he hoped wasn't as dorky as it felt. He couldn't make a bigger fool of himself than the gaggle of man-children showboating up and down the field. "I can't wait to crash one of your practices."

A hint of color appeared in her cheeks, and she lowered her gaze, shuttering the flash of annoyance that flared in those mesmerizing eyes. She tipped her head just enough to free the curtain of silky, brown hair. He had to curl his fingers into his palm to keep from touching it.

He heard Mike's warning cough, but it sounded a million miles away. It didn't matter anyway. Nothing in the world could have pried his eyes from the pearly flush creeping up her throat. The urge to chase it with his mouth hit him like a two-by-four upside the head.

She swayed slightly, and he followed, leaning into her as if they were connected by an invisible string.

A string their esteemed athletic director seemed to be determined to snap. Thank Christ.

Mike executed an expert pivot and inserted his shoulder between them, effectively drawing Danny's attention. "Other than the green-gold game, Coach Snyder doesn't hold open practice sessions."

Glancing from the AD to the glorious woman across from him, Danny forced a tight smile. "Yeah, I never did either, but I guess there's no way to block the lookie-loos out here."

Kate's eyebrows rose. The effect was almost as potent as the smile she'd used to subdue his players. Lines creased her high forehead, but the marks only made her more attractive. They spoke of a life lived open to surprise and amusement. The sudden need to know every little thing that tickled her funny bone or ticked her off made Danny's mouth run dry. He needed to know so he could figure out how to rank number one in both of those categories.

"Lookie-loos?" Her smile was syrupy sweet. She leaned in closer and lowered her voice. "If that's the case, I hope you can find some soon." She made a point of scanning the nonexistent sidelines for equally nonexistent fans. "Seems kind of…sad out here."

Kate glanced down, and he had to force himself to unclench his fists. Of course, he was a second too late. Her smile widened as she backed away.

"The *Sentinel* is looking for an interview," she announced, darting a glance at the boss man.

Danny frowned, confused by the swift change in

topic. "The *Sentinel*? Why are you telling us this? You the new secretary or something?"

Mike nearly cracked one of Danny's ribs with his pointy elbow. Kate, of course, caught the not-so-subtle warning. Her eyes narrowed, and her jaw tightened. She hesitated for a moment, as if weighing her options. But when she spoke, her drawl was as thick as molasses.

"Or something. I'm pretty booked up with the filming for NSN, but I figured I'd mention this to you." She fixed him with a disconcertingly direct stare. "Hey, they did a profile on you once, didn't they?"

They did a hatchet job on him just after the debacle, but he saw no need to acknowledge what they all knew.

"Caught it on a replay last week."

She flashed her championship smile again, but there was no warmth behind it. As a matter of fact, it felt a helluva lot like a shank of cold steel piercing his gut.

"Anyhow, I was thinking maybe you'd want a shot at a more friendly news outlet, so I thought I'd pass it along. I'm nothing if not a team player."

Message delivered, she turned on her heel and started back toward her car. Ice queen or not, he watched her walk away. He couldn't help himself. Hell, there wasn't a man alive who wouldn't be drawn in by the subtle sway of her hips.

"Don't even think it, man," Mike said, his voice low and ominous.

Danny shot him a glance. "Think about what?"

"You know what."

The edge in Mike's tone barely registered. Another male voice called, "Hey, Coach! Heads up!"

Danny jerked his head up, but once again, no one

was looking at him. They were all focused on Kate. The wind caught her hair as she turned, plastering a few wisps to her cheek and neck while the rest danced in the whirling spring breeze.

A young man in a cropped practice jersey cocked his arm and let the ball fly. The high, tight spiral arced nearly the width of the field. A gust of spring wind pinned Kate's shirt to her lithe frame. She stepped into the pass, her palms open and her fingers spread wide and welcoming. A low, throaty laugh rippled across the field as she secured the ball and feinted to her left. The players on the field erupted into whoops and catcalls, and she shook her head, grinning as she brushed the hair from her face. She tossed the ball underhand to a nearby assistant and then waved to the boys before starting for her car.

Danny stood transfixed until she reached the driver's door, willing her to look up once more. But he got no sneaking peeks or coy smiles from Kate Snyder. No, when she looked up, she stared directly at him, her chin lifted, her hair dancing in the spring breeze. They stood there, locked in silent challenge, and all the sounds of the drills being run on the scrubby field faded away. Then she cupped her hands around her mouth and shouted, "Hey, Coach, get your head in the game!"

Danny had to laugh. At last, he'd met a worthy opponent. And all the warnings in the world couldn't stop him from getting in the game. He lifted a hand in a half wave.

"Get crossways with her, and there's nothing I can do to save you," Mike reminded him.

He spared his friend a glance. "I thought you and your pal Millie wanted us to get crossways."

"You know what I'm saying."

Danny nodded once and turned his attention back to the field. "Who threw that?"

"Kilgorn. Wide receiver," Mike answered without missing a beat.

"He's our new quarterback."

An engine roared to life, but Danny didn't look back. Clapping his hands to get their attention, he strode onto the overgrown field and held up one hand to call for the ball. "Okay, men, bring it in. Time to get down to business."

# Chapter 4

"A HUNDRED AND TEN PERCENT FROM NOW ON. NOTHING less. You got me?" Danny gazed at the sea of sullen faces in front of him, searching for a flicker of response. He got zero. "Champions aren't born—they're made. If you're not willing to bring your all to the game and leave everything you have on the field, I don't have room for you on my team."

Silence. Not even the shuffling of shoes or a sniffle. Stone-cold silence. His voice echoed off the dry-erase boards that lined the walls. Shadows of last season's busted plays hid behind the thousands of X and O marks left by basketball. The jumble had to be Kate Snyder's brand of alphabet soup. Her season lasted to the very end. The men's team didn't even make the tournament.

Tearing his gaze from the boards, he stared up at the strips of fluorescent lighting. Talking to this bunch was like trying to break through the toughest defensive line. But he'd do it. Eventually, he'd find the hole and punch right through. He just had to keep pounding.

Pitching his voice lower, he gave them his best "I'm leveling with you" stare. Only a few hearty souls dared to meet his eyes. "This is Division I football. You're here because you have the brains and the drive to be here. Now, I'll admit that most of the guys you're going up against can barely tie their shoelaces..."

That earned him a couple of snickers. Danny grabbed them and ran, hoping he might find a way to channel their classroom discipline onto the gridiron. The principles of hard work and determination should translate. Unfortunately, it was hard to infuse confidence into a team that hadn't won a single conference game in four seasons.

"But they can play ball. So can you. You're big enough, strong enough..." Crap. Tapping old Stuart Smalley routines for inspiration—a new low for him. "We'll win because we work harder and play smarter than anyone else. I expect those of you willing to give that hundred and ten percent to spend your summer sharpening your skills. We can win. We *will* win. I won't accept anything less."

With a bob of his head to his coaching staff, Danny stepped out from behind the lectern.

At last, his players stirred. A few grumbled as they shuffled from the room. Danny's gut wrenched when he realized that none of them would even attempt to catch his eye. Not one suck-up in a whole pack of born over-achievers. He was in deep shit.

He gravitated to the door, as anxious to leave the claustrophobic meeting room as the rest but hoping he hid it a little better. Most of the coaches would be taking off on vacation as soon as the students finished final exams. He had precious little time to make inroads with this program. Some of his staff and a handful of seniors would be back in a few weeks to help run the camps for teenagers who dreamed of playing for powerhouse schools in Florida, Alabama, or Michigan. He found it hard to believe many potential all-Americans had visions of wearing Warrior green and gold, but you never knew. The school had roots that ran deep, and the camps were a good way to spot talent and build relationships early.

When he turned back to switch off the overhead lighting, he spotted Mack Nord still parked in his chair.

Mack was exactly the kind of coach Danny admired. The type he'd always wanted to impress as a player. The man was a football fundamentalist so fervent, Danny wouldn't have been shocked to hear he had his own Sunday morning show on local access cable.

The man cut no corners in putting every player through his paces. Danny appreciated that kind of old-school grit. He also liked listening to Mack's assessments of each player's strengths and weaknesses. Just the thought of those terse rundowns made Danny smile. On his first day there, Mack had certainly wasted no time sharing his opinion that Danny had been a fat-headed punk who let his dick make career choices for him.

He also said he hoped Danny had learned his damn lesson.

The same assessment had chased Danny from one no-name school to the next, but this time, he wanted to disprove it once and for all. "Mack? Did you need something else?"

The man's white hair shone silver in the harsh overhead light. He tipped his head back and jerked his chin at one of the mottled whiteboards. "I'm taking the wife to Destin for a couple of weeks as soon as we wrap up the school year." A wry smile twisted his lips. "She says it's the price I pay for scribbling formations on every napkin or envelope in the house." He chuckled and gave his head a rueful shake. "Once, I used one of her makeup pencils to sketch something out on the mirror. She damn near scalped me with her Pink Lady shaver."

Danny couldn't help but laugh. He'd spotted Mack's wife bringing the old coot his lunch more than once since he'd started at Wolcott. She topped out at five feet tall and couldn't have weighed much more than 110 pounds. Just the same, he had no trouble envisioning the scalping scene.

Tucking his hands in the pockets of his khakis, Danny stepped back into the room.

"Don't let her complaining fool you. The woman never misses a game. She stores decades of stats in that pretty little head of hers and puts up with a guy who spends all year obsessing over a four-month season." Mack gave a one-shouldered shrug, then sighed. "I guess she deserves a couple of weeks at the beach."

"And a medal."

"Oh, she has plenty of those. Every one of them set with diamonds." He rose with an audible groan and turned to face Danny head-on. "They're beat down. Calling them a bunch of losers isn't going to make them any better."

Mack's blunt words stopped Danny in his tracks. "I didn't call them losers."

Mack still wore that smirk, but the sharp edge of his tone cut through Danny's protest. "Not in so many words."

"Not in any words," Danny snapped, pissed off to find himself playing defense once again.

How the hell did this keep happening? He wasn't a lineman, for Christ's sake. He was the quarterback. The coach. This guy's boss. He'd be damned if he'd spend one more minute apologizing for his past. Tucking his wounded pride under his arm, he charged right into the fray.

"I believe it's reasonable to expect players who compete at this level—"

"Level," Mack sneered. "Son, you need to stop worrying about who's above you and below you and start worrying about what you have right up in your face."

Danny stared at the older man for a moment, mentally rifling through a half dozen snide remarks about the above and below part, then tossing them aside in favor of driving straight up the middle. "What's that supposed to mean?"

Mack shuffled over to the nearest whiteboard and picked up the eraser. Danny bit his tongue to keep from protesting the obliteration of what might have been the most brilliant basketball play ever. Not that he would know. Hell, he didn't even know if Kate Snyder had been the one to draw it.

"You forget you're not dealing with those meatheaded numbskulls you had at Northern."

The gravelly admonition jolted Danny from his fugue. "What?" He blinked twice as the implication sank its hooks. "Are you trying to tell me these kids are too smart to play good football?"

Mack took one last swipe at the play, then tossed the eraser onto the table as he turned to face him. "No, I'm telling you that they aren't talented enough to play anywhere else."

The bald statement set Danny back on his heels for a second, but like any good quarterback, he recovered quickly. "Well, then I guess we'll need to work on our recruiting."

"You can recruit until you're blue in the face, but you know as well as I do that no ballplayer worth his salt wants to play on a losing team."

"Is this some kind of super-loser circle jerk?" Danny regretted the snappish retort the instant it popped out, but like a fumbled ball, there was nothing he could do but fall on it. "There has to be a way to break the cycle."

Mack nodded once. It was an achingly slow tip of his head but a nod nonetheless. "There is, but I can tell you it has nothing to do with playing on any of your levels. I had a nun who used to yell at us to keep our eyes on our own papers. That's what you need to do, son. Look at what's in front of you. Make the best choices you can. Stop worrying about what everyone else has. It's time for *you* to play smart."

The sneer was back, and the damn thing made Danny feel about two inches tall. Crossing his arms over his chest, he planted his feet wide and lifted an eyebrow. "Are you going to share your thoughts, Yoda, or am I supposed to use the Force?"

Mack looked confused for a moment, then his face lit with a smile. "*Star Trek*."

"Wars. *Star Wars*."

"Whatever." Mack continued to smile, but it softened a little as he gave an easy shrug. "The love of the game. You forget, these guys are playing because they love it. There's not one of them with a snowball's chance in hell at playing pro ball. They play because they've always played. Talent or no talent, a player is a player as long as he suits up."

Danny's arms fell to his sides as the truth of Mack's wisdom burrowed in and started to take root. Still, he had to find some way to get through to his players. "But at this level—"

Mack cut Danny off with a pitying look, turned his back, and headed for the door.

"Football is football, no matter what *level*," Mack said, practically spitting out the last word. "Whether it's peewee or the NFC, you still have to find a way to get the ball over the line. That's why they call it a goal."

Danny felt like he'd just taken a hit at the knees. One delivered by a crusty old man in blindingly white sneakers.

"Your job is to show them how to do that. If they can't run it straight up the middle or airmail it in, you need to think smarter. Play smarter. Find a way for a bunch of brainiacs who simply love football to play the game to win."

Humbled. Hobbled. Helpless. Danny wanted to grab Mack and beg him to hand over the key, tell him how a guy who'd never played on a team that was less than a contender for a title was supposed to connect with kids who had nothing but participation trophies.

"They love it just as much as you do, hotshot. Start with that, and see what you can do." Then the mouthy old man ambled from the room as if he hadn't just told off his boss.

Danny watched him go, a mixture of awe and ire swirling in his gut. One thing was certain: he needed to talk to Millie Jensen about getting Mack his own Sunday morning show. He'd kick ass at it.

Casting one last glance at the hieroglyphics left on the whiteboard, Danny chuckled to himself as he pulled the door to the meeting room closed behind him. The corridor off the main hall was dim and deserted. A couple of aging display cases featured the few moments of glory the men's basketball team had known. Another paid homage to a mishmash of baseball, softball, and golf.

Rounding the corner, Danny trailed his fingers over the ancient plywood sign mounted to the wall. It was a relic from the old basketball arena and now served as a touchstone for all Wolcott athletes. Every student and staffer ever to wear the green and gold touched the peeling paint and plywood every time they passed. Being an athlete and as superstitious as any, Danny did the same.

Then he came to a complete stop in the center of the hallway. Sleek, frameless trophy cases stretched from the main entrance to the athletic department administrative offices and beyond. Discreet recessed lighting made the most of each shining silver tray and gleaming gold cup. Hunks of cut crystal shot rainbows on the walls.

He'd been scrupulously avoiding the proof of Kate Snyder's legacy since his first and only press conference. The urge to follow that multicolored trail proved to be too much to resist. Danny checked over his shoulder before tucking his hands in his pockets and giving in to temptation.

Jerseys from her playing days vied with more than a dozen framed team photos. As a player, she wore her game face for every photo. There were a few of those stern shots from her early coaching days too. It took a minute for him to spot her standing slightly behind her former coach and mentor, Buzzy Bryant. But as her career progressed, Kate seemed to learn how to smile. A photograph of her surrounded by her team after she'd helped them secure their first championship as a coach captured a wide smile of undiluted joy.

Mack's words came at him like a five-man rush. *Love of the game*. That's what he saw when he looked at Kate Snyder. She'd never lost her love of the game, and that was what made her a champion.

"I have a key. Let me know if you want to pet something."

Danny jumped and whirled. Busted. By the woman herself. Gritting his teeth, he shoved his hands deeper into his pockets as if that would make it look like he was just casually walking past. "What? I was just…"

His train of thought jumped the tracks when she tilted her head, those amazing amber eyes fixed on him with what appeared to be bottomless patience. She wore a thin, clingy sweater that was exactly the same shade of pale pink as her lips. The ends of her hair slipped over her shoulder and brushed her cheek. She tucked the hair behind her ear in a move he was beginning to memorize. The glossy, brown strands looked silky and soft. Danny damn near shoved his fists through the seams of his pockets to keep from reaching for her.

Those pink lips twitched at the corners, but she didn't quite smile. "Personally, I think some of the less prestigious awards give better trophies. My personal favorite is the crystal phallus I scored when I was named collegiate coach of the year by *Sports Nation* magazine." Her brow furrowed. "Women's division, of course." Pursing her lips, she tipped her head to the other side and widened her eyes. "I wonder if the guys get dildos to take home too."

Her feigned innocence, the husky timbre of her voice, and the crudeness of her observation startled a laugh from him. "I wouldn't know."

Kate chuckled, shaking her head ruefully. "I can't believe I just said that. You're a bad influence on me."

Danny shrugged and pulled his hands from his pockets. "I seem to be bringing out the best in people today."

She laughed again, but this time, her smile looked almost sincere. "Having a hard time with your troops?"

Giving in to impulse, he gestured in the direction of their offices. Not that his was anywhere near hers. She had a corner office with a quad view. His was little more than a janitor's closet at the very end of the hall, but he wasn't about to complain about office space.

He cast a sidelong glance as she fell into step beside him. "Let's just say I'm having a little trouble finding the handle."

She nodded as they approached her door. "Well, give yourself a chance to take a breath. You have a couple of months, and you have Mack." Her keys jingled as she turned the lock. "If anyone has a bead on what's going on around here, it's him."

Danny ran a tired hand over his face. His teeth and jaw ached from clenching. He pressed two fingers to the joint and rubbed at the tension, reminding himself that this was part of his penance. He should be used to receiving unsolicited advice and lectures from people who hardly knew him. They were the price he paid for fucking up in a spectacularly public way. But that didn't mean he had to like them. "Oh yeah, Mack has opinions."

Another one of Kate's fire-starter laughs drew him out of his pity party. He looked up just as she switched on the office light.

"I guess he's been on his soapbox already?" she asked. She shot him a look so heavy with sympathy, it should have pissed him off. But it didn't. If anything, it stirred him up on a bunch of different levels. Sure, there was a physical attraction, but Danny felt the tug of something more. She was giving him a glimpse of the woman behind the game face and big talk. The superstar who knew exactly how it felt to be condescended to on a daily basis but still held her ground with grace and dignity.

Swallowing a cold lump of pride, he craned his neck to peer into her office, uncertain if sympathy was enough to get him across the threshold. He didn't chance it. No point in giving her cause to wipe that sweet little smile off her face.

"I know I should listen to him. Logically, I know that."

"But it's hard to take advice from a guy who's never even been near the top of the heap," she concluded.

Stunned by her quick and highly inaccurate analysis, he took that dangerous step over the threshold. "That's not it at all—" He jerked to a stop just inside the spacious office and looked up in shock. "Whoa."

One wall of her office was dedicated to mounted wire racks holding dozens of pairs of shoes. Everything from the newest in the Jordan line to those pointy-toed white sneakers cheerleaders used to wear. Sneakers in every color and style. Some were leftovers from another era, and others looked like they'd never been worn.

"You were saying?" she prompted tersely.

"Do you wear all these?"

"When the mood suits me."

He tore his gaze from the wall of shoes, but she kept her eyes averted as she rifled through the papers in her inbox. "The mood?" Nodding to the feminine canvas sneakers, he asked, "What mood are those?"

She jerked a sheaf of papers from the stack and stuffed them into her oversized shoulder bag. "Those are for when I'm feeling a little 'no one invited you in here.'"

Pleased to have put her on defense for once, he stroked the acid-green laces on a pair of gunmetal-gray running shoes. "I bet these are your 'I feel pretty' shoes."

She stepped out from behind her desk and nodded to the door. "Right now, I'm wearing my 'the lead anchor from the biggest sports network in the country is waiting for me' shoes."

Danny glanced down and for the first time noticed that she was wearing sandals. They were flat and black, but they had those super-long laces that wound around her ankle a half dozen times. Like a gladiator. She'd tied the ends in a neat bow front and center. Her toenails were polished fire-engine red, and she wore black capris that clung to every single inch of never-ending legs.

He wanted to unlace those sandals with his teeth, peel that pretty sweater over her head, and drag those snug pants down her legs. Visions of Audrey Hepburn and Mary Tyler Moore danced in his head. Obscene visions in which he did unspeakable things to Dick Van Dyke's TV wife. The blood rushed from his head, and his dick grew hard. He might have seen a few other kinds of stars too, but Kate grabbed his arm and propelled him toward the door.

"You're wrong," he croaked.

She pushed him into the hall and whirled to pull the door closed behind her. "Wrong about what?"

A creak in her voice gave him courage. Then again, it might have been his hard-on talking. Either way, for

the first time since he'd stepped foot on campus, he
felt emboldened.

"I'm not having a hard time listening to Mack because
he doesn't have a winning record. It's because he's right,
and I have no idea how to change my game plan."

"Oh."

She looked up at him, her face a picture of confused
annoyance, and he smiled. It was a slow, cocky smile.
The kind he hadn't been able to muster for quite some
time. But pointed at the very fair Kate Snyder, it seemed
as natural as breathing. A pretty pink blush rose in her
cheeks when she realized she still had a grip on his arm.
She let go as if she'd been singed, but it was too late.
He'd seen stars in her eyes too.

"And you're wrong about the shoes," he added.

"Shoes?"

The husky timbre of her voice told him she wasn't as
unaffected as she'd like to be. That knowledge gave him
strength. Treating her to the same kind of slow, deliberate once-over she'd given him, he let his gaze travel all
the way down to her feet again. Then he leaned in, not
quite touching her. "Be careful with those shoes, Coach.
I don't think you know exactly what they're saying."

With that, he turned and walked away. But he felt her
eyes on his back as he sauntered toward the no-man's-
land that housed his cracker box of an office. At last,
he'd found a place comfortable enough to unpack his
collection of ball caps. He just wished he'd thought to
ask her where she'd scored those display racks.

# Chapter 5

DANNY'S STEPS SLOWED AS HE CRESTED THE HILL, A MIXTURE of anticipation and dread pooling in his gut. He'd asked the school grounds crew to do something, anything, about the condition of the practice field, but he hadn't brought himself to look yet. He'd also asked Mack to arrange for a half dozen of their most promising players to meet him there. Truthfully, he wasn't exactly certain the boys would show.

The grass was freshly mown, the field itself cut an inch shorter than the surrounding area. It looked more golf green than gridiron, but someone had taken the trouble to run chalk stripes at precise five-yard intervals and plant neon-orange pylons to mark every ten yards. He caught a gleam of silver and spotted Mack standing in the far end zone. The players Danny had requested milled around the old man.

The young men jostled and jockeyed, but none of them dared bump into Mack. Their semiscruffy faces wore smiles as they peppered the seasoned, old coach with questions, jokes, and jibes. To Danny's mind, nothing solidified Mack's status as a Wolcott staple like the boys' open, carefree interaction with the assistant coach. These were the cocky jock grins Danny rarely got to see.

It didn't take a PhD in psychology to figure it out. With Mack, they were players. The best he had. But next to Danny, with his gameday glory past and a gaudy Super Bowl ring to his name, they felt like they were nothing. He made them feel like nothing.

Now it was time to fix that.

Mack looked up as Danny approached. Like a flock of birds rising on an updraft, the boys dispersed, putting space between themselves and Danny. Danny smiled at them all, but only the boldest—Kilgorn, the wide receiver soon-to-be quarterback—had the guts to flash a grin. The others just shuffled their feet and tugged at their practice jerseys.

Danny turned to Mack, nodding to the field and the mesh equipment bag at the older man's feet.

"Thanks for getting all this together." He reached into the bag and pulled out a single football. "I think this'll be all we need." Danny couldn't help but smile when that pebbled leather settled into his palm and his fingertips found the laces. He curled the ball into his chest, cradling it like it was a damn security blanket, then eyed his players. "You're welcome to stick around if you want, but we're going to keep this pretty low-key," he said to Mack.

Mack snorted, then nodded to the aluminum-framed lawn chair he'd set out on the sideline. "Whatever the hell this is, I wouldn't miss it for the world."

The old man shambled toward his chair, leaving Danny alone with his handpicked players. He eyed them as closely as they watched him. Jerking his chin toward the center of the field, he said, "Follow me," and took off at a jock trot, not daring to look back to see if they actually did. He turned to face them at the fifty-yard line. His players stood assembled a safe five yards away.

He tossed the ball from hand to hand. Though he knew exactly what he wanted to say to them, he'd be damned if he knew how to get the conversation to kick off. Thankfully, Kilgorn wasn't afraid to wade into the silence.

"Are we in trouble for something, Coach?"

Danny caught the ball and tucked it safely into the crook of his arm. "Trouble? No. Should you be?"

"How come it's only us?" a deeper voice asked.

Danny's mental roster clicked. Oswalt. Defensive end. Junior. Six four, two seventy. Quick off the blocks. Leading the team in sacks. Which meant he actually broke through one of the massive Mid-American Conference offensive lines last season and caught the quarterback's ankle. He might lack confidence but certainly not intelligence.

"I picked you guys because I'm looking to you to be team leaders next year."

"We're not all seniors," Kilgorn was quick to point out.

The cornerback, a wiry kid named Nelson with kami kaze instincts, snorted as he eyed the true freshman wide receiver standing on the other side of the linemen. "Some of us aren't old enough to be out of our red shirts yet."

No, Danny's bench wasn't deep, and moving Kilgorn to QB meant he would have to play green in the passing game. But young Marcus Landry refused to rise to his teammate's bait, proving he was part of the reason Wolcott put up such a high grade point average each year. Before they could start ripping into each other, Danny smacked the ball against his open palm and dropped back a few yards, ending in the passing stance he'd learned in the peewee league. "Spread out."

They stared at him blankly.

He smacked the ball again, then zipped one straight at the freshman's gut. Landry wasn't without skill or instinct. He caught the ball right in the breadbasket and cradled it close. When he looked up, his dark eyes were wide with surprise. Danny nodded, confirming that he did indeed just catch a pass from a former Heisman candidate and NFL quarterback.

Tossing off a shrug, Danny took a few more steps back and clapped his hands, signaling for the return of the ball. "Sorry. That's gonna leave a mark."

To his credit, Landry did his best to wing it back at him, but as soft as his hands were, the kid didn't have much of an arm. Danny caught the ball one-handed and dropped back again. This time, the players started to back away.

"Let's play a game of five hundred," he challenged.

"What's that?" Russell, the leader of the offensive line, asked.

Danny cocked his head in disbelief, then shook it slowly. "You never played five hundred as a kid?" A couple nodded, but most wagged their shaggy heads. He tsked and pointed the end of the ball downfield. "Get down there around the twenty-five or thirty."

The players backed downfield but spread out along the line as if he were about to put them through a series of Mack's favorite drills.

He shook his head and waved them in. "No, bunch up together," he called to them. When they complied, he tucked the ball back under his arm and rubbed his palms together in anticipation and raised his voice. "Okay, here's how it goes. I throw the ball, you fight to be the guy to catch it. Whoever snags it gets a hundred points. First man to five hundred gets to throw."

"We're supposed to catch it?" his senior defensive tackle called back.

"Yep." Danny nodded. "And anything goes. Well, no shots to the sac or eye gouging," he amended, "but, you know, go for it."

"But, Coach, we're on D," Oswalt protested.

Danny stared at the kid, letting his incredulity show. "Are you telling me that you never once dreamed of snagging some hotshot QB's pass and running it straight down his throat?"

Oswalt shrugged. "Well, yeah."

Grinning, Danny stepped back into his stance and held the ball like he was posing for a goddamn trading card. "Well, here's your chance, kid. Get ready."

"Do we run it?" Landry yelled, glancing from player to player, then back at him.

"Not for this." The defensive players' faces fell so dramatically, he almost laughed out loud. "Unless you're on D. If one of you guys"—he pointed to the three defensive players in the group—"grab it, you can try to get past me. But if I get two hands on you, you're down. Deal?"

The players nodded and shuffled, smiles cracking their wary expressions as Danny lobbed a high, arcing spiral into the air. Youth, exuberance, and uninjured knees were the keys to pulling down that jump ball. Forgetting the fact that he was still fresh meat to his teammates, Landry snagged the ball. His victory dance was inventive and amusing, but his crowing came to an abrupt halt when his wobbly pass back fell five yards short of Danny's feet.

Chuckling, Danny trotted forward to retrieve the ball. Palming it easily, he pointed a finger at his youngest player. "Good thing you can catch, because my mama can throw deeper than you."

The players hooted and hollered, bumping each other as Danny lobbed another up for grabs. This time, it landed square in Oswalt's hands. The big guy looked up, more surprised than anyone that he had the ball. Laughing, Danny backed off a few steps and waved the big man toward him. "Come on, muscle man. Wanna make me eat that pass?"

Oswalt took off, but the man was more of a cannonball than a bullet. He tried to zig, then zag, but his massive body wasn't meant to juke. Danny let him have another ten yards before tagging him with both hands and plucking the ball from his meaty paws.

"Way to go, big guy," Danny commended. Patting the kid's shoulder, he gave him a playful shove back toward the group. "Make sure you tell Coach Jenkins to give you more cardio work. You can't run it back if you're winded after twenty yards."

"Aw, man. I hate that damn treadmill," Oswalt complained as he took his position in the group.

Danny jerked a thumb at Mack. "Would you rather I have Mack run you through wind sprints?"

"Shit no."

"Didn't think so," Danny replied mildly. "And watch your language. It may just be a few of you here, but this is practice, not a pickup game."

Oswalt grimaced and bobbed a quick nod. "Yes, Coach."

By the time he put up four more passes, the scores

were fairly even, and the boys' competitive instincts were beginning to sharpen. Danny's smile grew wider as their eyes narrowed. He threw short and made them scramble to get under it. He threw long, just to see who had the jets to go after it. He talked a little trash. As expected, they couldn't stop themselves from trying to give it right back to him. Picking at his age and injury, doing their best to psych him out.

All the while, Danny laughed. He laughed more than he could remember laughing on any playing field since his high school days. The days before the big schools came recruiting and his love of the game was consumed by stats and the fight for starts.

When Landry shagged his fifth pass, it was almost a relief. Danny was tired of being the guy standing at the front all the damn time. He wanted to get in there and mix it up. He wanted to play. Just for a little while.

And he did. Moving as a mob, they came in about ten yards to accommodate for Landry's puny arm. Danny crunched Anderson's foot to get one. Jabbed an elbow into Kilgorn's ribs to nab another. As Landry tossed up his sixth pass, the mass of bodies fighting for the ball looked more like a rugby scrum than anything related to American football. Danny, Oswalt, and Nelson were wrestling for the ball like bridesmaids after a bouquet when the shrill *threeeet* of a whistle sliced through the commotion. They all looked up to find Mack standing on the sideline, his hands on his hips and a disapproving scowl dragging the corners of his mouth.

"Are you the head of this program or some kind of head case?"

Danny sat up, the ball clutched to his chest.

"What the hell is this supposed to teach them?" Mack demanded.

"Uh-oh," Anderson muttered. "Someone's in trou-ble."

Eyes locked on his assistant, Danny searched his semiscrambled brain for anything resembling a plausible answer. What came out was, "It was fun."

Mack started toward the center of the field, wearing his "I mean business" face. Knowing he needed a more substantial response—and fast—Danny tossed the ball up to Kilgorn and rolled to his feet.

"Take a knee, fellas," he ordered, running a hand down the front of his grass-stained dry-weave polo. Before Mack had a chance to light into him, he held up a hand to get everyone's attention. "That was fun, wasn't it?"

His players nodded. A few mumbled, "Yes, Coach." Landry grinned and added, "A blast."

"Sometimes we forget football is a game," Danny said quietly. "I mean, we know it's a game, but let's face it. These days it's more like business, right?"

The players nodded in unison. When he turned, he saw Mack nodding too, his lips drawn into a tight line of disapproval.

"But it's a game. A game we all love playing." A lump of emotion formed in his chest. Pressing his fist to his sternum to hold it all in, Danny continued. "I'd forgotten how much I love it until just a few minutes ago. I think maybe a few of you had too."

"But, Coach, that wasn't actually football," Nelson said with a smirk.

Danny met the kid's supercilious stare with what he hoped was an expression of benevolence and not the malevolence he felt toward the little snot in that moment. He'd be damned if he let one snide kid steal his fun.

"We threw the ball, caught the ball, and—in a few cases—ran the ball," Danny added, nodding to the defensive players. "There were points, and we kept score. We fought the good fight, and we all wanted to win." Turning to Mack, he asked, "What do you think we learned here today?"

The old man held his gaze for a moment, then inclined his head in acknowledgment. Turning to the players, he shrugged. "You learned how to play to win."

"Exactly." At that, Danny took a knee too. "Listen, fellas, we all know we play in the toughest conference in the nation. We all know we haven't had a winning season in longer than anyone wants to think about, right?" That scored him a few sullen nods. "But that doesn't mean we can't win. Now, I can go all Al Pacino and give you the *Any Given Sunday* speech…"

"The what?" Landry whispered to Kilgorn.

"It's a movie. Look it up," Danny said impatiently. "The point is, we have to learn to fight again. As a team. I need you guys to be the pillars of that team. I need you guys to learn to fight for each other, count on each other. Then I need you to be the guys all the other players can count on."

Groaning as he unfolded, he pulled himself up to his full height and waggled his fingers at Kilgorn, signaling for the ball. Pigskin snug in his hand again, he searched the upturned faces in front of him. "Can you do that for me? Will you?"

A moment passed when there was nothing but the sound of spring wind and birds chirping. Then Oswalt lumbered to his feet. "I will, Coach."

"Me too," Anderson said, surging up next to him.

He got an "I'm in" from Kilgorn and an "I'm willing to go all in" from Marcus Landry, who obviously needed to stop watching poker tournaments on late-night television.

Danny felt his chest fill with pride as one by one, his players rose to the challenge. Half-afraid he'd say something sappy, he turned to Mack. "You'll work with Coach Jenkins? I want each position to have an individualized training plan for the summer." Turning back to his players, he pressed the ball between both hands. "I expect you guys, as this team's leaders, to be in tip-top shape when you come back for two-a-days. You get me?"

"Yes, Coach." They answered almost in unison. And not one man looked away.

Gripping the ball, Danny forced himself to meet each player's eyes. "I'm not promising we can win big," he said gruffly. "But I'm pretty damn sure we can grab at least one conference game if we play hard. Play smart. Play this game to win. But play because you love it. Otherwise, this is a job, not a game."

Tucking the ball under his arm, he stuck out his hand palm down. "Who's a Warrior?" he asked, using the school's pregame mantra for the first time.

One by one, his players added a hand. On a silent count of three, they broke the huddle with their battle cry: "We are Warriors!"

Danny hung back as Mack and the players made their way back toward campus. Tossing the ball he'd used from hand to hand, he paced the red zone as he replayed the quasi-practice in his head. By the end, he'd forgotten to be the coach. Laughing to himself, he gave his head a shake as he tried to recall the last time that happened. "Years," he mused aloud.

"Talking to yourself already? I thought it would take longer for them to break you."

Whirling, Danny spotted a spectator standing atop the rise at the edge of the practice field. For one heart-stopping moment, he thought the backlit figure might belong to Kate Snyder, but then he realized the shadow was too long and too broad. He shielded his eyes against the glare of the sun and squinted as he started up the incline. Tyrell Ransom smiled as he approached. They'd been introduced in passing but had yet to exchange more than cursory greetings.

"Hey, how's it going?" Danny asked, tucking the ball into the crook of his left arm and offering his hand.

"Good. I just saw some of your guys heading back. From the smiles, I'm guessing they weren't running wind sprints," Ty said, giving Danny's hand a firm shake.

Gripping the football by one end, Danny held it aloft. "Just horsing around a bit. Trying to break the ice, you know?"

Ty nodded. "Oh, I know. The first week I was here, half the team refused to look directly at me."

"Hard to coach someone else's recruits."

"And hard to step into shoes worn by the same guy for decades," Ty added. "But it looks like you've got Mack on your side, so that helps."

Unsure whether the comment was innocent or a dig, Danny responded with generic man compliment number one. "He's a good guy."

"Oh yeah. A really good guy," Ty concurred. He glanced toward campus, then hooked a thumb over his shoulder. "Well, I should get going. We'll catch a beer at Calhoun's sometime, okay?"

Surprised and pleased by the possibility, Danny nodded. "Sounds great."

Ty smiled wide as he backed away. "I'll need to remember to horse around with my guys when I get 'em back this fall. I liked what I saw."

"Can't hurt," Danny answered with a shrug.

Ty pointed one long finger at him. "But I feel compelled to remind you that H-O-R-S-E is a baller's game, Coach."

The taunt coaxed a grin out of Danny. "Tell you what, you hang an old tire from a tree, and we'll see who can throw for letters, Coach."

~~~

Kate's first indication that there'd been a shift in the force was the sudden influx of football players wandering the halls of the athletic center. Usually, the big guys went to ground the minute spring scrimmages ended, but not this year. Rumor had it that Coach McMillan not only extended his program's spring practice schedule into May, but also made it mandatory for returning seniors to participate in at least part of the summer football camps, unless they presented a written request for recusal. Her spies told her that only one player had asked to be excused and then only because his family would be traveling abroad during those weeks.

The other big change was that the training center was now crammed full of meatheads clanging plates and talking trash about the amount of weight they could lift in a clean and jerk. She'd always had the facilities to herself early in the morning, but now the place crawled

with enormous linebackers, tight ends who lived up to
their titles, and wideouts whose purpose was God only
knows, what with shoulders as broad as a compact car.
And for better or worse, they seemed to love having her
there. They all wanted to talk training with her, even
though their conditioning coach, Scott Jenkins, was
standing right there, his ever-present clipboard in hand.

Kate found herself equally annoyed and amused
by their antics. One morning, one of the overfed
jockstraps—most likely hopped up on an extra bowl
of Wheaties—asked if he could bench-press her. Kate
graciously declined his offer, then countered with one
of her own—a phone call to his mother. She explained
that she wanted to ask how his mom might feel about
her son speaking so disrespectfully to a woman. The
boy immediately apologized, then made his way to the
circuit equipment, where he now retreated each time
she came in.

Still, she liked talking to them. A new hopefulness
fueled their determination. Though none of them dared
to mention Danny McMillan to her by name, she was
pleased to see them coming around. It was heartening
to hear big talk coming from players who'd looked like
puppies who'd been whipped with the newspaper mere
weeks before.

"Hey, Scott," she said, drawing up beside the assistant coach as he made an indecipherable mark on the
paper trapped in the clipboard. "How are they looking?"

"Awesome," he answered without looking up from
his notations. A line bisected his sandy brows as he
scribbled. "I've got the special teams, receivers, and
quarterbacks regimens sorted out. Just need to get the

O-line, D-line, and backs mapped out, and I'm running away to Tahiti."

She started, taken aback by the uncharacteristic hyperbole. Scott was usually as unflappable as they came. It took a lot of intestinal fortitude for a guy who weighed little more than a buck and a half to stand over a three-hundred-pound tackle and demand two more sets of reps. "Wow, he's really working you all that hard?"

"How many more, Coach?" the big guy asked, grunting and straining as he pushed the bar off his chest.

"Seven," Scott replied without missing a beat. He looked at her at last, blinking as if he were the one with a steady stream of sweat pouring into his eyes. "Who's working what?"

"McMillan. Is he really that much of a hard-ass that you're willing to run all the way to the South Pacific to get away from him?"

Scott tilted his head, his confusion etched into every crease in his face. "Huh?"

"You said you were running away to Tahiti," she reminded him.

"Oh! Yeah. For three weeks." He smiled and tapped his eraser against the clipboard. "Twentieth anniversary. I went big."

Just like that, the tips of her ears burst into flames. Thanking God for Scott's oblivion, she waved a hand in front of her face to ward off a full-on blush and returned his smile. "Wow. You sure did."

His gaze shifted to the mountain of muscle stretched out on the weight bench, and he gave an encouraging nod. "Three more, Pinky." Before Kate had a chance to reconcile the massive young man in front of her with his nickname, Scott turned back to her. "Coach McMillan was cool with it. I'll be back long before two-a-days start, even with the revised schedule."

Kate glanced over her shoulder, curiosity gnawing at her insides as she surveyed those closest to them for potential gossips. Each of the young men seemed intent on his task, so she gave her natural inquisitiveness free rein. "Revised schedule?"

"Yeah, we're staggering the practice units for fall workout. Bringing some of the squads in earlier, then bringing the team together as a whole later." He smiled and patted Pinky on his quivering bicep. "Way to go, man."

"What's the point of that?" she asked, following Scott as he moved to another player. "Isn't he afraid that will erode team cohesiveness?"

"Not at all."

Kate jumped and whirled, meeting Danny McMillan's eyes but pressing her hand to her throat to keep her heart from popping right out of her big, fat mouth. "No?" she managed to croak.

"I think it will allow us to focus some time and attention to areas we know need help." A smirk twisted his handsome features as he crossed his arms over his chest and stared her down. "I appreciate your concern though. It's nice to know someone's worrying over us, isn't it, guys?"

He boomed the last, the deep baritone of his voice cutting through the clangor and clamor of the crowded weight room. A few born ass-kissers answered with a jaunty, "Yes, Coach."

"Thank you, Coach Snyder," Danny said with an overly solicitous grin. "It means everything to the team to have your support. Doesn't it, fellas?"

This time, a few more voices bounced off the walls, but all Kate could hear was the roar of blood in her ears. The son of a bitch was patronizing her. He dared to stand there, in the athletic center built on the success of her program, and smirk at her. Like he'd accomplished something more than requiring a bunch of beefy boys to spend more time in the gym when the only thing he ever did successfully was blow his entire career sky-high.

It was too galling.

She wouldn't let him get to her. She couldn't say anything. Not here, in front of his players and coaches. Not in her house.

Squaring her shoulders as if preparing to shoot a free throw, she raised her chin a notch. "Well, I hope it works out for you," she said coolly. Turning to one of the players, she let her smile warm a few degrees. "I'm counting on you guys to make us Warriors proud." Focusing her attention back on Danny, she let the smile drop. "If you'll excuse me, I'm here for a quick workout."

Brushing past him, she set her sights on the cardio units lined up at the far end of the training center. She nodded greetings to a couple of players huffing and puffing as they punished the elliptical machines, waved to one of the staffers seated on a recumbent bike, then tossed her towel over the rail of the last empty treadmill.

Jabbing at buttons until the belt whirred to a walking pace, Kate forced herself to draw deep, even breaths as she unraveled her earbuds and crammed them into her ears. Her player clipped to the hem of her tank, she tossed the wires down her back and upped the pace. By the time she hit a comfortable stride, the young man next to her slowed to a walk. Her machine rocked when he jumped off the belt and landed heavily on the side rails. She caught the apology he mouthed, then returned her gaze to the television mounted on the wall.

Someone claimed the machine beside her, but she was too absorbed in trying to lip-read what Greg Chambers and his cadre of NSN talking heads were gabbing about to pay much attention to her neighbor. The closed captioning had been turned off in favor of being able to see the ticker scroll at the bottom of the screen. Whatever the argument, the mood looked to be intense. She toyed with the idea of plugging directly into the machine to get the audio, but it was baseball season. In her opinion, the only things duller than baseball were watching grass grow or paint dry. Instead, she zoned out on Chambers's perfectly tousled hair, amped up the speed, and let the Black Eyed Peas tell her what a good night they were destined to have.

It wasn't until the song's driving beat faded into silence that she noticed the heavy footfalls and slightly uneven gait of the runner beside her. She pressed the pause button on her music and listened intently. Weights still clinked and clanked in the background, but the whir of machines had decreased dramatically. The runner beside her huffed, then added a few degrees of incline to his workout. With no more than a glimpse of his hand out of the corner of her eye, she knew who her new neighbor was.

Suddenly, the silence surrounding them grew more oppressive. She didn't need to look to know they had an audience. A glance in McMillan's direction confirmed her suspicions. A flood of unchecked fury rushed through her.

"I just wanted a goddamn run," she muttered as she upped the ante and lengthened her stride. She'd gone three steps when she realized, too late, that he wasn't wearing earbuds.

"Same goes," he grumbled.

"I was here first," she said through gritted teeth. "In every possible way."

He shot her a scowl, then increased his speed to match hers. "I'll go, but not before I'm done." Blowing hard, he swiped an arm across his brow. "I try to get at least three miles a day. Don't worry. I'll be out of your way before they go to *Sports Roundup*."

Kate glanced at the clock. The daily sports recap started at the bottom of the hour. If what he said held true, that meant old Danny could still run an eight-minute mile. Well, so could she, damn it. Increasing her speed again, she ignored the screeching pain in her bad knee and stretched her stride even farther.

"Seriously?"

She didn't look at him. Didn't acknowledge his incredulous tone or the edge of accusation undercutting the simple question. "Seriously," she replied.

By the time they started mile number two, every machine in the cardio section was full once again, but no one else was in motion. Their audience talked in a low rumble made indecipherable by the pounding of their feet. At the 2.5 mark, they were in perfect unison. She heard the telltale *whir-snick* of a phone camera but couldn't be bothered to care what those kids posted. At least, not at that moment. She was winning. She would win. And just to make certain, she bumped up her pace a smidge more.

As she closed in on three miles, she glanced over at him. "Go for 10K, Coach? Might give you a shot at catching up."

He snorted and mopped his face with his towel. "I think I just lapped you."

"You wish," Kate answered, pitching her voice low so only he could hear.

She heard the sickening screech of his sole scraping the belt, then felt a heavy *thunk* as the handrails bore the brunt of his weight. She turned in time to see him press into his arms and lift his feet from the belt. His shoes touched the side rails at 2.93 miles. A collective groan went up from the crowd when the pedometer on her machine clicked to 3.00.

Gripping the handrail, she hopped lightly off the speeding belt. The machine beeped as she downshifted the speed to her normal pace and jumped back on. "So that's a no on the ten?" she asked, flashing him a winning smile.

Danny punched the stop button, and his belt slowed to a grinding halt. "I think I'll pass, thanks."

Kate nodded but didn't break stride. "I understand. But keep training. You'll get there." She flashed him a smile so sweet it tasted like a maraschino cherry.

Danny leapt from the treadmill without deigning to answer. A little pang of guilt twisted her gut. It turned into full-blown regret when she glanced back to see a couple of his players giving their coach a consoling pat as he passed.

She pulled the plug on her own cooldown and snatched her towel from the rail. Without acknowledging a single "Way to run, Coach," she draped the towel around her neck and set her sights on Danny McMillan's sweat-soaked back.

She didn't turn as she called over her shoulder, "I find out any of you posted a picture of my backside anywhere, and I'm coming after you." The warning was met with a couple of nervous chuckles. So nervous that she felt compelled to shout a reminder to her audience as she hurried to catch up to McMillan. "Remember, you can run, but I can run faster."

She drew up short when the man himself whirled, his blue eyes ablaze. "I get it. You won," he bellowed, flinging his arms out wide. "I stumbled, as usual, and you are the champion." He all but sang the words as his lips curled into a sneer. "Congratulations, Coach. We'll have that treadmill plated in gold and put it in one of those display cases."

"Hey," she said, breathless from the exertion of the run and the vehemence in his tone. "Listen, I'm sorry. I shouldn't have done that."

"Done what, exactly?"

The bite in his tone was enough to take a chunk out of someone with less pride. Unfortunately, she'd just proven she had more than enough for both of them. Swallowing just a little of it, she looked him dead in the eye. "I shouldn't have let that happen. Especially not in front of your—"

The *whir-snick* of a camera shutter stopped her cold. She spun to find the lineman who'd asked to bench-press her grinning at them over the top of his phone. "How about you? You up for running a 10K today?" she snapped.

Proving he had a few brains to go with his brawn, the player ducked behind the nearest stand of free weights, mumbling something about the nutty PR lady.

"You don't get to talk to my players like that," McMillan growled.

"I either threaten him with a run or shove that phone up his ass. I chose the one that won't get me fired."

He opened his mouth, but she held up a hand to stop him. Her knee burned like fire, and the last thing she wanted was to go another ten rounds with him. They'd given Millie and her minions plenty of fodder for one day.

"Hey, just let me get this out, then we can hit the locker rooms and go to our separate corners. Okay?"

He snapped his jaw shut so hard she heard his teeth click.

"I'm sorry. I was… Well, I guess it's pretty obvious that I'm a competitive person," she began.

"It's pretty obvious that you're an egomaniac…"

He crossed his arms over his chest, and she couldn't help noticing what nice arms they were. Muscular but not bulked up. Silky, dark hair on his forearms. Thick wrists. Broad palms and long fingers. Quarterback hands. Hands that knew how to put just the right spin—

"…and you're threatened by me."

Just like that, her sanity returned. Blinking away the sheer audacity of his statement, she scoffed. "Threatened? By what? Your stellar coaching record?"

"By the fact that I'm even standing here."

Tipping her head down, she gave him the same look she gave her freshmen when they couldn't believe she wouldn't be bumping an all-American senior just to start them. "You do realize we had a football coach before you got here, right?"

"You don't like the fact that the media knows my name better than yours."

"I'm not sure I'd be as proud of the reason as you seem to be."

"I'm not the one struggling with my pride here." His voice dropped enough to make his point strike home. "I got on a treadmill for a quick run. You're the one who turned it into a scene."

"And I was trying to apologize for that," she retorted.

He nodded once. "Apology accepted. But just so we're straight, I'm not apologizing to you or anyone else for taking this job. I'm good at what I do. And if you doubt that for even one second, I suggest you take a good look around, Coach." He waved one graceful hand toward the crowded weight room. "My guys have every right to be here, and so do I."

He turned and pushed his way into the men's locker room. Frustrated and flustered, Kate tugged at the neckline of her tank as she blasted a gust of air at the hair that escaped her straggling ponytail.

She looked up just in time to see a player holding a phone pointed directly at them. Her suspicions solidified when he attempted to hide behind a circuit machine half his size, but there was not much she could do if he had snapped a picture. The phone was his. They were in a common area. But she was a coach, and that did give her some leeway in dealing with student athletes.

Her mouth pulled into a grim line, she started toward him. "Okay, big guy, it looks like you need a hobby, so you're going for a run." She snagged the sleeve of his athletic department T-shirt and dragged him out into the open. "And guess what? I'm going to be your head cheerleader."

Coach Jenkins just smirked and shook his head as she hauled the hulking young man along behind her. She

shoved the kid toward a treadmill, then stepped around
to the other side so she could stare straight at him as he
ran. "Tell you what else." She held her hand out palm up
and wiggled her fingers. "Seeing as how I'm so nice and
all, I'll even hold on to your phone for you."

# Chapter 6

"THIS ONE?" MILLIE YANKED A LOW-CUT, LEOPARD-PRINT top from a rack and held it up for Kate's verdict.

Kate huffed a laugh. "For me or for you?"

Red lips pursed, Millie tilted her head as she inspected the blouse. "You're right. Mine."

Hangers clicked as she added the top to the clothing pile draped over her arm. Kate glanced down at the skirt dangling from her fingers. She should have insisted on the wine first. A little dutch courage to get her through what Millie kept calling the "day-to-evening" department. God, she hated shopping.

"May I help you ladies?"

Kate automatically shook her head. "We're just look—"

With the agility of a point guard, Millie stepped into the space between Kate and the salesclerk. "We're looking for date outfits for my warrior princess here."

Kate glared, but Millie was undeterred.

"I must warn you, she hasn't had lunch yet, and the guy she's seeing has a stick up his ass and, frankly, isn't worth the wax. But she wants to look pretty, and I want her to have what she wants." Millie tossed a playful glance in Kate's direction. "What do you have in super-tall, I'm-too-sexy-for-you?"

The saleswoman threw her head back and laughed, but the genuine amusement in it made it hard for Kate to take offense. "I'm Julie, and I just love customers like you."

She beamed at Millie, then plucked the skirt from Kate's hand and studied it as if she were drawing up the play for the game-winning shot. Kate closed her eyes, teetering between hope and humiliation. A gentle hand on her arm forced her to open them again, but instead of seeing a fashionista's disdain, Kate caught the sparkle of challenge in Julie's eyes. Game on.

"Not a bad choice, Coach," Julie said, wiggling the hanger so the skirt's filmy overlay flounced.

Kate stiffened, momentarily discomfited, but quickly resigned herself to the recognition. She was a big fish in a tiny pond.

Julie flashed Millie a conspiratorial smile and dove deeper into the sea of racks. "Come with me. I know just what we need."

"And we need a dress for the banquet tonight," Millie decreed as she prodded Kate away from the cashier's station.

"I have a dress for the banquet."

Millie rolled her eyes. "You wear the same boring black dress every year. What do you say we try living life in color this year?"

An hour later, Kate adjusted the two carriers filled with purchases and planted her feet in a WNBA-worthy pick to catch the slippery dress bag sliding off her shoulder. "I need to put this stuff in the car, and then I need the wine you promised."

Nodding, her friend motioned toward the exit closest to where they'd parked. "Fine, but after that, we shop for shoes."

"And underwear," Kate added in a hushed tone.

"Underwear!"

Millie's voice carried over the music pulsing from the cosmetics counters and ripped right through the adjacent men's sportswear department. More than a few heads turned.

"You do love a spectacle," Kate muttered.

A harried-looking woman wearing a stretch bracelet loaded with keys jabbed a finger toward the far corner of the store. "Lingerie, floor two, southeast," she said without breaking stride.

"Underwear," Millie repeated, dropping it down a notch but infusing the word with more consideration than it warranted. "So you're planning to sleep with Jim?"

Embarrassment set Kate's ears on fire. Within a heartbeat, the heat of a blush consumed her. Jim wasn't the first person she envisioned when she decided she needed something new from the lingerie department, but she'd quickly stuffed thoughts of Danny McMillan down deep. He wasn't the man she needed to be thinking about when it came to sexy things.

"I was only planning to find a bra that doesn't have a racerback."

"Bullshit." Abruptly, Millie started toward the door closest to where they'd parked.

It took Kate three seconds and two full strides to catch up to her friend. "Where are you going?"

"You said you wanted to drop your bags," Millie reminded her.

The rigid set of her friend's posture somehow filtered down to her voice. "What's wrong?"

"Nothing. I'm just hungry."

Kate wasn't fooled by the explanation or put off by Millie's dismissive wave. "I don't get it. You're the one who's always getting on me about how my relationship with Jim has been at a standstill. We were just shopping for date clothes." She stepped up the pace to get ahead of the tiny torpedo of a woman. "You're the one who's always after me to…"

She trailed off, smiling as she held open a door for a young mother pushing a double stroller. By the time she let it go, Millie was halfway to the car.

"Hey," Kate called as she hustled after her friend. "What's the matter?"

"Nothing." Leaning back against the fender of Kate's car, Millie glanced up at the sky as if she were reading the time by the alignment of the sun. "Hurry up. I need that wine."

Kate dumped her purchases into the trunk and then slammed it with a little more force than necessary. When her friend jumped away from the car, Kate caught her arm. "Tell me."

"It's nothing," Millie replied too quickly. Her mascaraed lashes fluttered, but she didn't meet Kate's eyes.

Kate stared at the thick fringe in wonder. "Do you have false eyelashes?"

Millie reared slightly, then looked up at last. "Extensions. You really should get some."

"You put extensions on your eyelashes? Like hair extensions?"

Millie rolled her eyes, showing off the long, subtly curled fringe. "I once told you I went to a party where they injected botulinum into my forehead, and you're shocked that I wear fake eyelashes?"

"Everyone makes questionable choices," Kate said with mock solemnity.

"Like sleeping with Jim Davenport?"

Kate threw her hands up and stalked away. "I thought you liked Jim."

Millie's kitten heels clicked on the pavement, but Kate didn't slow. She was still struggling to get a handle on the disturbing ambivalence she felt each time she thought about her upcoming date. She didn't need Millie's razzing on top of it.

The dating dance she and Jim had been doing had gone on long enough. Their timing was finally on target. And now, after months of haranguing Kate to push for more, her best friend was doing a one-eighty.

So Kate pulled one of her own.

She spun, and Millie thumped into her, carried by the momentum she'd gained in those ridiculous shoes. "Hey!"

"You've been after me for months to do this," Kate hissed.

Millie smoothed her hair back from her face and straightened to her full five foot three. "That was before Danny McMillan came to town."

Kate's eyes popped in disbelief. Did Millie have some kind of psychic power? She needed to deny, deflect, de-Danny this conversation as quickly as possible.

"You can't be serious. The man—"

Millie held up a preemptory hand. "I'm not saying you should sleep with him." She paused, pursing her lips as she considered, then shook off the thought. "No. Definitely not. It would spoil the chemistry."

"There's no chemistry!"

"Sweetie, the two of you have so much chemistry there's been talk of handing out hazmat suits to the entire athletics department, but I need you to hold off for a while."

"I'm not going to sleep with Danny McMillan," Kate said through gritted teeth.

"Yet." Millie threw an apologetic smirk in with her qualifier. "I need some time to build the story, so don't jump him yet."

"I'm not jumping him." Kate huffed. "And wasn't the picture you posted on Twitter bad enough?"

The snapshot of Kate and Danny had been taken at a staff meeting. Whoever snapped it just happened to catch the moment when the two of them had swiveled away from one another. But the earnest look on Mike Samlin's face made it appear intentional. As if his two high-profile coaches couldn't bear to look at one another.

"It's working. People like the whole Bobby Riggs versus Billie Jean King angle."

"We aren't tennis players."

Millie's face brightened, and the worry lines that defied her beauty experiments disappeared. "I didn't think of an actual matchup," she murmured.

Wary of the speculative gleam in her friend's eye, Kate decided it was time to put a stop to this nonsense once and for all. She spoke slowly, so Millie couldn't blame her enunciation skills for any lack of understanding. "I'm having dinner with Jim Davenport. That dinner will most likely lead to sex. At least, I hope it does. It's been too damn long, and I'm starting to worry about rust."

Millie's face softened as she linked her arm through Kate's and propelled her toward the mall entrance. "You're not going to rust."

"Just last month, you were giving me the 'use it or lose it' speech."

"Then I saw what you *could* have."

"What makes you think I could have Danny McMillan?"

"I've seen the way he looks at you when you aren't looking."

"When?"

"Staff meeting."

Unable to resist, Kate asked, "How did he look at me?"

"Like he thought you'd be tastier than the Danish."

"Bull." Kate sighed. "Besides, you just told me I couldn't sleep with him."

"Yet." Millie held one finger up to make her point. "It would be awkward. And probably against some rule." She added the last as an afterthought, then promptly brushed it away. "But you might want to hold off on doing anything with Davenport too. I have a deal brewing with one of the local affiliates for you and Coach McYummy, and it might involve our old pal Jim."

"Are you telling me I'm about to get cockblocked by the evening news?"

"God, I love it when you talk dirty."

"Sleep with him, don't sleep with him," Kate muttered, her sights on the Italian restaurant that anchored the food court.

"To be or not to be," Millie intoned gravely.

"You are the queen of mixed signals."

Millie chuckled. "Sweets, you have no idea. Now tell me what shoes you're wearing to the banquet tonight."

<hr />

If Millie Jensen's intention was to win the award for most awkward seating arrangement, Danny would have to give the woman her due. By the time he'd arrived at the round table closest to the stage, there'd been only one empty seat. The one next to Kate Snyder and her flame-red dress.

Danny caught the glare she shot at the PR director's back as she sashayed away and took no offense at Kate's cool greeting. He wasn't particularly fond of being set up either. But Mike Samlin sat on Kate's left, and the rest of the table's occupants—as well as nosy nellies at neighboring tables—were watching his every move. If there was one thing he excelled at, it was playing under pressure.

Danny took the time to shake Mike's hand and plant a kiss on his wife Diane's cheek. "You don't look a day over twenty," he said, meaning every word. The streaks in her hair obviously hadn't come from the sun, and a fine webbing of wrinkles fanned from her eyes, but her all-American smile was still the same. If they could get her back into her old cheerleading uniform, he and Mike could pretend their gilt-edged futures still lay ahead of them.

"You always were such a smooth liar, Danny," she chided.

"Truth, Di. I speak only the truth these days," he insisted as he moved to take Ty Ransom's outstretched hand.

The men's basketball coach looked dapper in a blue suit so vivid it would have looked ridiculous on any man under six five. Ty introduced his wife, Mari, a diminutive platinum blond who, by all appearances, took her role as an athlete's wife to heart. A good bit younger than her husband, Mari flashed a practiced smile and pointed a stunning set of fake tits straight at him as they exchanged greetings. Her barely-bigger-than-a-napkin dress matched her husband's suit to perfection.

Unfortunately, the orange cast of her spray tan clashed with Ty's mellow mocha complexion.

Danny moved on with both relief and trepidation. Richard Donner, Wolcott's biggest booster, and his wife, Jacinda, rounded out their party. As he took his seat between the trophy wife and the trophy magnet, Danny couldn't help but note that Kate was the only woman at the table who hadn't somehow altered her God-given good looks. Her dark hair tumbled thick and lustrous over her shoulders, untamed by stiff sprays. The color in her cheeks came from good health, not a cosmetics counter.

She looked absolutely delicious. And he was going to do his damnedest to ignore her and the fact that the neckline of her siren-red dress did everything a dress should do to accentuate the positive without pushing… things…over the top.

He made small talk with the table at large as he studiously ignored the come-hither glances Mrs. Donner shot him from under a thick fringe of fake eyelashes. Oblivious to his wife's flirty looks, Richard launched into an enthusiastic accounting of all the lucrative opportunities that would come to the university once they brought the football program up to snuff. Hoping to refocus the conversation on the athletic program in general, Danny smiled at Diane and dropped a broad wink.

"The twins need braces, huh? Don't worry. I've come to save the day."

Diane rolled her eyes in response. "Yes, Uncle Danny, and we're all counting on you."

But humor, self-deprecating or otherwise, wasn't Dick Donner's strong suit. "We've been leaving millions of television dollars on the table by allowing our program to languish."

Kate snorted and muttered something that sounded suspiciously like, "Perish the thought."

"Once we prove that we can play with the big boys"—Richard clapped his hands then rubbed them together—"there's no reason we can't get just as big a slice of the pie as the other guys."

Danny shook his napkin and leaned closer to Kate as he settled it on his lap. "No reason other than they have multimillion-dollar facilities and an excess of kinesiology majors, and I have future doctors, economists, and engineers running drills in a cow pasture."

Kate smiled as she reached for her water goblet. "Horse, I think," she murmured. Perfect pink lips pressed against the rim of her glass, and a sharp stab of envy pierced his gut. "Or maybe there were goats. I can't remember."

"We get the money, we get the facilities," Richard stated with an impatient wave. "We need a team first."

"Tell me, Coach," Jacinda Donner interrupted, placing a bold hand high on Danny's thigh. "Do you really think we can go all the way?"

He was saved from answering—and the awkward business of removing the woman's hand—by a student server who chose that blessed moment to serve their salads. He beamed up at the young girl as she plunked the plate of field greens onto the table in front of him.

"Thank you so much. I appreciate it."

"Iron deficient?" Kate asked, lifting an innocent brow as she picked up her salad fork.

"Hungry. Mere moments from passing out." Eyeing

her plate with wary skepticism, he raised an eyebrow. "No dressing? Don't tell me you're on a diet."

A faint smile curved her lips, but she didn't glance at him as she replied. "No, I never diet."

"My kind of woman."

That made her look up. Those startling amber eyes met his directly. "I just don't see the point in wasting the dressing when I have no intention of eating these weeds."

He couldn't help himself. Those golden eyes drew him in like a tractor beam. Leaning closer still, he whispered, "You're just going to push them around a bit?"

"Or a lot."

"Bully," he chided.

"Wait until you see what I do to the poor croutons."

"Vivisection?"

"I devour them whole."

He chuckled, but a shiver of excitement ran down his spine. He eyed the stemmy lettuce as if it warranted closer scrutiny. To his credit, he didn't jump like a scalded cat when Jacinda Donner's hand landed on his thigh again. Shooting Kate a sidelong glance, he murmured, "I wish I had one tenth of your strength of character."

Kate rewarded him with one of those wide grins. "Maybe when you grow up."

With a grimace he hoped would pass for a smile, he turned to the ballsy blond on his other side. "Would you mind passing the ranch dressing?"

Danny spent the entire salad course thanking God above for making Kate Snyder tall. Had she been a few inches shorter, he'd have had a clear sightline down the neckline of that chili pepper of a dress. Just the thought of it was enough to make him sweat.

He should have hated her. Resented her at the very least. This woman made a chump out of him in front of his guys. But despite his competitive nature and her prickly disposition, he had a hard time making himself dislike her. She was her own woman—strong, capable, and completely unapologetic about it. He wasn't sure he'd ever met a woman like her. If she had insecurities, and surely she must have some, she kept them well hidden behind her game face.

In short, the woman made him itch to touch her. Every time he came near her, all he could think about was feeling those lean, taut muscles soften and grow lax. The memory of short, sharp puffs of air hitting his skin haunted his nights. He wanted to hear her panting in his ear. Preferably his name. With maybe a "more," "please," or "harder" tossed in just to keep him motivated.

Apparently, he'd let his leg wander along with his thoughts, because the next thing he knew, Mrs. Donner had her hand on his thigh again. This time, she didn't seem to be the least bit concerned with subtlety, because she came high and decisive. He flinched, his torso jerking forward in response to the demanding squeeze. Heat flared inside him, but not the welcome warmth of desire. He looked around in a panic, but everyone seemed to be engrossed in other conversation.

Everyone but Kate, whose gaze drifted toward his lap before moving on to some point in the distance beyond his private hell. Then she knocked the folded program that marked the line between his place setting and hers to the floor.

"Oh!" She smirked as she turned to meet his gaze. "How clumsy of me. Would you mind?"

"Not at all."

Shifting his chair back, he managed to dislodge Mrs. Donner's hand as he swooped down to retrieve the program. Kate's eyes met his as he rose. They glowed with amused sympathy.

"Thank you so much," she said, her voice husky with overdone sincerity.

"You're so welcome," he replied.

Kate placed the program in the center of the table. "There." She nodded, satisfied with her save. "Now we'll have a little more room."

Danny scooted his chair back to the table and a few inches closer to Kate. He made it through most of the main course by keeping his leg far enough away from Jacinda Donner to make her ploys obvious. Unfortunately, there was no easy way of avoiding Richard Donner and his never-ending pontification. The man ran on and on about television rights, expanding seating for bigger ticket sales, and branding and media rights.

"Let's face it. You've done a real good job of keeping Wolcott in the running conference-wise, Coach." The moron actually nodded to Kate and then brushed her achievements away with a dismissive wave of his manicured hand. "But girls' basketball will never be where the big money is."

Hectic color lit Kate's cheeks. Danny's spine stiffened when he saw the mottled splotches of red creeping up her neck. Kate remained stoically silent—a feat Danny thought should have earned her a medal—but they all knew the rules to the donor dance. They had to nod, smile, and somehow refrain from reaching across the man's groping wife to jab a fork into the back of Donner's hand.

On the other side of the table, Ty Ransom's eyes were so hard they gleamed. Danny didn't need to look at Mike to know he'd be in total accord. The tension at the table was palpable. There was no way in hell they'd let a hairless dweeb who probably never caught a ball in his life insult an athlete and coach as fine as Kate Snyder.

They needed a distraction.

"Excuse me, Mrs. Donner, I believe that's my napkin," he said, pointedly removing the woman's hand from his lap. "Let me get yours for you." He made a show of bumping his elbow against her chair as he presented her with the square of Warrior-green linen he swiped from her lap with a smile so innocent his cheekbones ached. "It's awful close in here, isn't it?"

"Yes. Yes, it is." Clearly peeved, the woman placed her napkin in her lap and reached for her nearly empty glass of wine. "Thank you."

"Too many helmet heads in one room," Kate murmured. When he glanced over at her, he saw that her smile was soft and a little rueful. "You boys should have left your shoulder pads in the locker room."

"We were told they were back in style," Danny quipped.

Kate's smile turned wicked. "I see so many of your players here tonight. Will you be handing out participation awards?"

He grimaced, but it quickly morphed into a grin as he acknowledged the hit. "Apparently I have a lot of graduating seniors on the team. They're just here for the free food."

"And more graduating with honors than most any other D-one school, I'd wager." When he rolled his eyes, she rewarded him with a husky laugh. "This could be a good thing. You'll get a fairly blank slate."

"Feels like a small consolation at this point."

"So, your team seems to have a new attitude, Coach. What did you do? Promise them all ponies?"

"I've been taking them out for ice cream after practice."

"Ah, well, that explains it." Kate beamed an open, cheerful smile at the young man who bent to remove her plate. "I'll do just about anything for ice cream," she whispered.

Danny choked back fifty filthy things he wanted to say and settled on scowling at the gangly, young waiter who held Kate's attention.

"Thanks, Robbie. How's the knee?" she asked.

"Better. Looks like I won't need surgery after all," the young man said, grinning at Coach Ransom as he collected the other plates. "Coach said to take it easy for a couple of months, then we'll start building back with the camps this summer."

Kate nodded, and her already-bright smile amped up a notch as she glanced from Robbie to Ty and back again. "That's very good news for the boys' team," she declared the moment the young man was out of earshot. "Maybe someone with a penis can win something around here for once," she added, not quite under her breath.

"Ouch." Danny chuckled as he and Ty shared grim smiles across the table. "I believe we've been challenged, Coach."

"Sounds like it," Ty agreed.

"In the meantime," Kate interrupted, blocking any chance he and Ty had to plot payback for the insult,

"I need to get ready to sing the praises of my girly little national champions. Coach McMillan, can I ask a favor?"

"Yes?" he inquired, keeping his tone light.

Her lips curved into a tight-lipped smile so serene it belonged on a portrait of a saint. He watched in rapt fascination as she worked the clasp on her evening bag and withdrew a small digital camera. "Since you won't be busy handing out awards, I was wondering if you'd mind snapping a few candid shots while I do mine?"

# Chapter 7

KATE YANKED OPEN HER FRONT DOOR AND ALMOST DROPPED her beloved Tea-Rex mug as she stared bleary-eyed at the surprise addition to her front porch. An oversized shoe box sat on her "Come back after basketball season" doormat.

She toed the mystery box, then glanced from left to right, making sure no one lurked in the shrubs waiting to snap a picture of her bending over in stretched-loose gym shorts and a faded T-shirt. The warm mug curled close to her chest, she squatted and flipped the lid off the box with one finger. Breath caught in her lungs, and she blinked in surprise.

The shoes nestled in the folds of tissue paper were a swirl of outlandishly obnoxious neon colors. So bright mere humans would need a pinhole projector to view them properly. She fell in love on sight.

"Come to me, my pretties," she whispered, setting her tea aside to draw the box closer. The tissue crinkled as she pushed it back. "Where did you come from, huh? Shoe fairies?" She touched one neon-orange lace and sighed. "Are you looking for a good home?" She peeked at the label on the box. "Look at that. Just my size."

Caffeine and nowhere-to-be-seen newspaper forgotten, she lowered the lid, gathered the box in her arms, and carried the precious foundlings inside.

Perched on the edge of the sofa, she stared at the prize in her lap. Her heart thrummed against her breastbone, and a giddy, bubbly rush of anticipation simmered in her veins. She couldn't remember the last time someone had given her a present, much less one this heart-trippingly perfect. She bit down on the tip of her tongue as she tossed the lid aside. A girly laugh of delight rushed past her lips the second she caught a glimpse of the shoes in the light.

Hooking her fingers under the laces, she plucked them from their tissue nest. The box fell to the floor unheeded as she gave the shoes an impetuous little hug. She knew it was silly but didn't really care. Let other women swoon over toothpick-heeled Jimmy Choos. She was a pushover for leather and mesh uppers with gel-filled insoles.

Setting one shoe aside, she gathered the tips of the laces to line them up. Her greedy gaze cataloged the number of eyelets and mapped the exact route she'd take through the tongue flap. It wasn't until she reached for the second shoe that she noticed the words inked inside the box lid. The thick, bold slashes of black magic marker seemed harsh and sharply incongruous with the colorful gift.

Dinner? D

She stared at the message, the pricey shoe dangling from her fingertips and her heart lodged in her throat.

Danny.

She shook her head hard. No. It couldn't be.

Or could it?

She'd caught him sneaking peeks at her all through the awards banquet. A couple of times, she thought he might have even been trying to look down her dress, but she quickly dismissed the notion. Why would he want a gander at her barely theres? Still, she'd had fun sparring with him that night. More fun than she'd had with a man in a long time.

She dropped the shoe to the floor, and her fluttering pulse slowed as the realization sank in. Of course the shoes weren't from Danny. And double-goddamn Millie for planting the seed. She and Coach McMillan weren't even on a first name basis, for cripes' sake. He didn't know where she lived, what she liked, or her shoe size. They couldn't be from him.

The *D* was for Davenport.

She hated Jim's habit of referring to himself by his last name. Hated that she'd picked up on it too. It made her feel like she was back in sixth grade, awkward and too tall, trying to be buddies with the boys for fear they'd reject her if she drew attention to the fact that she was a girl.

She gazed at the rainbow-colored trainers and shook her head, trying not to wish they'd come from another source. It wasn't fair. The terse message was Jim to a T, but the gesture was unprecedented. Romantic gifts left on her doorstep? Not a part of their game plan. At least not so far. Then again, they'd never been as close to sealing the deal as they were now.

Turning the shoe, she inspected the intricate pattern of tread and tried to ignore the pang of disappointment reverberating in her gut. She should have been happy. This was easily one of the most thoughtful gifts any man had ever given her. These shoes said he knew her and liked her just as she was. A chick-flick sentiment, but one that worked like a damn charm.

But charm, sentiment, and surprises weren't Jim's forte. He liked khaki pants, polo shirts, and brown loafers.

His athletic shoes were never even stark white or inky black but a neutral silver-gray. Kate found his mono-chromatic bent ironic for a guy who'd told her he once dreamed of becoming a color commentator.

She frowned as she wove the laces through the eye-lets. They already had a date for dinner scheduled. Why would he buy her the world's brightest shoes when she was already locked in for a night of pasta and stats?

Then again, it was gratifying to see him finally step up to the line. Of course, she wasn't naive enough to believe she'd inspired it all on her own. The video of her encounters with Coach McMillan always received a little play on both local and national sports news. Then there were the candid shots students kept snapping and Millie kept leaking. The crazy woman had started adding cryptic comments and pseudo-challenges to the department's social media posts. And it was all working like a dream. The world was clamoring for another Kate and Danny sparring match.

The only trouble was, the last thing she wanted to do was fight with Danny McMillan.

Maybe these shoes signaled a turning point in her relationship with Jim. There might not be any scary sparks or sharp-edged baiting, but she didn't have to worry about a clash of the egos each time they went out. They'd settle into their semiregular banquette at his favorite Italian place. It had to be Italian this week, because last week they'd gone to the steak house. But it would be good. Satisfying.

Wasn't it better to be with a man who made her feel cool and comfortable than one who made her bristle like a porcupine each time he came near?

She gazed at the new loves of her life and hugged herself tight. If they did indeed come from Jim, she'd have to give him credit for bringing his A game. These shoes were awesome enough to bump him solidly into double-bonus territory.

———

The building was empty but for two members of the maintenance staff Danny spotted emptying trash cans, their headphones clamped to their ears. The quiet closed in around him.

The day had been fairly easy, and he'd planned to unpack the boxes crowded into his office. Inspired by Kate Snyder's shoe collection, he'd ordered some racks for his hats. They'd been delivered and were ready to be filled, but a call from the athletic director informing him that good old Dick Donner was on campus put an end to that plan. Housekeeping and the best intentions were no match for a guy with deep pockets.

That was how Danny spent most of the day mapping routes with a computer nerd who considered himself a gridiron tactician. Richard never failed to let a conversation pass without reminding Danny that he'd been instrumental in giving a certain disgraced former football player a second chance at coaching Division I. Danny had known from the moment he accepted the plane ride up here that he'd be at the guy's beck and call, but he'd hoped for an off-season grace period with no armchair quarterbacking.

Donner was so smug, it was hard for Danny to keep a lid on his inner smart ass, but he had. For Mike's sake as much as his own, he made it through the entire meeting without acknowledging the fact that the Wolcott Warriors hadn't had a winning record since the Reagan administration—a stat that sports analysts and a few of his fellow coaches had mentioned a time or twenty since the day he was hired. That bottom line wasn't going to magically change overnight. Progress would be slow, but it would happen. There was no telling Dickie that though. He wanted results, and fast.

Heaving a tired sigh, Danny shoved his binders and tablet into his battered briefcase. As he gathered his things, he thought about Kate and the look of total understanding they'd shared at the banquet. He'd liked the intimacy of that look almost as much as he enjoyed the barbs they traded. The peachy-pink that colored her cheeks when their knees touched under the table. The sly curl of her lips when she had a zinger locked and loaded, just waiting for the opportunity to sling it at him.

Earlier that day, he'd caught himself searching the severed nets and framed jerseys lining the hallways for hints of what she might be like when she wasn't wearing her game face. The pantheon of gleaming wood, brass, and crystal proved she had every right to be cocky. But he liked the pictures best. The determination. The drive. Most of all, the joy lighting her smile in those moments of triumph.

And though every meeting with her felt like they were squaring off at center court, he liked seeing her smile. Live and in person.

Danny pulled the office door closed behind him without bothering to lock it. Come to think of it, he wasn't entirely certain there was a lock. He had a sneaking suspicion that his office might have been an equipment closet. When he'd mentioned something about his predecessor's decorating skills, Mike had grudgingly admitted that the former football coach had a bigger office that now belonged to Ty Ransom. But Danny didn't push it. Basketball ruled here. It would take at least three acts of God to change that.

His thoughts drifted back to his conversations with Donner and Mike. Historically challenged or not, the Wolcott football program did have potential. They had a handful of players with some talent. And the coaches were good enough for now. Mike was right about Mack. The old guy's insights were invaluable. And Mack was right about him too. He was a punk-ass screwup who needed to get his head in the game.

He had to stop comparing his team to others and quit worrying about what the press thought of them. They needed to make the most of the team's strengths and minimize the weaknesses. Priority one would be to strip the program down to basics and focus on the fundamentals. Everything else would fall into line.

He wasn't some ego-driven ex-pro-turned-coaching-wunderkind anymore. He was older. Wiser. And best of all, he had virtually nothing to lose. Money wasn't his motivator. He wanted his good name back.

Pausing in front of one of the trophy cases, he thought back to booze-fueled inanities Donner'd babbled at the awards dinner. Most people didn't even bother adding the gender qualifier to the athletics around here. A phenomenon particularly unusual in collegiate sports, where the sting of Title IX still smarted.

The topic of the federal regulation that prohibited sex discrimination in education was a sensitive one for a lot

of men, but not for him. He'd been at schools where the
disparity in funding between women's sports and men's
was so blatant it was shameful. Not that he was about
to give up any of his funding to buy the field hockey
team new sticks. There were times when having the best
helmets and pads saved life and limb, and his job was to
make sure his players had every damn thing they needed
to play hard and safe. But when Dickie dared to dismiss
those amazing athletes—those champions—as nothing
more than mere "girls," Danny's blood had boiled.

A muffled *thunk* followed by a series of high-pitched
squeaks drew him up short just as he reached the doors.
The steady drumbeat of a ball hitting hardwood drifted
up the concrete ramp that led to the arena. Curious, he
hooked a right and started down the corridor toward
the court. The pulse of continuous dribbling grew
louder. The squeal of rubber soles on varnished floor
made the tiny hairs on his neck stand at attention, but
it was the sight of the lone shooter that stopped him
dead in his tracks.

She was slim and supple, her body curved into an
airborne C as she launched the ball from her fingertips.
The spinning orange orb arced through the air, but she
landed almost silently, bouncing on the balls of her
feet. The cotton-nylon netting sang its siren song as the
ball passed through, a soft, seductive taunt, daring the
shooter to try it again.

Kate caught the ball after a single bounce and trapped
it against her hip as she walked toward the foul line. The
textured orange rubber pressed against the gauzy spring
skirt and sleeveless sweater she paired with blindingly
bright sneakers. Warmth gathered in his belly, and a

slow smile crept across his face. Somehow, neither the
gaudy shoes nor the utterly feminine clothes looked the
least bit out of place on Kate Snyder.

The shoes were an impulse buy. It seemed that since
the moment he took her hand in his, every reaction Kate
elicited from him was completely beyond his control.
He had no other way of explaining why he wanted her to
have those crazy clown shoes. He just knew the minute
he saw them that they belonged with her. From the looks
of things, he hadn't been wrong.

The soles squealed again as she made a break toward
the basket. Long, loping strides made her skirt swirl
around her knees. Incongruous as they were, the outra-
geous sneakers couldn't hold his attention. Not when
the taut muscles in her calves were on display and he
had the opportunity to watch toned biceps flex under
smooth skin.

She took the layup in stride, oblivious to her audience. Drawn like a fly to honey, he set his briefcase
aside and made his way courtside. She dribbled around
the top of the key and shook her hair back as she toed
the foul line. The nylon netting hissed as she sank free
throw after free throw without grazing the rim.

The woman was magnetic. Mesmerizing. Magnificent.

Like him, the ball kept coming back to her time and
time again. He stood on the sideline, entranced by the
glow the exertion gave her skin. The ball bounced wide,
and she snagged it easily, bringing it under control with
the barest flex of her wrist. Dribbling sure and easy, she
kept her gaze fixed on the goal as she backed to the top
of the arc.

Danny found himself holding his breath as she let the

ball fly, but he didn't follow its trajectory. He couldn't tear his eyes from her. There was a dull thud followed by a soft swish of net, but Kate shook her head in disgust as she reclaimed the ball. An incredulous laugh rumbled in his chest, but he didn't dare let it out. Her perfectionism didn't surprise him. He lived with the same drive.

"It was a beautiful shot."

Kate froze, her arm wrapped protectively around the ball, but she didn't turn to look at him. Instead, she cast an assessing glance at the basket. "A little short."

"Still a beautiful shot."

Danny knew he was taking a chance, stepping onto her court without permission, but there were forces stronger than common sense at play here. He needed to move closer. Needed a better look at the well-defined muscles in her arms and intimidating brace she wore on her right knee. His fingers itched to touch that filmy skirt, to smooth the thin sweater where it bunched at her flat stomach, to feel those small, high breasts in the palms of his hands. She pivoted, and he stopped, arrested by the sight of her. Pink lips, damp and parted. The pearly flush of exertion riding high in her cheeks.

He liked what he saw in her wide-set eyes. Wariness. Welcome. Just a flash of something he didn't recognize but wanted to know better. Much better.

"What are you doing here?" she asked.

He couldn't help but smile. He heard the proprietary note in her voice. "I work here, remember?"

The smart-assed reply seemed to give her the boost she needed. Rolling those beautiful eyes, she shifted the ball to her hip. "I meant now. I thought everyone was gone."

"I had a little heart-to-heart with Dickie Donner."

A wry smile twisted his lips. He was gratified when Kate returned it with a smirk of her own. "You'll be glad to know you aren't the only one manning the welcome wagon."

Her nose wrinkled when she grinned. Just a little but enough to make him want to kiss her senseless. "He didn't come over here and lick your cleats?"

He managed a sage nod. "He had some plays drawn up."

"Oh, I bet he did."

An optimistic man might think he saw sympathy in those amber eyes, but Danny had given up optimism years ago. This woman was more likely to skewer him than offer consolation. Still, he stubbornly refused to step back when she gave the ball a couple of hard bounces.

"Play your cards right, and he'll keep you in Gatorade and mouth guards for years to come," she said.

"Play them wrong, and I'll be lucky to get a job striping the field," he finished.

Her smirk transformed into a smile so brilliant he had to resist the urge to shield his eyes. "I bet you'd be so good at it. I hear you've been working real hard on walking the straight and narrow."

Torn between the urge to flee from another fruitless confrontation and the other urges wreaking havoc with his self-control, he shifted from defense to offense. He let his gaze roam down her body and slowly back up again.

"Love the new uniform. Of course, see-through or not, everyone in the place will be hoping that skirt flies up when there's a jump ball."

She blinked, a frown transforming the clean, classic

lines of her face as she glanced at her skirt. "It's not see-through."

He widened his eyes, trying for an innocent look. "No? Must just be my overactive imagination."

Sticking her chin up in the air, she turned her back on him and started toward the sideline. There, he spotted the open shoe box and fought back a smile. A profusion of discarded tissue nearly masked a pair of shoes comprised of two thin straps of black leather and spindly heels.

Four-inch heels. They stood eye-to-eye as it was. The addition of those shoes would make her tower over him. A prospect he found oddly arousing.

Odd, because he'd always liked the tiny girls. Little, delicate things he had to stoop to kiss. The kind of woman he could sweep off her feet literally and figuratively. Willowy figure notwithstanding, there was no doubt in his mind Kate Snyder could take him down. Hard. Physically, psychologically, and professionally.

And damn if that didn't make him want her more.

She dropped into the chair beside the box and toed off the retina-searing shoes. Eyeing him skeptically, she stripped off snowy-white ankle socks and balled them in a swift, practiced move. "Was there something I could help you with?"

The slight quaver in her voice sparked his curiosity. "Would you?"

Her sleek, brown hair cascaded over one shoulder when she cocked her head. He stared transfixed as she reached for one of the discarded sandals.

Shoe dangling from the crook of her finger, she raised an eyebrow. "Would I what?"

Discomfited by the directness of her gaze and the

beginnings of what would certainly be a hard-on of epic proportions, he shoved his hands into his pockets and gave a stilted shrug. "Help me." Her look of shocked innocence made him laugh. "Yeah, well, call me crazy, but I get the distinct feeling you don't want me here."

"Crazy." Kate tipped her head back and stared straight into his eyes. "Why on earth would you think I wouldn't want you?"

He froze, but God help him, his dick stirred. Resisting the need to adjust the growing tightness in his pants, he fell headfirst into that steady, golden gaze. "Do you?"

She wet her lips with the tip of her pink tongue and, for the first time in his life, he wished he had access to slow-motion replay. He tossed whatever half-assed game plan he had, stepped out of the pocket, and threw a Hail Mary.

He bent at the waist, his hands closing around the biceps he'd just been admiring as he pressed his mouth to hers. Her lips were sweet and damp. Impossibly soft, despite the fact that her body stiffened in surprise. Then she relaxed into the kiss with a soft gasp of surrender, and he lost all semblance of reason.

He dropped to his knees. A jolt of pain sailed through his body, but then her arms were around him too, and he couldn't care less. One hand slid up his neck. Her fingers were in his hair. Fingernails scored his shirt and bit into his shoulder as she arched into the kiss.

"Jesus," he panted when they came up for air. Pressing his forehead to hers, he ran his hand over her hair and then tucked it behind her ear just as he'd seen her do countless times. Mustering superhuman strength, he pulled back far enough to whisper, "This is insane."

"I have a date."

Her voice was faint, tinged with shock. Danny fell back on his heels, what little air he had left exploding from his lungs. He watched as the hands that mussed his hair and wrinkled his shirt groped for the sexy sandals. Fuck-me heels she planned to wear for another man. She wriggled her polished toes under the toe strap, and a surge of white-hot jealousy and anger balled in his gut.

"Who?"

Tugging the other strap up over her heel, she ducked her head to avoid his eyes. "None of your business."

"The hell it isn't." He stifled a groan as he rolled to his feet, ignoring the creaks and pops of his joints. He glared at her, but she remained stubbornly silent.

They sized each other up, looking for chinks in the armor they both wore. Recognizing a little of himself in her defiant gaze, he nodded shortly. "Fine. Yeah. Okay. Go on with your date. I hope you enjoy it."

He let his insincere good wishes hang in the charged air between them.

"But remember who kissed you first tonight, Kate."

She stared up at him, her lips parted and wet, hunger gleaming bright in her eyes. He had her just where he wanted her. She was off balance. Rattled, like he was. And that was good. Damn good.

"Remember who kissed you first. Then tomorrow, you come tell me who kissed you best."

He turned on his heel and strode the length of the court, gratified to note she didn't recover until his foot hit the bottom riser.

"What makes you think you were so great?" she called, her voice high and tight.

He chose not to chase after that ball. Instead, he snagged the smooth leather handle of his briefcase without breaking stride and headed for the steps. His heart hammered as he took the stairs two at a time. At the mouth of the tunnel, he turned back.

She stood with her feet wide, those heels doing incredible things to her shapely calves. Her hand perched on one hip, lending extra definition to the outline of her slender curves. God, she was incredible. The harsh overhead lights caught planes and angles of her face, sketching her classic beauty in sharp, bold lines. He let his gaze fall all the way to her pink-polished toes, then he took his time meandering back up to meet her eyes.

Determined to get the last word, he held her gaze. "That knee brace is sexy as hell."

Her jaw dropped, and her eyes widened before squeezing into a cringe. But she didn't look down. The hell of it was, he really did find everything about her sexy as hell. Including the knee brace. Lifting one hand in a resigned wave, he attempted a modest shrug.

"Be gentle with the poor guy, Coach. We *are* only men."

# Chapter 8

THE DATE WAS A BUST. OF COURSE IT WAS. DANNY McMillan guaranteed that the second he decided to plant that big, wet kiss on her lips. Okay, it wasn't all that wet. In truth, it was just the right amount of soft, slippery, and hot. Maybe a dash of demanding in there. Or was it commanding? Either way, he was hungry. She'd tasted desire on his tongue, and damn if she didn't feel the answering ache deep inside.

"I had a great time tonight."

Jim leaned in, startling her from her thoughts. She squelched a perverse impulse to insist he tell her which parts he thought were so great. Was it the predictability of his restaurant choice, or the fact that the food they'd eaten looked exactly like its photo representation in the menu? Did the framed jerseys and aging pennants that adorned the restaurant's walls psych him up? Was he turned on by the replica of one of her old WNBA jerseys hanging over the bar?

Kate smiled, an automatic response, but she could hardly bring herself to nudge her internal date-o-meter out of the "pleasant" zone. As far as she was concerned, there'd been nothing great about the evening. Aside from the pregame warm-up.

Jim propped a hand on the doorjamb, and she quickly stowed all thoughts of the capricious Coach McMillan and his marauding mouth. At least, she tried to. The kiss

Jim brushed over her lips was barely more than a glancing blow, as easy to miss as a hip check on a rebound. Danny's had been a game stopper. A foul so flagrant, he should have been tossed from the game. But Lord, she wanted to keep facing off with him.

"So, you and the prince of pigskin planning on going at it anytime soon?"

She blinked up at Jim, thrown by the shift in topic: "What?"

"I figure the triple chocolate cake should buy me at least a heads-up if you plan to put the guy in his place again."

He actually said it with a smile. He stood there on her own doorstep, the tips of his shoes touching her toes, and dared to imply she owed him a floorshow to go with the lame-ass dinner he'd bought her. Shifting her weight and squaring her shoulders, she moved out of the kissing zone. If he thought he was coming in after an implication like that, he was cracked.

"I don't know what you're talking about."

His eyebrows rose, and he ran a hand down her arm. "Millie's got this idea that it's like watching Billie Jean King and Bobby Riggs going at each other, but I don't see it. Still, the guys at the local affiliate are interested."

She stiffened, mortified at being caught in the middle of this ridiculous ploy to score media coverage. "There's nothing to be interested in. I simply welcomed him to Wolcott."

"And let him know who ruled the school." He crowded her a little. "I have to admit, you're a lot hotter than Billie Jean."

She blinked, taken aback.

"Thanks," she said dryly and stepped away. With his

tasteless kiss a faint memory and the insinuation that she owed him something hanging heavy between them, she didn't want to be within striking distance. She'd cracked a rib or two with a well-thrown elbow. "I didn't realize dessert came with strings attached."

His brow puckered. "I wouldn't call them strings."

"What would you call them?"

He tilted his head, studying her carefully. At last, the corner of his mouth ticked up in a rakish smirk she was certain he practiced in front of a mirror. "Inducement?"

She matched his fake rake with wide-eyed guilelessness. After all, if insincerity was good enough for him, it should be for her as well. "Is that what this was all about? A bribe so I'd tip you off on nonexistent stories? What about the shoes? What are they worth?"

He gave her a crooked smile that should have been more appealing than it was. He glanced down at the strappy heels she wore and came up with a shrug that marked him clueless. "Your shoes are great."

Her heart sped up as realization and vindication kicked it into high gear. *D* didn't stand for Davenport. *D* was for Danny. Danny, who kissed her hard and hot and left her feeling wobbly all night. The one man she shouldn't want.

She tried instead to focus on the one she was supposed to want. Jim's smile became a bit lecherous as he leaned in to kiss her again. Her stomach turned over, and her fingers curled into his shirt. She let it happen. Not because she wanted it, but because she needed a time-out. Just a few seconds to draw up the next play. And nothing would clear the slate like another one of Jim's zestless attempts at seduction.

He knew nothing about the shoes. She was sure of it. The tip of Jim's tongue tripped along her firmly sealed lips, but she didn't want to let him in. Some crazy, irrational part of her mind worried that he might be able to detect the lingering taste of Danny McMillan on her tongue. The sane part refused to take the chance on having an incredible kiss replaced by one that was forgettable at best.

She wasn't interested in playing springboard for yet another underachieving man.

Planting her hands on Jim's shoulders, she pulled away with what she hoped would pass for reluctance. "I'm sorry," she whispered, though she wasn't. "It's, uh…" She groped for an excuse and came up with the tried and true. "Sorry. This isn't a very good time." She forced a grimace of apology. "Maybe we…another time."

His brow furrowed and then smoothed as her implication sank in. "Oh." He nodded, his Adam's apple bobbing as he cast a longing glance at his car. Color rode high in his cheeks. "So…maybe next week?"

A guilty flush warmed her skin. "Maybe," she replied. But there was no way in hell.

Jim ducked his head to peck the usual chaste kiss to her cheek. "Night, Coach."

Annoyed by the use of her title and not her name, Kate bit the inside of her cheek as she slipped her key into the lock. "Night, Davenport."

Safe inside her house, she kicked off the sadistic sandals and flopped onto the sofa in a huff. The straps left livid pink marks crisscrossing her feet. She rubbed at them, frustration—intellectual and physiological— roiling inside her.

Closing her eyes, she drew a deep breath in and let it go slowly. Her body hummed, but it wasn't the result of her date with Jim. She tried to dissect the attraction that sizzled and popped every time Danny McMillan came near, but she couldn't parse it. Everything about him got to her. The dark hair and electrifying eyes. His solid, muscular build. The swagger in his step and the arrogance in the lift of his square chin. Maybe it sprang from nothing more than the allure of forbidden fruit, but oh, the man did something to her.

Kate licked her lips, closed her eyes, and let her head roll back. Two fingers under her skirt. That's all she needed. The vibrator in her nightstand could take care of her problem in seconds. The pulsing jets of her showerhead could drown out the low-frequency hum in her blood, but she knew damn well that none of those options would be enough. It would take more than simulated sex to scratch the itch that had niggled from the moment Danny's mouth touched hers. The man was fucking with her head even if he hadn't fucked her body.

Yet.

The stark acknowledgment of inevitability made her eyes pop open. She sat still, hands curled around the edge of the sofa cushion, her thighs pressed together.

Her mind raced. One by one, she rifled through possibilities and scenarios, each more impossible, and therefore more desirable, than the last.

She could call Millie and get his number. Millie wouldn't think twice about it. Kate used to call Stan Morton when he was head football coach. But she never wanted Stan's hands on her the way she wanted Danny's. She called Ty every now and again to talk shop, but frankly, she avoided it for fear of having to socialize with Mari. Still, a phone call from one coach to another wouldn't raise any eyebrows.

She could make up some bullshit story about the boosters and coordinating summer athletic camp schedules. Millie'd give her his number, and she could call him, and…

Two fingers. Hell, one would do it, she was so keyed up. Almost of its own volition, her right hand uncurled, releasing its death grip on the cushion in favor of pushing up under her skirt. Her panties were damp. Damn him. She brushed the tips of her fingers over the silky nylon blend.

Friggin' Davenport. He didn't deserve these panties or the pretty matching bra. She scowled as she edged a finger under the elastic. The chocolate cake wasn't that good. But oh, that was. Right there. A shuddering sigh rolled through her as she began to stroke her clit with the quick, feather-light flicks that no man would ever dream of employing.

She'd bet anything Danny McMillan wouldn't. He'd charge in, take control, and claim that tender swell of flesh as his due. She arched her neck, straining against the too-soft touch and picturing him looming over her like he had on the court that night. In her mind, it wasn't her finger working the magic. It was his. Big, blunt, a little rough, but still too maddeningly gentle. She didn't want gentle. She wanted him to drive her up, fast and sure, relentless in his pursuit of her pleasure. Hold her hands over her head. Thrust into her. Over and over…

Kate cried out as she pushed her own finger into the tight, wet channel, gasping and groaning as she climaxed.

The rasp of her breathing echoed in the quiet room.

She blinked at the blank television screen. The magazines on the coffee table seemed to be written in a foreign language. Perhaps it was the civilized tongue of people who didn't get themselves off on the living room sofa the minute they got home from a bad date. She blinked and pulled her hand out from under her skirt, careful not to touch anything with the glistening digits.

With a grunt of disgusted disbelief, she sunk into the sofa. "Well, shit."

Draping her left arm over her eyes, she focused on regaining control. Her muscles felt heavy with the special kind of languor that only sets in when one is replete. Or exhausted. Her brain latched onto the thought. Maybe that was the key. A few hours in the gym wouldn't hurt. She could build up the stamina she needed to keep up with middle and high school students who would cycle through her summer basketball camps. Burn off some energy in a manner that wouldn't make her look like a fool, get her fired or, worse, risk falling in love with another man incapable of seeing past his own ambition.

---

Danny grabbed the safety bar and jumped onto the side rails of the treadmill. Sweat streaked down the sides of his face and dampened his hair. His brand-spanking-new Wolcott Athletic Department T-shirt clung to him, and he tugged at the neckline as the belt continued to whir. The smart thing would be to stop and walk it off. A six-mile run with no cooldown was enough to guarantee screaming knees.

But he didn't want to walk. He wanted to keep pounding away. Needed to work off all the excess energy bubbling inside him. At least working out was productive. He'd already spent too many mornings thinking about Kate Snyder and exercising his right hand.

The blare of Nine Inch Nails in his ears did nothing to cool his blood. The song was almost an anthem for how he felt from the second he'd decided to kiss her. Desperate. Unstoppable. Exposed. One stupid kiss, and he wanted more. So much more. Like the song said, he wanted to crawl inside her.

The hell of it was, he wasn't thinking about her tits or her high, round ass when he jerked off that night or again in the wee hours of the morning. He was thinking about her eyes. Whiskey-colored and every bit as intoxicating, they were as fascinating as the ever-shifting glass in a kaleidoscope.

The whimsical thought jolted him from his reverie. Intoxicating? Kaleidoscopes? He snorted and yanked the buds from his ears. What the hell was going on with him? He wasn't a poet or an artist. He was a football player. He stared hard at his reflection in the mirrored wall and jammed his thumb on the button that would slow the pace.

*Get a grip.*

Ah, but he had. He'd had a good grip on her. He would have had her on her back if she hadn't come to her senses. Damn, she felt good. Lean and muscular, but soft. Indescribably soft. Grasping the handrail, he closed his eyes until he found rhythm in the measured steps.

The ferocity of his attraction to Kate Snyder caught him off guard. Lust didn't begin to explain it. If it were as simple as needing the physical release, he had plenty of opportunity and had never been shy about exploiting it. Older women were a little more brazen than the younger, but that was okay with him. He preferred easy pickings to the complications the young ones toted around like handbags. Didn't hurt that he was a decent-looking guy with a seminotorious reputation. Women loved that crap. And he was still in pretty good shape. Maybe not underwear-model material, but fit, and not so beat-up he scared the villagers.

But he couldn't stop obsessing over Kate's hitchy little hiccup when she'd pushed away. Did she make the same kind of noises when she fucked? Christ, he'd give his left nut to make that throaty moan he'd tasted explode into a scream. The realization that it had been too long since he'd even thought about sinking deep into a woman's body scared him. It was easy to convince himself he had been too focused on resurrecting his career to think about a relationship, but sex? What could possibly make him never think about sex?

Well, he was thinking about it now, and he needed to stop. Hell, just thinking about how she'd tried to humiliate him on these very treadmills ought to have been enough. But it wasn't. Apparently, his libido had the power to override his ego these days. And if that wasn't a dangerous set of circumstances, he didn't know what was.

Frustrated, he hit the button to cancel the session and planted his hands on his hips. These days, the Warrior workout room was empty in the early morning hours. Later on, a few regulars would shuffle in, but the campus was becoming more deserted every day.

He'd been pleased to note that quite a few of his players took their new strength-training regime seriously. He hoped he'd be able to use some of that raw determination to overcome the team's lack of any outstanding talent. Grit could get a guy a helluva long way if he was willing to work hard enough. If he could just convince a few of the leaders that they had it in them, they could pull the rest along with them.

His steps slowed until the treadmill ground to a halt. LED numbers flashed his stats, but he paid them no mind. As far as he was concerned, the workout had been a failure. Speculating about his absent football team wasn't proving to be a strong enough distraction. His blood still boiled with wanting Kate.

Stepping off the treadmill, he peeled the shirt over his head and took a quick inventory. The muscles in his chest and arms were well defined but not as inflated at they'd been back in his playing days. He'd need to see the doc about getting cortisone injected in his shoulder. Running a hand over the damp hair that led to his waistband, he had to admit his abs weren't as sculpted as they'd been when he was younger, but overall, his belly was still flat and somewhat ripped. He vowed there and then to spend the summer months reclaiming his six-pack rather than consuming them. Turning away from the mirrors, he mentally added more ab work to his routine as he started toward the weight room.

The chink of heavy metal plates touching and a low grunt of exertion drew him up short of the entrance. He glanced down at the wringing-wet shirt in his hand and shuddered. He loathed the thought of struggling into it again, but he was vain enough to know the body he'd been admiring moments ago would look battered beside even the softest twentysomething. He was shaking out

the damp cotton when the weights clanked a bit louder
and an exhalation of relief marked the end of a set. A
very feminine exhalation.

Curiosity piqued, Danny poked his head around
the corner. Shiny, brown hair pulled into a ruthless
ponytail. Long, toned arms spread wide to grip the
bar dangling over her head. Neon-rainbow trainers
planted on either side of the padded bench, Kate drew
the pulley down, the muscles in her back tensing and
bunching beneath her tank top. The metal bar grazed
the ponytail, setting it to sway as she controlled the
slow, steady ascent.

His feet moved without thought. He caught the count
she murmured under her breath, measuring his steps
to her reps. By the time she huffed, "Ten," he stood
directly behind her.

His shirt fell to the floor in a heap. Kate tensed but
didn't turn. The buzz of electricity humming through
the room had nothing to do with the fluorescent bulbs
mounted to the drop ceiling. The whiteness of her
knuckles told him she knew damn well it was him. He
straddled the end of the bench, pressing his knees into
her lower back as he gripped the cool metal bar on either
side of the center chain and eased it from her grip.

She raised her head and let her arms fall limp to
her sides. Their gazes met and held in the mirror. The
silky strands of her ponytail grazed his stomach as she
tipped her head back. But instead of the chastisement or
indignation he felt sure was coming, she said, "I have
another set."

Wordlessly, he hauled the bar down so she could
grasp it without rising from the bench. Long, strong

fingers wrapped around the grips, and his hands came to rest on her traps. She stiffened, but only for a moment. "You like the shoes?"

She cast him a sidelong glance. "Love them."

"So I have a chance?"

Graceful muscle moved beneath silken skin. He stared transfixed as she counted off the first rep. "Chance for what?"

"Dinner. I'd like to start over. See if we can't spend five minutes in each other's company without sniping."

"I'm told the sniping is media gold." She huffed and pulled the bar down once more. "Didn't Millie call you? The local station has booked time for us to do a weekly show. We're supposed to film the first one this afternoon."

"She told me." The show would be kind of a sports-themed point/counterpoint thing with Jim Davenport as their monkey in the middle. He wasn't crazy about the idea of picking fights with Kate for public consumption, but he'd take the opportunity to spend more time with her. He trailed his fingertips over her delts. "I just want to know if there will be Telestrators. I've always wanted to play with the Telestrator."

She pulled two more reps. "You are the handsiest spotter I've ever had."

He chuckled and slid his palms over her arms, feeling each muscle tighten as his fingers wrapped around her forearms. She held for a moment, but he urged her to proceed with gentle pressure. "I can't help myself," he confessed as she puffed out number eight. "I want you. God, I want you."

She froze, her shoulders and elbows locked and her arms quivering with the effort of holding the weights. "More than a TV show with a Telestrator?"

"I've had a TV show, you know. Nothing glamorous or exciting about standing in front of a green screen. The Telestrator is tempting, but it pales…" He stared, transfixed by the rosy flush coloring her fair complexion. "I can't think about anything but wanting you."

The plates hit with a jarring clang. She didn't turn to look at him, but tremors of exertion—or was it excitement?—shivered under sleek, pink-gold skin. "Do you always get what you want?"

He chuckled again. "I think you know I don't." She lowered her arms, but he couldn't stop touching her. "They've all warned me."

"Warned you about what?"

"You. To stay away from you. But I can't."

She closed her eyes. Dark lashes fanned flushed cheeks, and her muscles relaxed. "This is a bad idea on so many levels."

Her words were tantamount to a confession. She'd been thinking about it too. About him. Them. That kiss.

"Horrible idea," he agreed, bending to press a slow, firm kiss to her damp nape. "I don't cater to prima donnas."

He spoke low and soft, smiling as he kissed a lazy path along her hairline.

Kate shivered and tilted her head, granting him better access. "I've never been a fan of the comeback kid."

"You're so smug here in your little kingdom."

"Queendom," she corrected, sliding him a sly smile as he trailed kisses along the smooth muscles he'd traced. "And don't you forget it."

"I doubt you'll let me."

Scooting forward, she twisted her torso to look him in the eye. "I don't have a Telestrator handy, but I have a coach's clipboard." She cocked her head, sending her ponytail swinging. "If I let you borrow it, can you draw up a play where this could work? I don't see how either of us can come out the winner here."

She held his eyes just long enough for him to see the golden light burning bright in hers. Then she dropped her gaze to his crotch and the obvious hard-on outlined by the clingy nylon of his shorts.

"Time to hit the showers, Coach. Best make it a cold one."

"I have." His confession came out in a hoarse rasp. "Every damn day since I met you. Doesn't help."

She shifted to rise from the bench. Lean quads bunched and stretched. The black compression shorts she wore clung to the flexing muscle but stubbornly refused to inch higher. Her body brushed his. It was the barest contact, but it set him off.

"We can't do this, Dan."

A slap across the face would have been less effective in snapping him back. "Danny," he corrected automatically. Dan was his deadbeat father's name, and he'd never answer to it.

"Daniel?"

The only people who ever called him Daniel were LeAnn and his mother. He refused to think about his messy affair with LeAnn, and the feelings he had toward Kate were a far cry from maternal. "It's Danny."

One dark brow rose. "Are you five?"

He scowled, refusing to be baited. "Are you trying

to pick a fight so you can ignore what's going on between us?"

"Nothing is going on between us."

"But something should be." Unable to stop himself, he tucked a stray wisp of her hair behind her ear. "And you know it as well as I do."

Something that looked like regret flickered across her face, but by the time she met his eyes again, it was gone. "I know we're in a public place." Her brows inched toward her hairline. "Our *work* place."

"No one is here."

"We both are," she argued. She darted a glance at the locker room doors. "Someone else could be."

Frustrated, he gave in and made the move she so obviously wanted him to make—he stepped back. "Fine."

She took the opening, swinging her leg over the bench and darting around him as if he were a player she'd instructed to set a pick. He turned to follow her progress as she made her way toward the door emblazoned with "Warrior Women."

He let her get within arm's reach of escape, then hit her with a zinger. "I've always hated the last two minutes of a basketball game."

She froze, her arm stretched for the locker room door, her palm wide and fingers splayed. She shot a puzzled look over her shoulder. "What? Why?"

He smirked. All she needed was a football tucked into the crook of her arm, and she'd have been almost an exact replica of the Heisman Trophy. But one a damn sight hotter than old Ed Smith—that famous trophy's inspiration—had ever been.

"Intentional fouls." He started toward her but forced

himself to make his steps slow and deliberate, giving her every opportunity to stop him if she wanted to. "I think intentionally fouling a player to stop the clock should be outlawed."

She blinked as she straightened to her full height and turned back to him, her body tensed as if it took all her strength to absorb the sheer absurdity of his statement. "I've heard you have issues with clock management."

He came to a stop right in front of her. "I don't see the point in delaying the inevitable. I play straight, I play tough, and I play through to the end. No trick plays, just the fundamentals."

Her lips parted, and it was all he could do to resist their pull.

"Make your fouls as flagrant as you want, Kate, but we both know the outcome is going to be the same."

# Chapter 9

SHE RAN. GOD HELP HER, SHE RAN LIKE THE NINNY SHE WAS, pushing through the heavy door like the devil himself was riding her ass. And she didn't stop until she stood with her forehead pressed against the cool metal lockers.

Her pulse raced, and in her mind, the war waged on. She was single. He was single. It wasn't like she was his superior, and he was nowhere close to being hers. She supposed there'd be hell to pay if Mike ever found out about them. No doubt Danny had more at risk than she did, and if he didn't care...

But there were even more complications. They'd signed a contract with the television studio. Millie wanted friction for the camera. Kate wanted friction of an entirely different kind. But she wasn't about to let the media dictate her sex life. At least not any more than she had let Jim Davenport and his remarkable lack of libido impact it.

No, the television show wasn't her problem. Neither was generating publicity for the school. This was her off-season. Shouldn't she be able to get off?

The sound of a shower running made her skin prickle. She flipped over and stared at the opposite wall, as if her super X-ray vision could map out the plumbing lines inside the wall dividing the men's facilities from the women's. Then again, if she had X-ray vision, she wouldn't be wasting it on a maze of copper pipe.

It had been all she could do to keep from gawking at him in the weight room. She closed her eyes and slid her hand to the valley between her breasts. Her heart beat fast and hard. Groaning, she compressed one aching nipple with the flat of her palm. It didn't help.

His skin had been so hot. He was leaner than she had expected. She'd thought most former football players ran to fat after their playing days ended, but Danny hadn't. Every bit of him was firm. So firm.

The loose shorts he wore did little to hide the outline of his cock. Her mouth had run dry when she'd first spotted the telltale bulge in the mirror. Her mouth was still dry, as a matter of fact. She tried to swallow, but her throat was thick and rough, and nothing happened. A moment of panic seized her. She pushed away from the lockers, her gaze set on the water fountain mounted to the wall.

The rub of her thighs against each other made it abundantly clear where all her moisture had pooled. Her cheeks flamed even as she bent for a sip, and a series of tantalizing thoughts danced in her head. They were all alone. The place was a ghost town in the first weeks of summer. She was wet. He was wet. There was no reason in the world they shouldn't be wet together.

Well, no reason other than common sense, pride, and the threat of public humiliation served up with a side of career suicide.

But at that moment, reason was more slippery than the desire pooling between her legs. She moved on instinct, breaking for the goal as if she had a ball in her hand and a clear path to the game-winning shot.

The hydraulic hinge on the heavy locker room door

shushed the nagging voice in her head. She hooked a sharp right and plowed into the men's facilities. The sound of water beating tile greeted her. A low groan drew her up short, just shy of the shower room door.

Pressing her hand to her throat, she peered cautiously around the corner. The new and improved Warrior facilities boasted the luxury of tiled half walls, providing a modicum of privacy for the athletes as well as some handy-dandy shelves for toiletry items. Danny stood in the nearest stall with a hand planted on the wall. Water beat down on his neck and shoulders. It ran like a river along the deep groove of his spine and spilled over the high, round curve of his tight ass. But neither those firm, pale globes of muscle nor the tantalizing hollows that led to his hips were what pulled her in. It was the sight of his right hand wrapped around his cock.

He stroked himself with a ruthless determination that made her gasp. She wanted to cry out. Tell him to stop. Be gentle. Go faster. Harder. Wait. Let her. But Kate couldn't seem to extract the actual words.

So she chose action.

Billows of steam enveloped her. The soles of her bright new sneakers squeaked. His shoulders tensed, and the jerky movement of his hand stopped. She placed her hand on his back to keep him from looking at her. "Don't turn around." She inhaled shakily. "Don't stop."

The spray soaked the front of her tank and spattered her legs. Being a woman with her priorities firmly in line, she spared her last rational thought for her shoes. Danny stood still as a statue as she toed off the sneakers and kicked them toward the door. He didn't move when she let her fingertips slide over his smooth skin, tracing the contours of his broad back. The rise and fall of his ribs betrayed his outward calm. She wanted to make him pant. The thought galvanized her. If she was going to do something this stupid, the man would have to exert himself.

Reaching around, she ran teasing fingertips over the back of his hand. He was still gripping his cock. "I said, don't stop."

His hand began to move, but slower this time.

"That's right." She brushed a glancing kiss to his shoulder blade, then ran her tongue over the curve of his neck, lapping precious moisture from his heated skin. She wrapped her hand around his as she plastered herself to his back.

"Slower," she whispered into his ear.

A gratifying shiver ran through him, and she smiled as she kissed the tender patch of skin beneath it.

"Let it play out."

To his credit, Danny made no arrogant remark or attempt at sexy banter. He simply did as he was told, slowing his strokes to match the pace she set. Unable to resist, she brushed the swollen tip of his cock with her thumb. Her heart tripped over itself as she pressed her cheek to his shoulder and closed her eyes.

"That's it," she murmured as he settled into the slow, steady rhythm.

"Every day." The words rumbled from his chest, enunciated through clenched teeth. "I've thought about this every day."

She didn't open her eyes. She couldn't. The last thing she wanted was to break the spell of sensuality billowing around them like the shower steam.

"Kate."

His voice broke, the single syllable spilling a torrent of desire and emotion. A flash of panic seized her. She wasn't ready for that. She wanted to float along on a stream of sensation that had nothing to do with emotion. She pressed against the taut mound of his ass, undulating shamelessly. Danny groaned loud and long, slowing his strokes as he pressed back against her.

She needed to keep control. Grab a branch and pull herself out before the current was too strong to fight. Get them back on the same playing field. Forcing her eyes open, she focused on the tile wall beyond them as she launched her offense. "You've thought about jerking off in the shower?"

He chuckled—a soft, sexy roll of unguarded pleasure that left her cursing the layers of sopping wet Lycra between them and the fact that she couldn't quite get herself off by humping his ass.

"I've jerked off in the shower every day thinking about you. You and me."

The correction came out gruff and terse, but her smile only widened. Wanting more, she scraped her teeth over his nape. "Really?"

"God yes," he groaned.

Unwilling to let her goad him into revealing more lurid thoughts, he released his grip on his cock and grasped her wrist. The none-too-gentle hold made her gasp. The quiver of barely restrained strength in his arm made her want to rub herself all over him. He pressed her palm to his straining dick. She wrapped her fingers around him and hummed her appreciation. "You and me…such a bad idea."

"But it feels so good."

He was close. She knew that in one stroke. Ripples traveled up that stretched-taut flesh. The velvet-soft head of his cock popped out of her fist, dark, swollen, and glistening. She pressed a lingering, open-mouthed kiss to the sweet spot behind his ear, then pressed her cheek to his shoulder blade.

"Don't hold back. I want you to come." Her whispered wish came out softer than the spray, but she knew he heard her, because every muscle in his body tensed.

He resisted for the space of a heartbeat, but she brushed a tender kiss over his shoulder, letting him know it was okay. She had him. She wouldn't let him down. He exhaled hard, his shoulders slumping as he surrendered to her touch.

Hot come spilled over her hand just as a low, guttural groan ripped through him. She pumped him sure and steady, milking the orgasm for all he was worth, though her knees trembled. Kissing his smooth skin, she stifled the urge to curse the steady stream of water for washing away his heat. She wanted to keep it, hold it, possibly commemorate this moment of triumph with a plaque she could hang in her office and admire whenever she wanted.

"Kate."

He didn't turn to look at her or press back against her body. Instead, he fell forward, planting his hands on the wall to catch his weight. She stretched her fingers under the spray, sending the last vestiges of this encounter spiraling down the drain, then took a step back.

The sopping wet Spandex made a disgusting sucking noise as she pulled her tank away from her skin.

Mortified by the sound and her reckless actions, she stumbled toward the shower room's entrance. "This didn't happen."

"Bullshit it didn't. Kate…"

A note of urgency filled his voice, but she didn't look back. Without breaking stride, she snagged her discarded shoes from the floor and started toward the door. "I'll see you at the studio."

"I never took you for a quitter," he called as she grasped the handle on the locker room door.

She turned to find him standing in the middle of the locker room, stark naked, dripping wet and semihard. The sight of him, at once brashly bold and wholly vulnerable, ratcheted up her desire. "I'm not."

"Why are you running away?"

"I'm not." She winced, wishing she'd taken a second to think of a new response, but how could she when he was just standing there like that? "I just…people are going to start showing up," she finished with a weak gesture toward the wall clock.

"Dinner. Tonight."

She blinked, a bit affronted by his presumption but too turned on to work up a decent amount of ire. "We can't go out. We're supposed to hate each other, remember?"

His eyes narrowed. "I never agreed to that."

"But you will," she said, and his jaw tightened. She saw the little muscle beneath his ear jump and wanted to lick the stray drops of water from that spot. Widening her stance, she cocked her head and softened her tone. "You need this publicity, Danny. The school does too."

"And you're willing to go along with it?"

The slight sneer in his tone didn't put her off. She

knew all about pride, and it didn't take a shrink to see that his was tragically wounded. "I'm a Warrior. My contract is up for renewal. I'll do what's good for the program."

He took a long step forward, completely unselfconscious. "And what about what's good for you?"

His implication rattled her. "You think you're good for me?"

"I think we could be very good together."

She pursed her lips to make it look like every hormone in her body wasn't agreeing with him wholeheartedly. Gripping the door handle hard enough to turn her knuckles white, she let him sweat it out a bit.

"My place after taping," she said as she opened the door just wide enough to peer into the weight room. Finding it empty, she heaved a sigh and pulled it open wider. "Pick up a pizza on your way over."

She'd almost escaped when he called after her, "What kind? Pepperoni? Supreme? Veggie?"

Poking her head back in, she scoffed. "Veggie? Really? Didn't you see what I did to that salad?"

He stared straight into her eyes. "You're beautiful when you're soaking wet."

She blinked at him, then shook her head. "Just for that, you're bringing the beer too. And none of that 'light' crap either. Real beer," she ordered as the door swung shut behind her.

---

"I'm just saying it seems like a cheap way to delay the inevitable, that's all. Who in their right mind thinks they can overcome a three-basket deficit when the clock has started adding the decimal point to the equation?"

Danny leaned forward in his chair, his hands planted flat on his knees. He'd tried to pound a fist on the arm of the chair to drive home a point earlier in the taping, but the hollow thud hadn't had the desired impact. All it garnered was a pitying smirk from the woman sitting across from him. The slim, snug pencil skirt Kate was wearing, on the other hand, packed all the wallop of an atomic bomb. Judging from the appreciative once-over he'd caught the sports anchor giving her, he wasn't the only one who thought so.

Turning back to the guy in the middle—Davenport, that was the string-bean reporter's name—Danny flashed a winning smile. "Come on, Jim. I know you're a basketball guy and all, but you have to admit the last couple of minutes of the game get a little ridiculous at times."

"Ridiculous?" Kate edged forward in her seat. "What's ridiculous is you telling me that managing the clock to my team's advantage is different from trying to ice a kid attempting to kick a twelve-inch ball through a couple of poles from fifty yards away."

"Eleven inches," he corrected. "A regulation ball is between ten and a half and eleven and a half inches."

A smile quirked her lips. Dark brows arched eloquently. "Wow. I have to say, I'm a little shocked. Most guys would try to add an inch rather than take one away."

"Some of us don't need to," he retorted.

Suddenly, the scarecrow perched between them pressed a finger to his earpiece and sprang to life. "And that looks like all the time we have for this week. Coach Snyder, Coach McMillan, thanks for joining us here on *The Warrior Way*."

The moment they were clear, Davenport turned toward Kate, effectively blocking Danny out. Not one to be put off by guys he could snap like toothpicks, Danny simply unclipped his microphone and stood. The sportscaster rambled on about the summer basketball camps, all the while darting glances over his shoulder as if waiting for Danny to leave the set. For his part, Danny wasn't a big fan of how close String Bean's knee was to Kate's. As a matter of fact, it rankled him enough to make him step up. If anyone was getting close to that sexy, black skirt, it was going to be him.

"If you'll excuse us, Coach Snyder and I have another meeting this evening," he said, interrupting the man midsentence.

Davenport turned to Kate for confirmation. "You do?"

"We do?" she asked at the same time.

The impertinent lift of her brow challenged him. One infinitesimal little quirk, and he found himself riding the razor's edge of annoyed and intrigued. He glanced at Davenport, then met Kate's gaze directly, brain and body willing to rise to whatever she threw at him. "Boosters. We were going to figure out a way to tap them to finish what was started in the shower rooms."

"Oh."

A rosy flush crept up her neck. It looked awful pretty with the pale-blue sweater she wore. In truth, he was becoming quietly obsessed with the sexy secretary look she sported in the studio. The costume, coupled with those disconcertingly frank stares, was enough to have him ready to climb out of his skin. That delicious blush was an added bonus. One he couldn't wait to taste.

"Shower rooms?" Davenport glanced from Kate to him and back again. "Didn't you just upgrade the facilities?"

She dismissed Davenport's question with a shrug and rose. Standing almost toe-to-toe on the tiny set, she looked Danny straight in the eye and flashed a game-winning smile. "There are a few…finishing touches needed."

The reporter stared up at them, his brow knit in confusion. "You're going together."

Kate stiffened and took a quick step back. The smile was nothing but a memory. "Well, we're going to the same place," she amended. She removed her own ear-piece and mic and dropped the equipment onto the chair. "Do you need directions?"

She asked the question with such an air of polite distance, Danny almost laughed. "No, I know my way around pretty well."

Her lips twitched, and she quickly bit the lower one as if she couldn't trust it to behave on its own. "Fine. I'll see you there."

She pivoted and stepped off the set without giving them a chance to respond. Danny nodded to Davenport, then made to follow suit, but she stopped beyond the camera range and raised a finger as if a thought had occurred to her.

"Oh. Sometimes parking can be a bit hard to find off campus, but if you stick to the side streets, you'll probably get lucky."

Danny nodded once to let her know he caught her drift, raised a hand in farewell to Davenport, and followed Kate through the studio at a discreet distance.

Once they were out the door, Kate glanced over her shoulder and added, "Don't forget the beer."

---

Thirty minutes later, Danny paused on the sidewalk, fidgeting with his car keys as he inspected the neighborhood. He'd parked around the corner from Kate's neat, little bungalow—per her veiled instructions—but it irked him to do it. When he'd dropped off the shoes, it had been the dark of night, but he'd still pulled up to the curb in front of her house. Heaving a sigh, he opened the passenger door and retrieved the pizza box and six-pack of beer he'd picked up on his way over.

Kate obviously didn't want him seen hanging out at her house. Probably wise, given that Millie was currently making them out to be Ali and Frazier, ready to go fifteen rounds at the sound of the bell. Plus, though he chose to ignore Mike's pointed glares, he wasn't oblivious to the risks in pursuing anything beyond a professional relationship with Kate. And yet another niggling voice in his head kept whispering that her reticence may have absolutely nothing to do with their current publicity campaign. Maybe she didn't want to be seen with him. If that were the case, she was destined to be disappointed. He was done living his life under a cloud of shame. While he might have been willing to round a corner for the sake of its-nobody's-damn-business, there was no way in hell he'd skulk down an alley like he was her backdoor man. They'd just have to figure out a happy medium.

As a concession to discretion, he snagged the green-and-gold Wolcott baseball cap off his dash and pulled it down low over his eyes. Hopefully any nosy neighbors who happened to be peeping through their blinds would think he was just a pizza delivery guy rather than the evil football coach come to debauch the Warrior princess.

Kate opened the door the second he reached the top step. To his relief, her smile was warm and welcoming. But judging from the speed with which she relieved him of his burden, she may only have been happy to see the pizza.

"I didn't know what you liked, so I ordered it loaded," he said as he relinquished the six-pack.

"Just the way I like it."

He tried not to stare at her ass when she bent to deposit the food and drinks on the low coffee table, but he failed miserably. She straightened, flipping back that smooth fall of dark hair with a toss of her head, and his vision blurred momentarily. He wet his lips, hoping to find something semiwitty lurking in his addled brain, but thankfully, Kate read his play.

She smiled as he advanced. They stood eye to eye. Their noses bumped as they sought just the right angle. His hand spread across her back, and he smiled when he realized she may even have him topped by an inch or so. For some reason, the discovery fired him up like a blowtorch. Her eyes widened, but she didn't flinch or draw away.

That small indulgence was all the opening he needed. "I hope you don't mind cold pizza and warm beer."

"My favorites," she whispered.

# Chapter 10

HE BOUND HER TO HIM, LIFTING HER ONTO THE TOES OF THOSE oh-so-demure black pumps and tipping his head back to kiss her. It was an odd angle for him, but the curve of her lips fit his to perfection. The skin was soft and supple but full to bursting, like a ripe red tomato left one day too long on the vine. He sank into her, relaxing his hold just enough to lower her and change the angle. She moaned sweet and gentle, parting for him when he ran the tip of his tongue along the seam of her lips.

His ball cap tumbled to the floor as her fingers tangled in his hair. She caressed his nape, then dragged the flats of her palms down the length of his back and up again. She gave every bit as good as she got, the wet velvet of her tongue twining with his in a dance so slow and sensuous he almost forgot he was supposed to be leading.

Almost, but not quite.

He broke the kiss, settling his hands firmly on her hips and opening his eyes. Her lashes fluttered, and she blinked twice. He literally saw her snap back into focus, and man, that legendary concentration was a thing to behold.

"What?" she asked.

Blunt, direct, and sexy as sin. Lord, she was proving to be hotter than he'd ever imagined. And he'd spent a lot of time imagining her lately. The thing was, in every single one of those fantasies, she was naked. Holding her unswervingly forthright gaze. "I want you naked.

In a bed." Her brows shot up, and he grinned as he set
a loophole in their agreement. "At least the first time."

She stroked down his arm, then threaded her facile
fingers through his. "Well, isn't it lucky that I happen to
have a bed handy?"

"Where?"

The urgency of his question must have hit the sweet
spot. Her eyes lit up like a scoreboard. "Right this way."

She turned and tucked their linked hands into the
small of her back. Danny found himself mesmerized
by the sway of her hips as she led him down a short,
dark corridor. Just inside the bedroom, she released his
hand and crossed to the bedside table. With the flick of a
switch, a small lamp bathed the room in pale-gold light.

Her bed was smaller than the California king he
hauled from state to state, but he wasn't about to quib-
ble. He noted two pillows in snowy-white cases propped
against a scrolling wrought-iron headboard and a quilt
done in pale blues and cream. Like her, the decor was
subtle but pretty.

"Will this do?"

Her husky tease jolted him from his inspection.
Turning his attention back to her, he caught a flash of
uncertainty in her eyes as she lowered her lashes. A faint
blush stained her cheeks, but she kicked off her shoes.
He could feel heat wafting off her skin in waves.

"It's perfect." Brushing her hair back, he threaded
his fingers through the thick, glossy locks and curled
them around the back of her skull. "This has to be some
kind of joke. You're way too pretty to be a femjock," he
teased, hoping to ignite the fire in her again.

Bingo. Indignation flared, then simmered down to a

sizzle as she narrowed her eyes. "You're way too hot for a guy whose glory days are behind him."

Grinning, he slipped his free hand under the hem of her sweater and lowered his head, telegraphing his pass. "I dunno. I felt pretty glorious this morning."

"Did you?"

He felt her smile when he pressed a tender kiss to her temple. "I want to make you feel that good too."

She tipped her head to the side, allowing him better access as he skimmed her cheekbone. "Jerking off in the locker room was the high point of your day, huh?"

"Most definitely."

He murmured the affirmation into her skin, kissing his way along her jaw, then nipping gently at her lobe. Her pulse throbbed against his lips. He laved it with his tongue, relishing the staccato effect he seemed to be having on her heartbeat. Her back was smooth and warm under his palm. He fisted his hand in her hair, pulling her head back enough to recapture her mouth. But the blitz he'd planned met no resistance, a fact that both thrilled and disappointed him.

A perverse part of him wanted her to make him work for it a bit. Hell, he'd probably even beg, if that's what it would take. But the lady was willing. Not just willing but eager, if the frantic tugs at his shirttails were any indication. He came up for air, gasping and groaning as she pushed both hands up under his shirt.

"Nuh-uh." He took a full step back, hanging on to the hem of her sweater while he disentangled his other hand. "You've seen me. Been all over me. It's my turn."

He whisked the thin knit up over her head. She laughed as she brushed her hair from her face. A full-bodied, hot rush of a laugh that shot straight to his groin.

"Not much to see here."

She cast a disparaging glance at her breasts, obviously thinking there was something lacking in the high, subtle swells encased in lace-edged satin. Proving she was cracked. He'd seen dozens of sets of tits in his life, and he could honestly attest that hers were perfect. Definitely not the biggest, but they suited her long, lithe body to a T.

"Good thing you're not a ref. Your vision is crap."

He dipped his head to nuzzle the shallow valley between her breasts. His hands slid down to cradle the curve of her ass. She gasped, and her nails bit into his shoulders when he claimed her nipple, but he didn't mind the little stabs of pain. He marked the pale-blue fabric with wet, open-mouthed kisses. The satin heated, but the taut tip only hardened more. He pulled her deeper, suckling hard through the thin barrier as he groped for the zipper on her skirt. When he came up empty, Danny pulled back with a frustrated growl and straightened to his full height.

Her cheeks were flushed, the hectic color making her eyes glow gold. A hot blade of lust sliced through him. If her clothes didn't disappear soon, he couldn't be responsible for their safety. Eyes locked on hers, he raised his hands in surrender.

"Take it off or I tear it off."

She blinked once, then glanced down. "The bra or the skirt?"

"All of it. Now."

A sly smile tugged at the corner of her mouth, but she

nodded toward him as she crooked an arm around her back. "Why don't we just go ahead and get rid of everything? That way neither of us runs the risk of…fumbling."

He snorted softly but reached for the collar on his shirt without hesitation. "I don't fumble."

Jerking the logoed polo over his head, he sent it sailing in the same direction as her sweater. Her bra fell at his feet. He fought the urge to drop to his knees when she reached for a tiny tab at the side of that sexy skirt.

"Part of me wants you to leave that on," he confessed, going to work on his belt.

"Too tight. We'd never get it over my thighs."

She shimmied the snug skirt down to her ankles, revealing lightly tanned stretches of curved, firm muscle. A faint tan line ran low across the tops of her thighs, and tiny white scars dotted the spots where surgeons had scoped her knee. A longer, puckered scar marked the end of her stellar playing career.

"Not very pretty," she said.

Danny jerked, realizing that he'd frozen with his pants halfway down his hips. Giving them a shove, he let the weight of his belt carry them to the floor. "There you go, being wrong again." He waved a hand at the scar that ran from groin to knee. Her gaze dropped to his crotch instead, and his dick strained against his boxer briefs, anxious to make a good impression. "We can compare war stories later, but right now, there are more pressing matters."

—∿∿—

Figuring she was too far gone to turn back now, Kate stripped out of her panties and watched in fascination as

Danny shed the remainder of his clothes. Anxious with anticipation, she stifled the urge to cover herself as he made quick, if clumsy, work of his shoes and socks. But the second he stood in front of her as bare and aroused as she was, all nervousness fled. He opened his arms—a simple, probably meaningless gesture, but one she appreciated nonetheless.

She stepped into the circle of his arms and sighed when he pulled her flush against him. The enticing length of his erection nudged her belly. Crisp, curling chest hair teased her nipples into aching points. She slid one hand over his broad shoulder and cupped the side of his neck. His pulse pounded against the pad of her thumb. Drawn to its siren song, she pressed her lips to the spot and simply stood there, absorbing the sure, steady beat.

When she felt grounded enough, she raised her mouth to speak directly into his ear. "It's been a while for me." He groaned low and rough, and she ghosted kisses along the line of his jaw. "I'd ask you to be gentle, but I don't think that's what either of us really want."

"No." His answer popped out, but then he shook his head as if befuddled by what she was saying. "Yes."

He slid one hand up her back as she caught his lobe between her teeth and bit. Hard. His palm cradled the back of her head, making it clear he didn't want her to stop. She traced the shell of his ear with the tip of her tongue and reveled in the shiver that shuddered through him.

"Both. All," he amended.

Kate smiled when he tipped his head away and pressed his body into hers. Smoothing her hands over the tight swells of his butt, she pulled him closer still. "I bought condoms." She scraped the shadow of his beard with her teeth, and if she wasn't mistaken, his knees buckled just a little. Emboldened, she snaked a hand between them and trailed her fingertips down the stripe of silky, black hair that bisected his abs, stopping short of his straining cock. "We both know how important it is to have reliable equipment."

His hand tightened in her hair, and he urged her head up. His lips were parted and wet, his eyes dark as the midnight sky. She could have sworn she saw him clench his teeth. Dark brows lowered, and his mouth turned down in a fierce scowl. "Play fair."

The glower might have been more effective if he weren't so damn delicious-looking. The fact that he was rubbing his stiff dick mindlessly against her stomach lessened the impact as well. Determined to flout his stern warning, she smiled and whispered, "Make me."

She yelped when he yanked her up off her feet. Tall as she was, there weren't many men who could man-handle her. The perverse girly-girl inside her squealed with glee when he turned to the bed and tossed her onto it with a bounce. The woman in her almost purred.

Husky laughter rolled off the walls. Hers. His. Theirs.

It spoke a language of its own. The sound of it filled her up, making her heart drum faster, her breasts swell, and her pussy almost embarrassingly wet. She might have been self-conscious about the slick arousal if the evidence of his weren't so readily apparent. He wanted her. Judging from the tension in his defined muscles and the tiny throb in the corner of his jaw, he wanted her bad.

She scrambled back a bit, grinning as she arranged

herself in what she hoped was an alluring come-hither pose at the center of the mattress. It worked. He followed her without hesitation, planting his hands on the quilt and crawling up over her slowly, deliberately, stalking her like a big, sleek cat.

A long sigh escaped her as he lowered himself to her. Her arms and legs wrapped around him, every instinct demanding she hold him there. Close to her.

*Keep your friends close and your enemies closer.*

The old adage popped into her head without invitation. She stiffened as his mouth touched hers.

Danny instantly drew back. Propping his weight on his elbows, he searched her face. Concern etched a deep divot between his inky brows. "Am I hurting you?"

She shook her head, as much to dissuade him as to loosen the niggling kernel of doubt. "No. You feel good." To emphasize this point, she pulled him down for a hard, fierce kiss. "So good."

He wasn't buying it. She could see the skepticism in his narrowed eyes. Fortunately, she was also in the perfect position to divert his attention. All it took was a little wriggle, and a hoarse groan broke in his chest. Their breaths mingled, and their noses bumped. He settled against her hips, his cock nestled into her damp curls. Her toes teased the soles of his feet.

He fit. They fit.

That transient bit of awareness chased the last of her cliché-ridden worry away. "Condoms. Nightstand." She punctuated the words with soft, lingering kisses.

She should have known it wouldn't work. He was an athlete at heart, filled with determination and a stubborn need to conquer even the smallest obstacles. She squirmed some more as he searched her eyes, but not in a sexy, don't-you-want-me-baby sort of way. "What happened just then? What were you worried about?"

"Nothing," she answered too quickly. When the corners of his gorgeous mouth turned down in a frown, she broke. "I just… It's stupid."

"Tell me."

Gritting her teeth, she inhaled through her nose and let it go slowly. Sometimes, in order to score, a player had to suck it up and charge the goal. She might get hacked—or worse, blocked—but she had to take the shot. "We're not enemies, are we?"

His scowl disappeared. In its place, he wore an expression of such blank surprise he almost looked like a cartoon character. Then he pointedly glanced down at their nearly joined bodies. "Enemies?"

"I told you it was stupid." She spat the retort at him but refused to turn away. She'd committed to this shot, and she'd follow through. "It's…with all this stuff. Millie, the reporters, the sparring and trash talk. Then this." She ran her hand down his back, fingertips tracing the valley of his spine while her palm mapped the hard ridges that led down to his ass. "It's a little…confusing."

The line between his brows deepened. "I thought that was for show."

The oxygen she'd been hoarding whooshed from her lungs. She didn't bother even trying to hide her relief. "So we're friends?"

He chuckled softly, clearly amused by the leaps in her logic, and lowered a bit more of his weight onto her. "I'd like to be."

She raised her face for a kiss, and he obliged. A

long, lazy kiss that would have made her feel foolish for asking if he hadn't tasted so damn good.

"I'd say this feels pretty friendly." He pecked kisses to each corner of her mouth, then shifted to concentrate on her neck and throat.

He found the sensitive spot beneath her ear, and she shivered. Then, like the masterful player he was, he exploited the weakness. Kate gasped and arched as he drew the tender skin into his mouth and sucked. She panted with a mixture of relief and disappointment when he let go.

He soothed the spot with his tongue, then scraped it with his teeth. The implication was a warning and a promise. One she hoped he planned to see through. But no. He just meandered along, covering her neck, throat, and shoulders with feathery kisses that left her head spinning.

At last, he shifted his body down. The move snugged the thick shaft of his cock against her clit. She parted her legs farther, a blatant invitation for him to give her the friction she craved. Instead, he chose to string feathery kisses along her collarbone. She moaned her delight and frustration, rolling her hips in a not-so-subtle reminder.

To her dismay, Danny pushed up on his hands, peeling his body from hers. She clutched at him with arms and legs, and they froze like that, two fierce competitors with strong bodies and equally enduring wills locked in a battle for something they both wanted.

Desperately.

"This isn't going to be a fast break," he said.

She laughed but didn't loosen her hold on him.

He smiled down at her, understanding softening his expression. "We're going to take a page from your playbook. It's your turn to let the things unfold." She caught her bottom lip between her teeth, but his gaze never wavered. "I promise you can be on top next time."

She held out for a handful of heartbeats, then whispered, "Okay, but I've got next."

Danny wandered his way down her body, perversely avoiding her breasts but sending delicious ripples of sensation through her as he staked claim on each newly uncharted erogenous area he uncovered. Who knew her navel was so ticklish? She would have bet on her ribs, but no. She only moaned and writhed when he outlined them with the tip of his tongue. God, she loved the bit of suction he used when he covered her stomach with hot, wet kisses. By the time he nuzzled the undersides of her breasts, she lay beneath him as tight as an overtaxed hamstring but as loose as a shooter with a hot hand.

Her fingers slid through his hair, toying with the waves as he tormented her. He had a scar at his hairline. She wanted to ask him about it, but he chose that exact moment to close his mouth over her nipple. She arched her back, bowing into the pain-tinged pleasure as his teeth rasped the pebbled flesh. She collapsed, panting, her eyes locked on the ceiling when he pressed her back down with the flat of his tongue. His hands were everywhere—grasping her hips, stroking her leg, cupping her breasts as if he'd found the holy grail instead of a couple of wannabe B-cups.

"Christ, Kate."

He ground the words out as he released her other nipple, having subjected it to the same delicious torment as its twin. His hips jerked, his cock massaging a streak of hot, sticky pre-come into her thigh.

"I have to taste you."

With that, he abandoned all pretense of smooth moves and steady seduction. Cool air teased her wet nipple into a painful point. She pressed her palm to her breast to either soothe or smother it, her eyes fixed on the man slithering down her body. Broad shoulders spread her thighs wide. He looked up. The stark longing in his eyes made her pulse race.

"Yes?" he asked, his voice rough as sandpaper.

"God yes," she answered in a rush.

He slid one blunt fingertip through her wet folds, then plunged into her.

"Oh!"

Her hips rose in a valiant bid to meet each glorious stroke. Then his hot mouth closed over her clit, and all hell broke loose. She moaned. Oh God, she moaned loud enough to make him chuckle against her hypersensitive pussy, sending another paroxysm of pleasure pulsing through her. She moaned so loud the neighbors probably heard her. He circled the demanding bundle with a laziness that boasted his intention to do nothing more all night long if he wanted. Thankfully, he had more tricks up his nonexistent sleeve.

He drew her clit into his mouth, alternately sucking and teasing the tender flesh with his tongue while he started to fuck her with that singularly inadequate finger. Kate gripped his hair, tugging at the soft strands, then digging her nails into his scalp. She circled her hips, shamelessly fucking him back, desperate to grab the release hovering just out of her grasp. Then the bastard withdrew his hand.

"Please. No."

He ignored her broken protests. She almost wept

when he raised his head, a wicked grin stretching his wide, wet mouth. "Oh, I'm not quitting, Coach."

Danny lowered his head again, opened his mouth wide, and closed it over her. His damp fingertips teased the crevice of her ass. She planted her feet and pressed up, offering herself to him without apology. In this moment, the tables had turned. She was open, vulnerable to him in every way, just as he'd been to her in the shower room, and she gave herself over to it. He thrust his tongue into her once, twice, then pulled back to apply the most mind-bending suction she'd ever experienced.

She came hard and fast, in waves of sensation almost too intense to be called pleasurable. They rocked through her, one riding the heels of the other, relentless and irrepressible. Not that she wanted to hold them back. She didn't want them to stop. Not now. Not ever.

Certainly not when Danny pushed back to rest on his heels, a self-satisfied smile crinkling his eyes and cutting the most enticing grooves around his mouth. He waggled his brows a bit, but she was too wrung out to muster more than a weak smile. Chuckling and obviously riding high on his accomplishments, the man of the hour rose onto his knees between her legs. His cock jutted straight out from a thatch of ink-black curls, thick and heavy, the swollen head taut and slick with need.

"Score's tied."

She was still trying to make sense of his raspy declaration when he pitched forward, catching himself on his hands so he wouldn't crush her beneath his weight. His blue eyes shone with victory. The white of his teeth was nearly blinding.

Needing to gain a little ground, she retaliated with a

smile of her own, then cocked her head to take him all in. "Tied?"

"We're both up one." He gave his hips a meaningful twitch and looked deep into her eyes. "Looks like we're heading into overtime. You ready, Coach?"

The challenging light in his eyes was all the spark she needed. Reaching up, she grabbed a fistful of silver-shot dark hair and pulled him down. They kissed deeply, lingering as they shared the taste of the pleasure he'd given her. When they broke apart at last, they were both breathless.

Opening her eyes, Kate waited until he swam into focus. She pressed a fingertip to his damp upper lip, tracing the bow of it as if she were pondering his question very thoroughly, even though she'd known her answer the minute he asked.

"Danny?" She spoke his name in a whisper so soft and sultry he tensed like a pointer on the hunt. Then she smiled, letting it unfurl slowly. "I was born ready."

---

Good Lord, she was hot. He was glad she couldn't see his eyes roll back in his head when he reached for the nightstand drawer. He had to jiggle it to get it to open. An action that resulted in an immediate reaction from Kate and even more eye rolling on his part, but the drawer slid open with a heavy *thunk*. Danny groped in the depths, expecting to find a box of condoms, perhaps a pad of paper and a pen, reading glasses or a book—the sorts of things he might find in his own. He didn't expect to wrap his fingers around a disconcertingly thick hunk of silicone.

Rearing back, he came up on his knees with an

eight-inch rubber dick in a shade of purple he was pretty sure would be indicative of heart failure. "What the—" He goggled at the dildo, then shifted his gaze to the woman pinned beneath him. "Whoa."

A blush burned bright in her cheeks, but she managed a shrug that looked almost nonchalant. "It was a gift."

Curling his lip in distaste, he leaned forward to put the vibrator back where he found it. "The gift that keeps giving, huh?" He located the condom box with his next grope and pulled back again. A smirk twisted his lips as he tore into the cardboard. "Let me guess, his name is Bob?"

She flinched as if he'd revealed her deepest, darkest secret. "You know about BOBs?"

Danny snickered as he extracted a foil-wrapped condom. "I've heard the term." It was hard to look cool and smug when fumbling with a rubber, but he did the best he could. "Not very original."

"Mine isn't Bob," she retorted.

"No?" He secured the roll of latex at the base of his dick, then trailed his hand up the inside of her thigh, hoping to get the conversation—and the action—back on track. "Good."

A shiver passed through her when he settled between her legs again. He closed his eyes, relishing the sensation of being on the cusp.

"It's LeBron."

His eyes popped open. "Seriously?"

"No, just joking."

He shook his head but growled his approval when she drew her leg up high.

"It's Michael," she whispered as she wrapped those thoroughbred legs around his hips.

An involuntary moan escaped him when he pressed into her moist heat. His brain stalled. "Michael?"

"Jordan." She ran a languid hand down the length of his spine. "Why settle for anything less than the best?"

He blinked, trying to wrap his head around the fact that he was discussing a dildo with her when his real, live, pulsing dick was poised at the edge of glory. But her eyes glowed bright with pleasure and anticipation, the golden lights in them as irresistible as the siren song of her teasing. "Why not Kobe or Kareem?" he asked, his voice hoarse.

A smile tugged at the corners of her mouth. "Kobe has had enough trouble with women, and Kareem just sounds a little too dirty."

She tipped her hips up, and he began the slow slide into her. Dipping his head to whisper directly into her ear, he asked, "Magic?"

Her husky chuckle rippled through him. "This feels like magic, but I like Mike." Once he was fully seated in her, she raked her nails lightly up his back. "I like to fly high. Maybe you can help me get some air again?"

He choked on a gasping laugh but began to move inside her. "There's nothing I'd like more."

She slid a hand between their bodies. He felt her knuckles graze his abs and heard her gasp when she touched her clit. He drove into her—sure, steady, and driven completely insane by the fact that she was taking her own pleasure in hand. "Christ, Kate, I feel like the top of my head's going to blow off."

"God, I hope not. I've been thinking about this all damn day." She arched her neck and bowed her body into his. "I'd hate to think we'd be a one and done."

"Oh, hell no."

Determination reinforced, he pulled her hand out from between them and pinned it to the pillow beside her head. Grasping her ass, he leveraged onto his knees just enough to drive down into her, dragging the shaft of his cock over her swollen clit with each stroke. The tiny, maddening moans and whimpers were back within a matter of seconds. Her muscles cinched him tight, holding him deep and snug. He slammed into her, losing his grip as she tightened around him.

The first spasm rolled through her, and he shot off like a rocket, pumping into her wild and free, emptying himself inside her.

He might have shouted her name. The bedroom walls reverberated with release. But whether it was him or her, he couldn't recall. He collapsed onto her, trusting her to hold his weight as he buried his face in her hair. She gentled him with her hands, feathery strokes interspersed with firm caresses. She unknotted her legs and ran the arch of her foot the length of his.

"We fit."

A long moment passed. He didn't realize he'd spoken the words aloud until she answered.

"Yes, we do."

"It's nice."

She laughed softly. "Yeah, it is."

Slowly, reality came seeping back into his consciousness. Danny roused himself enough to peel his weight off her chest. He peered down at her, unable to repress his smile when their eyes met. "Know what else would be nice?"

Her stomach rumbled, and it vibrated through him, pressed as close together as they were. Kate laughed, and making Kate laugh was suddenly number two on his list of favorite things to do to her.

"Pizza?" she asked, eyes sparkling.

# Chapter 11

IT SHOULD HAVE FELT WEIRD, HAVING HIM THERE. FIRST OFF, he was a man, and it had been a very long time since she'd had a man in her bed. Second, she barely knew the guy. She had no clue what his favorite color might be or what television shows he watched. Did he read anything other than playbooks? Could he make her come that hard again? And all those questions aside, he was Danny McMillan. This was the cocky fuckup who'd blown into town demanding half the attention and twice her salary. She was supposed to hate him.

Too bad she didn't.

He didn't feel like a rival. He felt mind-blowingly good. And comfortable. Their conversation flowed. Yeah, it was peppered with jabs and jokes, but there was no longer much heat behind them.

Unlike their kisses.

He should have looked ridiculous in her bed, but he didn't. His thick, muscular thighs looked so good tangled up in rosebud-printed sheets. When she slipped out from under the cover he'd pulled over them, he simply lay there with his hand behind his head, staring at her as if she were a supermodel/centerfold combo and he was trying to figure out how to get the magazine staples out of her stomach. With his teeth.

And Lord, she wanted him too. Boy, was Avery going to be pissed. Her friend had spent the last few weeks researching salary inequities based on gender and preparing her attack on the patriarchal establishment. And here Kate was, sleeping with the enemy.

Self-conscious, she reached for the robe she kept hanging on the back of her closet door. "Don't you think you should do something with…"

She waved her hand toward his crotch but trailed off when he rolled up and off the bed in one fluid motion. She stood frozen, mesmerized by the sight of him as he crossed to her. Despite her helpful reminder, the condom still clung to his semierect penis. She couldn't help but stare. Even when not shown to its best advantage, every damn inch of the man was impressive.

She slipped one arm into the robe, but he caught her free hand in both of his and squeezed.

"Please don't."

A spurt of indignation shot through her when he gently slid the robe down her arm. She opened her mouth to protest, but he shut her down fast.

"You don't need this. Not with me." He shot a pointed glance at his own battle-scarred leg, then stared straight into her eyes. The short terry cloth robe dangled from his fingers in the no-man's-land between them, hers for the taking if she truly wanted it. "You can pretend this is a locker room, if that makes it easier, but I like looking at you naked."

A hot flush of pleasure prickled the back of her neck. Her nipples tightened in instinctive response to his roving gaze. She took the robe from him and placed it back on the hook, casting a glance over her shoulder. "Okay, but for your information, women don't strut around naked in locker rooms like men do."

He pulled her against his hair-roughened chest and kissed her hard. Stalking toward the bathroom, he grumbled, "Another fantasy shot to hell."

Kate laughed, appreciating the view of his tight, white buttocks as he disappeared into the room. "I'll heat the oven."

And that's how she came to be standing stark naked in her kitchen, tapping her foot impatiently as the oven heated and wondering if she should be worried about the six-pack of beer he'd set next to the pizza box.

"I'm okay with cold pizza."

She jumped. The blush that warmed her cheeks burned faster and hotter than the glowing red coil in her oven. He held the carrier of beer out to her, silently offering a bottle. She must have hesitated a second too long, because he huffed an impatient sigh and plunked the six-pack down on the counter.

"Let's clear this up right now."

The steel in his deep voice made her quiver, but not with fear or intimidation. That firm, terse tone turned her on like nobody's business. Arousal flooded her, making her head swim and her knees wobbly. Embarrassed, she ducked her head to peer into the empty oven. Swallowing the lump in her throat, she tapped the cool, unaffected tone she once used to trade insults with other players on the court. "Clear what up?"

"My past sins. For the record, I don't have a drinking problem or an anger problem, and I'm not a sex addict." His hand closed around her arm, compelling her to turn and face him. When she did, she found his blue eyes dark with frustration, but his gaze was steady. "Yes, I'd had a couple of beers the night all the crap came out about the recruiting violations, and yes, I exchanged some words with that reporter, but I never touched—"

"You don't have to—"

His fingers tightened on her arm, but it was the brisk shake of his head that cut off her arguments. "I wasn't drunk. I was angry. A completely justified anger." He bit off the words. "You *know* how it is. When you're the head coach, you're the head coach. Everything stops at you."

"I do know that."

"And you know as well as I do that the violations they supposedly nabbed us on were things every D-one school does—"

"Not every school."

He sneered a little at her holier-than-thou tone. "Fine, not *every* school, but most. And you know that nine times out of ten, the NCAA looks the other way."

She shot him an arch look but grasped for a way to lighten the conversation. "Are you calling yourself a ten?"

He didn't bite. Instead, he ran his hand through his rumpled hair. "There were other complications. I was already having issues with the AD and the administration, and I hadn't exactly scored a lot of friends in the community. But as long as I kept winning, they couldn't really get rid of me, could they?"

"No."

"I was an asshole, but not a complete asshole." He swallowed hard but fixed her with a direct gaze. "And then there was LeAnn."

She flinched when he spoke the young woman's name aloud. A part of her resented him for making that sordid bit of the story real when she stood there in her kitchen with him, exposed in more ways than one. "The student," she said stiffly.

He grabbed her arm and turned her to face him. "You make it sound like I was parking outside the high school, hoping some girl would pick me to be her prom date. She was a graduate student. I was thirty-five, and she was twenty-six."

"Kudos."

"There's a much bigger age gap between Ty Ransom and his child bride." When she didn't fire back, he let his grip on her arm fall slack. "Think whatever you want to think. Everyone else does."

The creak of old aches tinged the bravado in his tone, making her feel about two inches tall. He hadn't only been humiliated and humbled in this debacle. He'd been hurt too. And badly. An inexplicable surge of jealousy choked off the smart-assed remark she had locked and loaded. The beautiful redhead she'd seen all over the sports networks in the weeks following Danny's firing was more than just an ego trip for a guy high on himself.

"When it became clear that I was going to be the poster boy for all that was wrong with college football, I did everything I could to keep her name out of things." His lips thinned into a tight line. "But she didn't really want to be kept out of the spotlight."

"She was young." It was a simple statement of fact, not a judgment or an excuse. Somehow, saying the words aloud made her feel even more naked. She was decades older than the girl they were discussing, and in that moment, she felt every minute.

"She was," he agreed. "And pretty and smart."

His mouth pursed as he searched for one more word. "Ambitious." He pulled two bottles of beer from the carrier, twisted off the caps, and handed one to her. His mouth curled into a smirk so bitter, it made her chest hurt. "Also turns out she had no interest in dating a guy on the unemployment line."

He toyed with one of the bottle caps, running the pad of his thumb over the ridged edge, then pressing it into his flesh. "You know what the funny thing was?"

He paused, but she knew a rhetorical question when she heard one, so she kept silent.

"No one ever asked me how I felt about her. They just assumed I was a lecherous creep getting his rocks off with some young girl." He dropped the cap on the counter and rubbed his thumb against the side of his forefinger, soothing the lingering effect of his self-abuse. "No one even asked. The press, my so-called friends...my mother...my brother."

The resentment in his tone took her by surprise. Turning to face him head-on, she asked the question he'd waited so long to answer. "Did you love her?"

An endless minute passed, but he didn't look away. "I thought I did."

"I'm sorry."

She whispered the words of sympathy by reflex, surprised to find she meant them. Neither of them were fresh young things. They'd both loved, lost, and lived to tell the tale. At last, he turned away, lifting the bottle to his lips and taking a deep pull. His mouth was damp and shiny when he lowered it.

"Do you want me to leave?"

The bluntness of his question shocked her out of

immobility. She slammed her untouched bottle of beer onto the counter. "What? No!"

He met her eyes again. This time, his luscious lips twisted into a self-deprecating smirk. "I'd understand if you did."

Her eyes narrowed. "Easy to be gallant when you've already got what you wanted."

Those blue eyes flashed. "Why do you sell yourself so cheap?" She opened her mouth to retort, but he pressed his finger to her lips. When she obediently closed them, his hand fell to his side. "If I wanted to leave, I'd have been gone by now."

His assertion was too cocky by half, but a grin still threatened her. Kate squelched it as best she could as she pulled a round pizza pan from a cabinet. Lifting the lid on the carryout box, she shot him a glance from under her eyelashes. "Well, there's pizza." That was as close as she'd get to asking him to stay.

"Yes, there is."

She pursed her lips, weighing the wisdom of laying her own cards on the table. But he'd shown her his, and if there was ever a good time to give a little of her own, maybe this was it. After all, they were both experienced enough to know the risk of playing games. "My husband left me because I was better than him."

"At what?"

She shrugged. "Just about everything."

"I can see that." He stood there, naked and silent, watching her every move as she transferred the luke-warm pie to the pan and slid it into the oven.

She straightened, trying not to feel so terribly nude, but it was hard to play it cool when she was hyperaware of every bump, bulge, and unsightly scar. It was easier to do when she caught sight of the blatant admiration in his frank gaze.

The corner of his mouth lifted in that familiar smirk. "I guess I'm lucky to have skills in at least one area."

Her lips twitched, but she did her best to keep her expression sober. "Oh, I'd say you might have two."

"Is one of them football?"

"Of course."

"And the other?"

She fixed him with an unsmiling stare. "Is not football."

"So I've got that going for me." He raised his bottle in a silent toast.

Relieved that he didn't force her to expound, she picked at the foil label with her thumbnail as she searched for a neutral topic of conversation. A thousand questions came to mind—everything from politics to books to coaching strategies and motivational techniques. In the end, she blurted, "What's your favorite color?"

Danny smiled, but his customary flash of teeth widened and warmed in direct proportion to the sizzle of embarrassment in her cheeks. "Green. What's yours?"

"Blue." It wasn't true. She liked red, but with his eyes locked on her, there was no other answer she could give. "I mean red," she amended, turning to grab an oven mitt.

"You're decisive. I like that."

Slipping her hand into the padded mitt was comforting. She wasn't completely naked anymore, and that made her brave. "And I like a man who's helpful in the kitchen. Grab some plates, will you?"

He snickered, opened the oven door, pulled out the

pizza, and dumped the entire thing back into its box. "Plates? What are you, some kind of girl or something?"

"Not a girl," she retorted, liking the way he tried to bait her. It almost made her forget she was standing in her kitchen totally naked. But she couldn't forget, so she figured she might as well use her nudity to her advantage. "I don't know if you noticed, but what you see before you is over seventy-four inches of grown woman."

"Oh, I noticed," he grumbled. Closing the lid on the box, he dropped his half-empty bottle into the six-pack carrier again and gave her a playful but surprisingly effective come-hither stare. "Come back to bed, Kate. I feel weird standing in the kitchen naked."

---

"You done yet?"

Danny shot her the glare that made three-hundred-pound linebackers quiver in their cleats. "Just what every man likes to hear in bed."

She was a picture of wide-eyed innocence. "I'm just asking."

He glanced down at the pizza box between them. She'd eaten exactly two slices. He'd demolished over half but still wanted more. More pizza. More of her. More lying naked in her bed, propped up on both pillows and dangling a warmish bottle of beer from his fingers.

"One more." He deftly snagged another piece, too quick to let her chop off his hand with the cardboard guillotine she'd made of the box lid.

She shook her head and slid off the bed, dragging the boxed remains over rumpled sheets. "Just when

I was starting to like you, you go and make me hate you again."

"You don't hate me."

"You need to grow a gut like any decent man your age," she muttered.

He offered a guileless smile when she looked back from the bedroom doorway. "I need fuel. You're too much for me."

"And don't you forget it."

He chuckled as he chewed. Though she made noises about watching what she ate, from where he was sitting, he saw no hint of the self-consciousness she'd shown earlier. She moved with the ease and grace of the athlete she still was, all toned muscle and silky-smooth skin.

Except for the scars on her knee. Battle scars. Badges of honor.

Energized by the twisted surge of lust brought on by those gnarled gashes, he mowed the slice down to crust. When she reappeared, he took a moment to drink in the messy perfection of her. Her sleek, dark hair was tousled, tossed into wayward waves that framed her oval face and clung to her neck. She paused at the entrance, bracing her hands high on the doorframe and cocking her head. All six feet two inches of her were on display for him. Only him. And suddenly, he couldn't care less about fuel. All he needed was her.

"C'mere."

He beckoned with his chin, but she just raised an eyebrow. High, small breasts tipped with surprisingly dark pink nipples stood at attention. If he closed his eyes, he could imagine the musky scent of their bodies trapped in the dark curls between her legs. But he kept his eyes open. Wide. He needed them to trace the patterns he'd run over her creamy skin.

"Every man's wet dream. Isn't that what they say?"

The husky timbre of her voice jolted him from thoughts of end-arounds involving her spectacular rear end. "Huh?"

She released her hold on the doorframe, her body arching as if she'd just scored a slam dunk. "This." She waved a hand at him as she planted that perfectly imperfect knee on the edge of the mattress. "Pizza, beer…naked woman." She cocked her head and crawled toward him. "Or is the naked woman supposed to turn into the pizza and beer?"

He was working up a full sentence, but then she had his junk in her soft palm, and the tips of those long nails were testing and teasing spots that rarely garnered much attention. He squirmed a bit, and she laughed—low, soft, and knowing. She lifted her head to look up at him from under dark lashes as she pressed the pad of one finger to the spot beneath his balls. The nearly empty bottle he held fell to the carpeted floor. With a hum of amused satisfaction, she bent her head, and the soft ends of her hair tickled his thighs.

"Feel good?"

One last shred of cognizant thought had him pitching the crust he'd crumpled in his hand toward the night-stand. "Christ yes."

Danny let his head fall back as her lips grazed his sac. His dick hardened even more, pressing up through the tangle of her hair, unashamedly begging for the same attention. She ran her tongue between his nuts, and a tremor coursed through him.

She took him firmly in hand, fondling him as she looked into his eyes. "You know, people used to complain about my ball-handling skills."

"Idiots," he gasped.

Her mouth closed around his sac, drawing first one then the other into her mouth and sucking gently. He braced himself with his hand on her head, fingers sliding into the tangles and getting hopelessly snared. She followed the vein that ran along the underside of his cock, licking, kissing, and sucking with enough playful tease to drive him straight out of his mind.

She swallowed him whole, taking him so deep the head of his cock nudged the back of her throat, and every trace of oxygen in his lungs exploded into her name. "Kate!"

He could feel her smile as she withdrew. "Hm?"

"Don't stop."

Whether the gasped words were an order or plea, he had no idea. All he knew was he needed to be wrapped in that wet heat more than he needed anything else in the world. Maybe even football.

She hesitated for a split second, and he dug his fingertips into her skull, silently imploring. Her eyes met his, and she released him. For one heart-freezing moment, Danny was afraid he might actually weep at the loss. And then she spoke.

"Don't stop what? Tell me what you want."

"Suck me." The truth burst from him raw-edged. "I want you to suck me."

She quirked an eyebrow. "And then? Tell me everything." She sank down just enough to maintain eye contact while she placed a chaste kiss to the very tip of him. "How does the play unfold, Coach?"

"You like the dirty talk, huh?"

She didn't answer, but her lips parted, and he finally felt the moist heat of her mouth on his skin. Danny pushed his head into the pillow and let his eyes slide shut in surrender.

"Take me in that pretty mouth of yours, Kate. Soft, short strokes at first." He groaned as she followed his directions. "Now deeper, faster." He wrapped his own hand around the base of his cock, holding it up for her to take while hoping to hold himself back as long as possible. "That's it, suck."

He watched through slitted eyes. Her cheeks hollowed. She wet her lips so they'd slide over him easier, and his balls tightened, aching with the need for release. He let go of his dick and thrust up into her mouth, fucking her even as she drew on him enthusiastically.

"Oh, yes," he growled.

Every muscle in his body clenched. Kate shifted, taking him deeper still. He knotted his fingers in her hair, his hips jerking wildly with each pull. "That's it."

Another long, ragged groan escaped, but there was nothing he could do to stop them, even if he wanted to. Like any good coach, he knew when to ask and when to push. Now was the time to push her to her very limits.

"You're going to finish the play, Kate." His breath came short and fast. "Take it all the way. Then I'm going to drive you out of your fucking mind."

He ground the last out as the climax rippled through him. He felt her still for a moment, then push on as he started to come. God, she was beautiful with her flushed cheeks and red lips. Through the haze, he watched her eyes close and her throat work. The pull of tongue, cheek, and throat felt incredible. He gave himself up to it, letting sensation roll through him like the roar of a crowd. His heart drummed double time. And when he came back to himself a few seconds, minutes, or hours later, he caught himself chanting her name in a hoarse whisper.

Kate pressed a deliberate kiss to his hip bone, then blessed the hollow of his pelvis with another. "I did well, huh, Coach?"

Laughter bubbled up from somewhere near his toes. Untangling his fingers from her hair, he grasped her arms and dragged her up to meet him face-to-face. "You did very well," he said gruffly. He kissed her hard and deep, tasting himself on her lips and tongue. "But remember, practice makes perfect."

She yelped when he grabbed her waist and hauled her up, but it turned into a giggle. She straddled his chest and glanced down at him, confused. He gave another tug, urging her to climb higher. It took only a second for his intent to sink in. A pink flush crept up her neck as her hands came to rest on his biceps. He resisted the urge to flex harder when she gave them an appreciative squeeze.

One arched brow rose. "Up there?"

He nodded and slid his hands down to cup her ass. Parting the muscular curves, he trailed his fingers along the crevice until he grazed her wet folds. "I'm going to lick and suck you just like you did me. I want to watch you come." He flashed a wicked smile. "I'm more than happy to let you come out on top in the bedroom."

She laughed as her knees sank into the pillow. Her weight shifted the filling enough to lift his head higher. Thanking God for whichever science covered volume and displacement, he stared, transfixed by the vision hovering above him. Her pussy was a mouthwatering shade of pink he'd swear he'd never seen anywhere else in nature. The lips swollen, dark curls glistening with desire. He barely gave her enough time to wrap her hands around the rail of the headboard before he pulled her down onto his face, burying his nose in her folds. He thrust his tongue into her, hungry for the tang of her arousal.

Kate gasped and then moaned, her hips circling in a silent plea that screamed yes-more-please. The tips of his fingers dug into her ass. He held her firm against his mouth, fucking her with an eagerness he hadn't felt in years.

He'd always enjoyed eating pussy but never considered it essential to his own pleasure. Until now. He circled her clit, then thrust again, desperate to consume her. And Christ, how she responded. Undulating against him, grinding against lips, teeth, and tongue. She was every bit as greedy for him as he was to give it to her.

She tossed her head back, her arms locking as she gripped the headboard. He sucked gently on the hypersensitive flesh at her apex and used his fingers to tease her swollen folds until she spread her knees even wider. Her soft, desperate mewls of excitement and frustration drove him. He slid a single finger into her slick channel but withdrew before she could fully engage.

"Dammit, Danny," she ground out.

He chuckled, nuzzling the impossibly soft skin on the inside of her thigh. "That's right, cuss me. You know I'm perverse. The more lip you give me, the more determined I am to fuck you every way I can."

His lips closed around her clit, employing gentle but persistent suction to distract her as he slipped a finger into her again. This time, he gave her two hard pumps, then pulled out and applied the slightest hint of pressure to the tight pucker of her anus.

"Oh!"

He slipped another finger into her pussy. "Now, you tell me, Kate. Is this what you want?"

"God yes."

He pressed the wet digit into her ass but made it only as far as the first knuckle when she began to unravel. Eyes wide open, he watched her. There couldn't be anything sexier than Kate Snyder in the throes. The woman gave nothing less than one hundred and ten percent. Her head thrown back in abandon. The creamy skin of her throat exposed and vulnerable. She was incredible. Bucking against him, fucking his mouth and fingers, taking what she needed from him and giving him…everything.

She moaned her release to the ceiling, her arms straight and locked, and the posts of the headboard banging against the wall. Her skin glowed in the low light. Flushed and dewy with sweat, she was as ripe as a fresh peach. For the first time in his life, he thought he might understand the world's fascination with vampires. And maybe fruitarians. Either way, he wanted nothing more than to sink his teeth into her.

The second the last shudder ran through her, she pressed up on the headboard and jerked away from him. He grunted, bewildered by her abrupt withdrawal. Her whimpers and pants whispered through the room. Her pink pussy remained suspended above him but frustratingly out of reach. He tried to pull her back down, but she resisted, shaking her head in emphatic refusal.

"Sorry. Sorry." She panted the words, breathless but heartfelt. The mattress dipped, and he bounced slightly when she threw herself onto the bed beside him. "Sometimes…too sensitive just after," she managed at last, shooting him an apologetic glance.

Relieved that she wasn't rejecting him outright, he reached for the limp hand she waved between them and grabbed her wrist. Contact was contact, and his need to keep touching her while she came down was almost overwhelming. He pulled her arm over and kissed the tender skin at the base of her palm. "I get you."

"You do, don't you?"

"I think so. I think you might get me too."

She drew three more deep breaths. He could feel the throb of her pulse slowing. "This is bad," she whispered at last.

His heart lurched, but he took a moment to get his synapses in line. "I thought it was pretty damn good, but if you're thinking we can up our game, I'm willing to try again." He forced a weak smile. "You might have to give me about thirty minutes though. I'm not twenty anymore."

To his relief, Kate chuckled and turned onto her side to face him, considerately curling her arm so he could maintain his hold on her. "I may need more than thirty after that."

He knew he was about to tread close to fishing, but he couldn't hold back. "Because it was so bad?"

"Because it was so good." She blinked, solemn as an owl. "Contrary to popular opinion and against all principles of common sense, I like you, Danny. And that's bad."

"It's good," he argued.

"You know what I mean. This thing…" She reached over and stroked his chest with a lazy casualness that made his heart turn over. "We're not supposed to be able to stand each other, much less this."

She added the last with a stern glare that was obviously supposed to drive the point home but instead sent him into Kate-induced a-fib.

"What other people think is their problem, not ours." He rolled onto his side and threw a leg over her, just in case she decided to make a break for it without taking the time to hash things out. "I think this is a good thing. Damn good. And you think so too."

"I do?"

He nodded once, decisively. He'd never been more convinced of anything in his life. "Yes, you do."

"Which is why it's so bad."

She reached that convoluted conclusion with such conviction, he couldn't help but smile. "Well, if that's the way you see it…I can be badder."

Despite her reticence, he saw the spark of interest in her eyes. "Can you?"

"Oh, hell yeah." With a laugh, he rolled forward, using his momentum to pin her to the bed. "I mean, I admit I was a little intimidated when I saw your friend there in the nightstand drawer, but I'm over it now. I never thought I'd say this, because I've never been good at sharing, but if you wanted to get old Michael involved for a little two-on-one, I'd be game."

# Chapter 12

Kate's stomach growled as she clicked through her email folder. Without looking, she reached into the mini fridge beneath her desk and snagged a container of yogurt. Her chair squeaked as she leaned back to check the expiration date. "Crap."

She pitched it into the garbage can, then ducked under her desk to hunt for another. The fridge was empty. It was the first week of June, the time when campus life hung suspended between spring and summer terms. The cafeterias were closed. There were no interns to make yogurt runs or ass-kissers bringing around bags of fast-food breakfast sandwiches. Another loud growl confirmed that her stomach was displeased. Making a mental note to bring more yogurt, she popped up in her chair.

"Way to put him in his place last night, Coach."

Kate jumped and winced when her knee connected with her desk. Her hand lashed out, sending her half-empty travel mug flying. Proving he still had the reaction time of an athlete, Mike Samlin stepped out of spatter range as the droplets of mocha arced through the air. His sandy brows shot up when she fumbled to catch the stack of camp brochures Millie had deposited on the edge of her desk.

"I, uh…" She gathered the glossy trifolds to her bosom and clung for dear life, wondering how the hell the AD could know exactly how many places she'd put his good friend Danny in the past couple of weeks.

"Millie tells me the ratings went through the roof."

The show. He meant *The Warrior Way*. They'd engaged in the Title IX debate Millie had campaigned for. Doing his best to play the misogynist, Danny'd made a crack about her using university money to order pink basketballs. It set her up beautifully for a line about her players knowing how to use their equipment.

She telegraphed a silent thank-you to Millie and gave her boss a tremulous smile. "Thanks."

Mike's focus sharpened, and his friendly brown eyes narrowed a fraction. This was the moment she'd been dreading. She was a horrible liar. Never had the talent for it. The little pantomime he'd just witnessed proved that she didn't have the reflexes either.

She'd been avoiding the boss man, of course. Millie too. Jim Davenport had proved to be a little more assertive than expected, but she'd managed to slip past him the minute they stopped taping. And thirty minutes later, Danny had slipped inside her with that strangled little "Mmm" she'd come to know as his special hello.

But Mike was a diplomat as well as an administrator. He didn't go straight for the jugular. "Looks like your camps are sold out."

Relief mingled with pride as she grabbed the change of subject and made a break with it. "Middle grades start this week. We'll have varsity in July. Don't worry. We'll be out of the way when it's time for the boys to play."

The look of wounded surprise in his eyes said he didn't think he deserved her sharp tone. Poor Mike had apparently been out of the game long enough to forget about offense being the best defense.

"I'm sure Coach Ransom will appreciate that," he said mildly. Without waiting for an invitation, he sat in the guest chair opposite her. "I got an interesting phone call from Jonas Matthews."

Kate braced herself for battle. This was it. She'd let her agent off the leash. Told him to go after everything he could get. And now, the battle would begin in earnest. "Did you? That's nice."

Mike smirked. "He was tossing around some crazy numbers."

The dire warnings she'd heard from Jonas rang in her ears. *Don't agree or disagree on anything. Don't let them play on your loyalties. Do not negotiate.* That was Jonas's job, and it was time for him to earn his cut. Still, the implication that she didn't deserve every digit rankled.

"I've put up some crazy numbers over the years. I'm sure someone will find a way to make them match."

The threat was barely veiled. Why bother? They both knew it was time for Wolcott to put up or shut up. Regardless of gender, hers or her team's, she was a proven winner, and many schools would be happy to have her. A few might even deign to let her coach their precious men's team.

"Kate, we've—"

"Blown the budget on football?" she asked, cutting him off. "Not my problem."

"It's not that—"

"I'm not discussing this. Talk to Jonas."

"I will when he stops talking crazy."

She held his gaze, summoning the glare she usually reserved for slacking point guards or blind refs. "Don't hold your breath."

Mike pursed his lips, then tipped his head back to survey the décor. "When do you leave for your three-hour tour?"

She smiled. The *Gilligan's Island* reference was an inside joke. Anyone who'd ever done the lecture circuit knew those weeks could feel like years.

"A couple of weeks."

"You gone two weeks in a row?"

"One and one," she said. "I'll be home for a week, then on the road again."

"Good."

She started, surprised by the satisfaction in his tone. "Don't be so sad to see me go," she drawled. "Watch out, or I'll ask you to come by and water my philodendron."

Mike's expression grew serious. "Better me than someone else."

Kate stilled. She'd tried to drown her contract worries with lust, and it had almost worked. Unfortunately, her physical need for Danny only seemed to intensify—and for better or worse, he seemed to be as caught up in it as she was. The sex part, at least. He didn't seem to be nearly as worried about everything else.

His nonchalance alarmed her. Three nights ago, he hadn't even bothered putting on a ball cap. He'd parked at the curb in front of her house the previous night. She had been ready to lay into him about it, but then he'd kissed her hello, and all the fight had gone out of her.

They lay limp, exhausted, and fixated on her kitchen ceiling by the time she got around to chastising him for it, and even then, Danny brushed her concerns away. And she'd let him. After all, how could the danger of him losing his job and her losing her heart possibly matter when they could have hot sex in every room of her house?

Heaving a heavy sigh, Mike propped a hand high on the doorframe. "Last night's debate was just a reminder of how inequitable things can be in collegiate sports. In all sorts of ways."

She smiled and began straightening the rumpled brochures. "Coach McMillan gets a little hotheaded when it comes to Title Nine."

It was an exaggeration, but she didn't care. Getting him hot under the collar during their on-screen debate seemed to get him as worked up for the postgame too. She had to admit, she was primed and ready by the time he dropped the bag of Chinese carryout onto her table and pushed her up against the fridge. Magnets and reminders had flown in every direction, but in that moment, Kate had never felt more focused or in tune with her own power. He'd taken her hard and fast, but she was the one who let him. And in allowing it to happen, she brought that strong, stubborn man to his knees. Literally.

"He has a tendency to chase flashes of red, but most of what he says is bull," Mike said.

"I know, but it played well for the cameras." Hoping to shorten the conversation, she kept her answer semi-neutral. "He can be a bit of a drama queen."

Her feigned nonchalance appeared to make Mike more focused. He stepped into the room and closed the office door. When he turned back to her, the man was fully tuned in.

"Danny leads with his heart. Something that works well in motivating others, but it doesn't always pan out when it comes to his own interests. Detachment doesn't come naturally to him, and he doesn't always think things through to their inevitable outcome."

Her own heart beat like a jackhammer. She placed the neat stack of glossies in the exact spot where Millie had left them earlier and cast Mike a cool look. "And yet you offered him a multimillion-dollar contract."

"There were some variables I couldn't assess at that time."

Tiring of the cat-and-mouse game, she sat up straighter and folded her hands on her blotter. "Such as?"

Mike stepped away from the door. Gripping the back of her guest chair, he blew out a gust of frustration. "Kate, we've known each other a few years now." She blinked in surprise, but he held up a hand to stave off any interruption. "I've known Danny since we were the same age as the kids you coach. I'm not a fool. I guess it was too much to hope that he wouldn't be one either."

Indignation sank its razor-sharp talons into her. "How, exactly, do you think he's being foolish?"

"There's a morals clause—"

"Not in my contract," she snapped, cutting him off.

Yes, she'd checked. The morning after Danny first rolled out of her bed, she'd pulled out a copy of her contract and checked to be certain she wasn't in violation. Now, she and Mike stared at one another, the air filled with tension and the faint rasp of agitated breathing. Undaunted, she forged ahead.

"There's nothing in my contract preventing me from

entering into a mutually agreed upon relationship with a man over the age of consent and not directly in my employ. If I were, that is," she added, holding his gaze.

"There's nothing in your contract as it stands, but that contract is under negotiation. Big money comes with big expectations."

"I've exceeded everyone's expectations."

"I'm not talking job performance, Kate, and you know it," Mike replied, unruffled. He dropped his voice to a conspiratorial level. "But you should know Danny's contract expressly forbids him from any extra-curricular relationship with anyone associated with the university—staff or student." He sighed so hard she could swear she felt the air stir.

Touching the tip of her tongue to her top lip, Kate crossed her arms over her chest and turned to stare out the windows. "Bet old Danny wishes he could have a hunk of Title Nine protection."

"This isn't a joke." He ran a hand through his hair as he paced, rumpling its Mr. I'm In Control perfection. "I don't want to be a hard-ass about this. If you're happy and he's happy, I would be more than okay with letting this ride…"

"I don't know what you're—"

"Like I said, I know Danny," he said, the intensity in his tone shutting her down. "And I know his truck. And shit, the whole damn town knows where you live, Kate."

The need to move, to act, to get her stance set in preparation for a direct charge brought her to her feet. "This is none of your business."

"But it is. The terms of Danny's return to Division I play aren't exactly a secret, and if things start to go sour for either of you, he's out on his ass." He paused, then cleared his throat. "Then there's the question of your contract."

He left the rest of the thought unspoken, but she had a pretty good idea where he was heading. Still, she wanted to hear him say it. "What about my contract?"

"Don't make me put that clause in yours too."

She stood quietly, absorbing the irony of their situation. Here she was, a former athlete stripped of the power to play at the level she craved, a champion who'd brought nothing but glory to her school, and still she was being asked to make the sacrifice. The university's terms were as crystal clear as Jonas's, and they felt every bit as crazy. She could play hardball and get the salary she deserved, or she could have Danny.

A lump of ice formed in her belly, but she welcomed the sensation. It was the same cool center she used to tap when standing at the foul line or taking the game-winning shot. She looked her boss dead in the eye. "I'm not sure it's appropriate for you to discuss the terms of Coach McMillan's contract with me. Do the two of you have long, cozy chats about how he's making more than twice the salary that I do?"

"Now, Kate—"

"It's Coach. I've earned that much respect, haven't I?"

"Coach Snyder," he said, straightening his shoulders and bracing his feet wide. "I don't want to do battle with you. I just want what's best for—"

"Don't you dare try to tell me what's best for me," she said in a tone so soft, it sliced straight through whatever he planned to say.

They stared one another down. Then Kate dove into

the icy resolve she used to fuel her drive. Holding her head high, she walked to the door.

"Tell me, how do you feel about gender inequity in collegiate sports, Mike?" Her fingers closed around the handle, but she didn't open it. Instead, she turned and gave him a level look. "I'm curious. You don't seem like an ass, but it can be so hard to tell these days."

"Kate, please—"

"Coach," she snapped, then stepped back as she opened the door wide. "If you'll excuse me, I have a few things I need to handle before I greet my campers."

"Hello, Coach."

She jumped and pressed the flat of her hand to her breastbone as Jim Davenport stepped into the open doorway, blocking any chance of shooing Mike out. "Jim." She gave her head a shake to clear it. "What are you doing here?"

"I wanted to follow up with you on something you said on the show last night. The bit about the pressure on young women to downplay their athletic abilities."

He raised his eyebrows as if he'd prompted her, but Kate couldn't find the actual question. "Yes? What about it?"

"Well, I was hoping you'd elaborate. Maybe talk a little more about your own experiences?" She shot him a sharp glare. Davenport went on, undeterred. "With your summer camps starting this week, I thought it would make an interesting angle. It's no secret that your success played a role in the dissolution of your marriage to Coach Sommers, and now you've got someone with Coach McMillan's history coming in..."

The mere mention of her ex-husband's name sparked

a white-hot flash of anger. The reasons Jeff had left her were not common knowledge. She'd told Jim in confidence. Pain and humiliation undercut her rage, but the words wouldn't come.

While she floundered, Mike stepped into the doorway behind her and unleashed a stream of rhetoric that proved he was the perfect man to serve as spokesman for Wolcott athletics.

"I think Coach Snyder's continued success is a testament to her fortitude and ambition as well as an excellent endorsement of Wolcott's continued dedication to furthering every young woman's growth in both the academic and athletic arenas."

Davenport's jaw dropped. "Director Samlin, I didn't see you there."

"We were just finishing up," Kate announced. She nodded to Mike. "Thank you for your input. I'll take your suggestions under consideration."

Mike inclined his head, shoved his hands into his pants pockets, and strolled to the door as if he didn't have a care in the world. "Thank you, Coach. Have a good time with your campers."

Jim's brows rose again as the AD moved past. Then he slipped into her office wearing a sly grin. "What was going on in here? Contract negotiations?"

She rolled her eyes, but a shudder ran through her. Turning her back on him, she moved to her desk, wondering what she could possibly have seen in him. "Hardly." She shot him a condescending look. "I have an agent who handles those things. We were discussing my schedule." Kate winced when she realized she'd handed him a huge opening.

Predictable as he was, Jim dove right in. "Speaking of your schedule, I was hoping to see you this week. I'm starting to get the feeling you're avoiding me."

"Don't be silly." But her denial rang hollow. They both knew Jim didn't have a silly bone in his body.

"And that makes me wonder why." He moved closer, effectively trapping her behind her desk. "Everything was going great with us up until McMillan came around." She opened her mouth, but he stopped her with a raised hand. "Don't get me wrong. The ratings are great, but I can't help but wonder…"

Every muscle in her body tensed. Her fingers curled around the pen she'd picked up. Even her eyeballs felt stiff as she forced herself to roll them. "Yeah right." Her laugh sounded more like a bark, but she couldn't do any better with his gaze boring into her. "Well, there's been the television thing, and I didn't want…you know, awkward." She checked her babble, corralling her runaway mouth like a ball that took a bad bounce off the rim. "You know what it's like. Summer is always a time of transition. I've got camps, lectures…"

"Good. I'm glad it's nothing more. Bad enough that the guy is using you to get himself a little publicity." He tapped his fingertips on her desk, then fired off his next question. "Dinner?"

The invitation sounded like a challenge. The kind she didn't dare refuse. "Tonight?"

His brows rose inquisitively, and she forced herself to smile as she bent toward her computer and grasped the mouse. In an instant, her calendar filled the screen. Camp obligations, local appearances, and speaking engagements littered the electronic grid. The flurry of reminders, both personal and professional, that her assistant pinned to the sidebar added an extra boost of credibility. She closed her eyes, made a mental note to send her Aunt Julia a birthday card, and thanked God for giving her sense enough to never touch this calendar.

"Looks like I'm free tonight." She clicked to minimize the screen and turned her best postgame interview smile on him. "Steak?"

"Sounds good." Jim took a half step closer to her. "I, uh, look forward to it. I could use a good steak."

Kate covered her involuntary groan by dropping into her chair and giving her bad knee a rub. "Sounds great. I'll be tied up until about six, but I can meet you there."

"Okay. No, wait…I'll pick you up at about seven."

She offered up a weak smile, knowing he was mentally mapping out his moves for the evening. Moves he'd never get to use. And the fact that she'd have to wait until seven to eat dinner. Was she the only person on earth whose stomach was set to five o'clock sharp?

"You don't have to—"

"Seven."

He turned away, his pivot jerky. A surge of irritation pulsed through her as she noted the lack of grace. Stubborn, cocky, indecisive, and unintuitive. Twisting in her seat, she placed her fingers on her keyboard and spared him the barest of glances. "See you then."

Instead of leaving, he lingered in her doorway, his eyes locked on her. "Will the addition of Coach McMillan impact your contract negotiations?"

She looked up from the screen and fixed him with the same stare she used on recalcitrant refs. Then she blinked, all sweetness and baffled innocence. "As far as I know, he isn't invited."

Jim threw his head back and laughed. His eyes crinkled, and attractive grooves bracketed his mouth. In that instant, she remembered what she once found appealing about him. A tiny lump of regret formed in her throat. But then something in the corridor caught his attention, and his smile slid into something fake and a little smarmy.

"See you tonight, Coach."

Kate flinched slightly, jarred by the volume of his announcement. Until that day, he'd been a stickler for keeping their personal relationship separate from the professional, afraid someone would think he was compromising his journalistic ethics. She wanted to cry foul or call bullshit, but he raised the tablet he always carried and saluted her with it.

"I'll pick you up at your place. Seven sharp."

Kate fought the urge to lower her head to the desk and thump it a couple of times.

"Hey, Coach McMillan," Jim called in a too-jaunty tone. "I was hoping to get a little time with you today."

Kate tuned out the low rumble of masculine voices. Worlds were colliding. There were too many variables. Too many men backing her into corners, getting up in her space, trying to force her to take shots she wasn't interested in taking.

"It's not tournament play that I object to—it's the use of a selection committee to determine who makes the tournament." Danny McMillan loomed in her doorway.

She blinked, too stunned to respond to his lack of segue.

He stepped into her office and started to swing the door shut. "Let's get this straight once and for all. I don't ever again want to hear you imply that I'm scared of a playoff system."

"Noted," she whispered as the latch caught.

His volume dropped, but the steel in his voice remained. One dark brow shot up. "Your place at seven?"

Sitting up straight, she locked eyes with him. "Yes."

"What do you mean, 'Yes'?"

"I mean, yes, he is picking me up at my place at seven."

Silver-blue eyes narrowed to slits, but the intensity was laser sharp. "Picking you up for what? A date?"

Kate lifted her chin high, staring down her nose at him. She was playing with fire, but she was tired of feeling trapped and defensive. He was the one with everything to lose, and if he hadn't learned how to protect his own interests by now, she sure as hell wasn't about to rescue him. She'd been in her office for less than forty minutes, and already she felt like that video game frog trying to cross a busy street. She'd be damned if she'd sit still while a passel of testosterone-charged morons tried to run over her from every direction. "What's it to you?"

"What's it to me?" He goggled at her. "What's it to *me*?"

He jabbed his chest with his index finger, and she winced. She'd fallen asleep with her cheek on his shoulder and her hand in that exact spot. She knew the tickle of the crisp, curling hair between his pecs. Kissed his flat, brown nipples until they rippled. She'd sketched every ridge in his abs and stroked the trail of silky black hair that arrowed down his belly. Pursing her lips, she forced herself to hold his gaze when she really wanted to let it drop lower. She swallowed hard and pitched her voice low to keep it steady.

"So far today, I've had your buddy Mike in here telling me all about the morals clause in your contract, threatening to put one in mine, and basically telling me I can ruin your career, my career, or both if I let this continue."

"*If* you let it—"

Too het up to deal with his indignation, she cut him off with a wave of her hand. "Then I had Jim Davenport practically grilling me about why I haven't seen him since you came on the scene."

"I didn't know that you and old Jim were that close."

She stepped out from behind her desk, ready to nip this argument in the bud. The last thing she had the patience for was another man barging into her office and dragging his baggage along with him. "I have had exactly two full hours of sleep, three sips of coffee, and my yogurt is expired. If you want to be pissy, I suggest you do it in your office and not mine. I've had enough guff from men today."

---

Damn, she was gorgeous. Spots of pink rode high on her cheeks. "Guff?"

Nope. He couldn't score a smile. Still, Danny held her gaze, just for the sheer pleasure of it. Sparks of gold shone bright in her eyes, and her feet were planted wide. She was a thousand times sexier than any female wearing track pants and a T-shirt had a right to be. The belligerent tilt of her chin warned him to tread carefully, but he couldn't help baiting her just a bit.

"But I want to be pissy here. There's no one in my office—"

She mumbled something that sounded like, "Lucky you," making him grin.

"—and I missed you."

She blinked, and those gold lights in her eyes went soft and melty. For about half a second.

"You can't do this, Danny." She threw her arms up in frustration. "That's the point. You can't come to my office and be pissy and sweet and tell me you miss me. You can't park in front of my house and ring the damn doorbell as if there's nothing at stake here."

She came right at him, stopping only when they stood toe-to-toe. He started to reach for her, anxious to wrap his arms around this breathtaking Valkyrie.

"You like to think you're invincible, but you of all people should know you're not."

He wrapped his hands around her elbows as if she were the one who needed steadying. Clearing the rasp from his throat, he shrugged and tried for a casual tone. "I've been fired before."

She nodded slowly, but her lips thinned into a tight line. "Maybe that's what you want."

"What?"

"Maybe that's what this is all about. Wolcott's your way back into Division I, but maybe I'm your ticket out of the basement."

A frown pulled at his brows. Confused, he searched her eyes for clarity, but all he found there was wariness. "I don't know what the hell you're talking about."

"You've been a good boy for a few years, racked up a little good press for a change. But hey, think about it: you can get out of a contract and a relationship in one play."

The accusation landed like a punch in the gut. He released her arms and stepped back. "That's ridiculous."

"It's plausible."

"It's complete crap, and you know it."

"Maybe it is, but your pal Mike made sure I knew your contract comes with an ejector seat."

"You let me handle Mike. Tell me what's going on with Davenport."

She shrugged. "Nothing. He wants to take me out to dinner."

"That's the guy you were dating," Danny concluded.

"It wasn't serious."

"But we are," he asserted.

"It doesn't get much more serious than this, Danny. You can get fired!"

"I get that." Heaving a sigh, he ran his hand through his hair and gave his head a helpless shake. "I just don't know when this became some crazy-assed plot to get myself fired so I could get out of a relationship with you." He shoved his hands into his pockets and tried not to grind his molars as he walked to the window and stared out at the red brick paths that crisscrossed the quad. "Christ. This is what I get for thinking everything was going so well."

Kate touched his arm, and he turned. "You think things are going well?"

Her voice was soft and tremulous, like she was scared to ask the question. But when he looked into her eyes, he had a hard time imagining this woman

being scared of anything. Her ramrod-straight posture
and tight-lipped scrutiny should have made her look
like a ballbuster. But she wasn't. He knew she wasn't.
He'd spent hours learning every one of her soft, secret
places. His throat tightened, and his arm tingled where
her hand rested. Biting the inside of his cheek, he shot
her a sidelong glare.

"I thought they were until I came around the corner
and heard you making a date with that douchebag."

"He cornered me. I didn't know what else to do."

"That guy couldn't corner on training wheels." He
grumbled the insult, but she smiled so wide that time
stopped. Unable to see anything but the earnest entreaty
in her eyes, he brushed her hair back from her cheek and
tucked it behind her ear. "I know you have a bad knee,
but the next time some guy backs you into a corner, use
it. You're aiming for soft parts anyway."

Dark brows shot up, but her smile didn't dim one
watt. "Does that include you?"

Danny gave his head a quick shake, then ducked to
steal a kiss. "No. When I corner you, I want you to show
me all *your* soft parts."

"We have to be careful, Danny. I'll just have a quick
dinner with him. Trust me, it'll be either steak or Italian,
and I'll be home by nine." When he opened his mouth
to protest, she pressed a finger to his lips. "Jim's not
known for his spontaneity, but he is a reporter. We have
to throw him off the scent."

Her eyes widened, then flared to life when he drew
her fingertip into his mouth and circled it with his
tongue. She grabbed his elbow and pulled him to the
side, away from the window. "Danny, stop."

"Okay, I'll stop. Right after this." Taking her hand, he pressed a soft, wet kiss to the center of her palm, then he let her go.

"Have dinner with me instead. Steak or Italian, you choose."

Kate laughed. "Danny—"

She spoke his name in a chastising tone, but the pink flush staining her cheeks showed her pleasure. "Katie," he teased, toying with the hem of her shirt. "Date me. I can be a dick, but everyone knows dicks are far more fun than douchebags."

He scored another laugh, but this time, she tossed her head to flip her hair out of her face. "Tonight, I'm defusing the douchebag. If it makes you feel better, I'll call you when I get home."

She touched his face. A fleeting caress, probably meant to soothe, but the tease of fingertips over his eyebrow, cheek, and jaw made him ache for more. "I don't think anything is going to make me feel better about you being out with someone else."

She stepped back a pace. "I think it might be healthy for you to worry a little bit."

"It might not be healthy for Davenport. I don't want you going out with him."

"Tough, because I said I would, and I am."

He fought for control, struggling to keep his game face in place. She had to know how hard this was, but if this relationship was going to work, he had to trust her to handle herself. As much as he wanted to launch into the white-knight routine, she wouldn't take it well. She wouldn't be bullied. By either of them.

Her smirk melted into a come-and-get-me grin.

"Don't you worry about Jim. I can handle him. I think you need to spin our good friend the athletic director."

Shoulders drawn up tight, he stalked toward the door. "I can guaran-damn-tee you that you won't have to wonder if I'm kissing Mike or not."

"Danny?"

He froze, his hand on the door handle and his back to her. "Yeah?"

"Will you be wondering about me kissing Jim?"

Turning to look over his shoulder, he scowled when he spotted the pleased smirk she failed to hide. "Damn straight I will."

"You don't have anything to worry about."

He turned the handle but held the door firmly shut, keeping the world outside at bay for a few seconds more as he faced her. "Regardless, you're going to pay the price, Coach. When I'm done with you, you're gonna wish you were running bleachers."

He opened the door and made it over the threshold, but her laughter-laced retort echoed down the cinder-block hallway.

"Promises, promises."

# Chapter 13

"THANKS AGAIN FOR DINNER, JIM." KATE UNLOCKED HER front door and turned back to face him, her feet planted, ready to block his charge. Her cheekbones ached from smiling. Not because she'd actually had a good time, but because she was afraid she'd grit her teeth through the whole interminable evening if she didn't. "I was in the mood for a nice, juicy steak."

She still was. The rib eye they'd served her at Jim's favorite restaurant had been as dry and flavorless as her companion. It was no wonder he liked the place so much.

"So, I suppose I should..." She gestured to the door. "Nothing like running with a pack of twelve-to-fourteens to wear a girl out."

But Jim wasn't about to let a bunch of middle school girls run him off. "I was hoping you'd invite me in for a cup of coffee."

"Oh, no. I can't drink coffee after five." She curled her hand, clutching her keys to her chest, and wrinkled her nose. "Keeps me up all night."

"Sounds like the perfect game plan."

He settled a hand on her hip, and she fought the urge to stiffen. She had to keep it cool and casual. Move him along. Nothing to see here. Unable to force another face-cracking smile, she opted for a fake pout and jammed her key into the dead bolt.

"It does, doesn't it?" Her sigh should have measured on the Richter scale. If there was any justice in the world, she'd have an Oscar sitting on her mantel this time next year. "I can't. I told you my niece was in my camp this session, remember? She's staying with me." A lie. A big, fat lie. Kylie was safely ensconced in the women's dormitory with the rest of the giggling campers.

"She's here now?"

"I have to go pick her up."

"So we have a little time." Jim nodded, then stooped to brush a dry kiss over her lips. "The next generation, huh? I might have to stop by and see if that wicked jump shot runs in the family."

The tumblers in the locks fell, but she was too tired to fall for his lame flattery. "Camp is closed to the press. These kids are minors. You can't get anywhere near them."

He smiled, but it did little to soften the steel in her spine. "Darn. I guess I'll just have to be happy with getting close to you." He pressed a damp kiss to the side of her neck. "Rumor has it your agent is going for the jugular." His teeth scraped her skin, and a shiver of revulsion ran down her spine. Unfortunately, Jim was never very good at reading signals. He latched on to that instinctual reaction and ran with it. "Maybe that's what you're looking for?" He twisted the handle, and the door swung inward, carrying them both into her house.

Kate gasped, grasping his arms as they stumbled into the foyer. "Jim!"

Caging her against the wall, he fastened his mouth to her neck. Normally, she loved having her throat kissed. When Danny did it, she melted into a puddle of desire. But Jim's slobbery kisses called to mind the old Hoover canister vacuum her mother used to sweep the stairs. His hands slid to her ass, and the artless grope was all she needed to spur her into action.

"Jim, no." She planted her hands on his chest and shoved him away.

Her sessions in the weight room paid off. He tripped over his own feet as he tried to catch his balance. Chagrin contorted his blandly handsome face, and the flash of malevolence she saw in his eyes made her take an involuntary step back. A muscle ticked in his jaw. She forced herself to stand her ground.

"I'm sorry." The words sprang from her lips, and she hated herself for them. She tugged at her slacks and straightened her top, needing to keep her hands busy as she mentally cussed herself up and down for spewing an apology he didn't deserve. "I think we should call it a night."

He wiped the back of his hand over his mouth in a move so insulting, her jaw dropped. "You blow so fucking hot and cold. No wonder Sommers decided you weren't worth the effort."

Her mouth snapped shut and anger flared. It grew inside her, a fierce, red glow that spawned searing flames. "Get out."

"You owe me—"

"Nothing! I owe you nothing but a fat lip," she spat. "Now get out, or I'll give it to you."

"Christ, you *are* a ballbreaker," he muttered.

She couldn't resist taking one last swipe as he yanked open the door. After all, she was a clutch shooter. "Color, Jim. You'll never make it as a broadcaster because you lack color." He stopped, his feet planted on the sisal welcome mat emblazoned with a basketball. The same spot where she'd first seen the beautiful rainbow-colored shoes Danny had given her. "And that steak sucked," she added, letting the door slam between them.

She flipped the locks and sagged against the wall. She wished her niece were staying with her. The silence of the empty house closed in around her. Had it been this quiet before Danny barged into her life with his lukewarm pizza and inane arguments?

She peered into the living room, her gaze darting from the multicolored throw pillows scattered across the couch and love seat to the overstuffed armchair Danny had claimed as his spot.

A deep-purple satin pillow was squished into the crack between the back and the seat. She closed her eyes, remembering the wobbly arc that pillow made as it sailed through the air. She'd aimed for his head when she'd lobbed it at Danny the night before. She would have hit her target if he hadn't had such quick reflexes. There was no resisting the cocky grin he flashed as he thanked her for her concern for his comfort and tucked the pillow into the small of his back.

She'd fallen for his unperturbed arrogance. Fallen for him. Hell, she'd stumbled all over herself in her haste to make it from the couch to that chair. He'd held her there, straddling him, towering over him. She had him inside her with little more than a handful of pregame kisses and rode him with the kind of driving determination some guys might have found threatening. But not Danny. He just took it—let her take him—and gazed up at her in bright-eyed delight.

What a difference a day made.

Pushing away from the wall, Kate trudged into the living room and switched off the lamp she'd left burning. She rubbed her hand over her eyes and started down the hall, blind to everything but the promise of a full night's sleep. But when she lowered her hand, she saw a strange light spilling from the open door to her bedroom.

She cocked her head and stared at it. This was not a golden streak of lamplight or even the overhead fixture but the flickering blue-white of a television. She squinted at the eerie light, trying to remember if she'd left the set on when she went out, but she was 99.9 percent positive she hadn't.

The fifty-five-inch flat screen mounted to the wall opposite her bed was a parting gift from her ex. Frankly, she would have preferred some car wax, but he got the Corvette she'd bought him for his fortieth birthday. Which was okay. Unlike Jeff, she was too tall for the low-slung car. Her head grazed the roof every time he hit a pothole. She would have taken the enormous TV screen down if watching game film in glorious high definition from the comfort of her bed wasn't so damn good. But she hardly switched the thing on in the off-season.

She backtracked to the foyer, where she withdrew an aluminum softball bat from her collection of sporting goods. Heart thudding against her breastbone, she raised the bat as she approached with caution. There generally wasn't a lot of crime around campus, and she was fairly certain most thieves would take the goods rather than test them. Most likely she'd accidentally hit the button on the remote and failed to notice. Still, she felt more secure with the bat in hand.

Just outside the door, she bent at the waist until she

could peek into the room. The clutter on her dresser looked undisturbed, the quilt on her bed smooth and evenly draped. The brightly colored trainers she'd toed off earlier that evening lay tumbled by the bed. Beside a pair of well-worn running shoes, toes pointed right at the glowing screen.

Danny McMillan sat on the cedar chest at the foot of the bed, his face lit in glorious Technicolor.

Pressing her balled fist to her hammering heart, she stepped into the doorway and glared at him. "What the hell? How did you get in here?"

He didn't look at her as the play he was studying unfolded. "You don't lock the side door on your garage. You really should."

Galled by his hubris—and a bit more thrilled than she would ever admit—she crossed her arms over her chest and waited until the refs whistled the play dead. "Maybe I don't worry about it because most people in this town would know better than to break into the house of a six-foot Amazon who busts balls for sport."

A slow, sexy smile creased his cheeks and crinkled his eyes as he looked her over. "I thought you liked to toss balls through hoops for sport."

He paused the next play and tossed the remote onto the bed. His eyes raked her from head to toe. He made no attempt to mask the adjustment he made to his worn jeans as he stood. Broad shoulders rolled back, and she curled her fingers into her palms. Lord, she loved running her hands over those muscles.

"Davenport had exactly thirty-two more seconds to get the hell out before I took him down."

He spoke so quietly she leaned in to hear him better.

When his threat filtered through the haze of lust that clouded her mind, she rolled her eyes, kicked off her flat sandals, and came to a stop right in front of him, her hands planted on her hips. "I told you I could handle him."

"I knew you could. That's why he had another thirty-two seconds." He reached to touch her arm, but his hand fell away without making contact.

Kate frowned at the hand hanging limp by his side. "What?"

He shrugged and turned to look at the television again. "I broke into your house. I've been sitting here for the last hour and a half, and I've only made it through fifteen minutes of film. Five minutes ago, some guy was crawling all over you, and now another guy is camping out in your bedroom because he's so eaten up he can't be anywhere else."

"Stalker." She whispered the taunt, hoping to goad him into looking at her again. He didn't take the bait. Instead, that delicious mouth tightened into a grim line.

"Imagine what your pal Jim could do with that story."

"I don't think we're pals anymore." She took his hand and carried it to her hip, holding it there until his fingers curled around her. She leaned into him, invading his space just like he'd invaded hers. "Do we need to have a talk about boundaries?"

His nose brushed her own. She tipped her head to accommodate the kiss she hoped was coming, but he stopped, his lips millimeters from hers. "Nope. I'm pretty clear on them. You're mine, and for the record, I would have torn him to pieces with my bare hands if he tried to cross one more line."

Heat radiated from him. Warm, moist puffs of air

teased her mouth. The taut muscles of his chest and arms were enticingly hard. But his eyes... That direct, blue gaze was soft, filled with apology, embarrassment, and enough stubborn righteousness to make her knees wobbly. That whole "you're mine" thing should have raised her feminist hackles, but it didn't. Not with this man. Danny respected her. More than that, he liked her. And she liked the note of wonderment in his voice when he made those gruff, grumbly declarations. He sounded almost as if he couldn't believe his luck.

"I meant boundaries with you," she said, running her fingertip under the collar of his T-shirt.

"No. No boundaries between you and me."

He kissed her then, sealing the pronouncement with a caress so tender and searching, she couldn't remember a single reason why she should resist. Just when she thought he might pull away, he ran his tongue over the seam of her lips. Asking, not taking. Tempting instead of demanding. Of course, she gave in. How could she not when he drew her bottom lip between his and sucked gently? She plunged her hands into his hair and hung on. His warm palm slid down over her bottom, but unlike Jim's adolescent grab, Danny knew how to hold her. Firm and unyielding. Safe and secure. His body aligned with hers, a fit so perfect the barrier of their clothes hardly mattered.

Wet, warm kisses. His tongue sliding against hers. The steely length of his cock pressing into her. The muscles of his thighs were every bit a match for hers. She liked that. She'd known few men strong enough to stand up to her, but this man could take her. And damn, that knowledge thrilled her to her bones.

Fevered kisses blanketed her cheek, jaw, and throat. He ran one hand up over her ribs, bypassed her breasts, and cupped the side of her neck. She opened her eyes as she tilted her head back, granting him all the access he needed. His thumb traced her jaw as calloused fingertips teased her hairline. Desperate to center herself, she tried to find a spot in the expanse of white ceiling to focus on. One tiny speck to anchor her to the earth. That was all she needed. He shifted a fraction of an inch, and she gave up the search. There was no point when she could come right there and then, without anything more than the contours of his body fitted to hers.

"Kate?"

He nibbled on her earlobe with the sharp edges of his teeth. God, she loved it when he did that, even if it did turn her brain to mush. "Hm?"

"I've been going crazy all day."

She bowed up into his caress as he started on the buttons of her blouse. The silky fabric slid from her shoulders. She'd barely extricated her hands from the fabric when the front clasp on her bra gave way. He cupped her breasts as if they were something to be treasured. Tender and reverent, he teased her nipples with the pads of his thumbs, abrading the sensitive tips until they furled into hard, tight knots. With a moan, she let her head fall back, surrendering to the unadulterated want this man unleashed in her. She smoothed the back of his head, holding him close as he marked the slope of her neck and her collarbone with fervent kisses.

"You had no need to worry," she assured him.

He chuckled as he bent to kiss her breast. Nimble fingers opened the button on her pants. She wiggled her hips as he tugged at the zipper. She wanted them gone even more than he did.

"The hell I didn't." Danny dropped to his knees, dragging her trousers and panties down with him. He steadied her with a hand on the small of her back and his cheek pressed to the curve of her belly. She stepped out of the puddle of fabric and shook the dangling bra from her arms. He looked up at her, those brilliant-blue eyes alight with pleasure even as his mouth twisted in anguish. Trailing his fingertips up her shin, he paused to trace teasing circles on the scars on her knee, then spread his hand wide over her thigh. "Christ, what if you'd worn a skirt?"

Kate stifled the urge to laugh. He'd uttered the speculation with such horror. Like her battered and scarred legs were some kind of secret weapon. "I wore a skirt the last time I went out with Jim. Didn't make him crazed with lust."

"He's an idiot." He gave her leg a gentle squeeze to reinforce the assertion. "Thank God."

A shudder ran through her as he slid both palms up her hamstrings. His biceps tensed and bunched. She yelped as he rose, lifting her off the floor. Grabbing the broad, strong shoulders she loved so much, she dug her fingertips into his tantalizing traps and hung on tight.

---

Danny growled deep in his throat as he circled the end of the bed. He loved the power in her hands. Had the most bizarre impulse to lick them. Not just the long graceful fingers, but the broad palms as well. Lord, he was a goner. He'd let her tear him limb from limb with those strong, capable hands if she wanted to. It would be a hell of a lot easier to endure than knowing that some other man was basking in her smile, smarting from her wit, or, God forbid, holding one of those perfect hands.

Without ceremony or apology, he dropped her on the bed, then extricated himself from her grasp. He couldn't look at her as he shed his clothes. If he did, he might make an even bigger fool of himself than he already had.

Balled-up jeans kicked aside, he finally chanced a glance. Color played over her skin. He watched the greens, golds, blues, and whites from the television screen wash over the smooth expanse of creamy skin. But he didn't need added pixels or high definition to paint his favorite parts of her. The soles of her feet were pink, the high arch white and achingly vulnerable. The pinks and whites repeated in the scars left from her surgeries but in more vivid shades. The dark curls between her legs made his mouth water with anticipation. Golden-brown freckles dusted her chest and shoulders but stopped abruptly at the milk-white slope of her breasts. Only one dared to mark that expanse of skin the sun had never seen. A tiny, dark-brown rogue clung to the sweet spot just beneath her left nipple.

Knowing that freckle was there made him feel smug and sly. Kissing it made him feel like a god.

He stroked two fingers along the inside of her knee. Like magic, she parted her legs for him. A strangled groan tangled in his throat. He stared down at her. She lay naked and exposed, completely open to him. Totally trusting. Heat pulsed in his veins. Kate reached for him. One beautiful hand beckoning for him to join her. She whispered his name, and the last threads of his self-restraint snapped.

He grabbed her hand and pulled it to his mouth. His lips parted as they pressed to the center of her palm. She squirmed while he traced her lines and creases with his tongue, memorizing her pattern and wondering if he fit into it somehow. Not just for a few weeks, but for years, maybe even decades. She gasped and bolted upright when he ran his tongue over the delicate flesh between her fingers. A low, heart-stopping moan seeped from her lips as he drew her index and middle fingers into his mouth.

"Jesus, Danny," she whispered when their eyes met and held.

He lowered his lashes and sucked, deep and greedy. She grabbed his arm, drawing him over her as she fell back again. He released her fingers with a pop as they wiggled and shifted, settling into each other. Angling his head, he squeezed her wrist to hold her steady, then ran his tongue over her palm in a long, languorous lick. Fingernails bit into his ass. He scraped his teeth over the flesh at the base of her thumb, and she moaned again.

"That shouldn't be sexy." She arched her back and undulated against him, a slow circle of her hips that proved her theory wrong.

He nipped at the pad of her little finger, then pressed a tender kiss to the afflicted flesh. "Is it?"

"God yes." She dragged her free hand up the furrow of his spine and cupped his nape. "But I need your mouth elsewhere at the moment."

Lacing his fingers through her wet ones, he trapped his desperate, depraved kisses between their palms as he raised his head. "Yeah? Where?"

"Fundamentals, Coach. Remember your fundamentals."

He smiled as she pulled him down. Their noses bumped when she rose to meet him halfway, but the second his mouth covered hers, she sank back, taking him with her. Kate hitched one leg high on his hip, and he groaned into her mouth as his cock settled against the hot, wet crevice of her body. Her slippery fingers squeezed his. The velvet plushness of her tongue stroking his made it impossible to think of anything but this kiss. This moment. This woman. The six-foot Amazon ballbuster who conquered him with her sharp comebacks, soft whispers, hard angles, and secret sweet spots.

She drew her other leg up to encircle him, and soon he was sinking into the sweetest spot of all. Her heat enveloped him. She was slick and ready. Open wide and waiting for him. Just for him. Pride and need rose inside him. He thrust into her, burying himself in that irresistible inferno and relishing the feel of her wrapped tightly around him.

A rush of pleasure rippled through him, starting at his toes and traveling up his legs until it pulsed in his dick. Then panic gripped him. The urge to come hard and fast knotted his throat and made his chest tighten to the point where he thought he might burst in more ways than one. He held still for a second, thinking he could get a grip. Then he realized exactly why everything felt different.

"Condom." He croaked the word, loss and longing weighing the syllables in equal measure.

Kate stiffened beneath him, but those exquisite muscles held him tight. She blinked up at him. He stared down at her. For one insane moment, he envisioned them facing each other from opposite ends of a dusty

frontier town. In the next, he pictured himself spinning
a chamber holding a single bullet and pressing the barrel
of a gun to his head. But this wasn't high noon, and they
weren't playing Russian roulette. They weren't enemies.
They were on the same team.

"I haven't been with anyone since my divorce."

Her confession rushed over him like cool, clear
water, washing away some of his worries, but not all.
"I'm clean," he panted. "The board required a physical
in the terms of my contract." His eyelids grew too heavy
to hold open as she squeezed his hips with her powerful thighs. "Birth control?" He exhaled the question the
second she eased up enough to make a deep lungful possible. Laughter was the last response he expected, but
damn, it felt good to be inside her as that husky chuckle
rolled out of her.

She stroked his back. Light, feathery strokes. "I can't
get pregnant."

Jaw set, Danny gritted his teeth and began to with-
draw. At the last second, those long, strong legs clamped
around him, holding him captive.

"What? Where are you going?" she asked.

He bit his lip hard. "I should…guufh." The final word
was nothing but an inarticulate gurgle, but it was the best
he could do. She was slick and hot, tightening around him,
drawing him back in. Steeling himself to resist, he pushed
up on his arms and stared down into frantic eyes. To soften
the blow a little, he forced a wan smile. "Did I ever tell you
my brother is twelve years younger than me?"

"No." A deep furrow of puzzlement bisected her
brows, then her eyes grew round. "Oh."

Laughter rippled through her again, and this time,

there was no biting back his groan. He rocked against her, dying to plunge in but preparing to pull out. In just one more minute. "So, yeah, I always use condoms."

She stroked a hand over his head, then pressed it to his cheek, forcing him to meet her eyes. "I have an IUD, Danny. That's what I meant."

"Oh, thank Christ." Squeezing her captive hand tight, he surged into her. "You feel so good." He panted the words, staring into her wide eyes as he thrust into her. "I didn't want to stop."

"But you would have."

The confidence in her response stilled him. He gazed into her eyes and nodded slowly. "Maybe."

"Maybe?" She stared at him, surprised by the admission. She hitched her legs higher, and he settled even deeper inside her. "You'd have taken that chance?"

He bit his lip, then nodded. "For you? Yeah, I'd take the chance."

Chance. Didn't she realize he was risking everything for her? That had to mean something, right? A decision made. He almost snorted at the thought. A decision meant there'd been a choice. But there hadn't been. Not for him. From the moment he'd first clapped eyes on her, there'd been no other option. Only Kate. His Kate.

"I'd take it too, if I could," she admitted.

Things moved fast after that. Faster than he would have liked, but once they committed, there was no breaking up that play. Not until they both scored. She broke before he did, but just barely. Minutes later, they lay sweaty and spent.

At least he was. Kate's skin was dewy and glistening.

Then again, their frantic pace had whipped her smooth, dark hair into a frenzy of tangles. He lifted his arm to straighten it out, but his hand weighed a ton. It fell to the bed again, and he sighed with contentment. Even her tangles were beautiful.

"So he was a menopause baby?"

The question wriggled its way through his postcoital haze. He gradually became aware of other things. Fingers smoothing his chest hair. Soft kisses along his shoulder. The sting of scratches on his back. Wetting his parched lips, he dredged up the best response he could manage. "Huh?"

"Your brother was an oops?"

"Oh. Uh, yeah." He ran his hand over his face to wipe away the rest of the cobwebs.

He felt her smile. "Poor guy. That's Tommy?"

"Yeah." A lump rose in his throat. The same ball of regret and resentment he tasted each time he thought about the brother who was barely civil to him anymore. As if he were the one who deserved to be angry.

"I had no idea there was such a gap between you."

He swallowed the lump along with the absurd urge to laugh. "Oh yeah, there's a gap."

"He's coaching in the NFL now?"

Danny closed his eyes as he nodded, once again sending up a silent prayer of thanks for Pate Wilson. The wily football legend was too smart to confuse his brother's talent for coaching with Danny's penchant for fucking up. "Quarterbacks coach."

"Did he play quarterback?" Kate asked.

Danny shook his head but couldn't muster the strength to speak out loud.

She sighed and drew little patterns through the hair on his stomach. "You were a quarterback. I bet it was hard growing up in your shadow."

Those maddening circles tickled, so he stilled her hand by covering it with his. "I bet he's happy to have operating knees."

"He probably worshiped you." Her remark held a note of teasing, but it struck too close to home.

"If he did, he had a funny way of showing it." Silence blanketed them.

"I only have my sister left. Audrey." She laced her fingers through his. "We've never had much in common, but my niece, Kylie, is more like me." She sighed contentedly. "She's at camp this week, but we have to pretend we don't know each other, because she doesn't want the other kids to know we're related."

"Kids," he said with a short laugh.

"Did you ever want any?"

He shrugged. "To be honest, I never really thought much about it." He turned to look at her. "You?"

"I figured if it was meant to happen, it would happen. It just never happened, and after my divorce, I figured it wouldn't."

They lapsed into silence once more. The television flashed and glowed. He squinted at the logo painted at center field, marveling at the sharpness of the display. "This is a great TV."

Kate snorted softly and burrowed deeper into the curve of his neck. "Better be. It cost enough to feed a small village for a year."

He chuckled. "Took me forever to find the DVD setup, but I figured you had to have one in here." His lips curved into a smile, and he kissed the top of her head. "You watch film in bed."

"It was Jeff's setup."

"Ah, the infamous Jeff Sommers." His smile faded at the mention of her ex-husband. He managed to hold back just a second. "What happened there?"

"Nothing much, really. Mike hired Ty Ransom as head coach. Jeff was offered a job in Texas."

"And you wouldn't leave Wolcott?"

She quirked an eyebrow at the surprise in his tone. "You think I should have? You think I ought to have given up a job as head coach in which I had already won two championships for my alma mater to follow my husband halfway across the country so he could take another assistant's position?"

"Well, no, but you were married."

The genuine confusion in his tone seemed to soothe her ruffled feathers. "Yes, we were." Settling back against him, she stared at the television screen. "So you'd think I'd at least rate an invitation, right?"

"He didn't even ask you to go?"

Kate's smile was wan. "Jeff blamed me for Mike not hiring him."

Danny started to sit up, but she pressed him back into the pillows. "Blamed you? How could he blame you?"

"I didn't go to bat for him, pull enough strings…"

She trailed off, but Danny picked right up on the trail. "You were too damn good, made him look like the loser he is."

This time, her smile came naturally. She pressed a kiss to his chest. "I guess I could have tried to be less awesome," she said.

"Wouldn't have worked." He planted another kiss on the top of her head and subsided into the jumble of pillows once more. "Another unworthy idiot. Boy, you sure can pick 'em, Coach."

She stirred only enough to stretch her legs, the tips of her toes sliding down his shin. The curve of her arch fit his instep as if they'd been made to match.

"Says the man in my bed," she teased.

He huffed and shook his head. "The ones who leave it are the morons." Notching his finger under her chin, he nudged it up until she tipped her head back to look at him. "The man in your bed is the smartest, luckiest guy in the world. I'm not idiot enough to give you up. And if they want to fire a guy for being too smart, that's their problem. Right?"

She nodded solemnly. "Right."

# Chapter 14

DANNY TUCKED THE RECEIVER UNDER HIS CHIN AND REACHED for a folder containing recruiting stats as he waited for the call to connect. "Hey, Ma."

"Danny."

As always, there was a tremor of relief in his mother's voice when she greeted him. Like she was afraid she'd never hear from him again, even though he called every Wednesday like clockwork. Eileen McMillan only took calls during the hour between daytime programming and the evening news. Mondays, she caught up with her life-long friend, Grace. She had a standing hair appointment on Tuesdays, just as she had since he was a boy. He was allotted Wednesday, because on Thursday, she checked in on some of the older members of Saint Andrew's con gregation, and Fridays were reserved for her precious whoopsie, his little brother, Tommy.

And heaven help anyone who attempted to deviate from the schedule.

"How are you?"

She inhaled as if she had to brace herself. "I'm just fine, sweetheart. How are you?"

It was only natural that she'd be wary. After all, he'd broken plenty of bad news over these Wednesday afternoon calls. Danny did his best not to let the conde-scension in her voice piss him off, but he was tired of her acting like he was walking around holding a pair of wire cutters. He'd done what he was supposed to do. Following the longstanding traditions ingrained in college athletic departments and the Mafia, he'd taken the blame and done his time. Now, he wanted a kiss on the forehead and a welcome back home, damn it.

"I'm good, Ma. Great, actually."

"Oh? You're settling in okay?"

He caught the hopeful note in her voice and let a smile warm his voice. "Yeah, I'm just fine."

"Tommy says you'll have your work cut out for you with that team."

Just like that, his smile disappeared. Tommy had no right to disparage any part of Danny's life to their mother. Everything he had, every bit of career success that his younger brother had ever enjoyed, was because of Danny. He had no patience for his brother's petty disregard. Not when he was the one whose personal life and public reputation were left in tatters. But as always, he did his best to keep their mother out of the middle.

"They need some work, but the administration is primed to rebuild the program."

"Well, I'm glad to hear that."

Awkward silence hummed between them. Danny glanced at the time and wondered if they'd even make it to the usual five-minute mark without extra effort on his part.

"So, Ma—" he began.

"Did I tell you—" she started at the same time.

They shared a laugh, then prompted one another to go ahead at the exact same time. That earned them another chuckle followed by Awkward Silence: The Sequel. Finally, Danny decided to break for open ground.

"Ma, I've met a woman," he said, unable to bite back his smile.

"I'm finally going to the podiatrist for that bunion," she reported, stomping all over his big news.

"You are?"

"You have?" And just like that, the wariness in her tone was back.

He waited a beat, squelching the urge to snap at her. Most mothers would be happy to hear their son say they'd met someone, but not his. The last time he'd said something remotely similar, their family imploded. Rocking back in his chair, he gripped the armrests and dragged in a calming breath.

"Yes, I have." The pause that followed became Awkward Silence Part III: The Sound of Static. Bracing himself for impact, he plowed ahead. "You may have heard of her, actually. Lord knows you've spent enough time watching for me or Tommy on NSN. Her name is Kate Snyder, and she's the women's basketball coach here at Wolcott."

"The coach?"

The quaver was back now too, and the dam Danny had so carefully built around his anger sprang a slow leak. "Yes, Ma, the coach. Did you think I was going to tell you she was a player?"

"No, I just…I'm just surprised, that's all."

Oh, he had no doubt about that. He just wasn't sure what was shocking about her heterosexual son announcing that he'd met a woman who interested him. Suddenly, he wanted her to explain it to him. "Surprised about what exactly?"

"Well, after all that happened…"

She trailed off, leaving the thought dangling like the belt around the monk's robe he was apparently supposed to put on the minute his last serious girlfriend had decided to marry his baby brother instead.

"After what happened," he repeated, unable to keep the edge from his voice. "You mean, after your precious Tommy set me up to get shit-canned and then married the woman I loved?"

Okay, so it was the *Reader's Digest* version of what went down, but hit all the high points. They just hadn't unfolded in that order.

"Daniel."

For once in his life, the use of his full name had little impact on him. "No, Ma, I'm not the one who screwed up. I'm not the one who betrayed his own brother. I'm done taking the flack for what he did."

"But is dating this coach woman even allowed?"

She stopped him dead in his tracks. It wasn't that she'd struck the nail on the head regarding his relationship with Kate but the fact that she still insisted on deflecting and denying on her baby boy's behalf. Ignoring her question, he decided to use a little razzle-dazzle himself.

"She's amazing, Ma. Smart, funny, and totally down to earth. A great coach. Her interaction with the players is amazing. Instinctive. And you've seen her, right? Six foot two and beautiful. You know, a natural kind of beauty," he added, knowing that his mother never approved of the overblown women that flocked to men who made their living in professional athletics. "Dark hair and really pretty, brownish-gold eyes. Like the color of good Irish whiskey, you know?" And because it never hurt to play on patriotism, he dangled the shiniest bit of background. "Has an Olympic gold medal too."

"But if she works for the school—"

"Ma, don't."

"I worry. You just got your job back."

Catapulting from his chair, he pressed his knuckles into the desk as he leaned over the phone and spoke directly into the receiver. "I've had a job all along. Maybe not at this level, but I've always been the head coach, no matter where I went. I'm no one's assistant. And believe me, no one called in any favors to get those jobs for me," he growled.

"I'm only saying—"

"I know what you're saying, but I'm tired of playing the fuckup. I'm not the one who did all this."

"Don't you use that language with me," she huffed.

"Stop acting like I'm the screwup," he barked. "I did everything right. I did everything I was supposed to do. I took the fall, but now I'm back up, and all I'm asking is for you to be happy for me, for once in your life. Just me. Not because I can do something to help you or Tommy, but because, right or wrong, I'm doing something for myself."

He hung his head, letting his gaze go unfocused as he listened to his mother's quiet crying on the other end of the line. A sound he'd heard too many times. One he shouldn't be listening to now, when he'd been trying to tell her he finally found someone who made him happy.

"I'm sorry," he said. After a lifetime of conditioning, the words came automatically. What he wasn't used to hearing was the rasp of tears in his own voice. He cleared his throat. "I am. Don't cry. Please don't cry, Ma."

Sinking back into his chair, he fanned the pages of the open file with the pad of his thumb. Each sheet featured a meticulously kept record of every attempt at player contact. He wasn't taking any hits he didn't deserve. Not from anyone.

"No, it's not allowed, Ma, but I don't care." Certainty settled deep in his gut. "You see? That's why I had to tell you. It's not allowed, and I don't care. That's how much I care about her. I just wanted you to know."

---

Calhoun's was quiet. The students were gone, and the summer crowd wasn't big on spending gorgeous, warm evenings in dank, dark bars. That made it the perfect spot for this particular meeting of the minds. Kate smiled as Avery glanced over her shoulder, pushed aside the scotch she'd ordered, and reached for one of the tall straws protruding from Millie's unguarded hurricane glass.

"Why don't you just order one for yourself?" Kate asked as Avery used the tip of her finger to siphon off a hit of strawberry daiquiri.

"I refuse to subscribe to society's preordained notions of what a woman should drink." With a shrug, Avery drew the straw from the glass, positioned the business end over her open mouth, and lifted her finger.

Kate grimaced as the sticky, sweet drink trickled from the straw into her friend's mouth. Reaching for the pint she'd ordered, she held it up for inspection. "I'm drinking beer. What does that say about me?"

Avery grinned and dropped the straw back into the daiquiri glass just as Millie returned from her sojourn to the ladies' room. "It says your taste buds are dead." The second their trio was complete, she lifted the whisky she'd ordered on convoluted principle in a toast. "May they rest in peace."

"Amen," Millie said as she repositioned her straws.

Kate rolled her eyes. "You do realize we look like the start of a bad joke, don't you? A jock, a priss, and a feminist walk into a bar. Who orders the umbrella drink?"

Avery's brow puckered. "How is that humorous?"

"It's not. That's why it's a bad joke." Kate reached over and gave Avery's hand a condescending pat. "No matter how hard you try, we're still a cliché."

"Well, you are," Millie said, her pointed gaze traveling from the tracksuit Kate wore to her half-drunk glass of beer. "And Betty Friedan over there fights it so hard she's turned herself into one." She pressed one perfectly manicured hand to her breast. "Me? I'm an original."

Avery snorted. "Are there any parts on you that are still original?"

"One nip," Millie shot back, referring to the eyelift she'd had the previous year. "I had one little nip, and it was medically necessary. My vision was compromised."

Kate rolled her eyes but made certain she opened them just a little wider. The truth was, she understood Millie's decision to have surgery better than she liked to let on. When a woman spent half her life defying gravity, it was hard to give in gracefully to signs of time.

Leaning in, Avery folded her hands on the sticky tabletop. "Yeah, well, you're old news. What I want to know is how many times our Katie here has been compromised."

The shift in topic startled her, but the change wasn't nearly as disconcerting as their probing gazes. "What?" she managed to blurt.

"You're fucking Danny McMillan," Millie stated bluntly. "A lot, I'd say." She turned to Avery for confirmation on her diagnosis.

Lips pursed, Avery surveyed her carefully. "I concur. Well and often, judging by the size of those bags under your eyes."

"What? How?" Kate sputtered. "Why would you—"

"Oh, please," Avery said, waving away her protests. "We're not judging you. I, for one, am proud. And more than a little jealous."

"And I'm a little pissed that you didn't tell me," Millie said with an arch look. "But I can get past it—"

"As long as you give us all the salacious details," Avery injected.

"Exactly." Millie stirred her drink, then plucked a wedge of orange from the rim of her glass. "Tell us everything."

Kate's cheeks burned. She wrapped one hand around her beer glass, hoping the condensation might help her keep her cool, but it was no good. Exhaling slowly, she caved to peer pressure. Oddly enough, making the decision to spill her guts felt good. Like someone finally stuck a needle into her release valve. Little by little, the weight of keeping her relationship with Danny a secret from her best friends lifted. She let go of her glass and pressed her damp hand to the scarred table. The fire under her skin died down to a warm glow. "Oh God, he's so perfect," she gushed at last.

Avery gave up all her pretenses and squealed like a teenager.

Millie clapped a stunned hand to her throat. "I swear, I never thought I'd hear those words come out of your

mouth. I mean, I know the two of you are combustible—
that's why I put you together—but dear Lord."

"She's in love!" Avery cooed. "Completely deluded
and utterly cursed. Willing to sacrifice her personal
autonomy for patriarchal approval. How sweet is that?"

This time, Millie handled the eye rolling. "She's got
the hots for a stud muffin, that's all."

Offended by her friend's dismissive tone, Kate sat up
straighter. "I'm not deluded, and it's not the hots."

"Notice she didn't deny the stud-muffin part," Avery
said with a sage nod.

Fighting the urge to snarl, Kate fixed them both with
her most intimidating stare. "And I'm not giving up
any autonomy."

"Puh-leeze," Millie murmured, taking a draw from
her straw. "I'm just looking at you, and I can tell that
you'd work here for free if McStud Muffin's services
were part of your contract."

Avery jerked up tall on her stool and narrowed her
eyes. "It's a ploy. Mike Samlin brought the stud muffin
in to distract you from contract negotiations."

Kate scoffed and reached for her beer. After taking a
bracing gulp, she tossed the idea aside. "Y'all are forgetting that I'm not negotiating my contract. Jonas is."

"Doesn't matter. You'll agree to anything as long as
you keep getting some," Avery said with a nod.

"Oh, she's not that far gone," Millie insisted.

"Not that far gone?" Avery turned her incredulous gaze on Millie. "Didn't you hear her? He's so
perrrrrrfect."

"Our personal relationship has nothing to do with our
professional ambitions," Kate said stiffly.

"Maybe not yours, but you aren't the one who has nothing to lose," Millie pointed out.

Dead silence blanketed the table. An excruciating minute passed. Then Avery sighed and sagged. "This isn't at all how I wanted this conversation to go," she muttered, lifting her glass of scotch to her lips.

Millie blew out a gusty sigh and planted an elbow on the table. "I just wanted to know how big a piece he's packing." Her chin dropped into her open palm, and she cast an apologetic look in Kate's direction. "And if he knew what to do with it."

Kate felt a little of her indignation ebb away as she studied her friends. They really did mean well, even if they were both shit stirrers.

"Why do we always say that? There's not much to knowing what to do with the actual piece," Avery mused, stirring her scotch with her fingertip. "The only thing to do with that is to stick it into an orifice." A devilish twinkle lit her eyes as she sucked the booze from her skin. "I mean, a guy's cock is a one-trick pony. More important they know what to do with their hands, or tongue, or—"

"We've got it." Millie cut Avery off before she could ramp up to lecture mode. Turning her full attention to Kate, she smiled benignly. "You can tell by looking at her that he knows what he's doing with...everything."

"Can you?" Kate asked, genuinely curious. "Can you really tell just by looking at me?"

"Well, maybe not everyone," Avery conceded with a shrug. "But we know you."

Millie nodded. "And we know what you looked like when you were with Jeff."

Kate frowned. "How did I look with Jeff?"

She flinched when Millie poked her in the forehead with one vermillion-tipped nail. "Like that."

"Quick, stop furrowing, or she'll whip a syringe of botulism out of her bag," Avery urged.

Game face in place, Kate settled an impassive stare on the other two women. "Better?"

Avery's lips curved into an affectionate smile. "Actually, I liked the grin you wore when you gushed about how perrrrfect he is."

"I did too," Millie agreed.

"Yet you both jumped me about it." Kate picked up her beer and saluted her friends with it. She took a healthy slurp, then gave her head a sad shake. "Sheesh, women."

"We're a pain, but we're still easier to deal with than men," Avery asserted.

Millie shot her an exasperated look. "Some of us are more of a pain than others."

Unperturbed by Millie's jab, Avery shrugged. "I'm low maintenance. I'm happy with a drawer full of double A batteries and my collection of rubber dicks. They don't make a mess or any demands."

"Speaking of messy..." Millie ran her hand over her blouse, then fiddled with her necklace. Curious, Kate watched as her normally confident friend fidgeted and fussed. "Something has come to my attention, and I wanted to get your take on it."

"Is it about the football coach doing the basketball coach? If so, old news." Avery blinked. "Oh, wow. I totally just pictured Coach McStud Muffin getting down and dirty with Ty Ransom instead of you, Katie, and I have to confess, I'll be taking that image to my bunk with me tonight."

Kate gaped at her friend, but even she had to admit the image Avery conjured wasn't exactly repugnant. "Nice thought, but it would never happen in a million years."

"In my mind, it's already happening." Avery grinned. "That's it, just move your right hand a little, Danny Boy."

"Stop," Millie ordered in a voice stern enough that they instantly obeyed. "Leave Katie's boy toy alone."

"Yes. Please." Kate added the last as an afterthought. Ready to escape the hot seat, she focused on Millie. "What's going on?"

"Well, it does involve Ty Ransom," she admitted with uncharacteristic caution.

"If I'm not allowed to picture them both, I'll take one of two," Avery allowed with a magnanimous wave. Settling her chin on her palm, she gazed at Millie with rapt attention. "Tell us what's going on with Tasty Ty."

Despite Avery's guffaw, Millie's expression remained grim. "I don't know anything for sure, but I need some advice."

Kate blinked, taken aback. Millie gave advice; she didn't ask for it. "Advice?"

Avery raised both eyebrows. "Well, this is a first."

"Hush," Kate hissed, concerned by Millie's unchecked frown.

"Well, you know I spend a lot of time poking around the various social media platforms," Millie began. "I have to tell you, I hate PicturSpam. There are some things a person just wishes she could unsee, you know?"

"Oh, I know," Avery agreed wholeheartedly.

Kate said nothing but gave an encouraging nod.

"I'm not certain, but I think Ty's wife might be fooling around on him."

Kate's stomach dropped to her feet. "You think this because of something you saw on PicturSpam?"

Millie pressed the heel of her hand to the center of her forehead, smoothing the wrinkles away. "God, don't these idiots realize that once you press post, things are out there for everyone to see? Forever?"

"And you saw Ty's wife with another guy?" Avery prompted.

Heaving a sigh, Millie picked up her glass. "I saw Ty's wife in ways I never wanted to see anyone whose spouse I have to face on a regular basis."

"Shit."

Kate muttered the word, but the heartfelt sentiment cut through the ambient noise of clinking glasses, piped-in rock and roll, and the groans of a few baseball fans with their eyes glued to a wall-mounted television.

Millie looked up, her blue eyes sad and troubled. "Do I say something?"

The three of them fell silent as they contemplated the question. On the television, the batter stepped out of the box to take a couple of practice swings. He was facing down a full count of balls and strikes. Kate stared at the screen, riveted by the man's expression as he stepped up to the plate to await the next pitch, his bat swaying over his shoulder, moved by barely contained anticipation.

Kate watched, unblinking. She hated baseball, but God, she loved that feeling. The pressure. Tension humming in her blood. Sweat beading on her forehead and upper lip. Unlike most people, she thrived on make or break moments. She often made it, but only because she knew better than to force a shot. A true player knew to run the route, let the ball roll off their fingertips, or wait for the right pitch to come. They trusted their instincts above everything else. And they refused to admit defeat until the last buzzer sounded.

There was no way anyone could have made her see her ex-husband for the parasite he was, no matter what proof they had. She had to find that out on her own. And though she had known deep down that her marriage to Jeff was over long before Ty Ransom was named men's basketball coach, she hadn't wanted to admit it. She'd signed a contract based on sentiment when she took the coaching job at Wolcott. That was her mistake. Not Mike's or Danny's or even her agent's. After all, Jonas had advised her to hold out longer. Not just ask for more but flat-out demand they pay her what she was worth.

But she didn't listen. Ty Ransom wouldn't listen either.

Poor Ty. He'd have to wait until his instincts kicked in. Millie wasn't entirely certain, and even if she were, it wasn't her place to say anything. No one wants to admit they made a huge mistake on something as fundamental as choosing the right person to love.

"No," Kate said at last. As if snapping from a trance, she jerked her head to look at her friend. "You can't say anything that'll make any difference. They'll just have to let things play out."

—◆◆◆—

She came home to find Danny's ball cap on her end table and the man himself propped against her headboard. He was mostly naked, or at least stripped to the waist, and propped on both pillows as if he owned the place. She tried to work up what Avery would think was an appropriate amount of ire at finding him in her space without invitation once again, but she couldn't. She liked coming home to him, as cheesy as that sounded.

Spotting her in the doorway, he muted the television. "Hey. How was your night?"

"Better now," she said, refusing to feel even a hint of shame at the confession.

A slow smile spread across his handsome features. He dropped the remote on the nightstand and gestured for her to come closer. Not even taking a moment to toe off her shoes, Kate dove onto the bed and into his arms. The skin stretched over his biceps was warm and smooth. Kate turned her head and pressed her lips to the tender flesh on the inside. Though he was ticklish, he didn't flinch or shy away. He just let her kiss him.

"You okay?" he asked, his voice raspy and rough around the edges.

"Long day."

He tucked his chin to his chest and peered down at her, blue eyes wary and watchful. "But this is okay? Me being here?"

She chuckled, then caught a little of that oh-so-tempting skin between her teeth. "Now you ask."

He squirmed a bit but mostly let her have her way. For that, she rewarded him with a slow, swirling flick of her tongue over the afflicted flesh. "I can go if you want," he said.

"I don't want." She turned into him and pressed her cheek to his chest. Crisp hair tickled her nose. She burrowed deeper into his embrace, not in the mood to implement strategies or play games. "I like having you here."

He kissed the top of her head, then smoothed her hair with an awkward pat of his hand. "I like being here."

"Millie and Avery think you're a hooker Mike hired to distract me from my contract negotiations."

He chuckled. "How many million do you think I'm worth?"

She barked a laugh. "Million? I was thinking I'd offer to swap the country club membership for you. After all, I get to see you swing your club in the comfort of my own bedroom. Why bother with the culottes and saddle shoes?"

"Nice."

She giggled and nuzzled his flat nipple. "They doubt my ability to keep my head in the game."

"Typical mathletes."

His unabashed jock snobbishness tickled her. Running her hand down his chest, she stroked the line of soft hair that bisected his abs. "I know, right?" She kissed his throat, enjoying the bob of his Adam's apple against her lips as she let her fingertips slide a few centimeters lower. "They have no respect for my...drive."

"Fools."

He exhaled the word in a rush that ruffled the hair he'd just smoothed. His chest rose and fell with gratifying quickness as her hand drifted lower still. His cock was hot and more than half-aroused by the time she wrapped her fingers around him. She pressed a tender kiss to his pec, delighted by the tremor she felt ripple through him.

"Kate?"

"Hm?"

"Don't give up the country club membership."

"No?" She released him long enough to push the covers down past his knees. "How come?" she asked, resuming her grip.

He answered with a low, strangled groan that made her smile. "Don't say come."

"Sorry," she whispered, but she didn't mean it.

"You can't quit the club." Danny pressed his head into the pillows and arched into her touch. "It'd be a damn shame to waste a strong backhand like that."

# Chapter 15

THE THRUM OF A DOZEN BASKETBALLS AGAINST HARDWOOD drew him like a vandal to a freshly painted wall. The lack of syncopation should have crawled all over his nerves, but it didn't. Those crazy, time-challenged thuds reminded him of the beat of Kate's heart just after she came. Frantic. Erratic. Beautifully untamed.

He hovered in the mouth of the tunnel, his gaze locked on the honey-colored court. She stood at the center of mayhem, the brightly colored shoes planted square in the middle of the stylized shield and crossed swords that served as the university's logo. Two dozen gangly preteens gamboled around her, skinny arms and legs flailing as they chased those bouncing balls.

Kate called something as one of the girls sprinted past her, a shining, blond ponytail streaming in her wake as she broke for the basket. The layup circled the rim but refused to fall through. The girl's shoulders slumped as one of her cohorts snagged the rebound and dribbled away. She turned toward center court, hope and dread written all over her face. Kate gave a casual wave that clearly said "Shake it off," captured a wayward ball, and winged it at the girl.

A flash of color at the far end of the court caught his attention. A huff of surprise burst from his lungs as he spotted a second Amazon among the milieu of munchkins. Another one of the WNBA's former all-stars bent at the waist to talk to a girl who wasn't much past the five-foot mark. A quick scan turned up two of her assistant coaches, a current NBA player, and Ty Ransom scattered between loose groups of middle school players.

Danny released a low whistle as he sidled into a row of bleachers and lowered a seat without taking his eyes off the action below. "That's a lot of firepower."

He'd mumbled the observation to himself, but a deep voice came from higher up in the stands. "You should see who she pulls in for the varsity camps later this summer."

"Mack?" Twisting in his seat, Danny scowled as he squinted into the gloom beyond the first tier of seating. "That you?"

His assistant coach grunted in reply. "Better move back into the shadows. She doesn't like people crashing her camps. Says it makes the girls nervous."

Barely containing a snort, Danny glanced around at what he'd thought was an empty arena. Then he spotted them. A dozen or so spectators sat high up in the stands, all with their attention fixed on the court. All but one, that is.

Danny started to rise, but a sharp jerk of the AD's head stopped him. Before he could seek refuge in the cheap seats, Mike made his way toward him, climbing over rows and bounding down the shallow steps three at a time. He read the intent on the other man's face as easily as he read defensive formations. The blitz was coming. Danny had a choice: scramble and run, or stay in the pocket and take it like a man.

"Probably should have stayed in your office, Coach,"

Mack stage-whispered. "I think the big guy's been looking for you."

Danny didn't bother to conceal his grimace as he
watched his old friend approach. "Yeah, thanks for the
heads-up."

"Mack." Mike acknowledged the older man with a
nod but didn't break stride. Mack didn't bother to move,
a fact that made it doubly uncomfortable when Mike
dropped down right beside Danny. "Coach."

Mike hadn't even left the customary one-seat man
buffer between them. A fact that did not bode well as far
as friendly conversation might go. Danny shifted in his
seat and eyed the other man. "Director."

Mike leaned forward to plant his elbows on his knees
and clasp his hands between them. He kept his eyes
locked on the court below, but tension rolled off the man
in waves. "I'd hoped I wouldn't see you here."

A pang of regret twisted Danny's gut. This man was
his friend. One of the few who had not only stuck by him
when the shit hit, but who also reached out on a regular
basis. Danny had been so busy avoiding his boss lately
that he hadn't noticed Mike had been dodging him too.

The warning Mike had given that day on the practice field came back to him. The man had gone out
on a limb for him. Danny was lucky to have this job.
Kate was too deeply ensconced in Wolcott for him to
fool with her and walk away unscathed. Every word
was true. Unfortunately, a warning was never going to
be enough to keep him away from Kate Snyder. Hell,
nothing short of a highly skilled assassin would have
done the trick.

"You can save the lecture," Danny warned.

The blunt assessment captured Mike's full attention. "Huh?"

"There was no way it wasn't going to happen."

Mike's eyebrows rose. "I'm scared of both the structure and the content of that sentence."

Danny had to laugh. Letting his head fall, he rolled the knots from his shoulders and dropped back another five yards to buy himself a little time. These days, Mike looked a lot more like an academic than an all-American. In reality, the man was both. Not only was he smart as a whip, but he also had the heart of a ballplayer. Danny needed to remember that. Unlike the front office guys he'd worked for in the past, he couldn't bully this one into letting him call his own shots.

"Listen—"

"No!" Mike hissed. "I get it, okay? She's beautiful, she's talented, she's friggin' six feet tall—"

Danny turned and dropped the heel of his foot on Mike's instep. Hard. Hard enough to make the man suck air. "Stop right there."

Mike gritted his teeth, then threw an elbow with enough force and accuracy to restore what little space the two had started with. "Dammit, Danny, just looking at her wrong can get you fired in the blink of an eye."

"You think I don't know that? You think she doesn't?"

Mike slid to the end of the seat and turned to face Danny head-on. "Then what the hell are you thinking? It took you years just to get back to this point."

The shrill *threeeep* of a whistle cut though the cacophony, and the disjointed thrum of bouncing balls ceased at once. Danny watched as the girls lined up to place their balls on wheeled racks parked at the far end of the court. One by one, they rushed to the middle of the floor, anxious to see what Kate had planned for them next.

Mike's growl of frustration was muffled by his palm. "Is she really worth it?"

The silence throbbed around them. Alive. Pulsing with adrenaline. And like a rookie spotting his first opening in the defensive line, Danny dove headlong into it. "How's Diane? Still worth it?"

It was a cheap shot and Danny knew it, but he was feeling cornered and didn't care. Mike's wife had been a cheerleader he'd fooled with on and off in their under-grad days. Then she turned up pregnant just after one of those "on" periods at the end of their junior year, and Mike showed up for practice that fall with a shiny gold wedding band on his finger.

All indications showed that the marriage was thriving. They'd had two more kids after Mike's pro career petered out. Danny had been to their expensive-but-comfortable house for dinner and spotted the pencil marks on the doorjamb that made the house a home. But still, it wasn't like Mike had been given a lot of choice once the dirty deed was done.

"I'm sorry." Danny issued the apology in an instant. "That was… I'm sorry. I didn't mean that. You know I love Di."

Mike sagged back against the seat. "I'm not trying to bust your balls, man. I'm just… The stakes are high. It's not just your job on the line here. I took a chance on you."

Danny slumped, the weight of Mike's reality pressing down on him until he slouched like a sullen teenager. "I know that."

Tugging at his bottom lip, he watched as Kate divided

her worshipful minions between the opposing baselines. Whistle clamped between her teeth, she walked backward until she reclaimed her spot at center court, then gave it a short, shrill blast. The soles of sixty sneakers slapped polished oak. When the first girl came close to touching her, another bleat split the air, sending them back in the opposite direction.

She toyed with them, sending them long then short, reversing their course on her whim, and smiling around the whistle's rubber guard as their squeals and taunts filled the air.

He closed his eyes. It took little effort to conjure the image of her straddling him. Toying with him. Tormenting him. Pushing him until it felt like everything would explode—his dick, his head, his lungs, his heart.

A long, trilling blast of the whistle jolted him, and Danny sat bolt upright as the girls ran to her. They surrounded her at center, their faces shiny with sweat and tendrils trailing from battered ponytails. They beamed at Kate. Every one of those young, fresh faces glowed with elation. He knew that feeling. It came to him each time he fitted his fingers between the laces of a football, cupped the curved leather, cocked his arm, and let one fly. *Love of the game*.

Love.

Eyes fixed on the woman towering over her gaggle of munchkins, he let go of the tension inside him. It was time to stop playing it safe and start playing to win. And to win, he needed to lay it all on the line. His job. Decades of friendship. The heart thumping hard against his breastbone. He hadn't lied when he told his mother Kate was worth the risk.

"I love her."

He spoke the words no louder than a whisper, but he knew Mike heard him. He couldn't be bothered with the knuckles glowing white beneath his old friend's skin. Not when he'd lobbed his heart right at the unsuspecting woman like a Hail Mary. Closing his eyes, he envisioned it slicing through the air in a high, tight spiral, unraveling the closer it got to her. Just like he did. Danny swallowed hard but forced himself to open his eyes. He couldn't stand envisioning his heart lying bloody and beaten at her feet. "I love her."

"Does she love you?"

Danny opened his mouth to tell the man it was none of his damn business if she did or she didn't, but at that moment, Kate raised her head and looked right at him.

Thank God he hadn't heeded Mack's advice to move higher up in the stands. For once in his life, he was more than happy to be too slow to outrun Mike Samlin. He answered the eloquent lift of her brows with an exaggerated shrug. A small smile curved her lips as she carried the whistle to her mouth again and blew hard. This time, she took off with the pack, her dark hair bouncing off her shoulders as she raced the girls for the racks that held the basketballs.

He watched as she ripped a ball from the grasp of a girl eight inches shorter and dribbled away. Her throaty laugh rose like smoke. Her erstwhile opponent went after her, bony arms flailing as the NCAA coach of the year squared up and stepped into her defender, unwilling to give even an inch when it came to the only thing that mattered—taking the shot.

He drank her in, memorizing the line of her. Eyes fixed

on the rim and toes pointed at the goal, her body curved into a graceful bow, her strength and power breathtaking to behold. She was his. And she loved him too.

"Yeah, she does."

Mike heaved a sigh heavy enough to crush a lesser person. Danny twitched when the man's hand landed heavy on his shoulder, but Mike's voice was quiet and calm when he spoke. "Are you sure?"

"I'm sure." And he was. He knew with every fiber of his being that she loved him back, even if they hadn't said the words yet.

Mike sighed. "I can't stand the thought of watching everything you've worked for blown sky-high because of some woman."

Danny turned to look at his friend. "Not some woman. *The* woman," he corrected gruffly. "Before I met Kate, the only thing I had to look forward to when I left the office at night was hours of game film. The only goal I had was getting back, getting better, and getting my hands on that trophy."

Mike held his gaze. "And now?"

The smile started, and there was no way he could stop it. Pure joy. Powered by love. Of the game, and of the right woman. "Now I want all that and her."

The AD rapped his wedding ring against the plastic armrest and stood. "Well, there goes Millie's publicity plan."

Squinting up at the other man, Danny shrugged. "Oh, I bet Kate and I can keep fighting for the cameras."

"Hard to buy two people going at each other if you know they're getting it on at night." Mike shoved his hands into his pockets and tossed down another put-upon sigh. "Bobby Riggs and Billie Jean King never fell in love."

Danny barked a laugh. "There were reasons for that."

"I suppose." As if the man thought he still had any room to maneuver, Mike cast a sidelong glance at Danny. "Keep it off campus."

"There goes my plan to bend her over the trophy case."

His words dripped with sarcasm. As it was, he'd been actively plotting payback for the locker room tryst for weeks, but the right opportunity never arose. He wouldn't cross it off the list, no matter what Mike wanted.

"I guess I'll have to make do with away games," Danny said.

"Okay, I've said what I needed to say." Mike patted his shoulder again but this time gave it a friendly squeeze. "I'll talk to you later."

He started to slide from the row, but Danny caught his arm. "I'm sorry about what I said. It was a cheap shot. You know I love Diane, right?"

"I do too. No matter how rough things were at the start."

Danny didn't even try to fight the flush that crept up his neck. He deserved every scorching bit of it. "I get you. And I *am* sorry. I shouldn't have lashed out like that."

The AD caught the apology with the same grace he used to show only when snatching footballs out of thin air. "Now you know how I know you're not bullshitting about Kate."

Danny watched his friend walk away without another word. Down on the court, the assistant coaches were herding the campers into lines for layup drills. Kate huddled with her two famous volunteers on the sideline. The lights above the court striped her dark hair with

streamers of gold. The green-and-gold lanyard around
her neck clashed with the neon-pink Nike shirt she wore
with black track pants. He caught the Y-shaped outline
of a sports bra beneath the high-tech fabric. The shirt
clung to the slope of her breasts and flowed smooth over
the curve of her hip. The urge to yank them both up to
her armpits made his fingers curl.

The squeak of a seat rising alerted him that he wasn't
alone with his X-rated thoughts. A pair of decidedly
low-tech sneakers appeared in his peripheral vision. At
least the damn things had laces and not Velcro closures.
He didn't need to look to know his inherited assistant
would have completed the look with polyester coach's
shorts and a polo.

Keeping his gaze on Kate, he asked, "You got something to add, Mack?"

Mack didn't scuff his shoes or clear his throat. He didn't
bother with anything as obvious as a tap on the shoulder
or whistle blast in his ear. Danny had seen the old coot
do it to players on occasion. The tactic was undoubtedly
effective but not as potent as stillness and silence.

At last, Danny gave in and looked up. "Well?"

Mack gave him the single nod that Danny was starting to think the man had trademarked, then gestured to
the court. "Just glad to hear you finally got your head in
the game."

Kate walked her guests to the ramp that led to the
locker rooms. Her thanks were effusive. Handshakes
turned into hugs and kisses. The guy from the Knicks
held her a little too long for Danny's liking, but she
simply laughed and punched the future Hall of Fame
candidate in the arm as she pulled away. Poor Mack

had to resort to a light slap upside his head to regain Danny's attention.

Shocked, Danny turned to glare into crystalline-blue eyes, for the first time noticing that the shade was startlingly similar to the reflection that greeted him in the mirror each morning. But this man was nothing like dodgy Dan McMillan. This man knew who he was, where he belonged, and exactly what the next play needed to be.

"Yeah, Coach?" Danny asked, his voice hoarse with anticipation.

"Just make sure you play every minute of every quarter. Right to the last down." He glanced at Kate and then back again. "Every second counts, kid. Hell, these basketball players, they'll even take it down to the tenths and hundredths of a second. Play hard if you mean to win."

"Gotcha."

The old man thumped his back, then rose. "We've been spotted." He jerked his chin toward the court. Kate stood in the center circle once more, a ball tucked under her arm and a gaggle of preteen girls gathered close. She raised a hand and waved him down. Of course, Mack was off like a shot. "Looks like you're about to get drilled, and not in the good way," he said with a chuckle.

Unable to resist her smile, Danny rose like a man in a trance. The soles of his athletic shoes were silent as he jogged down the steps, but the second he stepped onto the polished hardwood, they sang out his surrender.

Smiling at the chorus of giggles that greeted him, he trotted out to meet the group, his shoes squeaking like someone had stashed a pair of rubber mice in the insoles. "You beckoned, Coach?"

"Think fast," she blurted, then winged the ball she'd been holding directly at his chest.

He caught it just before it knocked the wind out of him. Palms stinging, he shot her an arch look. "Fast enough for you?"

Kate simply smiled that saccharine smile he'd come to know and love and pointed to the far goal. "Hit it."

Without breaking eye contact with her, he dropped the ball into an easy dribble. "Hitting it, Coach," he replied with a smirk.

She let him have two steps before she unleashed her gaggle of flying monkeys with nothing more than a simple, "Get him."

—⁓—

Kate drew up short when she spotted Danny lounging against the trophy case outside her office door. "Oh. Hi."

He didn't straighten or return her burgeoning smile. In fact, he didn't look happy to see her at all. He looked…determined. She'd become fluent in Danny McMillan's body language over the past few weeks. The tightening of his abs when her fingers bumped over his ribs marked him as ticklish but unwilling to admit it. A quick downward tug at the corners of his mouth signaled amusement he was reluctant to show. The sharp, jerky nod he gave her told her he was holding himself on a tight rein. His fingers were curled into his palms, not quite fists.

"You and your minions have fun making me look like a slug out there?"

Her ears burned, and her nipples went on high alert. That old saying about someone being beautiful when they're angry came to life. He stood there, pissed off and gorgeous in all his high-definition glory, and, Lord, she wanted him. It had been less than six hours since he'd rolled out of her bed, but that didn't make her any less eager to have him in it—and in her—again. Judging by the heat flaming in his blue eyes, he felt exactly the same way.

"You looked like you wanted to play." She brushed against him as she aimed her key at the lock on her office door. He stiffened just the slightest bit, and she shot him a sidelong glance as the door swung open wide. "I would have introduced you to Alec and Shaundra, but they couldn't stick around for the slaughter."

"Your friend Alec can shoot, but he plays golf for crap." The words sounded like a typical jock jibe, but Danny wasn't wearing the requisite smirk to go with them. Instead, he kicked the door shut, twisted the lock, and started toward her, blue eyes locked on her like laser beams. "And given how I did against a bunch of twelve-year-olds today, I'd say I've got more than enough trouble trying to handle one Amazon woman. Two would probably kill me."

"I wasn't offering to set you up." She leaned back to perch on the edge of her desk, bracing her feet wide and tipping her chin up to hold his gaze. Invitation or challenge, he could read it either way he wished. "Besides, you're not her type."

That cocky smirk she loved so much finally made its appearance. Danny stepped between her legs. Her eyelashes fluttered when he ran his big, rough hand over her hair. But when he wound a hank of it around his fist and tugged not so gently, her eyes snapped open, and her head tipped back.

"Haven't you heard?" he asked. "I'm every woman's type."

"I hate to break this to you, lover boy, but I can tell you for a fact that I'm more her type."

It took a half second for the full impact of the taunt to sink in. The metamorphosis of his expression was priceless. So was the sheepish but delighted smile he settled on at last.

"Day-yum," he drawled. "If that's not a thought to keep a man up at night, I don't know what is."

Kate grabbed his belt buckle and pulled him a little closer, all the while staring him straight in the eye. "Stop being a pig. Besides, she's not *my* type."

He blushed as he rubbed his thumb along the base of her skull. "Sorry, I know that was bad, but…can't I keep it? Just for…inspiration."

"You're playing with fire, Coach," she warned.

"Never did develop a healthy fear of it." He lifted a shoulder in a helpless shrug. "Now, with you, I think I might be turning into a damn pyromaniac."

She wet her lips, then let her hand fall away from his waistband. "I saw Mike up there too. I assume he was warning you off."

"He tried."

"Danny—"

"He failed."

The stark ferocity of his assertion stopped her. Whatever she was about to say crumbled to dust on her tongue. She stared hard at him, searching for a crack she might slip through to inject a little reason, but all she saw was the impenetrable granite of sheer determination. Still, she was a champion, and champions

never stop. Even when faced with seemingly insur-
mountable odds.

"He's going to fire you."

"No, he's not."

His rapid response startled her. She squinted at him,
trying to read whatever convoluted thoughts had led him
to his new certainty. "How do you know?"

"I know."

A slow smile curved his mouth. Riding the wave of
impulse that seemed to swell whenever this man was too
near, she rose up and pressed her lips to it. The smile
blossomed and spread as she moved to give the other
side of his mouth equal playing time. She loved kissing
him happy. Danny's smiles had a taste all their own,
spice and heat, as if each bump of his lips served as a
thermostat. Oh, she loved his other kisses too. The ones
rich and intense as dark chocolate. Those quick pecks
that were savory but also achingly sweet. She particularly relished the moments when his innate coordination
failed and he got a little sloppy.

She angled her mouth to fit his, then parted her lips
enough to make him throb as much as she did. His
answering groan was gratifying, so she parted them just
a teensy bit more. His other hand came to rest on her hip.
She was about to break the kiss when he stepped closer.
His knee banged the front of the desk, but it didn't seem
to faze him. He kissed her slow and soft. Languid nips
and brushes that made her squirm. His hand tightened
on her hip. She knew she should do the sensible thing
and pull back, but he yanked her to the edge of the desk,
pressing her firmly against the hardness beneath his fly
as his tongue swept into her mouth. And oh, it felt good.

Their kisses went on and on. Deep, drugging, and dangerously tempting, each swirl of his tongue made her ache in places that had no business aching in this place where she did business. She grasped at the last straw of sanity.

"Danny," she gasped when he relinquished her mouth at last.

His fingers curled around the elastic waistband of her pants. She tried to protest, but his lips found the pulse in her throat, and all she managed was a strangled moan. She closed her eyes as his hand traveled from her nape to her breast.

"We can't…not here."

He pinched the hardened tip of her nipple, sending pain-laced pleasure coursing through her like a shot of adrenaline.

"We're… We might… Anyone."

He let go of her breast, and every objection she meant to voice melted away in a burst of white-hot desire. "God yes."

Chuckling, Danny shoved the rubber tip of her whistle between her lips and crooned, "Shh."

Her teeth clamped down on the whistle. The rubber ball trapped in the chamber trilled softly as she exhaled her surprise.

"Watch your breathing." He leaned into her, pressing her back on her desk, forcing her to splay her hands behind her to catch her weight. He tugged her pants over the curve of her hip. "Lift up."

He uttered the command in a voice so gruff, she obeyed without thought. Papers slid beneath her palms as she leveraged herself up. A proposed endorsement contract for a line of performance-enhancing protein supplements, camp schedules, drafts of the talks she'd be giving to overfed businessmen who considered an elite female athlete something of an anomaly. She smiled when he grappled with the zippers at her ankles.

Her T-shirt flew across the room. He pushed at the wide elastic of her sports bra with frantic hands. It rolled up like a broken blind. He caught a hank of hair and yanked. Her scalp screamed in protest, but she remained silent. The little rubber ball trapped in the whistle vibrated with each exhalation, but she kept it steady. The last thing she wanted was for him to stop. His hands were on her, and she was the sexiest, most desirable woman on earth. Even if she was clad in nothing but a pair of obnoxiously bright sneakers and some no-show socks.

Her fingers sank into his thick hair. The silky softness of the waves slipped through her fingers as he suckled her. The insistent tugs at her breast wound her up tighter than a spring. She inhaled through clamped teeth but carefully let the air seep from her lungs in measured exhalations, afraid she'd elicit another trill from the whistle.

He pressed the tip of his finger to her entrance. "Yes?"

She nodded, and he thrust deep inside her. The whistle fell from her mouth on a gasp. Wide-eyed with shock and desire, she gaped at him. Eyes locked on hers, he fumbled with his belt as he finger-fucked her fast and hard. "It doesn't matter, Kate." He ground the words out like gravel from his throat. "You and me. It's what we say that matters."

Her body bowed as he pressed the pad of his thumb to her clit. "Yes."

The rasp of his zipper caught her attention. She tucked her chin to her chest, watching with interest as he worked his jeans and boxer briefs over his hips without missing a stroke. His cock sprang free, thick and hard. She shifted, eager to touch, but Danny wasn't having any of that. He slipped his finger from her wetness and loomed over her, bending his knees to align their bodies. Then he was inside her.

"You feel so good," he said. "Nothing should feel this good."

Gratified as always by the wonder in his observation, she smiled. He pushed her back, oblivious to everything but his obvious need to dominate her, and in that moment, she was more than happy to let him have the upper hand. Even if it meant having the imprint of her red Swingline stapler permanently tattooed on her back. She ran her hands over the mesh polo he wore, felt his heart thrumming hard and fast beneath the placket, and smoothed the clingy knit over his rock-hard abs. The bunched fabric of his jeans abraded her inner thighs. She punished him for his state of half dress by hitching her hips higher and digging the heels of her shoes into the flexing muscle of his bare ass.

"I love making love to you."

A flashbang of heat and hunger flared inside her. The confession was rough and rasping, its content not nearly as shocking as its phraseology. Usually his talk was edgier, dirtier, and used four-letter words that didn't include the letters $L$, $O$, $V$, and $E$. A lump rose in her throat as the sensations he stirred inside her reached fever pitch. He made that hoarse hitching noise that signaled the fraying of his control. He slipped a hand between them, his aim unerring. He circled and stroked her, matching the maddening thrills incited by the combination of hand and cock, kisses and whispers, and love…

Oh God, she loved him, and he loved her, and they were on her desk, for God's sake.

"Kate…"

That helpless croak was all it took. She flew, her fingernails digging into shoulder and scalp, her hips bucking against the unyielding wall of his pelvis, demanding more, taking him deeper, contracting around him until she wrung every shudder from the big, tough ballplayer cradled in her arms. The one who just "made love" to her. On her desk. In broad daylight. With their boss just down the corridor.

She stroked his hair, loathe to break the spell but all too aware that they'd crossed yet another line. "This is insane. We can't do this." She tempered the words with a tender kiss on the top of his head.

"I know. Mike warned me specifically not to do this." He nuzzled her ear. "Maybe that's why I went a little crazy."

"Just a little?" She couldn't repress her grin as he sagged against her. "Nuh-uh. Up, big guy." Balancing precariously on one hand, she gave his shoulder a shove. "I have a stapler in my back, and I'm pretty sure we just desecrated a letter from the president of the NCAA."

"Consecrated," he corrected, lifting his head to look her in the eye. "The man would be ecstatic to see this much action."

"Danny." She gave him another fruitless push. "I wasn't kidding about the stapler."

With a reluctant sigh, he began to disengage. "Sorry."

He put himself back together in the time it took her

to locate her bra. A smirk twisted her lips as she pulled
the lace and satin off Wilt Chamberlain's head. Her staff
had given her the life-sized cutout as a gag gift on her
last birthday. Now, the basketball legend stood sentry in
the corner, his short-shorts exposing miles of leg and his
knowing eyes following her every move. She refused to
flinch. With supposedly twenty thousand women under
his belt, Mr. Chamberlain had no room to judge. Surely
he'd seen things more scandalous than some stray lingerie and a desktop tryst.

Snatching her T-shirt from the floor, she shrugged
into it and yanked it down until it covered her bare ass.
"I don't want to sound like I'm complaining, but…" She
turned to find Danny standing in the same spot, his feet
braced for battle and her pants and panties in his hands.

"But you are," he answered with a terse nod.

Unwilling to give another inch of ground, she untan-
gled her clothes and bent to finish dressing right in front of
him. She managed to get her panties on and one foot into
her pants. Then she felt his fingers trailing lightly over the
spot where the stapler dug into her skin. She froze when
he bent and pressed a tender kiss to the impression.

"I'm sorry. I just…" He let the thought trail off as he
straightened.

Kate thrust her other leg into her pants and yanked
them into place. Pivoting on her heel, she met his gaze.
"You just?"

"I think I'm in… I mean. I…"

Panic flared in his eyes, and for a second, she was
tempted to take pity on him. But that second passed.
She wanted him to say what she thought he wanted to
say. And she wanted him to say it first. She raised both

brows and plastered her best patient-coach expression on her face. One she hadn't needed with the twelve-to fourteen-year-olds that morning, but it looked like Danny would need every bit of encouragement she had if he was ever going to work up the nerve to tell her what she wanted to hear. He opened his mouth, and she drew a shallow breath, holding it deep in her lungs as a damper on her own need to say how she felt about him.

"I'm picking you up at seven," he blurted. "We're going out to dinner. In public."

The air rushed from her lungs. She turned her glare on his back as he strode to the door.

He paused, his hand gripping the handle, but he didn't look back at her. "Wear a skirt. I like looking at your legs."

She spewed the first words that came to mind. "Screw you."

"Just did," he retorted, finally glancing at her over his shoulder. "Loved every second of it, and so did you."

"And you love me," she shot back.

A smile twitched his lips as he opened the door. He stood framed in the doorway as it took hold and grew, stretching those too-lush lips into a wolfish grin. "Yeah, well, I'm going to call it even on that score."

# Chapter 16

Kate drifted through the doors to the athletic complex, certain the perma-smile on her face looked every bit as goofy as it felt but too happy to care. Danny had taken her to Caprice for dinner. The restaurant was not only the home of an award-winning chef, but also a favorite with the locals. The place had been packed when they walked through the doors.

She'd stood inches taller than Danny in the heels she'd worn in retaliation for the skirt demand, but it didn't seem to make much difference to him. He guided her through the crowded tables, his hand warm on the small of her back and his smile wide. They'd endured the drive-bys from friends and fans and even signed a few autographs. Danny didn't seem to mind that she signed three to his one, but he grew impatient with the speculative glances halfway through their appetizer. The second she set her fork aside, he took her hand in his, making it clear they were anything but enemies.

Even Millie's late-night phone call did little to dampen the evening's perfection. If anything, the older woman's raspy harangue added fuel to the fire.

Kate smiled as she strode down the deserted corridor. For the first time since her affair with Danny began, she'd awakened to find him nestled into the pillow beside hers. He looked so delicious in his sleep—an overgrown boy with whiskers speckled with silver and a mouth so kissably soft it wouldn't have shocked her to discover it was outlawed in some conservative states. By unspoken agreement, they'd moved their early-morning workout session from the weight room to the bedroom. But unlike the joyous pillage and plunder of the previous night, their lazy, languid coupling in the gray light of dawn seemed more of a celebration of freedom.

She didn't even mind that he refused to let her out of the bed to brush her teeth. He loved her, morning breath and all. She was his. He was hers. And they didn't care if the whole world knew it.

Her smile grew to the Joker proportions as she tapped the faded plywood Wolcott Warriors sign permanently mounted to the cinder-block wall. Not that she needed extra luck. She'd gotten lucky a total of three times in the past eighteen hours. The wicked smirk Danny wore as he strolled from her front door to his truck told her she was bound to come into more good fortune soon.

She rounded the corner at full speed but slid to a stop when she spotted Jim Davenport leaning against the wall outside her office. He had a copy of that morning's *Sentinel* and his ever-present tablet curled in one hand. An insolent sneer twisted his beigey-bland features into something almost interesting when he pushed away from the wall. Kate opted for offense. No way she was letting a loser like Jim force her into playing defense.

"Jim. How did you get in here?"

He snorted as if her questioning a reporter's ability to gain access to a building closed to the general public this early in the morning should have been obvious. And it was. "I know people," he said with a dismissive shrug. "Other than you, that is."

He unfolded the paper to show a grainy photo printed under the "Out and About" header. "To think I bought all that bullshit you used to spew about preferential treatment. I actually admired how *scrupulous* you were about it." The sneer seeped into his voice as he took a step toward her. "So stupid of me. I should have realized that a good screw would have meant so much more to a woman like you than some pesky scruples."

Kate blinked, unsure how he managed to knock the ball out of her hands so quickly. But she recovered soon enough. Shaking off the commentary on her sex life and whatever the hell he meant by *a woman like you*, she charged at him, over six feet of woman pissed off about having her exceptional mood pissed on.

"What exactly *were* you after, Jim, sex or a story? Because I could never figure that out. Maybe if I'd been a little clearer on what our relationship was, I might have been more forthcoming, but I *owe* you nothing."

The once-over he gave her made her skin creep and crawl. "I wouldn't have minded the sex," he conceded at last. "Lucky for me, I got the story without having to go that far."

A chill raced through her. She froze in place, willing every muscle in her body to be still as she scanned his face, searching for any hint of his next play. Only her rebellious heart dared to move. Each thump against her breastbone felt like a blow. She focused all her energy on holding his gaze and tamping down the swell of panic rising inside her. "What story?"

Jim smirked as he tipped his head to study the photo in the paper. "You and your guy look good together. The sparks fly on camera, but you know that already, don't you? Got you both national airtime. Not that you really needed it, but then again, people tend to forget about women's sports once the highlight reels stop running."

Her hands curled into fists, but she held back the punch she desperately wanted to throw. Her hands were too important to her to risk breaking a knuckle on this bonehead. She was still attempting to summon a scathing retort when he droned on.

"Of course, your little dog and pony show scored lots of free promo for the university. Tell me, Kate, were you the dog or the pony?"

"Get out." She ground the words from between clenched teeth.

Davenport just laughed her off. "Hey, look on the bright side. Your new boyfriend had enough pull to remind NSN that you're still around. They finally shot the fawning feature film you've always wanted, and it's all thanks to Dreamboat Danny."

"That documentary was contracted two years ago," she retorted.

"And they managed to get a crew on campus just two weeks after Coach McMillan's inaugural press conference." He tossed the paper at her feet. The photo of her and Danny holding hands across a table stared up at her. "Well played, Kate. Too bad you won't be able to leverage your boyfriend's notoriety too much longer. You'll have to find some other schmuck to set a pick for you."

Her head shot up. "What's that supposed to mean?"

"It means lover boy is in violation of his contract. The board can fire him today." He raised his eyebrows, daring her to refute the statement.

Hands on her hips, she curled her fingers around

the bone like she did when she was trying to catch her wind. It was the exact same spot Danny grabbed when he pulled her hips high in the air and plunged into her until she screamed his name. Powered by the memory of kisses feathered along her skin, she planted her feet and prepared to take Jim's charge full force.

"We're colleagues. We had dinner."

"You're holding hands," he pointed out.

She tried to match his snide tone but fell short as she fumbled for plausible deniability. "We were shaking hands. He'd just agreed to reinflate all the basketballs in the storage closet each week if I brought him a Cubs hat back from my trip to Chicago."

Jim nodded as if he might actually swallow that load of bullshit and flipped open the cover on his tablet. "Good, 'cause I doubt he'll be wearing the green and gold much longer."

He turned the pad to show a photo of her kissing Danny goodbye that very morning. She wore nothing but a faded Warrior Women T-shirt and a pair of panties that showed as she stretched into the kiss.

"Not that it matters. It seems there are a few programs looking for a new head coach. Now that Samlin popped his redemption cherry, Danny Boy may have other options. We all knew this was a stepping stone, but I guess we thought we'd get to see the guy call one play before he skipped."

Danny had teased her about giving a floor show as she shoved him out the door. She stared at the photo, memorizing every crease in his rumpled slacks. She'd put those pleats in the front of his dress shirt with her very own hands. The green-and-gold Wolcott hat he wore to cover his bedhead was hers. He was hers. Or she thought he was. But for how long?

Squaring her shoulders, she looked Jim straight in the eye. "What story are you looking for, Davenport?"

"Something better than another up close and personal with the NCAA basketball's reigning queen."

His words proved to be a timely reminder of who and what she was. "That's the only story I have to tell."

"I bet I can get a juicier story from your lesser half. I want to know what really went down at Northern and what he expects to get out of coaching a team like Wolcott." He snapped the cover closed on the tablet and brushed past her as if they hadn't shared the world's most anticlimactic courtship. "Tell Coach McMillan I'll be in touch to set up my exclusive."

"He won't give it to you," Kate called after him.

"He'll give it to me," he said without turning back. "You can call the dinner a business meeting if you like, but I can email this little scrap of evidence straight to the chancellor's office." He paused, derision contorting his bland features into something ugly. "Nice panties, by the way. If I'd known you were wearing something that girlie, I might have tried a little harder to get a peek at them."

---

Thirty minutes later, Kate was wedged into Danny's broom closet of an office with a wall of unpacked cardboard cartons boxing them in close. She and the university's athletic director were the only things standing between her stubborn alpha male of a lover and the phone on his desk. He'd threatened to plow through them both to get to it, but Mike hadn't flinched, and Kate figured she was safe enough taking her cues from him.

She crossed her arms over her chest. "Don't give in to him. It's blackmail. He doesn't have the balls to follow through anyway," she asserted, hoping she sounded more confident than she felt.

Danny glared at her. "It's not about the balls. It's the cockblocking that's got him pissed off."

"I don't think so." The tips of her ears warmed at the compliment, but she snorted nonetheless. Casting a sidelong glance at Mike, she shook her head. "If he really wanted to get into my pants, he would have made it a while ago."

Danny's jaw tightened. "He didn't try because he knew you were too much for him."

The AD feigned interest in a box labeled "Special Teams and Other Shit," but the color rose in his face. "All that aside, we can do more damage control internally. I've called Millie. She was scheduled to have a root canal this morning but ended up canceling it." He chanced a small smile. "That alone should get you a little forgiveness for blowing her battle-of-the-sexes strategy."

"Yeah, but now she'll want to exploit the sex," Kate muttered.

"I don't care what either of you say," Danny interjected. "I'm talking to Davenport. Whether he has a hard-on for Kate or for me, it doesn't matter. I'm tired of taking the hits. The media's been coming at me from all sides for the past four years." He turned his full attention on Mike. "I'll talk to the chancellor and the board myself, and I'll do it before I talk to Davenport, but I'm not keeping my mouth shut on this one. I will tell the truth. Whether people choose to believe it is their problem."

Mike pursed his lips as he considered Danny's play-calling. "Enforcing the morality clause is optional," he mused. "It's not automatic termination, so if you can talk a good game with the chancellor—"

"I don't need to talk any game." Danny planted his hands on his hips. "I just need to know if you guys are going to cover my blind side."

"I saw that movie." The words popped out. Kate clamped a hand over her mouth, but it was too late. Both men stared at her.

While Mike wore the expected "are you crazy?" crease between his brows, Danny's eyes danced with affection and amusement. "Then you know one bad hit can end a career."

She blinked, and the common denominator finally seemed so obvious, she was embarrassed to have missed it. All this time, it wasn't about her versus Danny or the two of them in collusion against Mike and the administration he represented. It was the three of them against everyone who didn't eat, sleep, and breathe pure love of a game. Any game.

"Aren't the three of us proof of that?" Kate asked. This time, the guys wore matching looks of puzzlement. "We all took hits that knocked us out of the game. Mine might not have come from a flying tackle, but believe me. When body parts bump from sixteen inches off the floor, the landing is rarely pretty."

"I can't imagine you being anything but pretty," Danny said, and the gentle gruffness in his voice made her knees wobbly.

"I, uh, sorry." Mike made a point of clearing his throat. "Still here."

Kate couldn't spare their boss a glance. Not when Danny was looking at her like that. His steely-blue eyes were deceptively calm, but in their depths, she saw determination burning bright as a gas flame. And there was nothing sexier than a man so cool he smoked like dry ice.

"Don't talk to him. Please," she added a bit belatedly. "Call that cute, little Barbie girl from NSN. She'd love to get to you."

The corner of Danny's mouth twitched, but he gave nothing else away. "Jealous?"

"I could snap her like a twig," she retorted.

"And I am *still* standing here," Mike chimed in.

"Why is that?" Danny asked without taking his eyes from hers. "Don't you think you should be calling the chancellor and prepping him for my call?"

"I never said I'd run interference for you." They both turned at that, and Mike gave them a meaningful glare.

"You will," Danny said quietly.

"Maybe I should just fire you now and save everyone the trouble," the AD said heatedly.

Kate scoffed. "You won't."

"How do you know?"

Mike's expression was hard. Holding his gaze was a challenge, but Kate was a woman born to smash any obstacle that got in her way. That was what she'd lost sight of in the years since her playing career ended. She was the type made to climb mountains to reach her goal. The kind of woman who fought for the man she loved and the life she wanted.

"You won't because firing him would be ridiculous, and you are not a ridiculous man." She turned to face Mike as certainty bloomed inside her. "You'll call the chancellor and anyone else you need to call because you don't want to lose the best thing Wolcott football has had going for it in…forever."

"That isn't saying much," Danny reminded her.

Shifting her attention to the man on the chopping block, she gave him a smile that felt more than a little shaky. "Just hold your horses and wait for Mike to grease the wheels. Don't talk to anyone but the two of us. And I mean anyone."

"Even my mother?" Danny shot back, hackles rising.

"Your mother is okay, but I'd appreciate it if you'd hold off calling your agent until we've had a chance to talk."

"What's that supposed to mean?" Mike asked, instantly defensive.

"It means we all know Danny has other options."

The AD whirled to face his friend. "You're jumping?"

"Only if someone makes me." The two men stood still for an endless moment, eyes locked on each other. Finally, Danny turned and looked directly at Kate. "I don't want to go."

"Then we have to see what we can do to keep you here." Her voice was embarrassingly husky.

She reached over and grabbed a sticky note and pen from the cluttered desk. Biting her lip, she scrawled an amount with a staggering number of zeroes attached to it, folded the paper in half, and thrust it at the AD.

"This is the minimum it'll take to keep me. It's less than Geno Auriemma, but more than everyone else," she said, referring to the winningest coach in women's basketball. "And when I top Geno's record, I'll be coming back at you, so you might as well break it to the chancellor while you're chewing the fat."

Mike goggled at the number on the paper. "I can't... No one—"

She held up a hand to stop his stammering. "Bullshit."

"God, I love you."

Danny's quiet declaration snared her attention. When she turned, she found him staring at her, his face alight with admiration. She clamped her mouth shut. A lifetime of living in locker rooms charged with the hormones of two dozen women had taught her that silence was often the most effective weapon when trying to get one's point across. The seconds crept past, each one ticking like a time bomb as the three of them sized one another up. Finally, she cracked the tension with a grim smile.

"So now we all know where we stand." Shooting a glance at Mike, she yanked open the office door and gulped in some less-testosterone-saturated oxygen. "Danny's not the only one with options, Mike. Make sure the chancellor and the board understand that when you show them that number. I think we can all agree I've earned it."

Mike said nothing, only nodded and tucked the paper into his pocket.

"Get to it, ladies," Kate ordered. "I have a camp to run, and I'm missing my morning session."

Their heads jerked back in unison. Mike scowled, but Danny just guffawed. "Ladies?"

She smirked. "You're right. I shouldn't insult women like that." Stepping into the hall, she started to pull the door closed behind her and paused. Meeting Danny's eyes, she smiled. "Stop by if you get a chance. I love having pretty cheerleaders watch while I work."

———

"See what I'm up against?" Danny asked his old friend. He sighed and shoved his hands into the pockets of his track pants. "I can't walk away this time, Mike. I won't roll over and play dead for you or for this job. Not again. *Never* again."

"Even if she asks you to?"

"Especially if she asks me to." Danny skirted the edge of the desk and dropped into his chair like a bag of rocks. "She doesn't want me to lose this job. I don't want to either, but I can't deny her, and I won't hide behind her skirts."

"She doesn't wear skirts very often."

"Actually, she does. She looks fucking incredible in them."

Mike sank into the lone guest chair as if he was scared it would be yanked out from under him at any time. "Listen, I know where you're coming from. Kate does too, if I'm reading her right." He sat back, caution slowing his movements. "But you can't just pound Davenport into the ground."

"Bet me."

Mike smirked and shook his head. "He knows people around here. Board members, boosters, former and future players. Don't let the size of the pond fool you. It may be small, but it runs deep. He's been in the loop for the better part of a decade, and he hasn't completely given up his hopes of a national spotlight. Don't make yourself his launch pad."

"You know what Tommy did," Danny said, looking his friend in the eye. "If I can handle getting torpedoed by my little brother, I can handle a small-time local reporter. I just wish I knew whether the guy's semistiffy is for me or Kate."

"I think he's after both of you." Mike shrugged. "All the more reason not to be hasty. You might be ready to charge in, but you're not the only high profile at risk here. You have to think about how this could blow back on Kate."

Danny exhaled in a slow, measured gust. "Fine. I'll wait for Millie to spin her magic web, but I'm dealing with Davenport one way or another. Damned if I'll have that pencil-necked geek lurking around Kate's house again. That's just damn creepy."

Mike smiled as he reached for the phone on the desk. "I'll hold him down for you."

―――⌇⌇⌇⌇――

Danny wound the frayed threads of his self-control tight. "We've been over this," he growled.

Millie didn't even blink. She just stared at him over the rims of her zebra-striped reading glasses, unmoved. "And we'll be over it a dozen more times before I let you do an interview." Her lips pursed, and she wrinkled her nose. "Even one with a wanker like Jim Davenport."

"You think he's a wanker too?"

Millie just rolled her eyes. "You won the fair maiden. No need to trample the knave into the ground. Hell, I doubt the guy could even lift one of those jousting things."

Danny grinned, tickled that Kate's friend found it so easy to brush away the competition. "Lance."

"Yeah, well, we'll all concede that your lance is bigger. Now answer the question," she prompted.

He heaved a heavy sigh as he slumped deeper into the chair. "I'm just proud to be a part of the Wolcott athletic program. Coach Snyder has been very helpful and encouraging with my players. I can't wait for the Warrior faithful to see our team in action this fall."

"He'll keep trying to trip you up, trick you into saying something personal about you and Kate," she said, tapping her stylus against the screen of her ever-present tablet.

"I've been down this road before," he reminded her.

Eyebrows arched, she leaned in and spoke slowly but with scalpel-edged precision. "Yes, but the last time, the woman in question decided to ditch you, spill her guts to the press, and marry your little brother." She fixed him with a piercing stare that had Danny squelching the urge to squirm. "I'm pretty sure Kate's not going to go that route, so you need to be prepared to protect her privacy."

"Her privacy is my privacy."

"Yes, well, that's something, isn't it?" She flashed a sweet smile so patently false he nearly burst out laughing. "It's not just her privacy at stake here. You know that, right?"

"I do."

"I mean, her heart is on the line too. Do you get that?" she prodded.

"Mine is too."

His blunt answer seemed to take some of the starch out of her. "That shithead she married hurt her, and now this jerkoff is going to give it his best shot—"

"He'll have to get past me to do it," Danny insisted, cutting her off.

Millie set her precious tablet aside, tugged at the hem of the snug skirt she wore, and rose from her seat. "Fine."

Danny stood too, relieved to be excused from this inquisition so he'd have time to prepare for the next. He had an appointment to meet with Mike and the chancellor at three. An appointment that might make all of Millie's diligent interview preparation a moot point. But he couldn't think that way. He wouldn't. When he'd first been offered the job at Wolcott, he thought the school was a bit of a joke. Now, he never wanted to leave.

He extended a hand toward Millie. "Thank you for all that you've done since I came here."

Without warning, the too-cool PR woman was gone, and he found himself being hugged. Hard. "Break her heart, and I'll break you into pieces so tiny all the king's horses and all the king's men wouldn't even find 'em. You get me?" she whispered in her three-pack-a-day rasp.

"Got you."

Her smile was a little watery when she pulled away, giving his arm an absent pat. "Just figure out a way to get through these next couple of days, and this will all blow over."

Though he admired her optimism, he couldn't quite buy into the possibility of a quick and painless end to all this. "Thanks. It might take more than a couple of days, but I plan to stick."

Millie picked up her tablet and tapped it with one scarlet-tipped finger to wake the screen. "The key is to minimize exposure. Try to keep this local. Trust me," she added, turning her attention to the screen with a grim smile. "There's always a bigger story."

——

Danny's chest felt too tight as he stalked through the empty halls. Back in his closet of an office, he couldn't settle. His skin was itchy. His talk with Millie left him itching to do something. Anything. He tried to busy himself with finalizing the schedules for the upcoming football camps, but Mack pretty much had them lined out.

The minutes slowed to a crawl. Feeling defiant, he unpacked the tower of boxes he'd ignored since the day he'd moved in. The need to see Kate built inside him like a pressure cooker, but she was scheduled for lunch at the Kiwanis Club. He'd spotted blue sky and green grass on the other side of Millie's window. Too twitchy to sit still, he decided to change into his running gear and hit the track. Mike could leave a message on his cell if he needed to. There was just no way he could sit there and wait for the ax to fall.

Mind made up, he started for the door. But the second he twisted the knob, his phone rang. Danny frowned as he answered. His old friend Mike sounded grim as he informed him there was no need to wait until three to come over to the administration building. Chancellor Martin would see him now.

# Chapter 17

"I ADMIT I HAD MY RESERVATIONS WHEN DIRECTOR SAMLIN put your name forward," the chancellor said, folding his hands atop the immaculate leather blotter protecting his antique desk. He peered at Danny over the tops of his half-moon glasses. "I'll also admit that I'm not the least bit shocked that you managed to violate the terms of your contract within mere months of signing." The man's already thin lips tightened to the point where they almost disappeared. "I have been in contact with our legal advisors, and I am told that we would be completely within our rights to terminate your association with Wolcott University."

Danny shifted his weight from one foot to another, swallowing a lump of red-hot anger along with another hunk of his pride. He was being called out on the carpet—literally—by a man he could pound to a pulp, but if he wanted to keep his job and keep Kate, all he could do was stand there and take it. Looking down at the Persian rug beneath his feet, he counted down from five before attempting any response.

"Yes, sir. I believe you are."

Chancellor Martin rose from his glove-leather chair and turned toward the windows that looked down on the campus green. He stared into the distance, letting the silence loom large in the room. Danny glanced at Mike, who simply shook his head.

"Why shouldn't I?"

Danny jumped, startled not so much by the sudden-
ness of the question as the unexpected challenge behind
it. "Why shouldn't you?"

The man turned to look at him, a smug smile curving his lips. "Yes. Why shouldn't I terminate your contract?" He spoke slowly, enunciating each word as if
he were being forced to converse with the village idiot.

Anger and adrenaline zipped through him. Standing
taller, Danny looked the man square in the eye. "Because
I'm the best thing to ever happen to this school's football program. Because I'm your best shot at making this
school something other than the laughingstock of the
Mid-Continental Conference."

Scorn replaced the man's supercilious smirk. "And
you think that's truly important here?"

Mike chose that moment to step in and smooth the
waters. "Chancellor Martin, improving our standing
within the conference would mean an increase in television coverage and increased visibility in recruiting."

The chancellor didn't even glance in his athletic
director's direction. His gaze remained pinned on
Danny. "And those are the things you believe are truly
important here?"

Before Danny could answer, Mike jumped in again.
"All of those things provide more scholarship oppor—"

The chancellor cut him off. "We have alumni who
are more than generous when it comes to providing academic scholarships." At last, he spared Mike a quick
glance. "Let's be clear. You're concerned with providing opportunities for athletic scholarships."

"Yes," Mike replied stiffly. His resigned expression

told Danny this wasn't the first time he'd gone a couple of rounds with his boss on the topic. "Athletic scholarships can be just as important to a school's vitality as their academic counterparts."

Danny cocked his head, fascinated. For the first time since he arrived on campus, he was getting a clear vision of how deep the divide between athletics and academics at Wolcott actually ran.

"Sir, the two are not mutually exclusive," Mike continued. "Many student athletes excel academically. No one expects Wolcott to lower their standards—"

"It will be a cold day in hell," Chancellor Martin interrupted. "Which is why I'm holding you to yours, Mr. McMillan."

The word *mister* hit Danny like a slap in the face.

Chancellor Martin sat back down on his throne and pivoted to look directly at Danny. "I can certainly understand the…attraction you might feel toward Coach Snyder," he said.

"Sir, it's more than attraction—"

The older man held up a hand to stop him. "I do not care to hear the details. It doesn't matter to me if the ghost of Howard Cosell himself came to you in a dream and told you to pursue Coach Snyder." He sniffed as if the notion itself were too much to bear contemplating. "Here at Wolcott, we hold our people to a higher standard, whether they are students, faculty, or staff. We expect our leaders to be beyond reproach, and unlike the leaders of many other institutions of higher education, I do not believe it is wrong for us to do so." He fixed his gaze on a crystal paperweight engraved with the university's motto. "I will not allow the integrity

of Wolcott University to be compromised in any way.
I will not allow these hallowed halls to be tainted by
scandal and sensationalism."

Once again, Chancellor Martin folded his hands and
looked up over the rims of his glasses. "But I am a fair man.
I will give you the opportunity to rectify this situation."

"Rectify the situation?" Puzzled, Danny looked to
Mike, but his friend's expression remained unreadable.
"Rectify it how? Kate Snyder and I are in a relationship.
A wholly consensual relationship, at that," he added
with a meaningful glance at Mike.

As if he'd been waiting for his cue, Samlin stepped
forward. "Coach Snyder has made it clear to me that her
future happiness here at Wolcott may hinge on Coach
McMillan's continued employment as the university's
head football coach."

Chancellor Martin's white eyebrows shot up. "Are
you implying that Coach Snyder intends to blackmail
the university into keeping her…boyfriend on staff?"

"No," Danny snarled.

"I'm simply reminding you that Coach Snyder's contract is currently under negotiation," Mike said impla-
cably. "I've given you her salary expectations. I'm also
letting you know that money alone may not be the decid-
ing factor in bringing those negotiations to a mutually
agreeable close."

"She thinks she can blackmail us into keeping him
on," the chancellor repeated. Turning his full attention to
Danny, he sat a little straighter in his high-backed chair.
"She is wrong," he stated flatly. "Mr. McMillan, you have
until five o'clock this evening to decide whether you wish
to continue your affiliation with Wolcott University."

The statement was bold and blatant, but Danny wasn't about to leave that room until he was clear on the terms and conditions attached to that decision. "So you're saying that I either end my relationship with Coach Snyder or I'm fired?"

Chancellor Martin inclined his head. "Precisely."

Though his insides were churning like a cement mixer, Danny felt the corner of his mouth kick up ever so slightly. Looking his boss's boss directly in the eye, he returned the courtly nod. "And now who's resorting to blackmail?"

He couldn't get out of the wood-paneled office fast enough. Desperate for a gulp of fresh air, he pivoted on his heel and marched out of the office.

---

Mike caught up to him as he hooked a sharp right in the corridor, heading straight for the doors. "Wait," his friend huffed. "Danny, wait!"

He didn't stop or slow or even turn his head. "No need to wait, Mike." He hit the crash bar on the door with both palms, sending it flying. "I told you which I'd choose, and I meant it."

"Just don't…" The athletic director's polished wing-tips skidded along concrete, but Mike hooked a hand around Danny's arm, and his grip was as sure as ever. "Don't do anything you'll regret."

Danny turned on his friend. "The only thing I'd regret would be losing Kate."

"You seem so sure about that. How can you be so sure?"

Danny searched his old friend's expression but found only genuine concern and more than a little perplexity.

A spear of warmth sliced through him. Smiling down at Mike, he shook his head, letting a little of his own wonderment show through the bravado that propelled him out of the chancellor's office.

"We're not twenty anymore, Mikey," he said gently. "I've had enough of what I don't want to know a good thing when I've got it." A rueful smile twitched his mouth. "Jobs are easy to get. Women like Kate are one of a kind."

"But jobs like this…" Mike had the good grace to grimace when Danny's brows lifted in an unspoken challenge. "D-one jobs, I mean." He paused for a second, then threw his hands up in frustration. "Where else are you going to have a chance to make an impact like you can here? You're already having an impact," he asserted. "And yeah, the program might not be a coach's dream, but look what you've done in just a couple of months."

"I choose Kate." Damn, it felt good to say that. The truth. His truth, simple and easy. Feeling lighter than he had in weeks, Danny started toward the athletic center.

"But even if you choose her, you lose her." Mike hustled to keep step. "No matter what she says, Kate won't leave here. This is her home. Her house. She built this place." He jogged a few steps, then turned to face Danny, doing a little hop-skip to stay a stride ahead. "I know what she said, but Danny, do you really think she'd leave it all for you?"

For the first time since he walked out of Martin's office, Danny's step faltered.

Of course, Mike was sharp enough to catch his hesitation. "I know you took this job just to get a toehold, but coaching football at Wolcott is pretty much like being handed a blank check. You've got guys like Dick Donner waving wads of money around, and all they want to see is some marginal improvement." He stopped walking and planted his hands on Danny's shoulders, bringing him to a halt as well. "You know the expectations that come with other D-one coaching jobs. You won't get this opportunity anywhere else."

Danny eyed his friend closely. "Do you really think I don't know that?"

"If you let Martin shit-can you, no one else will touch you." Mike's jaw tightened. "We both know any interest will dry up."

Shaking his head, Danny let a slow smile unfurl as he savored the vehemence of Mike's argument. He had to admit it was damn nice to have someone fighting for him for a change. "You know as well as I do that's bullshit. There's always someone willing to scrape the bottom of the barrel."

"But that doesn't change the fact that you're tying you career choices to a woman who has every option."

"That's exactly the point," Danny shot back, jumping on the one bit that neither could dispute. Kate had choices, and she chose him. "Who says she has to follow me? What if I follow her?"

"Jesus Christ, listen to yourself!"

"I am," Danny said calmly. "You're the one who's not getting it."

"There's not a whole lot to get. Even if she were willing to move on, what makes you think you'll end up even close to each other? What then? You looking forward to Saturday nights spent having Skype sex with your kick-ass girlfriend?"

Danny refused to be ruffled. Swallowing his impatience, he stared down one of the few friends who'd stuck with him through thick and thin. "Kate loves me."

Mike pushed a hand through his hair as he exhaled his exasperation. "Points for that, but this is one of those instances where the love of a good woman isn't going to save you."

Clapping his old friend on the shoulder, Danny shrugged. "I appreciate the effort, but I'm not looking to be saved."

"At least take the time. Think about it. Talk to Kate about it," Mike implored. "Maybe you can agree to... cool things down—"

"Hell no."

"—just for a while."

"Not going to happen."

Mike growled his frustration. "Talk to Kate," he repeated, teeth clenched. "At least she has some sense."

Danny treated his friend to a self-deprecating smirk. "Not as much as you'd think, given the fact that she fell for me."

"Yeah, well, I'm hoping she'll snap out of it when she figures out she might get saddled with another loser head-coach wannabe."

Danny's head snapped back like he'd just been horse-collar tackled. Mike's earnest brown eyes filled with horror as the words sank in.

"Oh, man," Mike murmured. "I'm sorry. That was low."

Biting the inside of his cheek to keep from lashing out, Danny took a step back and cut a wide swath around the athletic director, his eyes fixed on the athletic

complex at the far end of the quad. "Yeah. You're right.
I'll be sure to do that."

—◦◦◦—

Danny was relieved to find the track empty when he
stepped out of the locker room but surprised to see members of the marching band stomping all over the infield.
The kids were dressed in shorts and tees—a far cry from
the heavy, dark uniforms they'd wear in the fall. Instead
of carrying their instruments, they each held an electronic tablet. He paused beside the bleachers to stretch,
his curiosity piqued by the odd syncopation of their
steps. From his vantage point, they looked like a writh-
ing mass of bodies, but judging from the ecstatic cry of,
"Yes! That's it! Back to the transition!" that boomed
from the PA system, something must have worked when
viewed from above.

He straightened from a hamstring stretch in time to
see the group disintegrate into even more chaos. Spotting
a few of the drumline guys standing off to the side, he
started toward them at a trot. "What's going on, fellas?"

The guys jumped, but then one of them hitched his
harness a little higher and smiled. "Hey, Coach. We're
just practicing some new choreography."

Danny's brow puckered. He didn't normally pay
much attention to the nonathletic elements of the game,
but he'd always appreciated the marching band. Though
some of these kids might never have touched a ball in
their lives, they were an integral part of the college football experience.

"Don't you guys get the summer off?"

The boy smiled and shrugged. "Some of it. We have

competition in two weeks, then we'll come back early to start rehearsals for the halftime shows."

Danny affected a fierce scowl. "Is that so? Well, I guess I'll need to get those slackers on my team back for two-a-days even earlier. I can't have the band running circles around the defensive line, can I?"

The boy snorted and tapped his sticks against the rim of his drum. "Yeah, Coach, better get 'em back."

Nodding to the two others, Danny shook out his arms and legs. "Well, I'd better get to it, or you'll be running over me too. Give me a little something to set the tempo, will ya?"

One of the other boys grinned and started to tap out a beat so slow, a metronome would have outpaced it.

"Christ, I'm not that old," Danny growled, and he set off at a respectable trot. The drummers soon caught on, and after he circled the track once, their beat forced him to pick up the pace.

It took a full mile to fall into just the right cadence. His rhythm section was called back to duty on the next lap, and he loped along for another mile. It pained him to admit it, but the braces he wore on both knees actually did provide more stability. By the time he passed the five-mile mark, he was drenched in sweat and flying high. When he passed the bleachers again, a pretty, dark-haired lady dressed in a pale-blue pantsuit let loose with a wolf whistle that would have done a construction crew proud.

He slowed to a trot but didn't double back until he reached the curve. By the time he made it to Kate, she was leaning against the rail on the bleachers. A hint of white lace showed just above the top button on her suit.

He wanted to dive in and see exactly how much lace there was.

"Whistling at a guy like that can get you into trouble," he huffed as soon as they were within talking distance.

She gave him that smug Mona Lisa smile that made him want to rip the buttons right off her neat little jacket. She leaned over and whispered, "Maybe I'm looking for trouble."

"Well, then you came to the right place." The last thing he wanted to do was tell her what went down in the chancellor's office. Hoping to distract her, he lifted the hem of his shirt and blotted the sweat from his forehead. Sure enough, he caught her ogling when he let the shirt drop, so he pressed his advantage. "You free tonight?"

"For a hot date?"

"Yep."

She gave a regal nod and straightened to her full height. "I just have to decide what to wear."

"I vote for nothing."

"One vote doesn't make it a consensus."

Bracing his forearms on the metal crossbar, he leaned in to give his calf muscles a good stretch. "Are we having this relationship by committee?"

"Seems that way sometimes. How much oxygen did you have to give Mike after I left?"

"I don't kiss and tell."

"Avery wants to know if there was mouth-to-mouth involved, but I don't think you should answer that. I think she's just being a pervert."

"I think so too."

"I have a surprise for you."

"Does it involve what you will or will not be wearing to dinner?"

"Not in the least."

"Okay, but just for the record, I don't see myself ever changing my vote."

"Ever?"

Planting the sole of his sneaker on a rusty metal bar, he lunged for the rail where her hands rested and grabbed hold. The muscles in his shoulders, back, and arms trembled as he hauled his bulk up until his chin cleared the rail. "Never," he growled.

"Show-off."

"A guy has to showboat when there's a pretty girl watching."

"Then you must be worn out."

"I only do it for you."

Her lips curled into that too-tempting smile, but she stepped back. "I have to get changed and get some work in with the girls. Ty's been covering some time for me, but I'm usually pretty hands-on with my camps."

He stole a glance at her. She didn't know he'd met with the chancellor. Couldn't know. If she did, she would have been all over him about it. But the meeting wouldn't remain a secret for long. Millie most likely had the man's phones tapped and office bugged. He couldn't put it off any longer.

"Mike and I met with Chancellor Martin. They're giving me until five o'clock today to decide."

She froze. "Decide what?"

"You or the job."

Kate gasped, then exhaled a soft, "Oh, Danny."

"I already told them I choose you."

She shook her head so hard, her hair tangled in her lashes and the glossy lipstick she wore. "Danny, no."

Unable to resist, he pulled himself up for a kiss, sealing those dark strands into place. "Kate, yes."

She gripped the rail so hard, her knuckles turned white. Dropping back to the track, he ran his palm over them, letting the sharp ridges wedge their way into the soft center. "My agent is working on it. I have options, but giving you up isn't one of them."

"Can't you try to stall them? Maybe Millie can work some magic," she urged.

"She'll be busy prepping for the press conference."

She blinked. "What press conference?"

Giving her a tired smile, he shrugged. "The one where they spew some bullshit about how this wasn't the fit we were looking for and that we've mutually agreed I should move on down the road." Wiping his brow with his sleeve, he squinted up at her. "You want to watch at your place or mine?"

Her jaw tightened. "That's it? You're just quitting?"

Danny stiffened. "I'm not quitting. I'm being fired. Again." Planting his hands on his hips, he hit her with his best "my decision is final" glare. It bounced off her like a jump shot with no air under it.

"We'll see about that."

"Just what do you think you're going to do?"

Kate balled her fists and dug them into the sweet spot just above her hip bones. God, he loved that spot. Loved putting his hands in that exact place and holding her tight as he sank into her.

"Believe it or not, some people think I have a little pull around here."

The sneer in her tone yanked him straight out of his daydream. "Kate, I don't want you doing anything to jeopardize your negotiations."

"They're my negotiations. I'll jeopardize them if I damn well want to."

He opened his mouth, then snapped it shut again. Arguing wouldn't get him anywhere with her. Instead, he leapt for the rail again, this time using every bit of momentum he could muster to haul himself over it. The soles of his shoes slapped the aluminum decking so hard the impact rang out, reverberating through his body. Kate swayed toward him. Instinctively, he cupped her elbow to steady her.

She stared at him blankly for a moment. Then looked down at their feet.

A smile tugged at the corners of Danny's mouth when he saw that he once again stood toe-to-toe with his warrior. And as usual, she wasn't about to back down.

He tried to clear the lump from his throat before he spoke, but his voice still sounded gruff and embarrassingly emotional. "I don't want you to sacrifice one scrap of what you've worked for because of me."

She stared back at him. "I don't intend to."

"Then what are you planning?"

Wetting her lips, she gazed past him at the marching band on the field. "I guess it's time to round up our team."

"Our team?"

The enigmatic smile she wore matched the calculating gleam in her eye. "I have to get back and make my campers happy. Meet me at my place at five."

"Your place?"

"You should know it by now. You're practically a

squatter," she said, lifting both brows in challenge as she eased away.

"I can't believe I'm asking this, but…what exactly are we going to do at your place?"

"Work on strategy."

"Strategy? There is no—"

She silenced him with a finger pressed to his lips. "I want to see how you are with the pick and roll outside the bedroom."

He narrowed his eyes. "You think I can't play ball?"

Her smile turned saucy, and she flicked her hair over her shoulder, like she'd scored a point off him. "Oh, I know you can. But the buzzer hasn't sounded yet, Coach."

# Chapter 18

Danny opened and closed the nightstand. LeBron/ Michael/Magic/Kareem hit the back of the drawer with a dull thud, and the man with the real dick smirked. That was the most action Kate's trusty vibrator had seen in a long time. He'd made damn sure of that. Sighing, he let his eyes skim over her long legs as he turned back to the television screen. The sound was muted, which was just as well. He was getting enough of an earful from his agent.

Traveling the path he'd worn in the polished hardwood, he headed for the bedroom door once more. On the threshold, he turned back. This was his favorite view. Kate, stretched out on her bed, wearing nothing but a faded athletic department T-shirt and a little popcorn butter on her chin. She had a sheaf of papers in her lap, but he didn't want to think about those. He didn't need to. That's why he paid the guy currently reaming him out a hefty percentage of his salary.

"I know, Gene."

He spoke the words by rote. He'd been chanting them like a mantra through three phone calls. Yes, he knew another scandal might make him unemployable, but there was no scandal here. He and Kate were both legal and unattached. There was no glaring age difference, no question of staff/student ethics or any conflict concerning parties in a position of authority over one another.

Kate may be able to kick his ass in the record books and on the basketball court, but that had no bearing on his ability to lead a football team. It also helped shore up his ego that he knew exactly where and how to touch her to get her to admit he was The Man.

He stepped back into the room. On screen, the NSN anchors flapped their lips. A live feed of the Wolcott University media room showed only a blank backdrop printed with the Warrior logo. The ticker scrolling along the bottom of the screen informed viewers that they were awaiting a special announcement from Wolcott Athletic Director Mike Samlin. Danny scowled at Jeff Sommers's ultra-high-tech media center. He couldn't help but wonder if Kate and her ex had spent an equally disheartening evening awaiting the announcement of Ty Ransom as the school's men's basketball coach.

"Tell him to look at the second clause in section three again," Kate said without looking up.

"Danny, are you listening to me?" his agent demanded.

"I know, Gene," he answered automatically, then turned toward Kate. "Ask him to what?"

"I want him to read through the part about the buyout clause again. They might choose to pay you off," Kate answered.

"You know," Gene scoffed, the two of them talking over one another. "You can't possibly know. I just told you."

"Do they have to buy me out regardless of the reason for termination?" he asked his agent.

"There's a buyout, and if they feel like keeping things cordial and low profile, they may pay part of it, but you're in violation, so they can terminate for cause, and you get nothing," Gene replied, his answer short to the point of rudeness. "Now, did you hear me about San Jose?"

At last, Gene's information clicked. Danny turned away from Kate and her high-definition television screen. "San Jose? As in California?"

Gene blew out an exasperated huff. "Yes, the last time I checked, San Jose was in California."

The papers crinkled again, but this time, he didn't dare look at Kate. "San Jose is interested?"

"They've put out feelers." Gene paused, and Danny could almost hear the smugness rolling off the man. "Idaho too."

"Boise State?" Danny's heart began to thrum. He might have to buy some special sunglasses to deal with the glare off that blue turf, but he'd—

"Idaho," Gene repeated more forcefully. "As in the Vandals."

"Oh." Danny's stomach dropped, but his heart continued its drumline cadence. "Nothing closer to home?"

"Home?" His agent repeated the word as if Danny had spoken in a foreign tongue. "What home?"

"Here," Danny said, spinning on his heel and heading for the bedroom door on the first leg of what he was sure would be an epic bout of pacing. "Close to where I'm at now." He paused on the threshold, closing his eyes as he awaited the answer he knew in his gut was coming.

"No. The only other nibble I've had was from UTEP, but I figured you weren't hot to move back to the Rio Grande valley."

"Not so much."

"And what makes you so sure Kate Snyder will go wherever you go? I get that the two of you are all cuddled up and shit, but unless you're packing a magic wand in your pants, I don't see her following you to the ends of the earth. Tough talk or not, she's a lifer, Danny."

As if taking her cue, Kate whispered, "It's starting."

Danny turned back in time to watch her exchange the copy of his contract she'd been dissecting for the remote control. A pair of green reading glasses with gold emblems on the earpieces held her hair back from her face. Green and gold. Warrior glasses. Her expression was all business as she pointed the control at the television and unmuted the sound.

Mike Samlin stood at the podium, his expression solemn, the lines bracketing his eyes and mouth more pronounced than ever. "On behalf of the Wolcott University administration, I thank you in advance for your time. I'll be reading a brief statement, but I will not be taking any questions at this time."

Danny ended the call with his agent without a goodbye and sank onto the edge of the bed.

"It was with high hopes and great expectations that we announced the addition of Danny McMillan to the Wolcott University athletic program. In the short time he has been on campus, Coach McMillan has already had a positive impact on our student athletes and staff. Unfortunately, circumstances have come to light which have placed our continued relationship with Coach McMillan in jeopardy. As of this afternoon, the administration has decided to release Danny McMillan from his contract. We will begin reviewing new candidates for the position immediately. On behalf of our players and personnel, we ask that the media refrain from speculation that may be damaging to either Wolcott University or Danny McMillan. Thank you for your time and your ongoing support."

With that, Mike folded the statement in half and turned from the podium. He almost made it out of camera range before one of the press corps shouted, "Is this because of his relationship with Kate Snyder?"

Kate groaned. "Oh, you horse's ass."

A turbulent moment of confusion followed as the cameraman swiveled to find the reporter who'd asked the question. Within seconds, Jim Davenport's supercilious smirk filled the screen. Danny shook his head, the urge to laugh bubbling up inside him. He had to hand it to the weasel. The man had his scoop, and he wasn't about to give it up. But the moron squashed whatever grudging respect he might have mustered when he opened his big, fat mouth again.

"He's been seen leaving her house in the early morning hours. Doesn't Coach McMillan have a morals clause written into his contract? Seems to me there's no need for further investigation. That is unless you're hoping for video evidence."

Danny was off the bed like a cannonball, his fingers curled into fists. "I'm gonna break that fuckin' stick insect in half."

"Ignore him. It's his moment in the sun." Pressing the mute button once more, Kate pulled her reading glasses down and picked up the contract. "Jim Davenport just delivered the only line of color commentary anyone will ever hear from him. Sad to be a one and done."

Danny swung a hand in the direction of the television. "Don't you want to hear what they're saying?"

She shrugged. "I've heard all I need to hear."

"Yeah. I got fired."

Kate went back to perusing the codicils and clauses as if she found legalese the most fascinating thing in the world. "Not exactly a surprise." She nodded to the television. The cameramen kept their lenses trained on Mike's retreating back as he left the podium. "He doesn't want you gone any more than I do."

Danny swallowed the lump of uncertainty balling at the base of his throat. "I may end up on the West Coast."

"I can't really see that happening," she said distractedly. "You're not the granola type."

He dropped down on the bed, purposefully jostling her to get her undivided attention. "I'm serious, Kate. The only interest I have so far is in California or Idaho. What happens then?"

She didn't answer.

Terrified by her silence and unable to think of a thing to say, he looked up in time to see dozens of the candid shots Millie'd leaked to the press over the past couple of months flashing on the screen. The feed scrolling across the bottom included the words *publicity stunt* and *media sensation*. Finally, NSN's Greg Chambers shook his head as the network showed the grainy photo Davenport had snapped of him kissing Kate goodbye at her door. Danny didn't need to be an expert lip reader to catch the anchor's incredulous, "Is this for real?"

Danny grabbed the remote and jabbed the power button. The screen went dark, and the soft hum of the surround-sound speakers filled the room. "Well, that's the nail in the coffin."

"What is?"

"The kiss. Mike and I managed to leave the bit about Davenport's pictures out of the conversation with Chancellor Martin."

The words were barely out of his mouth when his phone rang. Danny glanced at the display, then held it up to show Kate the caller's name.

Swiping his thumb across the screen, he managed a brief, "Hey."

"I'm afraid I've been instructed to contact Gene to let you know we'll be terminating your contract for cause," Mike said in a stiff, formal tone. "The termination papers will be drawn up within forty-eight hours."

Danny heard the hitch in his old friend's voice. "Yeah. I caught that. Hey, thanks for trying, man. For everything."

"I wish…" Mike paused for a second. "Well, I was going to say I wish things were different, and in this case I do, but only some things."

His friend's circular reasoning made him smile. "I'm gonna pretend that made sense."

"Be happy. That's what I was trying to say." Mike chuckled. "But I guess you already made that choice."

"Yeah, I did." Danny glanced at Kate and found her watching him with a worried frown. Shifting closer, he pressed a tender kiss to the lines between her brows, then turned his attention back to the call. "I'll be in tomorrow to clean out my office."

Mike snickered. "Should be fairly easy, since you never unpacked."

Danny thought about the cardboard boxes he'd methodically emptied and flattened that afternoon. So much for his rebellion. It was a damn good thing he hadn't been ballsy enough to haul the pile of cardboard out to the Dumpster. All he needed was a roll of tape and he'd be good to go. Again. "Piece of cake."

Flashing a weak smile in Kate's direction, he ended the call. "They'll have the papers ready in the next forty-eight hours."

Pink lips set in a thin line, she nodded once. "Two days. Got it."

"Kate, sweetheart…" He tucked her hair behind her ear and ran his knuckles down the soft slope of her cheek. "It's done."

"Nothing's done until the papers are signed." The gold flecks in her eyes shone warm but dull, like the ancient track-and-field trophies tucked at the back of the lesser display cases.

"I want to ask you a question," he said.

Her startled gaze met his. Those pretty pink lips parted. He saw the hope flare in her eyes and wanted to gut himself with the ballpoint pen she'd been using to mark up his contract. More than anything, he wanted to cash in on that unspoken invitation. Right there and then, his future—or lack thereof—be damned.

A marriage proposal tingled on the tip of his tongue, but he pressed his lips together until the urge passed. He didn't know exactly where the impulse had come from, but he knew he couldn't blurt "marry me" and expect her to jump at the offer. He needed to think things through. He needed to have a plan. But the realization that she was it for him wasn't surprising. He'd been feeling this… rightness…since the moment they first touched. And now he was about to lose it. Lose her. No, he needed a more solid play. She deserved more than a Hail Mary proposal from a guy who didn't know where he'd land next.

"What question was that?"

Danny hesitated only a moment. He might not have been prepared to throw for the win, but he could test her defensive line. "The West Coast," he managed at last, quirking a brow. "California? Idaho? Would you consider going?"

She wet her lips and looked down at the papers in her lap, her disappointment palpable. "You said San Jose or Boise State?"

"University of Idaho. Not Boise."

Like a switch had flipped, the teasing light flashed in her eyes. "Wow. Not even Boise? You really are in trouble, aren't you?"

"Hey, it beats Rio River College." He tried to fix her with a stern stare, but he couldn't hold on to it. "Yeah, I guess I am."

"I'll have Jonas test the waters in the Bay Area." She wrinkled her nose, tapped the rumpled printout of the contract, then picked it up and tossed it to the floor. "But I have to tell you, I'm not giving up yet. I like my house, I like my bed, and I like the way you look in it."

Danny allowed her to push him back onto the pillows she pummeled and plumped each morning. "You're kind of a female chauvinist pig, you know?"

"Oh, I know." She tossed her hair over her shoulder. "It's one of the things you like best about me."

"Damn straight it is." Grinning up at her, he counted down from three in his head, then flipped her over with practiced ease. Pinning her hands high above her head, he leaned in close and dropped his voice to a whisper. "But right now, it's time to show your man a little sympathy and consolation. Stand by me like a good little woman should."

"I've never been called little, but I'll give it my best shot." Kate raked one hand through his hair and slid the other down his belly. "Oh, poor baby," she purred, stroking him through the slick nylon of his gym shorts. "Does this make it better?"

He closed the distance between them, capturing her lips and stretching the kiss out slow and deep. Her body bowed beneath his, and he took the kiss deeper, hoping she could taste the promises he wanted to make. Trusting she'd choose him the way he'd chosen her. Praying she'd never want to stop touching him. Wanting him.

Loving him.

---

Kate paced her office from window to door and back again. The next time she made the turn, Millie rolled the desk chair over just enough to stick a leg out and block her path.

"I'm gonna put you in a kennel if you don't stop it," she threatened.

Kate had to admire her friend's powers of concentration. Millie'd pulled the whole maneuver off without tearing her eyes from the computer screen. Tapping a bright-coral nail to the glass, she drew Kate's hop-scotching attention to the monitor.

"This is still my favorite," Millie said. Kate squinted at the photograph someone snapped the day she'd crashed Danny's introductory press conference. Her hair flew wild around her head, but her jaw was set and her eyes were locked on her quarry. "You look like you belong on the prow of a ship."

Unimpressed with her friend's idea of a compliment, Kate rolled her eyes. "Great. Just what I was shooting for that day."

"She'd need bigger boobs." Avery didn't look up from the papers in her lap. With a practiced flick of her wrist, she circled a section of text. "No such thing as a flat-chested figurehead. You know those suckers were carved by men."

"Thanks for that," Kate said with a snide smile. "Reading anything good?"

Avery held up her hand. "I'm not done yet."

Kate turned to stare out at the quad. The space should have been deserted, but it seemed that every sports reporter who wasn't covering baseball was on campus, hoping to catch her and Danny together. She was all for giving them what they wanted. After all, Danny was being terminated. They had little to lose. But he wouldn't do it. For once, he was the one reminding her about her own contract negotiations and playing it cautious, claiming they needed at least one steady income to keep them both in Tiger Balm.

She glanced at the contract in Avery's lap, hoping her friend might use her experience as a former paralegal to confirm what Kate already suspected. They might have a way out of this mess.

Maybe. Possibly. With a little luck, a giant leap of faith, and some skillful loophole diving.

She hadn't said anything to Danny that morning. He had his hands full as it was. His agent was due in on a midmorning flight. His voicemail had gone to overload within minutes of Jim Davenport's accusation. He'd come in early to beat the press, wanting to talk to Mike face-to-face one last time. Now, he was down the hall, packing his things. For either California or Idaho.

He'd asked her a question, but it was one she didn't want to answer.

Which was ridiculous, considering she'd threatened to do exactly what he was asking her to do. She was already putting her career on the line for a man. One who shouldn't have any claim on her but somehow did from the minute she met him. After just one night with Danny, she knew they were right together. She knew it the same way she could tell if a shot was good the second it left her fingertips.

But she'd been wrong about one thing. She'd thought he was going to propose to her when he said he wanted to ask her a question. And in that magical moment, every princess fantasy she'd stowed deep down inside her sprang to life. It was a damn good thing she'd been speechless.

Idaho, for cripes' sake. What does someone say to that?

But oh, she'd wanted him to pop the question. She'd wanted a poofy dress and a tiara and a bevy of woodland creatures to help her dress. She'd wear high heels so she'd tower over him as they said their vows. He'd like that, perverse as he was. She wanted a real wedding this time. She didn't want to pretend fifteen minutes in a judge's chambers was good enough for what she felt for him.

But dreams and reality didn't always play out that way.

Being the industrious woman she was, she knocked her man out with a vigorous round of screw-'em-all sex, waited until he started to snore, then slipped out from under his tree trunk of a leg to reclaim the pages of the contract they'd tossed aside. Closeted in the bathroom, she read and reread the morals clause until she could recite it. If her hunch was right, a quickie ceremony at the courthouse might be just the ticket. And she'd do it for him. Otherwise, she might be saying hi-de-ho to Idaho soon.

She'd lain awake until he crept out of bed and shuffled off to the shower. Then she'd called Millie and Avery. They might not be cute, furry woodland creatures, but they would help her get her man.

Avery tossed the contract aside with a dramatic sweep of her arm. Pages fluttered to the ground all around her.

The commotion was startling enough to capture Millie's full attention at last. Peering at the smug bohemian seated in the guest chair over the rims of red-polka-dotted glasses, she quirked an inquiring brow. "Well?"

The stretched neckline of Avery's tie-dyed T-shirt slipped off her shoulder as she heaved the world's largest sigh. "As much as I hate to say it, I think you're screwed."

Kate's stomach plummeted to her feet. "There's nothing I can do?"

"Just the one thing," Avery said with grim twist of her lips. "You're gonna have to buy the cow if you wanna keep him."

Millie yanked her glasses from her nose and fixed their friend with her hardest stare. "For once in your life, can you cut the crap and just give a straight answer?"

Avery rolled her eyes, then turned her full attention to Kate. "The clause specifically states 'inappropriate or immoral relationship.'" She shrugged, and her T-shirt slipped a little more. "If you buy into all that bogus morality crap created by misogynists and supported by a patriarchal establishment, there's nothing *inappropriate* or *immoral* about marriage."

Millie barked a triumphant laugh. She glanced up at Kate, her eyes sparkling with anticipation, then turned back Avery. "Thank you for not using air quotes."

"Air quotes are always inappropriate and immoral," Avery answered. Beaming up at Kate, she cocked her head. "So…think you'll take the bull by the horns?"

Kate froze, her lips pursed and her gaze fixed on the rack of shoes mounted to her wall. She never left the pair Danny gave her here. They were too important to her. No, even though she had room on the wall for another half dozen pairs, she carried those sneakers back and forth each day in her gym bag, afraid to let them out of her care.

Was that why she wanted to marry Danny? Was it just a way of pinning him to her side? If she didn't marry him and the administration followed through, would she be able to go too? Wolcott had always been her home. This was the place where she first became a champion. It was her safe haven when her playing days ended far too soon.

"Is it crazy?" she asked her friends.

"Yes," Avery answered without hesitation.

"Shut up, you," Millie admonished.

Avery sighed and pushed her hair back from her face. "Listen, I don't believe a piece of paper is proof that two people love each other more than anyone else, but I have to admit it might be nice to see a shotgun wedding for the purpose of saving the *guy's* reputation for once."

"Do you love him?" Millie asked, her trademark rasp unnaturally gentle.

The answer shot out of Kate's mouth like a bullet. "Yes."

Smiling, Avery stood and smoothed her gauzy skirt. "I'll go buy a bouquet of whatever the grocery store has." She turned to Millie. "Judge Baxter still a season-ticket holder?"

"Will be till the day he dies," Millie answered, reaching for the phone.

Bobbing a decisive nod, Avery gripped Kate by the arms and propelled her toward the door. "Go line up your groom. The clock is ticking on those forty-eight hours."

Without another word, Kate yanked open her office door and sprinted down the hall. She dodged a couple of media types snapping pictures of the trophy cases, lifted a hand in acknowledgment as she zipped past Mack standing in the doorway to the bullpen, a smug smile creasing his face, and skidded around the corner that led to Danny's closet of an office.

"Danny!" She caught the doorframe with her fingertips and let the laws of physics rein in her momentum. "I've got to ask…"

Kate trailed off as she scanned the tiny space. It was empty save for the sea of cardboard boxes cluttering the floor. The walls were covered in old team plaques and team photos. Decor that hadn't been there the day before. The wall beside his desk was eaten up by a giant metal rack exactly like the one that hung in her office. But instead of shoes, Danny had ball caps—dozens of them. Each sporting a different team's logo or mascot. Every one with the bill curved just so. Even the one with the rattlesnake appliqued to the front.

Closing her eyes, Kate curbed her impatience by conjuring the memory of the morning kiss Jim Davenport's photo captured. The warmth of Danny's mouth. The morning gravel in his voice. Those rough, ready hands curling the brim of his hat, getting it just how he liked it before pulling the visor down low over his brows.

Too late. They'd been caught. Game over.

"Hey."

She turned and found the man of her daydreams slowing his steps as he approached, his hands buried deep in the pockets of his jeans. "Hi."

The corners of his mouth twitched. "You come by to help me pack?"

Kate shook her head, trying to dislodge the lingering memory of that early-morning kiss, wishing she could shake off her nerves. Inhaling through her nose, she focused on him. Only him. That craggy, handsome face was her backboard, his smile the square she could bank on if she needed to, but the light in his eyes was her goal. She stared deep into their electric-blue depths, knowing it was time to take her shot.

"No. I came to ask you to marry me."

# Chapter 19

EVERY TIME DANNY HAD HIS LEGS KNOCKED OUT FROM under him, he'd always crashed to the ground. But the moment the quasi-proposal popped out of Kate's mouth, he started flying high. It proved he hadn't been crazy to make that extra stop after dropping Gene off at the hotel. While his agent was deploying career damage control, Danny focused on kicking his own ass into line. Staring at the breathless, beautiful woman standing stock-still in his office, he knew he'd made the right decision. Even if it came twelve hours too late.

Only a fool would think a woman like Kate would just up and move without a guarantee. A contract. A promise that he was in it for the long haul. Even if they ended up in Idaho. He smiled, picturing her in hiking boots and a cowboy hat. Maybe a plaid shirt with the snap pockets on the chest. Knotted at the waist. Just above her shorts. Not athletic shorts, but the khaki short-shorts that hiking, outdoorsy women who lived in the Pacific Northwest wore, at least in his mind.

"Or not," she said tartly, then tried to push past him.

"Hey! No, wait." He caught her around the waist and pulled her close against him. "I haven't given you my answer yet."

"I take it back."

He grinned, shifting to the left just enough to make their bodies align. "You can't. It's against the rules."

"There are no rules," she retorted.

She put up a token resistance. He'd give her credit for that. And hot damn, the way she wiggled felt good. So good. And right. Things had been…sticky between them the night before, and not in the usual way. She'd expected a proposal, and he'd flubbed it. Then he was stupid enough to think that by letting his actions speak for him in the language of sex, he'd somehow prove how much he loved her. It wasn't until she'd slipped out of the bed to hide in the bathroom that he realized sometimes a guy just had to say the words.

"Yes." The furrow he loved so much formed between her finely arched brows. She opened her mouth to speak, but before she could get another word out, he kissed the frown away. "Yes, I want to marry you."

Kate blinked. "You do?"

"Yes. Yes, I do." He brushed her hair back, letting the sleek strands slide through his fingers. "And for the record, I wanted to ask you last night."

She cocked her head, her eyes gleaming gold with challenge. "And you chickened out?"

Danny laughed, more than happy to concede the point to her. "I chickened out." He trailed his thumb over her cheekbone, then tipped her jaw up a fraction of an inch. "You're so much braver than I am."

"About time you realized that."

This time, he didn't rise to take the bait. "I've known it all along. That's why I fell for you. And exactly why you're way too good for a guy like me."

"Wow, you really *have* seen the light."

Refusing to play along, he held her gaze. "I'm unemployed. Every relationship that's meant anything to me has failed spectacularly. I can't tell you where I'll end up, but I'm enough of a selfish bastard to ask you to give up everything you've built to come with me."

"Danny—"

"You deserve so much more, Kate, but you offered, and I'm gonna take it." Releasing her abruptly, he dropped down on one knee and reached into his pocket. She gasped, and her hand flew to her mouth the second she saw the ring box. "I was a fool to blow my chance to ask you last night, but I'm not stupid enough to choke twice. Yes. My answer is yes."

He flipped open the lid on the box to reveal the round-cut diamond he'd chosen. "The guy called this one a 'halo setting,' but I thought it looked like the rock was a ball dropping through a hoop."

Tears filled her eyes. Her fingertips trembled against her lips, but still she didn't say anything.

"If you don't like this one, there are some shaped like little footballs."

"Marquise cut," she whispered at last.

"Whatever."

Her tears finally broke the barrier, spilling over her lashes and streaking down her cheeks in twin rivulets. His heart seized, even though he knew—or hoped—that they were happy tears. For the love of God, she was the one who did the proposing. Taking her hand in his, he gave it an urgent squeeze. He tried to clear the lump from his throat, but his voice was still little more than a rasp. "Hey, don't do that."

"Don't tell me what to do."

"You asked, and I said yes. You shouldn't be crying. Isn't there a saying about no crying in basketball?"

Kate sniffed and gave him a wobbly smile, but at least there were no more tears. "It's from a movie. And they were talking about baseball."

Danny shrugged, then looked up at her from under his lashes. He hoped to look appealing but had a sinking sensation he might just look pathetic. Still, he needed to use every down he had to score this. "Do you want this ring?"

Without hesitation, she nodded. "Uh-huh."

He waited for her to make a grab for her prize. When she didn't, he pulled her hand to his lips and kissed it fervently, watching her face for a clue as to how he could set the play in motion again. He followed her gaze to the ring box, then back to him. Finally, it snapped into place. "You want me to ask you?"

Kate looked away briefly, and a rosy blush colored her cheeks. When she answered, she spoke in little more than a whisper. "Yes."

Relieved and excited to have put his thumb on the issue, he grinned as he kissed the back of her hand again. Gazing up at the woman towering over him, he held her hand firm in his grasp. "Kate Snyder, will you marry me?"

She started to nod but stopped abruptly, her eyes narrowing. "Do I have to change my name?"

A laugh burst out of him. Leaning back, he stared up at her, thoroughly amused by the strategic play of her agile mind. "Only if you want to, but I'm not paying to have all those trophies redone."

"I don't think they do that."

"Just making my terms clear."

"And if we get married, I get an equal say in where we end up?" she persisted.

Danny snorted. "Equal say? You're the only one with viable employment options. I'm the one who'll end up making the Shake 'N Bake every night."

"You can't cook worth a damn."

Knees aching, he tried to glare at her, but the smile on her face told him he'd come up short. "You know I've had this knee scoped three times, right? You're going to have to seal the deal, or we'll need a winch to get me back on my feet."

She pulled a face. "Maybe I should look for a model in better condition."

"Like you have any room to talk."

"True," she conceded.

"Take me as I am?"

"It *is* a pretty ring."

Taking that as his cue, he released her hand and pried the ring from its velvet bed. The platinum setting gleamed under the fluorescent lighting. The diamond shone, but not as bright as the pleasure in Kate's eyes. "It's a simple yes or no question," he nudged.

"Yes."

Her long, graceful fingers shook as he slid the ring home, and a surge of pride pumped through his veins. He turned her hand over to press a kiss to the center of her palm, then gently curled her fingers in. "Good. Then it's settled."

His joints creaked as he rose to his feet, but every second of pain was worth it. Kate threw herself at him, winding her long limbs tight around him and burrowing into him as if she wanted to crawl into his skin. He smiled as he kissed her, wondering if she didn't know she'd gotten under it the first time they met.

She kissed him hard but sweet. He tipped his head to part her lips, and she met him there, her tongue matching his stroke for stroke. God, he loved this dance they did. The tenderness tempering unapologetic need. The perfect meld of give and take. Power and surrender. Like football, life was a game of inches that made up yards, and yardage converted into points. Now that he knew he'd have her by his side, Danny had no doubt they'd find a way to win. As a team.

—∞—

"Stop dragging your feet." Kate took hold of his arm and started hauling him up the courthouse stairs.

"This is idiotic. We are not doing this now."

"I asked you to marry me, you said yes, and I have a pretty, sparkly ring." She gave his arm another yank, knowing damn well if he truly decided to dig in, she'd never be able to move him. "We have to do this now."

He allowed her to pull him to the doors, then screeched to a halt. Gesturing to their reflection in the glass, he shook his head. "Look at us, Kate."

She did as he asked. It must have been her fairy godmother's day off, because she still wore the same yoga pants and "Nothing but Net" T-shirt she'd left the house in that morning. Danny was only marginally better in blue jeans and a polo shirt. They both looked haggard from the nearly sleepless night.

"I want to do this right." He spoke low and soft in her ear. "Unlike some people, I've never been married before."

The comment felt like a low blow, so she fell back on defense. "You should have told me you were a virgin that first night. I would have been more gentle with you."

His lips curved, but she closed her eyes. She couldn't bear to see him smile and laugh her off. Not when she was fighting so damn hard to save him. Save *them*.

"You were gentle enough," he assured. She squeezed her eyes shut tighter when he pressed two fingers to her jaw and turned her face toward his. "Kate, look at me."

"Don't smile," she blurted before she could stop herself.

"What?"

"I'll look at you, but don't smile. You can't smile. This isn't a joke."

"And here I thought you were trying to convince me this is the happiest day of my life."

She chuckled. She couldn't help herself. The man's humor was darker than an eclipse. Rather than risk looking at him, she let her head fall forward. Her forehead came to rest on his broad shoulder. She had a hard time suppressing her own smile when he wrapped his arms tight around her.

"I want us to have a real wedding, with our friends and families there." His voice was gruff, but his hand was gentle as he smoothed the ends of her hair against her back. "I don't want to sneak off like we've done something wrong. We haven't done anything wrong, Kate."

"We got you fired." Lifting her head, she searched his eyes. "It may not be wrong, but we can prove beyond a shadow of a doubt that it's right. All you have to do is let me make an honest man out of you."

"Ha-ha."

"We can still have a wedding. I want one too. We can have it next week, next month, or next year, but if we want to have a snowball's chance in hell of slipping through this loophole, we need to do this today. We can't risk having the marriage license and termination papers dated the same day."

"Well, there's a compelling argument for love," he grumbled.

"I love you." Desperation took over, fraying the edges of her voice. "It may not work, but then again, it might. This is our half-court heave."

"A Hail Mary," he corrected.

"The best play we have."

"You're the best thing that's ever happened to me." He framed her face between his big, broad palms, and her legs turned to jelly. "I just want you to have everything you want to have."

"I will," she answered. "Just as soon as we get in there, sign that license, and get Judge Baxter to wave his 'I do' wand over us, I'll have what I want."

"Not even close."

She shrugged, then turned her lips into his palm. "Anything else is just showboating," she murmured against his skin.

"Kate, look at me."

Feeling keyed up and languorous at the same time, she roused herself from her Danny-induced stupor and rocked back to stand on her own two feet. "Yes?"

"I promise I'll do everything I can to stay."

Wetting her lips, she slid her hand down into his and gave his fingers a squeeze. "Save your promises till we're on the inside, big guy."

Within minutes, they were signing their marriage certificate and a few extra autographs for the county clerk. Five minutes after that, they stood facing one another on a faded Aubusson carpet in Judge Baxter's book-lined office. Danny had just taken her hands in his when the door flew open and Millie and Avery blew in with Mike in tow, the boss man looking shell-shocked.

"What are you doing here?" Danny asked the athletic director.

Mike blinked as if he'd been hoping the whole scene was nothing more than a dream, then shrugged. "Being your best man. Probably getting myself fired too."

"Hush. This is America," Avery said, thrusting a weary-looking bouquet between Danny and Kate. "They can't fire you for attending a civil ceremony, can they, Judge?"

"No, I don't believe that would give them cause, but this is an employment at-will state..." the judge began.

"You hush too." Avery stepped back, gave Kate a critical once-over, then tugged the bottom of the bride's T-shirt down so it covered her butt better. "Besides, we're all on our lunch hours."

Millie stared at Avery, clearly astonished. Then she burst out laughing.

"Oh, can it. All of you," Avery blustered. "It's the maid of honor's job to do the flowers and the fluffing the train thing."

Millie pounced. "Maid of honor? Who said you get to be maid of honor?"

"I've never been married. You have." Avery flashed a smug smile. "You can be matron of honor if Kate wants you to." She turned to Kate, wrinkling her pert nose in distaste. "But personally, I think having both might be a little pretentious for a civil ceremony."

Kate looked at Danny, and he stared back at her, bewilderment etched into every handsome line on his face. Mike stepped up behind Danny and nodded solemnly to Judge Baxter. With some hushed squabbling about who'd hold the place of honor for Kate, Avery and Millie jostled until they stood side by side facing the bride.

Kate shot them an amused glance, then looked down at their feet. "I think Millie's a half inch closer."

"Only because she has gunboat feet." Avery corrected the deficit, then tossed a triumphant glance at Millie. "There. We're even."

"Are we ready?" the judge asked. He pinned each participant with a stern stare, but the corners of his mouth twitched with amusement.

The cellophane wrapper on the grocery-store bouquet crinkled as Kate lifted it to her nose. She took one long sniff, then handed the flowers to Millie so she could reclaim her hold on her man. "I'm ready."

Danny stared straight into her eyes. "Me too."

—⁓—

"Trust me on this, you do not want to come in there with me," Mike said firmly.

Calhoun's bar was quiet midafternoon, but they still pitched their voices low so passersby wouldn't overhear. "I had Judge Baxter look at the contract, and he agrees," Kate said in a warning tone. "The way it's worded, Danny would have grounds to fight termination for cause."

Mike closed his eyes in a blatant and unapologetic attempt to find the handle on his patience, and Danny knew his old friend well enough not to be offended by it. Kate, on the other hand…

"Chancellor Martin may succeed in getting rid of him, but it's going to cost him," she continued, undaunted.

"It's the old 'cheaper to keep her' bit played out in reverse," Avery said, lifting her glass of scotch in salute.

They'd retreated to Calhoun's immediately following the ceremony to sketch out a game plan. So far, all they'd agreed on was the fact that he and Kate were well and truly married. Everything else seemed to be up for debate.

"It's my job," Danny pointed out.

"You don't have a job," Mike countered. Lifting his beer in a toast, he smirked at the happy couple. "To the bride and groom. I hope somebody thought to bring shoes and rice. They may need them."

"The shoes weren't to wear," Millie said, taking a sip from her daiquiri without looking up from her phone. "They were supposed to symbolize the groom taking over responsibility for the bride's upkeep."

Mike snorted and toasted Danny again. "Good luck keeping this girl in shoes. You'd better find a job real soon."

"This *woman* can buy her own damn shoes," Kate shot back.

Tired of his friend's double-sided razzing, Danny plucked the beer mug from his grasp, returned Mike's salute, and drained the contents for him in three long gulps. "Fine then," he gasped, setting the empty mug down with a thud. "Deliver the message. Kate and I will share the happy news with Gene and Jonas."

"Sounds like a pop group, doesn't it?" Kate asked, her smile a mile wide.

Danny couldn't help but smile back. She'd gotten her way, and her pleasure was utterly undimmed by their dank surroundings or their friends' unchecked cynicism.

God, he loved that smile.

"Let Martin know we've gotten married, and see if that smooths things over a little," Danny said, buying in to her enthusiasm. Why not? They were already all in. Might as well hope they'd turn the right cards.

"I keep trying to remind you all that we've already made your termination public. Even if he wanted to back down, he can't now. It's out there." Mike snatched Danny's beer off its cardboard coaster and returned the favor. Wiping his mouth with the back of his hand, he placed the empty mug back where he found it, then slid off the bar stool.

"He was one of those guys who spent the fourth quarter moping on the bench if you were down a few points, wasn't he?" Kate asked, nodding to Mike.

"Yes," Danny replied.

"I was not," Mike refuted at the same time.

Clapping a hand to his friend's shoulder, Danny looked him straight in the eye. "Thank you for coming today."

Mike gave a jerky nod. "You didn't need to send Thelma and Louise after me. I wouldn't have missed it."

Danny opened his mouth to tell him that he hadn't sent anyone after anybody, but Kate stopped him with a firm hand on his thigh.

"We know that," she assured him. "But it was more fun to send the Despotic Duo in."

Avery sniffed at the implied insult. "I'll have you know that we honored every one of the rights granted to him under the Geneva Convention."

"Except this isn't wartime, and he was kidnapped and transported, not taken prisoner," Millie interjected, setting her phone aside with a sigh. Looking up at Mike, she tapped her fingernail against her glass. "I'm not sure you should bother much with Chancellor Martin. I think we need to take this to a higher authority."

Mike cringed and closed his eyes. "Why do I have a feeling I'm going to hear something I can't unhear?"

Millie cocked her head, her eyes unfocused. Danny could practically see the wheels turning in her head. Conscious that he'd most likely already put his friend at risk, he held up a hand to stop the calculating woman from saying anything more.

"Go," he told Mike, nodding toward the door. "Go tell him. If nothing else, you can claim you tried to warn him about whatever idea Thelma has wriggling away in that steel trap of a mind."

Millie scoffed and lifted her glass as if she were sipping mai tais on an island terrace and not watered-down premix in an off-campus dive. "I'm Louise," she informed him primly, then took a gulp big enough to give an Eskimo brain freeze.

Mike nodded and stepped around Danny to plant a polite kiss on Kate's cheek. "You were a beautiful bride," he mumbled as he took off for the door before any of them had a chance to recover.

"Good thing he's not an umpire," Avery observed. "You guys would be so screwed."

"Referee," Kate corrected.

Her friend leveled her with an arch stare. "You say referee, I say frustrated ex-jock who's into zebra cosplay."

"God, I love you guys," Kate blurted, reaching for Avery's and Millie's hands.

"Wow. Drunk on half a beer," Millie murmured, but her eyelashes fluttered a little faster.

"You are the best friends I've ever had."

"Stop," Avery groaned. "You're not supposed to say this stuff until you're kneeling in front of a toilet and one of us is holding your hair back."

"I mean it," Kate argued, leaning in. Her knee brushed Danny's, and he could almost feel the earnestness wafting off her. The three women exchanged some kind of telepathic message with a few darting glances, and then Kate sat up straight and reached for her beer. "Now tell me, what are we going to do to save Danny's bacon?"

At that moment, a long shadow fell over the table. Kate looked up to see Ty Ransom looming over them. "Hey, Ty."

He lifted his chin in greeting. "Did I hear that right?" He cast a wary look at Danny, then turned his attention back to Kate. "Did Mike just call you a bride?"

"He did." A hot flush rose in her cheeks. "I'm sorry I didn't invite you. It was kind of a...spur-of-the-moment thing."

Ty nodded as he digested the information, then lifted his highball glass in salute. "Congratulations. And good luck," he added before taking a hefty slug of the amber liquid.

"Look at us. We're nothing but a bunch of day drinkers," Avery commented. "You'd think we were in college or something."

"Did I also hear you say something about saving Coach McMillan's bacon?" Ty prompted.

"Wow. No need to fit this guy with a Miracle-Ear," Avery muttered.

Millie shot her a quelling look, then turned to look at

Ty. "Yes. They're invoking his morals clause, and we're trying to figure out a way to get them to let him stay."

Ty fixed Danny with an unflinching stare. "Seems to me you've already figured it out."

Danny bristled. "Hey, getting married was her idea."

Kate leapt into position to set the block. "It was my idea."

Ty shrugged. "Well, congratulations, Danny Boy. You have your leverage." He leaned down and brushed a soft kiss to Kate's cheek. "Just make sure you use it to get what you want too," he added before wandering into the gloom of the bar, his uneven gait more exaggerated than usual.

Millie leaned in. "Things are not going well there," she confided.

"Oh no." Kate twisted in her seat, trying to spot Ty again. "With Mari, you mean?"

"With a lot of things," Millie answered, an ominous note deepening her voice. Straightening on her stool, she slapped the sticky tabletop with her palm to draw their attention back to her. "But that isn't today's problem. Today, we will take the case of McMillan and Company versus Wolcott University to the airwaves."

"Taking to the streets!" Avery crowed, thrusting a fist into the air.

"To the National Sports Network," Millie corrected. "The sports media version of *The People's Court*."

Avery nodded, lifted her glass high above her head, and shouted, "Power to the people!"

# Chapter 20

DRESSED AND READY FOR HIS TIME ON THE AIR, DANNY stepped into an empty conference room off the main hall of the hotel and pulled his phone from his coat pocket. It wasn't a Wednesday, but it was important that he let his mother know what they'd done before one of her cronies let it slip. Or worse, Tommy tattled on him.

"Hello?"

His mother sounded cautious and a little scared. As if the person who was calling at an unscheduled time might somehow be able to leap through the phone and make demands of her.

"Hey, Ma, it's Danny," he said quickly, hoping to reassure her.

A pregnant pause followed. "Danny? It's not Wednesday today, is it?"

"No, Ma, it's not. I just…I have some news, and I wanted to tell you before anyone else did."

."You got fired again," she said on a sigh.

Annoyance spurted up inside him. "You know, Ma, technically, I've never really been fired from a job. I was asked to resign from Northern, and if you'll recall, they had to pay me a truckload of money to get me out of there."

"Did the new school ask you to resign because of that woman?" she persisted.

The tremor in her voice and the fact that she couldn't

seem to retain the names of the schools where he'd coached in recent years reminded him that his mother wasn't a young woman anymore. Hadn't been for quite some time. And the misadventures of her only sons were probably not adding to her chances at longevity. But how could he answer her without lying or setting his marriage to Kate up for failure in his mother's eyes? He had been asked to resign because of her. And though his mother hadn't already heard the news, she would soon. Danny decided it was time to throw the long ball.

"Kate and I got married this afternoon, Ma."

His mother's gasp rang sharp in his ears. "You what?"

"We were married in Judge Dennis Baxter's chambers this afternoon. I wanted to let you know because we're doing a kind of a joint interview on the National Sports Network tonight. Live," he added. "You can watch, if you want."

"Watch?" she repeated, sounding bewildered.

"The interview with me and Kate," he clarified gently.

"Have you called Tommy to tell him?" his mother asked.

Heaving a sigh, Danny rubbed the back of his neck. "No, Ma, I haven't called Tommy. I called you."

"You should call your brother. Tell him about this Kate woman. Maybe now that you're both married, you can put this whole thing behind you," she insisted.

"Ma, it was never about Tommy and LeAnn. I've told you that a million times."

"Yes, but now you're doing well on your own and he's doing well, you're both married... Please, Danny, I'd like to have Thanksgiving like a normal family."

"We never had Thanksgiving like a normal family, because Thanksgiving is on a Thursday. You take dinner to other people on Thursdays," he said, remembering all the times he and Tommy had seen their own portions of turkey and dressing dwindle away to nothing because someone else needed it more.

"Being able to give to others is a blessing, Daniel," his mother reminded him sternly.

"I agree, Ma." And his exorbitant salaries had made it possible for his mother to grant more blessings than most, but he didn't bother reminding her of that fact.

"And you only have one brother," she added, segueing into her favorite fallback. "When I'm gone, you won't have any other family."

"I'll have Kate," he reminded her. Thinking back on the sadness in Kate's tone when she talked about her strained relationship with her sister, he straightened his spine and steeled his resolve. "We'll be each other's family."

His mother released a long-suffering sigh. "One can never have too much family."

Danny begged to differ, but now wasn't the time to argue. "I have to go, Ma. It's time for us to get ready for the interview. Kate and I are going to take a little honeymoon when she gets done with her summer commitments, but we'd like to fly up to see you when we get back."

"Oh, I'd like to see you too, sweetheart. And your Kate."

His Kate. She was his Kate now, for better or for worse. And he was going to do everything in his power to make it for better as far as his new bride was concerned.

"I'll talk to you soon, Ma."

"Talk to you on Wednesday, Danny," she said, the correction a gentle rebuke for his daring to call off schedule.

Danny ended the call but stared at the phone long and hard. He could call Tommy, but he didn't really see the point in it. The guy was an NSN junkie anyway. He had to have seen the news about the coaching job by now. His brother was a professional strategist. Any connection between Danny's job and his marriage was not going to be flattering, and Danny didn't feel up to taking hits from anyone else at the moment.

Pocketing the phone, he smoothed his tie over his stomach, then stepped out into the deserted corridor. It was time for him to find his Kate and get this show on the road.

---

Kate checked her phone for the fiftieth time, then dropped it into the pocket of her pale-blue suit jacket. She'd left a voicemail asking her sister to call her, but so far, there'd been no word from Audrey. She and Danny had agreed it would be best to call their respective family members before the live broadcast, but it looked like she wouldn't have the chance to forewarn her sister.

Not unless she did so via message.

Fired up by the notion, Kate extracted her phone again and started typing with her thumbs. It would serve Audrey right to get the news via text. Maybe next time, she wouldn't be so quick to ignore Kate's calls. The text read simply: Tried to call U. Married Danny McMillan today. Wanted to tell U B4 you saw it on news. K.

Her duty done, she edged closer to the wall and let her head fall back. It seemed that in the last twenty-four hours, she'd done nothing but revise strategy and set play after play in motion. Truth be told, all this

maneuvering was a bit wearing on a girl who simply
wanted to stay put.

"Looking good, Coach," one of the crew members
said as he hustled past her and through the double doors.

She did look good. One hell of a lot better than she
had at the courthouse, and if that wasn't ass-backward,
she didn't know what was. A few hours before, she'd
gotten married in yoga pants, a yogurt-stained T-shirt,
and her fifth favorite pair of sneakers, but for the
National Sports Network, she had to dress up. Men
wearing earpieces scurried past her, carrying equipment
and cable into the hotel ballroom. Kate couldn't think of
a time when she had done an interview anywhere other
than a basketball arena.

At center court.

She glanced down the blandly decorated hotel corridor and shuddered. Yards of cable stretched from the
front doors to the sectioned-off ballroom. They had to
squeeze the interview in quick. Apparently, there was a
bat mitzvah scheduled for that evening.

She peeked into the room and spotted the customary
canvas chairs placed in the center of the room. There
would be no cozy Costas setup for this interview. They'd
promised Brittany, the perky, blond junior reporter NSN
had sent to cover Danny's welcome, an exclusive. This
interview would be the last hurrah in the Wolcott battle
of the sexes.

The girl sat in the middle chair, the tip of one french-
manicured finger poised above the tablet in her lap.
Her platinum hair spilled over her shoulders, carefully
arranged sections veiling her no doubt perky breasts, the
rest a shining fall so smooth it looked like a sheet of ice.

She wore the heavy makeup the cameras demanded, but even from this distance, Kate could see her face was smooth and unlined.

Twenty-five, twenty-six at the very most, Kate guessed. Millie had mentioned something about her playing on an Olympic volleyball team. Kate thought about her own Olympic jersey hanging in one of the Warrior Center's many display cases and grudgingly acknowledged the unexpected kinship with the reporter.

But that was as far as her sense of solidarity went. She didn't want this pretty, young thing seated between her and Danny. What viewer in their right mind would look at Brittany, then look at her and imagine that Danny McMillan would choose her? Despite the normally healthy state of her ego, Kate was having a hard time buying it herself.

She jumped as a warm, broad hand claimed the small of her back. Danny chuckled, and scents of male aftershave and a hint of makeup wound around her.

"Hey."

Danny stood close, his broad body bracing her back. Strong. Solid. Set. She gave up a little of her weight, and he took it, wrapping one arm snug around her waist. She stroked his sleeve. The wool of his suit coat was smooth beneath her fingertips. The knot of his tie pressed into the back of her skull. Still, she'd wager it had taken him a lot less time to get ready for this circus. While she'd been worked over by an army of minions operating on Millie's behest, he'd been holed up with their agents.

"Are you still fired?"

"Yeah."

"How are things looking?"

"How does North Dakota sound to you?"

"Cold."

His chest moved in a laugh, but no sound came out. "Yeah, well, I touched the people's princess. I'm sure most of the top-tier schools are busy locking up their women."

"I'm the queen, remember?" She turned her head and pressed her cheek to his lapel, inhaling the skin-warmed spice of his aftershave. "And there will be no other women for you. I'd crush you with my powerful thighs."

"Not them?"

"Only you."

"What a way to go." He brushed his lips over her hair. "My mother can't wait to meet you."

"I tried to call Audrey, but she didn't pick up. I texted her. I was thinking maybe we could meet in Nashville for dinner one night, but we don't have to if you don't want to," she said in a rush.

"I'm going to meet her sooner or later." His arms tightened around her. "You can't undo the damage now, Coach. You called the play, and now you're stuck with me."

She let her head loll against his shoulder. "I can't believe we're stuck doing this interview."

"I'm just glad we had Millie on our side. That woman could overthrow dictators."

"I think maybe she has." Craning her neck, she peered up at him. "And Mike?"

"He's working it as best he can," Danny assured her. "Too bad Martin's such a stubborn ass."

With a shaky sigh, she turned her head to gaze straight into his piercing blue eyes. "Please tell me they put mascara on those eyelashes."

"Sorry. No mascara."

Poking her lower lip out, she sulked. "So not fair." She relaxed against him, letting him support a little more of her weight. "Would you let me?"

"Let you what?"

"Put mascara on those inch-long eyelashes."

"No," he said firmly, but his hesitation indicated a willingness to let her do just about anything she wanted to him.

Turning her face into his neck, she brushed a kiss to the corner of his jaw. "You'd look so pretty."

"You're a cruel woman."

Another crew member rushed past them, waving some kind of gewgaw that must have been a vital cog in the works, because the minute he ducked into the ballroom, the frenzy of activity became more purposeful. Kate tugged at her skirt and forced herself to stand tall. "I prefer the term 'tough broad,' if you don't mind."

Danny stepped in front of her, putting himself between her and the scene of their soon-to-come public hand slapping. "I'll just play it safe and stick with beautiful."

Only halfheartedly imagining the mile-long lashes coated in glossy black, she searched his eyes until she found the confidence she'd momentarily misplaced. It was there, as always. Right there with the smirks, the stares, and the cocky jock swagger. It was no wonder she hadn't recognized it at first. This man's unswerving belief in them looked a hell of a lot like real love, and she'd never loved anyone the way she loved him.

He brushed her hair back, tucking a piece behind her ear. "Why do you do that?" she asked.

"Hm?"

"You always push my hair back behind my ears. Why?"

He cocked his head, studying her quizzically. "I don't know. I guess I just see you do it, and I like…" Finally, he gave a helpless shrug and traced the curve of her exposed ear with his fingertip. "I like your face. I like your ears. It's fun to watch them turn pink."

As if he'd given the damn things a cue, they started to burn. A sly smile cocked one side of his mouth. He planted his hand on the wall and leaned into her. She couldn't have torn her gaze from his if she'd tried.

"They're tender and soft and taste so damn sweet."

"All that from ears," she whispered.

He gave a slow nod, his expression solemn but his eyes bright. "Just imagine how I feel about the rest of you."

"I love you," she blurted.

"Coach? And, uh, Coach?" a young man called, breaking the spell.

"Good. Otherwise, we made a big-ass mistake today." They both turned toward the scrawny assistant fidgeting in the doorway, tablet in hand and headset draped around his neck. Danny pushed away from the wall, but instead of distancing himself from Kate, he took hold of her arm and urged her forward. "You ready for us?"

"Yeah, we're all set," the kid called back.

Danny's hand slid to its usual spot in the small of Kate's back as they made their way to Brittany's side. "Just let me handle most of this, okay? I made the mess, I'll clean it up."

"I have a stake in this too. Aside from you, I mean," she clarified.

"You do?"

"The world doesn't revolve around you and your drama, Danny."

"I never meant to imply that it did."

His placid tone set her off. He could pretend to be panicked or at the very least ruffled, damn it. She pulled away from him just shy of the baseline. "That figure I gave Mike? My salary? I asked for more than they're paying Ransom."

"Whoa."

"I won't settle for less."

"You shouldn't. Your record has his beat to shit."

"Just so you know," she said, straightening her hem, "it's possible they won't pony up. And I wouldn't be here come fall anyhow."

"If this doesn't work, I won't be here tomorrow," he countered.

"Always trying to one-up me."

He smiled and tucked her hair back behind her ear again. "No, just letting you know that, although the choices we've heard so far aren't ideal, it doesn't matter to me where we end up now. I know we'll be together."

"Are you two ready?" the assistant asked again, turning the clipboard in his hands nervously. He grimaced in apology and shrugged. "We're live in three minutes."

Her heart hammering, she gave Danny's hand a squeeze and started toward the semicircle of chairs, adding a little extra sway to her step as a reward. "I'm set," she said, smiling sweetly at the production assistant, "but I think the pretty boy could use a little pancake. Looks like he has a pimple."

Danny barked a laugh and caught up to her in three long strides. "She thinks I'm pretty," he said, affecting a simpering tone. But when the makeup woman hustled across the floor clutching a plastic tube and a sponge, he waved her off. "My face is fine." He shot Kate a glance out of the corner of his eye. "And she thinks so too."

Kate refrained from further comment, her focus set on the chair to Brittany's left. Positioning oneself on an opponent's weak side was a strategy so fundamental old Mack Nord probably used it to determine which side of the bed his wife could sleep on each night. In watching the young woman prepare for the interview, she'd noticed that Brittany was right-handed. That meant she'd be naturally inclined to focus on the person to her right. Kate would cover the left. Out of the line of fire, but right there to protect Danny's flank if push came to shove.

She was really good at pushing and shoving.

The interview unfolded at a slug's pace. To start, Brittany aimed a volley of razor-edged questions at Danny but lobbed only softballs at her. The knowing looks the younger woman darted in her direction made Kate wonder if she was supposed to thrust a fist of feminist solidarity.

Frankly, the sanctimonious little twit was pissing her off. Who was she to question Danny's integrity? Who were any of them? Everyone made bad choices. People lived with consequences. Danny had, and every time they knocked him down, he got right back up and called his next play.

The questions and answers flew. Brittany kept trying to make each one a knockout blow. She must've forgotten she was dealing with a man who spent the majority of his adult life staring down three-hundred-pound behemoths hell-bent on smashing him into the turf.

The reporter paused to take a drink of water, and

Danny's gaze met Kate's above the young woman's head. He tried to smile, but the misery he must've felt each time those manicured nails picked at another old wound dulled the luminescent blue of his eyes.

Millie had been all about controlling the story, but at the moment, it felt like they had no control. Funny, just a day ago, all Kate had been thinking about was cutting Jim Davenport off at the knees. Well, the schmuck got what he deserved for taking the cheap shot at the press conference. His piddling newspaper story was about to be scooped on air by the biggest sports network in the nation.

But whatever triumph Kate felt in besting Jim was dampened by having to sit quietly and watch Danny field one hostile, impertinent question after another without stepping in. Biting her tongue and sitting on her hands was nothing short of torture. But she couldn't interfere. Millie was right. He needed to come clean about what happened in his past once and for all, before they could deal with their future.

"Do you ever hear from LeAnn Cushing?"

The question jolted Kate from her reverie. Brittany spoke the woman's name as if it should be known in every household. This time, Kate didn't bother trying to mask her scowl.

"Well, she *is* married to my brother, so I'm on the Christmas card list."

His answer was stiff and terse. It hurt Kate to hear the pain in his tone, but the realization that the mere mention of LeAnn still had so much impact on Danny cut her to the quick.

Brittany pounced. "She married your brother?"

Danny glanced over at her, his eyes a vivid plea for

help. In that moment, she understood why he never spoke about the relationship that caused his fall from grace. The woman wasn't the one he missed; it was his brother. Sitting up tall, Kate charged into the fray and swatted the question like she was blocking a shot.

"Family connections can be complicated," Kate said, inserting herself into the conversation for the first time since the interview started. "But I don't see what his relationship with his brother and sister-in-law have to do with football."

Brittany blinked as if Kate had ripped a strip of hot wax from between her perfectly arched brows. "I'm sorry?"

The woman's blank expression made it too damn easy for someone with the instincts of a natural-born winner to go on the offensive. "My ex-husband was too threatened by my success to stay married to me, but no one ever asks why. I just think it's funny that you're peppering Coach McMillan with asinine questions that have absolutely no bearing on his ability to be a successful football coach."

Kate thought she heard Danny groan softly, but Brittany shot ramrod straight in the canvas chair. "I'm sure Coach McMillan has the technical skills to be an adequate tactician," she said coolly. "What I'm questioning is whether a man who dates students—and according to rumor, fellow staff members—should be the man we look to as a role model for young men in sports."

Danny leapt into the argument. "Ms. Cushing might have been a graduate student, but she was twenty-six years old when we started seeing each other. I wasn't that much older—"

"But still quite a bit older," Brittany interjected.

"Huh. I wonder how much is too much?" Kate turned

to Brittany, a frown deep enough to make Millie's head explode bisecting her brows. "Is three years a better spread? Would five be stretching it?"

"I'm not sure I know why you're asking," Brittany replied cautiously.

"Well, you seem to think you're an expert, so I'm trying to get a feel for what would be an appropriate life choice for Coach McMillan and what wouldn't."

"Kate, please…" Danny started.

"Does it vary from man to man? Ty Ransom is eighteen years older than his wife, but I don't see anyone heating up tar and plucking chickens." Kate looked directly into the camera. "Sorry, Ty. Nothing personal. I just want to get the rules straight."

"We're not here to talk about Coach Ransom," Brittany said primly.

"No, we're here so you can peck more holes in Coach McMillan." She shuddered delicately. "It's like watching an old Hitchcock movie."

"Kate, don't engage."

Danny's attempt to intervene was well intentioned, but she had a head full of steam and needed to release it. The poor guy was trying to fight back a hailstorm with a flyswatter.

Swinging her crossed legs toward Brittany, Kate widened her eyes in feigned confusion. "Does it work both ways? Is there some exponent I should be working with to calculate the male-to-female conversion?"

By now, Brittany looked utterly confused and just angry enough to come at her. Kate couldn't resist. Dusting off her rusty acting skills, she threw her career and life choices down to flop at the reporter's feet.

"I was six years older than Jeff Sommers." Her voice dripped with mock outrage. "Where is Mike Samlin? I can't believe the university would willfully allow a woman who preys on younger men to roam the campus freely."

"Oh God," Danny muttered as he propped his elbow on the arm of the chair and dropped his forehead into his hand.

Poor Brittany glanced down at the tablet in her lap, obviously trying to find the spot in her notes where she'd lost the thread. Kate almost felt as sorry for the young reporter as she did when she pounded a Division II school in the preseason using only her second stringers. It was time to stop playing cat and mouse with the poor girl. After all, she was only trying to make a name for herself. Kate respected her ambition. But Kate wasn't interested in trading courtesy baskets with a journalist. If there was one thing her coaches taught her, it was that true champions showed mercy for the teams they outmatched. Of course, they didn't let up entirely until the victory was assured. It was clearly time for her to put this game away.

Kate glanced at the red light on the camera and leaned in close to Brittany as if she were about to share a secret, even though she knew the mic would pick up anything she said. "Danny's three years older than me. Is that okay?"

The reporter's head jerked up. The overhead lights made her blond hair gleam like spun gold. Her eyes were still clouded with confusion, but instinct kicked in. Her nostrils flared as she smelled blood. White teeth gleamed as she flashed a deceptively sweet smile. "Is the age difference between you and Coach McMillan significant? Are the accusations Mister, uh"—she checked her tablet—"Davenport made true?"

"Kate."

Danny spoke her name softly, but the underlying note of warning rang through. She ignored it. She was the woman who always made the clutch shot, no matter what the distraction.

Propping her elbow on the back of the chair, she stared past the twentysomething between them and fixed her eyes on her prize. "Well…"

She drawled the word, infusing the single syllable with a myriad of meanings. Of course, Brittany pounced.

"So you're confirming that you and Coach McMillan are involved?"

"You haven't seen the pictures?" Kate smiled, slow but sure, letting it unfurl as she raked the man across from her with an impudent stare. "That's why I'm wondering how this whole age thing figures in and if it swings both ways in terms of the gender issue." She rolled her hand, gesturing for the young reporter to be more forthcoming. "Hey, is it a problem if a female coach seduces an older man?"

"Seduces?" Danny's bark of laughter drew every eye to him. He sat forward in his chair. His body language was challenging, but the light in his eyes was the product of pure pleasure. "Are you trying to say *you* seduced *me*?"

Recrossing her legs, she let the delicate high-heeled sandal she wore dangle from her toes. "I'm not trying. I'm saying."

"I seduced you," he asserted.

"Not at all the way I remember it." She pressed a thoughtful finger to her lip. "I had the upper…hand, if I recall correctly."

"Kate."

This time, she acquiesced with a smirk and shrug. "Relationships are all about compromise, right? If it's easier on that fragile male ego to think it was the other way around, I can afford to be generous."

Brittany's head swiveled like a Wimbledon spectator as she tried to keep up with the volley. "So the two of you are a couple. Has all this fighting been fake?"

"Oh, it's not fake," Danny answered without breaking his gaze. "We don't agree on much of anything."

"And I never fake anything," Kate answered with a sly smile. "But there are a few things we don't argue about." She straightened from her insolent little slouch and got right down to the business of disarming the press. "But I have no problem letting him buy dinner. I consider it my way of closing the salary gap."

---

Admiring Kate's ability to look so damn beautiful and composed as she launched grenade after grenade into the conversation, Danny gave his head a shake and held up both hands in mock surrender. "I'm not touching the money thing."

Brittany's preternaturally thick eyelashes fluttered as she tried to grab hold of the interview again. Age and experience gave them an edge. Unfortunately, she was too young and ambitious to realize that she was outmatched on both sides.

"Just as well, seeing as how you have no salary now." Kate arched one eyebrow at her new husband. "But you agree that our salaries don't accurately represent our contributions to Wolcott Athletics."

"I'm not agreeing to anything without a bomb squad present."

"Oh, you were pretty agreeable earlier today."

"Kate," he growled.

Kate turned to Brittany with a sweet smile. "He'll land something pretty quickly, no matter how hard you guys try to tear him down. He's very dedicated. Watches game film instead of Netflix. Knows just when to blow his whistle."

Danny narrowed his eyes, knowing damn well it wasn't his whistle she was thinking about. Poor Brittany looked completely lost. And miserable. This interview was her big break, and he and Kate's antics were ruining it for her.

Feeling an unprecedented benevolence for Brittany and more than ready to launch a little shock and awe of his own, he readied his ammunition. He lounged in his seat as if he hadn't a care in the world, then he craned his neck until he could look Kate square in the eye. "I don't see how it matters. What's yours is mine now, right?"

He had to give her credit. She didn't even flinch. Instead, she picked up the live round and tossed it right back at him. "I knew I should have insisted on an iron-clad prenup covering those glass cases lining the halls." She leaned closer to Brittany and spoke in a low, confiding tone, but her eyes never left his. "You know he's only after me for my...trophies."

Danny laughed again. Out loud. On camera. Damn, but this woman did things to him. Awesome, wonderful things. Tearing his attention from her, he fixed Brittany with an unwavering stare, willing her to catch on. "She drives me crazy. In every possible way. That's why I'm keeping her."

The reporter searched his face for clues. "Is this… Are you… What's going on here? Is this some kind of joke?"

Sometimes there was nothing sweeter than toying with a newbie who thought they had game. Then there were the times you had to cut them a little slack and let them *in* the game. The fear and uncertainty he saw in those wide, blue eyes told him they'd played keep-away long enough.

"No joke. You just snagged the headline of the week." Slipping out of his chair, Danny came around to Kate and kissed her full on the mouth. "You're stubborn and mouthy and totally wrong about the designated hitter."

Tears filled her green-gold eyes. One tangled in her dark lashes, but she didn't try to dash it away. "Spoken like a man who never had to play defense in his life."

He stared at that glistening tear, enthralled by its tenuous hold. "Oh, but you're wrong. I've been playing defense too much lately. I'm ready to score." He pulled her hand to his mouth and gently kissed her knuckles, then looked straight into the camera. "That's why I married her."

"Nice," she hissed, throwing an elbow.

Danny flashed his cockiest grin. "Seemed like a good idea at the time. I need a big, strapping girl like you to guard my flank."

"Wuss."

"Wait. You're saying the two of you got married?" Brittany asked, practically falling out of her chair to get closer to them.

Kate lifted her right hand to reveal the sparkling ring on her left. She grinned when Brittany gasped, and waggled her fingers. "We did. Just this afternoon."

Danny gave the perky blond gaping at them an "aw shucks" smile. "I need someone to coach me through the next thirty or forty years, and I hear she's the best."

Kate started to nod, then stopped abruptly. Her fingers tightened on his. "I told him I couldn't take him to the next level unless he was willing to commit one hundred percent."

"I promised a hundred and ten."

Crew members whooped and clapped as he snatched his amazing Amazon woman from her seat as if she were barely more than a feather. Kate wound her arms around him. Her toes grazed the laces of his shoes. At last, their lips met. He kissed her sweet but deep. The muscles in her thighs tensed, and he could tell she was fighting the urge to wrap her legs around him. God, he wanted her to.

They'd exchanged vows that afternoon, but the day had been too jam-packed to spare the wedding night more than a passing thought. He angled his head and slid his hand into her hair, taking everything he wanted from the kiss, cameras be damned. He was thinking about the wedding night now.

Kate crushed two of his toes when she turned back toward the cameras but thankfully retained enough presence of mind to place herself between the lens and the insistent erection now pressed into the soft cheek of her ass.

"That's the only way he can ever win an argument," she said, giving her head a pitying shake.

Her silky hair teased his nose as she cast an affectionate glance over her shoulder. She covered the hand he'd placed over her stomach and wove her fingers through his. All around him, signs and insignia proclaimed pride in a school he used to think of as a joke, but standing there with Kate secure in his arms, he finally discovered exactly how a warrior felt after winning the battle of his lifetime.

"I've already won everything I need to win," he said.

Kate smirked and cast a glance at Brittany, who'd scrambled from her chair but stood there looking lost. "And he always has to have the last word."

"I do not."

"Prove it."

"What? How?"

"By keeping your mouth shut so you can't shove your foot in it." Turning back to the camera, Kate aimed the full wattage of that magnificent smile straight at the lens. "Good evening, sports fans. Allow me to introduce y'all to Mr. Kate Snyder."

# Chapter 21

Keeping his mouth shut wasn't an option. Not when he had a bride to kiss again. He was smiling from ear to ear as Kate unhooked his microphone and transmitter and tossed them onto the chair she'd abandoned. And there was no way he could keep his lips zipped when Brittany threw her own version of a Hail Mary.

"What are you going to do now?"

Danny stopped, Kate's hand tucked securely in his, and turned his attention back to the reporter. Some fast-thinking crew member lowered a boom mic just as he started to speak. "Now? Well, right now, I'm going on my honeymoon."

"I meant in terms of coaching."

He looked at Kate, and she looked back at him, one shoulder hitched up in a shrug. He smiled at her. "I guess that will be a family decision."

He released her hand in favor of wrapping a secure arm around her waist. Lame gesture or not, he wanted her to know that no matter what happened, he'd have her back.

Brittany took his equivocation as an invitation. The cameraman swung around as she grabbed a handheld mic and thrust it at Kate.

Kate glanced at Danny. Not one to back down from a full-court press, Kate leaned in, forcing the younger woman to ease back a step. "Well, you know my contract is up, and with salary negotiations not moving in the direction they should be moving and Danny looking for a new position…" She paused to give the implications of their current status a moment to sink in, then looked directly into the camera's lens. "I guess it's safe to say we'll both be free agents soon."

Before the reporter could produce a follow-up, Danny and Kate made for the ballroom door. The corridor, which had been deserted just a short time earlier, was now crammed with a mishmash of press and fans. People reluctantly gave way as Mike Samlin shouldered his way toward them. Planting himself between the two of them, he gripped their elbows in a hold that made it clear he didn't intend to let either of them pop loose.

"Excuse us. Excuse us," he said as he propelled them past the shouting reporters.

A fan shoved a Wolcott Warrior baby shirt at Kate. She took it automatically but stared down at it in befuddlement.

Suddenly, Mike hooked a left and pushed them through a set of swinging doors. They stumbled into a bustling kitchen, but not one of the busy workers bothered to look up at the intrusion.

Kate tossed the tiny green-and-gold jumpsuit thingy at Danny's chest. "Well, there's a fine wedding present."

He caught the scrap of fabric, then shook it out. "I think it's kind of cute."

"I'm not twenty, Danny, and this isn't 1953. I won't be popping out 3.2 kids now that we've been married for four hours."

He tossed the baby shirt onto the counter and planted his hands on his hips. "Hey, I'm not the one who gave it to you, so don't come after me."

"I have an offer, if anyone's interested," Mike interrupted.

Both Danny and Kate swiveled to face him. "An offer?" she echoed.

Danny scowled as the hairs on the back of his neck prickled. "Why are you talking to us? You know where Gene and Jonas are holed up."

"I've already run it past Judas and Jezebel, but they laughed me out of the room," Mike muttered.

"Judas and Jezebel," Danny repeated. "I like it."

Kate took a step forward. "What was the offer?"

"Danny can stay, but you'd need to agree to remain here at your current salary, Kate."

To his credit, Mike's voice was steady as he served up that morsel of ridiculousness. But that was all the credit Danny could find to extend to him. "Bullshit."

"For how many years?" Kate asked.

"No. There's no way." Danny shook his head so hard his vision blurred, but one thing remained perfectly clear to him. There was no way he was letting his wife settle for anything less than everything she deserved.

"But this could buy us time. Buy *you* some time to prove what you can do," she argued.

"You've already proven what you can do. Over and over again." Danny turned back to Mike. "No one knows what she deserves better than you. I can't believe you had the balls to come down here and try to serve us this steaming pile of crap on today of all days. The same day you stood next to me as I vowed to love and honor her," he snarled, his voice rising.

Mike raised both hands to hold off the onslaught. "I'm doing what my job requires me to do, just as we all have from time to time. Right?" He fixed Danny with a pointed glare. "But now that I can say that the offer has been rejected…" He paused and turned that unflinching stare on Kate. "You *are* rejecting this offer, aren't you?"

Her gaze zipped toward Danny and then back to Mike. "I, uh, yeah. I am." She squared her shoulders and lifted her chin a notch. "As a matter of fact, my price just went up another half mil. And I think we need to look at schools with better football facilities. That practice field is ridiculous, and no one converts their stadiums between football and baseball anymore."

"Actually, a lot of them still do," Danny murmured in her ear.

"Shut up. I'm trying to get you a wedding present." She made a face. "Besides, who in their right mind enjoys watching baseball?"

"More exciting to watch snail races," Danny agreed.

She beamed up at him. "I knew I liked you for a reason."

Mike made a show of clearing his throat. When neither of them looked over, he resorted to shouting an "Ahem!"

Danny chuckled and turned his attention back to his friend. "Yes?"

"I thought I might mention that when I was in the war room with the wonder twins earlier, I heard the names Tulane and Baylor being bandied around. There's a room service elevator off the other end of the kitchen. You can use it to join your agents in the temple of greed." Mike backed off a step as his cell rang. A sly smile curved his lips as he checked to see who the caller was. "Speaking of greed, will you look at that…"

Activating the call, Mike pressed the phone to his ear and boomed. "Hello, Mr. Donner. Yes. Yes, it's true," he said, making shooing motions with his hand. "No, I don't want to lose them either."

Trusting his friend to come through with the clutch catch, Danny took Kate's hand and started through the kitchen. "Come on. Let's see what Tulane has to offer besides gumbo."

"I do love a fresh beignet," Kate said, trotting to catch up with him in her heels.

---

Twenty minutes later, their respective agents were debating the relative merits of swampy Louisiana summers versus all the things that seemed to go wrong in and around Waco when an insistent knock rattled the door. Kate kept her eyes glued to the list of offers and terms she'd received from various universities as she murmured to Danny, "I think that'll be for you."

Her new husband huffed a laugh and pushed himself off the suite's sofa and stalked to the door. "Are you claiming to be clairvoyant now too, Coach Everybody-Wants-Me?"

"Nope, just busy looking over my options. I figured it'd be best to keep you occupied while I work."

"Funny girl," he grumbled, reaching for the handle.

"You're not fired," Mike announced, then brushed past Danny, barreling into the room as only a man who'd downed one too many energy drinks could. Stopping short of Gene's spot at the quasi-conference table, he crossed his arms over his chest. "We're not drawing up papers. There will be no termination."

The agent eyed him shrewdly. "There was a verbal offer and acceptance of Coach McMillan's resignation."

"We're prepared to pay a modest bonus to offset any distress we may have put Coach McMillan through over the past couple of days."

Kate dropped the legal pad she was holding when she spotted Richard Donner framed in the doorway. "I thought you were on your way to Hong Kong."

Richard pursed his lips. "Funny thing about planes. You can turn them around."

Mike plowed ahead, his movements jerky but purposeful. He reached into his pocket and pulled out a small neon-green slip of paper. She gasped when he unfolded the sticky note she'd given him with her salary proposal and slapped it down onto the table in front of Jonas.

"Congratulations, Coach Snyder. This should make you the highest paid women's basketball coach in the NCAA. By a mile."

Kate narrowed her eyes as she rose from the sofa. "And the half mil we discussed earlier?"

"I added it on."

Jonas peeked at the figure written on the scrap of paper, and his eyebrows flew toward his hairline. A laugh escaped him as he looked up and nodded. "He did. I almost feel bad about taking a cut of that."

"Feel free to waive your percentage on any terms you didn't negotiate," she said mildly.

"I said almost," her agent quickly replied.

Smirking, Kate turned her attention back to the athletic director. "And the other terms?"

Mike shook his head, conceding defeat in the face of her persistence. "I can't do anything about the stadium situation until we have ticket sales to justify the change, but we do have a donor who has pledged a generous sum toward the improvement of the practice facilities."

"Have you now?" Kate turned toward Richard Donner, an amused smile tugging at her mouth. "I wonder who it could be?"

"Of course, there are some stipulations on the money," Richard warned.

"What kind of stipulations?" Danny asked, speaking up for the first time, his wary gaze on the wealthy alumnus.

"The Richard W. Donner Athletic Complex," the man announced, a wide smile spreading across his face. "Has a nice ring to it, doesn't it?"

As always, Kate was both amused and annoyed by the man's desperate need for glory. She'd been so sure he'd be unable to resist, she'd banked her entire career on it. "Sounds wonderful. As always, thank you for your generous support of our programs."

"Yes, thank you," Mike echoed, then elbowed Danny sharply.

"Thank you," he managed to grunt.

Donner nodded, accepting their gratitude as his due, then turned to Kate. "I'm just glad you caught me in the flyover states. It's a helluva lot harder to file a change of flight plan when you're out over the Pacific, you know."

Danny, Mike, Gene, and Jonas all turned to her in unison.

"You did this?" Danny asked.

"I should have known," Mike muttered.

"Way to go, Coach," Gene said, leaning back in his chair and gazing up at her with blatant admiration.

Only Jonas dared to laugh. "That's our Kate. She plays hard, and she plays to win."

Richard Donner turned to Danny and offered his hand. "You're a lucky man, Coach McMillan."

"Don't I know it," Danny said, fixing an unsettling, blue stare on her.

A few beats of awkward silence filled the room, and Kate forced herself not to fidget under her husband's intense scrutiny. If he thought he could psych her out when she already had the game in hand, the man had another think coming.

"Speaking of lucky men," Donner prompted, breaking the tension.

Mike sprang into action like a windup toy. "Oh! Right." He pulled a key card out of his pocket and held it out to them. "I can handle the nitty-gritty stuff with Gene and Jonas. You two have better things to do."

Danny glanced at the key card. "We do?"

"It's your wedding night," Donner boomed, grinning expansively. "Chancellor Martin thought securing the honeymoon suite for two important personnel would be a nice gesture on the part of the university."

Danny shrank back from the key as if it were a snake. A dull red flush crept up his neck. "Oh, he did, did he?"

Before things got too far out of hand, Kate snatched the key from Mike's fingertips and reached for Danny's hand. "Well, that was right nice of him," she drawled. "Wasn't that nice, sugarplum?" she cooed, fluttering her lashes at her husband.

In an instant, all that intensity zeroed in on her. "No. No sugarplum."

Tugging on his hand, she started for the door. "Come

on, honey lamb. Let's leave the nice vipers to earn their cut off the top."

"No honey lamb either," he said, shooting a warning glare at his old friend when Mike started to snicker.

"How about hot stuff?" Kate asked as she pulled him out into the hall.

"Getting warmer." He stopped dragging his feet and caught her up against him. "Only one problem with your plan, mastermind."

A puzzled frown pulled at her brows as she tried to figure out what she might have missed. "Oh? What's that?"

He jerked his chin at the doors lining the hallway. "We don't know which room that key opens."

Temporarily stymied by his reasoning, she had to laugh. "Yeah, well..." She glanced over her shoulder at the room they'd just escaped. "We could go back in there and ask, but I really don't want to. What if they try to take it back?"

"They can't take it back. I'll crush them if they try," he growled.

Kate beamed at him. "Oh, so macho. I like it. Well, we can either go down to the front desk and ask, or" — she scanned the deserted corridor once again — "we employ a little deductive reasoning."

He kissed her hard and fast, stamping the latter idea with his approval. He set her down on her too-high heels once more but held on until he was certain she was steady. "Okay, Detective Snyder. Wow me."

"Oh, I plan on it." She pressed a finger to her bottom lip, then tapped it. "We're on the top floor already. Stands to reason all the best rooms would be up here."

"You're brilliant."

"I know." She smiled, warmed by the affection in his tone more than the compliment itself. "That room on the other end of the hall has double doors and what appears to be some kind of plaque on the wall. I'm going to put my money on that one."

"Quick and bold. I like that." He squinted at the far door. "I can't read it from here. Can you?"

"No," she admitted as she stepped out of the nosebleed pumps Millie had forced her into. Swooping down, she caught the pair by the toothpick heels, then used them to gesture toward her pick. "Race you for it."

Their eyes met, held, and then they both took off down the corridor at a full sprint. Hampered by her snug skirt, she touched the brass plaque engraved with the words "Honeymoon Suite" a fraction of a second after he did.

"I let you win," she panted, falling back against the door and letting her shoes clatter to the floor at his feet.

"Bull."

"My feet hurt from those stupid shoes."

"Sexy shoes," he corrected. "Whiner."

"I'm wearing a skirt," she cried, gesturing angrily at the knee-length instrument of torture that hobbled her stride.

Bracing his hand against the door, Danny caged her in. "Excuses, excuses."

She looked up at him from under her lashes. "I love you."

"I love you too," he answered, his lips hovering just above hers. "Even if you do play dirty."

He closed the distance before she could draw breath. Thankfully, the man was more than generous about sharing his. They kissed slow and deep, taking their time, savoring one another and the victory.

"You have no idea how dirty I would have played," she whispered as he peppered her throat and neck with those little sucking kisses that made her insides clench and dissolve all at the same time. "I would have done whatever it took to keep you. You're mine."

Capturing her face in his hands, he tipped her chin up. "And you're mine. Forever."

"Forever," she agreed on a sigh.

This kiss was hotter, deeper, and more demanding than the last. She moaned into his mouth when he slipped one hand down to stroke her ass. Kate tugged impatiently at her skirt, lifting it up just enough to hook a leg over his. Danny pressed into her, lining their bodies up with mind-melting precision. He slipped his hand under the hem of her skirt and shoved it a few inches higher.

"God, I love it when you wear skirts. Skirts and sports bras," he rasped against her cheek. "I love seeing you in both, but I love seeing you out of them more."

"I have to admit, I prefer to do without them both."

She arched against him, and he groaned. "For the love of all that's holy, where did that key go?"

Kate slid a hand between them and stroked the hard ridge of his erection. "I think I dropped it with the shoes."

He groaned again, but this time, it was laced with pain and frustration. "You'll have to get it. I might put an eye out if I try to bend over."

She snorted and wound her arms tight around his neck, holding him there for just a moment longer. "Think pretty highly of yourself, don't you?"

A low growl rumbled in his throat. She felt it roll through her as his mouth covered hers again. "Get the key, or I get to have you here and now."

The all-too-familiar whir of a camera shutter made her laugh tangle in her throat. Danny froze, one hand up her skirt, the other palming her breast through her jacket. "Millie, you have half a second to run before I take you apart piece by piece," he said in a deep, menacing tone.

"Sweetheart, I only run if there's a shoe sale involved," Millie answered with her sandpapery laugh.

Poking her head around Danny's shoulder, Kate glared at her friend. "What the hell are you doing?"

"I needed one more shot. Just in case." Unfazed by Danny's threats, Millie sauntered over to the shoes Kate had ditched and pulled out the hotel key card.

"In case of what?" Kate asked, holding Danny snug against her as she took the plastic key from her friend.

"In case I need a distraction." She leaned up on tiptoe and kissed Danny's cheek. "Congratulations—you won the girl." She kissed Kate's cheek next and then pulled back, tears shining in her eyes. "Best wishes to the bride."

"Thank you," Kate called after her.

Millie simply raised a hand in acknowledgment. "Strawberries and champagne in the room. Not that you two look like you need them." The elevator chimed, and she called out, "Enjoy your sexy times."

The second the elevator doors whooshed shut, Danny pressed his forehead to Kate's. "We have to get you some new friends."

She laughed and rocked her forehead against his. "Nope. I like the ones I have just fine."

"They're cracked."

Kate pressed a playful kiss to his lips, then swung her arm back to grope for the key slot. "And they say such nice things about you."

Danny gently freed the key from her fingers. A quick swipe, and Kate had to make a grab for his forearms as the door swung inward. He pulled her upright, then took her with him as he stepped away from the open door.

"What are you doing?"

But before she got the question out, he'd caught her behind the knees and cradled her to his chest. When she giggled, he pretended to stagger under her weight. "Man, I'd better get back in the weight room."

"That's it. I'm crushing you with my thighs just as soon as we get your life insurance straightened out."

He grinned and stole a hard, fast kiss. "No life insurance. You're going to have to deal with me for a good long time, Mrs. McMillan." He swiped one more smacking kiss. "It's a good thing you can afford to keep me."

She snorted. "It's still a pittance compared to what you guys make."

He shook his head. "Don't dismiss what you did today, Kate. You scored big, and I know you're going to come at them even harder next time. You deserve everything you got and more."

Offering him her sweetest smile, she pressed her cheek to his shoulder. "Were you planning to carry me over that threshold, Mr. Snyder? If so, you might want to step up your game a bit."

"Yes, Coach," he answered agreeably. "Whatever you say, Coach."

"I say I love you, super jock."

He kissed her soft and sweet, then stepped into the

room. Setting her on her feet once more, he tucked her hair behind her ear. "I love you too, my little flower."

Beaming, she wriggled from his grasp, unzipped her skirt, and stepped out of the pool of fabric with exaggerated delicacy. Shooting him a flirtatious glance, she turned toward the bedroom and called over her shoulder, "Race you for the bed!"

# Epilogue

KATE TUGGED ON DANNY'S HAND, DRAWING TO A STOP JUST outside the door of Calhoun's bar. "Okay, we have a six a.m. flight, and we still have to pack. We're in, we drink, we're out."

He chuckled. "You are a party animal."

"Danny, I'm tired. I've been on the road or on the phone with my agent for the past two weeks. I just want to get on that plane and get away for a while."

"You just want to go home and watch the NBA draft."

She flashed a sheepish smile. "Well, it's been twenty years since Wolcott has had a first-round prospect coming out of the men's program. I'm excited for Ty."

He leaned in and placed a tender kiss at the center of her forehead. "Okay. We'll make it quick. Then we'll go home and turn on NSN while you pack your bikini."

She snorted, then hauled him back for a better kiss. Right smack on the lips. "My bikini isn't the star of the show. Wait until you see the Speedo I scored for you. We're talking Mark Spitz 1976 red, white, and blue for my all-American boy. I thought it would be fitting, with the Fourth of July coming up and all."

Unperturbed by the threat, he disentangled himself and gestured toward the door to the bar. "I bet I'll look awesome in it."

"I bet you will too with your big, powerful, former football player bod," she cooed. But competitive annoyance surged as she yanked the handle on the heavy wooden door. He would look awesome, even in a ridiculous suit like that. As if she'd allow him to wear such a thing. The man attracted enough female attention just walking around in his coach khakis and a golf shirt.

Glancing back over her shoulder, she found him wearing his mind-reader smirk. She was conjuring a zinger to wipe that smidge of smug off his face when they stepped across the threshold and were hit by a wall of noise. Not the usual cacophony of clinking glasses and shrieking coeds but one cohesive shout of "Surprise!"

Before she realized what was happening, Millie enveloped her in a perfumed hug. "Happy wedding day!"

"Wait, what?" Kate squirmed, trying to break free from Millie's grasp. Her resistance was futile. She may have had a height and muscle advantage on her friend, but Millie had a strength of will that made fire-forged iron look as flexible as aluminum foil.

"You said you were going to have a wedding, but then you didn't do anything," Millie shouted over the barroom hubbub.

"I've been gone," Kate reminded her.

"And tomorrow you leave for your honeymoon. Well, you can't have a honeymoon without a wedding, missy," she said starchily. She clamped a hand around Kate's wrist like a manacle and pulled. "Come on."

In the blink of an eye, Kate found herself torn from Danny's side and swallowed by the crowd. Summer sessions had started early in June, but the crowd was still much thinner than usual. She waved to Mike Samlin and his wife, and they raised their hands in return. She spotted the track and field coach, her own assistants, as well as a couple of Ty's from the men's team, and, surprisingly enough, Dominick Mann, Wolcott's enigmatic baseball coach.

"How'd you get Dom Mann to come?" Kate shouted into Millie's ear.

Millie shrugged. "I asked."

"I've invited him to a hundred things," Kate complained. "He never comes to anything."

Millie's steps slowed as they wound through a knot of revelers near the dartboards. "I'm a lot more charming than you are," she replied with a saccharine-sweet smile.

Kate laughed. "Bullshit."

"And less intimidating," Millie added. "Believe it or not, Katie, not all men are as enthralled by your Wonder Womanness as dear Danny."

Craning her neck, Kate scanned the crowd for more familiar faces. Her steps faltered when she caught the profile of a man seated at the small table she, Millie, and Avery usually shared, but Millie yanked her along like a steam engine. They were heading for the ladies' room at the back of the bar, full speed ahead.

Once inside, Millie released her arm, but Kate was immobilized by a spindly missile aimed right at her torso.

"Oh, Aunt Katie," her niece Kylie crooned as she hugged her tight. "You're getting married."

Kate ran her hand over the girl's dishwater-blond hair, a soft smile curving her lips as she allowed herself to be squeezed with the anaconda-like enthusiasm of an almost-thirteen-year-old. No point in quibbling over the technicalities that took place at the courthouse weeks before. With Kylie here, whatever Millie had cooked up for these festivities would be family official.

Patting her niece's bony back, she nodded. "That's what I hear. Too bad no one told me, or I would have dressed better."

Kylie drew back and stared at the cropped capris and washed-thin T-shirt Kate wore with a look of horrified distaste only an adolescent girl could pull off. She hesitated when she spotted Kate's brightly colored sneakers.

"Well, the shoes are pretty," Kylie said at last.

Kate preened, both at the compliment and the fact that she and her beloved girl shared some similar interests. She and her sister, Audrey, had struggled their whole lives to find common ground, but Kylie seemed to be the perfect meld of the two of them. Someone cleared their throat with a loud "Ahem," and Kate looked up to find her sister standing beside the lone toilet stall, a long white garment bag suspended by her fingers.

"Oh. Hey, Aud," Kate said, reluctantly untangling herself from Kylie's gangly embrace. "You're here."

"Well, I finally got invited to one of your weddings," her sister said with a sniff. "I could hardly pass that up, right?"

"Audrey, I tried—"

But her sister stopped her with an outstretched hand. "I know. I get it." She shot an affection-filled glance at her daughter, then smiled. "We're just glad to be here." Tipping her head toward the door, she said, "Mark's here too," referring to her husband. "He was excited to get to watch part of the draft with all you basketball types."

"Speaking of the draft," Millie interrupted. "We need to get you changed and this show on the road, or we aren't going to be able to pull this off before the first pick." She tugged the zipper on the garment bag all the way down. "Dress."

Kate caught a glimpse of traditional white satin and organza, then realized something was missing. Kate found herself awaiting a lecture on patriarchal traditions and the suppression of feminist ideals by the wedding industry. "Where's Avery?"

"She's handling things out front. She said to tell you that if you find it hypocritical to dress yourself up as a vestal virgin en route to ritual sacrifice, you can find her by the pool table and she'll protect you from Bridezilla." Millie pursed her lips. "I think she means me, but as usual, Avery misses the point." She pulled a flat, white box out of her ever-present tote bag and thrust it at Kate. "Bridal undergarments."

"Wait until you see the shoes, Aunt Katie," Kylie gushed. "They're like Cinderella shoes."

Millie snorted. "As if Cinderella could afford Jimmy Choos."

Kate blinked. She'd spent enough time with Millie to know that the name meant some serious shoe dollars spent. "Jimmy Choos?"

A beatific smile lit Millie's face. "I got them at a trillion percent off. You are so lucky to have those enormous feet. The sale racks were practically begging me to relieve them of their burden." She nodded to the stall. "But shoes last. Get changed, and we'll get you hitched up."

"Millie's a romantic," Kate called to Kylie as

she stepped into the stall. "Every day, she whistles 'Someday My Prince Will Come' to all the little mice and bluebirds." She smiled at her sister as she draped the garment bag over the top of the stall. "Thanks, Audrey."

Audrey nodded. "We'll be out here if you need help with the zipper or something."

As Kate swung the stall door shut, she heard Kylie say, "That song was from *Snow White*, and she didn't sing it to mice and bluebirds. She sang it to the dwarves. *Cinderella* had the mice and birds, but Aunt Katie can never keep them straight."

Eyeing the garment bag with a mixture of excitement and trepidation, she stripped out of her clothes and opened the box first. Millie had chosen lacy, white bikini panties and a matching strapless bra. Simple. Beautiful. Exactly what Kate might have chosen herself.

Clad only in the new lingerie and her sneakers, she tuned out the running commentary coming from the other side of the door and zeroed in on the dress bag. It wasn't overly puffy, thank God. And Millie hadn't selected any kind of special underpinnings, so whatever was inside had to be fairly simple.

Nudging the bag open wider, she gasped when the faint opalescent sheen of the satin came to life under the harsh fluorescent lights. A thin layer of organza covered the satin from the softly draped neckline to the hem, like early-morning mist clinging to a rippling river. She pushed the protective cover off the hanger, anxious to get the full impact.

The dress was perfect. A long, slender column of fabric so sumptuous it needed no beading or embellishment.

A sob rose in her throat and caught on a loud hiccup.

"Everything okay?" Millie called out worriedly.

Okay? The word was nowhere close to what she needed to describe this dress. It was everything she had dreamed of and like nothing she'd ever imagined.

"Katie?" Audrey prompted.

Kate swallowed hard. "Perfect," she managed to croak at last. "It's perfect."

---

While Kate was in the bathroom with the girls, Danny sauntered over to the bar and found Mike standing there beside his wife, a suit bag hanging from the brass rail beneath the bar.

"Hey, thanks for bringing this for me. I didn't know how I was going to get over here with the full suit on without Kate getting suspicious."

"No problem," Mike said. "Happy to help."

Danny smiled at Mike's wife, Diane, and leaned in. "Hey, sweetheart, how are you?"

Diane stretched onto tiptoes to hug him hard. "I'm so happy for you, Danny. So happy to see you happy."

Chuckling at her gushing, he shook his head as he drew back. "You are the happiest girl I know, so if you're happy, and you're even happier that I'm happy, this place might explode from happiness."

Mike hesitated only for a second, then leaned in to speak in a low tone. "Hey, listen, it may not all be great news. There's someone here that you may not want to see."

Danny looked at him quizzically. The only person he might not want to see would be the big boss, and only because he was getting tired of that guy looking down his nose at him. "Chancellor Martin?"

"No, it's not the chancellor." Mike shot a glance at the back of the barroom. "Danny, your mom couldn't make it. She said that the travel was too much for her, and she wanted you and Kate to come up to see her when you get back from your trip."

Danny nodded. "I kind of figured. She's having trouble with her hip, and I knew she wasn't crazy about the idea of flying."

"But she sent a proxy," Mike said darkly.

It took only a moment for Danny to key in on his friend's pointed look. "Tommy. She sent Tommy," he concluded flatly.

The fixed smile Diane wore melted off her face. "Yeah, she did. And LeAnn is with him."

"Of course she is," Danny muttered.

He looked down at the floor for moment, digesting this latest development in the McMillan family drama. A couple of hours. If he could take hit after hit from massive defensive linemen, he could handle a couple of hours in the same room with his brother, right?

"I can make them leave," Mike offered.

"But I don't think you should," Diane interjected.

When both men turned to look at her, she raised her hands in a gesture of futility. "What does it matter anymore?"

Danny blinked, and Mike scoffed, but Diane went on undeterred.

"Seriously, Danny, does it matter?" she prodded. "You're happy, right? You have everything you want right here. They have everything they want out in

Seattle. Think of them as just another couple of boosters. Smile, nod, move on."

Unhooking the hanger from the bar, Danny draped the suit over his arm, nodded to his two oldest friends, and started toward the back of the bar. Along the way, he shook hands with new friends and colleagues, accepted back slaps and high fives from the few students in the bar, and, with each step, came to realize that Diane was right. As usual. This was his turf now. His home. He had the woman of his dreams and a future he couldn't wait to share with her.

He and Tommy didn't have to be close. Hell, they didn't even have to see each other, unless their mother organized some kind of command performance. All he had to do was be polite and cordial. He'd shake the man's hand and treat LeAnn with the same respect he'd give any acquaintance's spouse.

The crowd shifted, then parted as he neared the table Kate and her friends usually occupied. His baby brother sat with his back to the bar. Danny used the opportunity to take in the changes the last few years had wrought. Though he'd always been smaller than Danny, Tommy was now thicker through the waist. His hair was the same dark brown. Maybe a bit thinner than it had been, but no gray yet. Unconsciously, Danny ran his hand over his own hair. He still had the thick waves he'd inherited from their mother, but he could almost feel the strands of silver tickling his palm.

Tommy.

He'd carried him around as a baby. Carried him his whole life. In a way, Danny understood his brother's need to break free from the fraternal grip. He just wished Tommy hadn't felt total annihilation was the only option.

LeAnn spotted him first. She looked exactly the same. Young, bright as a copper penny, and sharp as a tack. As he approached, it occurred to Danny that his ex may have once been a grad student ten years his junior, but she had to be at least a year or two older than his brother.

"LeAnn," he said, drawing to a stop beside the table. Tommy looked up, startled by his sudden appearance, but Danny didn't wait for him to adjust. "Tom." His heart ached as he looked into his brother's eyes, but he held it together. "I understand Mom couldn't make it, but thanks for coming." He extended his hand, and Tommy gave it a long stare before returning the grip.

"You're welcome. Congratulations."

"We're very happy for you, Danny," LeAnn chimed in. "And so glad we could make it out here for this. I promised your mom I'd take lots of pictures."

Danny forced a tight smile. "Great. She'll love that." He took a step back and held the suit bag up like a shield. "Sorry, I have to get changed."

Always fast on her feet, LeAnn recovered first. "Oh! Yes. Go," she said, making a shooing motion. "We can't wait to meet Kate. I've always admired her."

The tightness in Danny's cheeks eased at the mention of his wife's name. "Yes, well, there's a lot of her to admire," he said, his nerves getting the best of him at last. "A lot of things about her," he corrected in a rush. Turning to his brother, he inclined his head. "Thanks for coming."

Tommy returned the nod. "We're happy to be here."

Out of the corner of his eye, he saw Avery making a beeline for him, and thank God she hadn't heard his slipup. "I have to go," he repeated. "We'll catch up after." He raised a hand to halt Avery's march. "I'm going. I'm going."

"You have exactly five minutes to be out in front of that jukebox, or I'm coming in after you," she warned.

He glanced at the relic from the 1980s, then back at Avery. "That's where we're having the ceremony?"

"I have it all queued up to play 'I Am Woman' the second I pronounce you woman and chattel."

He leaned down and pressed a smacking kiss to Avery's cheek. "What church was it that gave you license to kill?"

"The Universal Church of Life," she pronounced primly. "If you want to continue living, I suggest you get changed and get out here before Millie finishes with your bride."

"Going," he repeated, brushing past her to get to the men's room.

Once inside, he changed with a haste he hadn't tapped since his locker room interview days. Unlike most jocks, he didn't relish getting caught on camera wearing nothing but a towel.

Humming under his breath, he turned to face the lone mirror in the room as he measured the ends of his necktie. The glass was foggy and smeared with God-knows-what, but there was no clouding the anticipation rising inside him. Soon, he'd see Kate in an actual wedding dress. Until Millie mentioned it, he hadn't realized how much he wanted that. Not just for her, but for himself as well. And yes, they'd be in a dank, musty bar and not a church, but it didn't matter. They'd be surrounded by friends, colleagues, and…family.

Snugging the Windsor knot up to his collar, he sighed as he studied his reflection, then reached into the pile of discarded clothes to retrieve his phone.

His mother answered on the second ring, breathless and a little agitated. He smiled when he realized he was most likely interrupting her bridge group. "Hey, Ma," he said by way of greeting.

"Danny?"

Her bewildered tone carried a note of annoyance that made him smile. "I know it's not my day to call, but we're here, and we're going to do the ceremony thing, and, well…" He paused to brace himself for what he needed to say next. "Thanks for sending Tommy out for the party. It's good to see him."

His mother covered the phone and called out, "I bid two hearts!" Danny chuckled, and his mother huffed as she came back to the call. "Sorry, it was my turn."

"I won't keep you, Ma. I just… I'll call when we get back, okay? Set up a time when Kate and I can get up there to visit."

"You'll call on the Wednesday after you get back?" she confirmed.

Ducking his head, he nodded. "Yeah, Ma. I'll call you on the Wednesday we get back."

"Okay, Danny. Love you," she said, though she was clearly in a hurry to get back to her game. "Take care of Tommy. Oh, and give my love to Kate," she added just before ending the call.

Danny pocketed the phone, scooped up his discarded clothing, and shoved it all into the suit bag. Wadding it

into a ball, he tucked it under his arm and stepped into
the noisy bar. A few catcalls and whistles followed him
as he made his way to the jukebox. He raised a hand
to acknowledge the jeering, but his smile stretched a
mile wide.

Avery nodded to a pile of bags jumbled in a corner,
and he added his to the collection. When he turned, he
spotted the crepe paper wedding bells hung from the
ceiling rafters and pinned to walls among the Wolcott
banners and pennants. Mike stepped up to take his
place at his side, just as he had at the courthouse. Out
of the corner of his eye, he saw Tommy and LeAnn
slide off their bar stools and make their way toward the
gathering crowd.

The ladies' room door opened, and Millie flew out,
her mouth drawn in a taut line of disapproval. When she
bustled up to take her place across from him, she pierced
him with a glare.

"Your bride is a pain in the ass," she announced to
the assembled group.

"Uh-oh," Avery said under her breath. "Someone
didn't comply with the plan."

Millie swiveled to glare at her, then froze when she
saw the dashiki-styled caftan Avery wore over her
clothes. "Our lady of cultural appropriation, preserve
us!" she said in a rushed whisper. "What in God's name
are you wearing?"

Avery extended an arm and beamed as her flowing
sleeves billowed. "Like it? I found it in my mom's closet
and thought it was perfect."

Millie rubbed the bridge of her nose with two fingers. Amused by their byplay but growing inexplicably

nervous, Danny searched the crowd for familiar faces. When he caught sight of the NSN talking heads chatting it up on one of the muted televisions, it occurred to him that he hadn't seen Ty Ransom yet.

"Hey, is Ty coming, or is he in New York for the draft?" he asked Millie, hoping to distract her from the topic of Avery's wardrobe choices. The question worked like a charm. Millie's head swiveled around, and her gaze narrowed as she searched his face. The hair on the back of his neck rippled. "What? What is it?"

She stared at him for a second longer. "Oh, he's not in New York, but I doubt he's coming."

"What's going on?"

At that moment, the bathroom door opened, and Kate's sister and niece emerged. Audrey nodded to Millie, who cast a worried glance at one of the television screens.

"Things aren't good on the home front. Tell you about it later," Millie murmured, then turned to signal someone in the corner.

Danny jumped when a six-piece pep band launched into a jaunty rendition of the school fight song. The bar's patrons fell silent as the band ramped up the tempo. The ladies' room door opened again. This time, Kate stood silhouetted in the frame, her long, lithe figure a shadow against the bright lighting behind her. And then, she started to walk toward him.

Though he preferred skirts that showed off her spectacular legs, even Danny had to admit the dress was perfect. The top of it draped softly below her collarbone. He was sure the effect was supposed to be soft and demure, but the way it left the tantalizing hollows

exposed practically dared a man to kiss her there. And
he would. Maybe even before he stripped her out of that
tempting column of floaty, white fabric.

But for now, he was content to look at her. Stare at
her, really. He always thought she was beautiful, but
he'd never seen her look quite this stunning before. At
least, not without a ball in her hand. He wanted to soak
it all in and let her milk the moment too, because if he
had his way, she'd never be a bride again.

She held a small clutch of flowers at her waist. He
didn't know what they were called, but he recognized
the thin stems of bell-like blossoms from the flower beds
his mother kept along the side of her house. He gaped
like a love-struck teenager as she moved slowly across
the dimly lit barroom, working every step. It wasn't until
she drew close that he caught a flash of color and tore
his gaze away from her long enough to look down.

Kate smiled, handed her bouquet off to Millie, and
lifted the hem of her dress just enough to expose the toes
of the multicolored trainers he'd given her.

Swallowing the boulder in his throat, he took her
hands in his and pulled her close. "Great shoes," he
whispered.

"Thanks. I like them."

"I love you."

Kate beamed at him, her hazel eyes dancing with dev-
ilment. "Well, then, I guess that makes me the winner."

Clearing her throat loudly, Avery stretched her arms
wide as if calling down the deities. "Dearly beloved, we
are gathered here today to deliver this woman and this
man into the bondage of eternal teamwork…"

*Keep reading for a sneak peek of the
next book from Maggie Wells*

*Play for Keeps*

# Chapter 1

MILLIE JENSEN RAPPED ON THE TINTED GLASS SLIDING DOOR off Ty Ransom's patio until her knuckles ached, refusing to let up. This time, she added a threat for good measure. "Ty, if you don't open this door in the next ten seconds, I swear I'll throw a chair through the glass."

He couldn't hear her, of course. The glass was the super-duper insulated kind. The type to not only repel the elements, but also empty threats and spin doctors in the midst of mild coronary failure. She cupped her hands around her face, pressed her nose to the glass, and peered into the gloomy room. The dark, combined with a vaulted ceiling, gave the space a cavernous appearance. Caught in the flickering light of the television, oversized furniture cast hulking shadows on the walls. She peered at the screen. A pair of talking heads yammered at one another. The National Sports Network logo anchored the scrolling ticker at the bottom of the screen, but the latest scores were taking a back seat to big-time gossip this night.

She was about to call to him again when she saw the display on his phone light up with the incoming call. "Don't you answer that!" she shouted through the glass.

He didn't even check to see who was calling, much less answer. Tyrell Ransom, head coach of Wolcott University's men's basketball team, sat sprawled in a massive armchair parked in front of the screen, his

long legs akimbo. The hand that held the phone dangled
over the arm of the chair. Millie squinted, wishing she'd
chosen high-beam night vision as her super power when
she'd clicked through the latest "Choose Your Super
Power" internet quiz. The second the call clicked over
to voicemail, she turned the meaty side of her fist to the
glass and began to pound with all her might.

At last, the shadowy figure stirred.

Millie pounded harder, urging him to hurry up and
unfurl his long, lanky frame. He rose from the chair so
slowly, she almost shouted again. Instead, she held her
breath as he approached. Each step he took was deliberate. His gaze never left her. A part of her—the part she
liked to keep tamped down tight, because her impulses
tended to get her in trouble—admired the lithe grace
of his movements. No doubt this man was an athlete.
Once, an elite one. He was still a man in his prime, even
though his days in the spotlight were long behind him.

He narrowed those startling amber eyes and peered
down at her through the glass door as if she were a spec-
imen on display. Falling back on old habits, she snapped
to full military attention before meeting his questioning
gaze. Her father had been a master sergeant in the U.S.
Marine Corps. It took a helluva lot more than one sulky,
washed-up basketball giant to intimidate her.

"Open the damn door." She enunciated each word
carefully, making lipreading possible in case her intentions were somehow lost in the shuffle. She'd slipped
out of the wedding party she'd helped put together to
celebrate her best friend's recent nuptials to come check
on him. She wasn't about to be turned away.

"Now!" she bellowed when he didn't move fast

enough for her tastes, giving the glass another thump with the side of her fist. The lock snicked, and he lifted the security bar. Before he could do the honors, she grabbed the handle and yanked the door open.

Shooting a disparaging glance at the glass in his hand, she brushed past him. "Yeah, because sitting in the dark getting drunk is always the best course of action."

"I hadn't thought about getting drunk," he mused, letting the door slide shut with a *thunk*. "Good idea." With a grace that always surprised her, he turned and walked toward the fully stocked wet bar. "Hey, aren't you supposed to be at Kate and Danny's party thing tonight?"

"It's still going on. Your absence was noted," she added pointedly.

"Yeah, well, I wasn't much up for socializing." He tossed the clear liquid he'd been drinking down the drain, then nodded to the crystal tumblers lined on a shelf. "Can I buy you a drink, Mil?"

She watched as he splashed less than a centimeter of liquid into the bottom of the highball glass he'd been carrying. This time, it was amber, and not clear. Crap. If he hadn't been drinking before, he was now.

Ignoring the offer, she opted to switch on a floor lamp. Warily, Millie peered down at her shoes. The nappy faux hide on her Jimmy Choo ballet flats was damp but otherwise appeared none the worse for wear in spite of her stealth approach. When Ty hadn't answered the ring of the bell, she'd had to activate plan B. Since there was no way she'd chance rolling ass over teakettle down his steeply sloped yard to get to the back door, she'd cut across the neighbor's yard for a stealth approach to his split-level McMansion.

Exhaling her frustration, she shifted straight into fixer mode. "Okay. Time to pull up your big boy pants and make a plan."

Without taking his eyes off her, Ty tossed the drink back with a flick of his wrist. He fixed her with an oddly defiant glare as he let the tumbler slip from his fingers and drop to the floor.

"My big boy pants?"

Millie goggled as the heavy crystal glass rolled across the wide-planked wood without shattering. She stared after it in wonder. Had it survived the fall because his arms were so long and it hadn't had far to go? Shaking her head, she thanked God she wouldn't have to add cleaning up shards of glass to her to-do list for the night.

"Right." She clapped her hands together. "Your woman has ditched you. No big deal. Happens all the time."

"Thank you for your condolences."

She let the sarcasm pass. He could expend his anger on her all he wanted. She was more worried about what he said to other people.

Moving past him into the still-shadowy great room, she spotted the remote control perched on the arm of the overstuffed armchair and made a beeline for it. She pointed the zapper at the screen and switched the power off, plunging them into thick, buzzing silence.

Feeling steadier, she faced Ty once more. "The real juicy part is she left you for one of your players."

Ty planted his big ball-handler hands on his hips. "Thanks for clarifying," he said gruffly. "I almost missed the juice."

Millie rolled her eyes. She didn't care what her friend

Kate said about an athlete's innate mental toughness. There was nothing trickier than handling a bunch of super jocks and their touchy egos. "I *am* sorry, Ty, but you had to have seen something like this coming, right?"

"Aren't you supposed to be making me feel better or something?"

"I'm not your mommy. I'm not here to kiss the boo-boo and make everything better." A shiver ran down her spine even as she spoke the words. Awareness. Hot. Tingling. Happened every time they shared air space. Which meant she'd had more than two years to get a handle on her attraction to him. Too bad being near him made her grip feel shaky. "No, my job is to help you put the best possible face on a situation that may reflect badly on the university."

He inclined his head slightly but still managed to look straight down his nose at her. "You're a real pal, Millie."

"I'm working," she reminded him. "I'll try to be a better pal when I'm off the clock."

"What do you want me to do?"

Setting her jaw, she studied him, measuring his readiness to step up to the line on this one. "First of all, we have to keep you off the phone. Then, we need to spin your marital situation: amicable split, coming for a long time, you wish her well, blah, blah, blah. When they start lobbing questions about Dante, we keep the focus on your contributions to his NBA career."

"So you don't think I should go on TV and tell the press I want to take a baseball bat to his shins?"

She blinked, surprised by even the hint of violence coming from this quiet giant of a man. "Do you?"

He shrugged one shoulder. "Kinda."

"Over her? Really?" The questions, three simple words tinged with seven shades of disbelief, popped out before she could stop them. "I thought you two were pretty much done before all this."

The air between them sizzled and cracked with tension. At last, he ran a hand over his close-cropped hair and down to knead the muscles in his neck. "No. Not over her."

"Then why?"

The corners of his mouth curled up in a rueful smile, but she didn't see even a glimmer of happiness in his eyes. When he spoke, he enunciated each word slowly, as if he were forced to explain his reasoning to a particularly slow toddler. "Because I envy his court time. His career. His future." He flung one long arm out. "He's just starting out. No injuries. Nothing holding him back. He's going to have the career I never had."

She raised her eyebrows. "Then this could be the strangest midlife crisis ever."

He held up both hands. "Hey, I'm not having a crisis, and this is not my fault."

His palms looked to be about the size of salad plates. A fact Millie had long found intriguing. But this wasn't the time or place to speculate about how great it would feel to have those big mitts all over her. She could let her fantasies loose later. When she was alone.

Besides, the defensive note in his denial told her he wasn't quite as cool with his wife leaving him for one of his NBA-bound players as he wanted her to think. Feeling the need to do something, anything, to make him realize she was on his side, she reached out and gave his arm an awkward pat. "No. No, it's not. And I am sorry."

He looked down at her hand, a smirk curving his lips as she yanked her fingers away a tad too quickly. "Wow. You really suck at the sympathy thing."

Millie had the good grace to grimace. "I've never been very touchy-feely."

Ty cocked his head. "I'm surprised."

"Are you?"

He took a half step closer. "You don't strike me as the kind of woman to shy away from anything."

Proved how much he knew about her. It was all she could do to hold her ground. Not because she was scared of him. More that she might not be able to keep her own impulses in check. Ty Ransom was not only tall, built, and too handsome for his own good, but he was sweet and funny in a self-deprecating way that more successful jocks never quite mastered. A flutter of nerves tightened her belly.

Flattening her hand on her midriff to quell the internal uprising, she plastered her public relations smile on her face. "Well, I do like a good fight."

"I've noticed."

"That's why I'm here. We don't have to let the press run this thing. Take control of your message instead of spouting off. Make the story the one you want to tell."

"I don't see what there is to control," he said with feigned nonchalance. "My wife left me for a first-round draft pick. Can hardly blame the woman for upgrading, can you?"

"Well, truthfully—"

"He's got two working knees, more vertical lift than I had on my best day, and according to our good friend Brittany at NSN"—he dropped his voice to a conspiratorial whisper as he referred to the perky blond reporter from the sports network—"charisma." He nodded to the darkened screen, then shrugged. "God knows Brittany would know."

"Brittany doesn't know squat."

He guffawed. "You do have a way with words." He crossed to the wet bar and plucked another clean glass from the shelf. "You're hired."

"Thanks, but I already have a job."

"See? You don't even want me," he muttered as he pulled the stopper off a decanter. "Charisma," he growled. "Don't think I ever had any, even when I had game."

She hated this. Hated seeing this proud, cocky man lose his swagger over a woman who was little more than a piece of dandelion fluff. Sucking in a deep breath, she approached with caution. "Ty—"

# Acknowledgments

First and foremost, I have to thank my parents, Robert and Suzanne Kidwell, not only for the gift of life, but for instilling in me their love of Broadway musicals, college football, and books. Not necessarily in that order.

On our first "real" date, my husband, Bill, offered me the option of seeing a production of *Damn Yankees* or tickets to an Arkansas Razorbacks football game. Because I am a bit like the infamous Lola, I get what I want, so when I cooed, "Ooh, I love college football," I got my man.

I would be remiss if I didn't thank the late coach Pat Summitt for providing the inspiration for Kate Snyder. A paragon of grace under pressure and strength of character, Coach Summitt was a true champion in every sense of the word. I also have to thank football coach Bobby Petrino. I'd be a big ol' liar if I said his departure from the Razorback football program under a cloud of scandal didn't provide a bit of fodder when it came to dreaming up Danny McMillan's trials and tribulations.

This book was truly a labor of love. I want to thank my agent, the always enthusiastic Sara Megibow, for falling for Kate and Danny as hard I did. I appreciate your unflagging support and your voracious appetite. You are a superstar!

To Cat Clyne, Laura Costello, Rachel Gilmer, and the entire Sourcebooks team, I thank you from the bottom of my heart. You have taken my vision for this book and these characters to the next level, and helped me step up my game as an author. It makes this former DuPage County resident proud to be published by a company founded and run by women, and based right in the center of my old stomping grounds. I'm so pleased to be a part of the Sourcebooks family!

A huge thank-you to my personal Dream Team. This book, and all my books, are written because Laurie, Christine, Michelle, Carol, and of all the Super Cool Party People believed in me from the start. Big thanks to the sparkling gems of the Diamond State Romance Authors, who keep me on track and semi-sane. A special shout-out to my long-lost-sister-separated-at-birth, Karen Booth, for hanging on to me as we ride this crazy train together.

Most importantly, I have to thank critique partner extraordinaire Julie Doner. Julie is the reason this book came to life. One night, I said, "I want to write a story with a heroine who is unapologetically kick-ass. Not the gun-toting, fancy martial arts kind of kick-ass. More the kind that comes from being the best at what she does and owning it." And the rest was...*Love Game*.

Oh! And if anyone is curious about Kate's shoe collection, know that it actually does exist, and it belongs to Julie Doner. She has promised to share pics in my Facebook reader group, so be sure to look for them!

Mostly, I thank you for picking up this book and reading my story. I appreciate you most of all.

# About the Author

By day, Maggie Wells is buried in spreadsheets. At night, she pens tales of people tangling up the sheets. The product of a charming rogue and a shameless flirt, you only have to scratch the surface of this mild-mannered married lady to find a naughty streak a mile wide. She has a passion for college football, processed cheese foods, and happy endings. Not necessarily in that order.